# Departures

# Departures

## Adrienne Bellamy

NEW AMERICAN LIBRARY

New American Library
Published by New American Library, a division of
Penguin Group (USA) Inc., 375 Hudson Street,
New York, New York 10014, U.S.A.
Penguin Books Ltd, 80 Strand,
London WC2R 0RL, England
Penguin Books Australia Ltd, 250 Camberwell Road,
Camberwell, Victoria 3124, Australia
Penguin Books Canada Ltd, 10 Alcorn Avenue,
Toronto, Ontario, Canada M4V 3B2
Penguin Books (NZ), cnr Airborne and Rosedale Roads,
Albany, Auckland 1310, New Zealand

Penguin Books Ltd, Registered Offices:
80 Strand, London WC2R 0RL, England

First published by New American Library,
a division of Penguin Group (USA) Inc.

First Printing, September 2004
10   9   8   7   6   5   4   3   2   1

 REGISTERED TRADEMARK—MARCA REGISTRADA

THE LIBRARY OF CONGRESS CATALOGING-IN-PUBLICATION DATA:

Bellamy, Adrienne.
Departures / Adrienne Bellamy.
p. cm.
ISBN 0-451-21294-0 (trade pbk.)
1. Women—Pennsylvania—Fiction. 2. Mothers and daughters—Fiction. 3. Philadelphia (Pa.)—Fiction.
4. Single mothers—Fiction. 5. Neighborhood—Fiction. 6. Girls—Fiction. I. Title.
PS3602.E6457D47 2004
813'.6—dc22                2004009317

Set in Adobe Garamond
Designed by Ginger Legato

Printed in the United States of America

## To Wendell Sawyer:

You and I have had our ups and downs and ins and outs and will continue throughout our lifetimes. I want to thank you for allowing me to be a part of your life in the seventies. You have provided my best memories. Our friendship, quiet times coupled with the adventures that I shared with you and Blue Magic certainly and beyond a shadow of a doubt played an enormous part in fueling and triggering my imagination and creativity and thus bore Departures. I chased my dream in writing this book and caught it. I am sharing it with you. I could not have learned from a better teacher. Thank you for demanding that my soul never become impregnated by insecurity so I could never give birth to the monster named Jealousy. Though I tried to replace you once in my life, I have learned that there could never be another you.

## To Bill Thompson:

May you rest in peace, my love. The angels must be mesmerized 24/7. I know you are looking down here smiling in satisfaction right about now. You've got to be wallowing in pride knowing I have followed your instructions and become an author. You knew what was in me long before I had a clue. I guess it takes not only a good and perceptive writer, but also an unselfish human being to notice another's dimly lit flame and help to channel her energies to create a blazing fire. Your words of encouragement are engraved in my favorite organ—my heart. I want you to read every word in Departures and share all of the emotions I felt in writing it. You owe it to yourself. You're gonna laugh your butt off, and I'll bet you a dollar that I have correctly guessed your favorite character. It's Lucy. I miss your face and I'll see you when I see you.

## To Alia Bellamy:

My little stinker. Thank you for your support, for fighting with me as well as for me. I actually needed it all. Thank you for saying "no" when you had to, and making me solve my computer problems. I'll be glad when you're not seventeen anymore and I know you'll be glad when I go to "the home." No matter what goes down, I'm on your side and you are my life. Don't you ever forget that, baby. You are Mommy's best girl even on a bad day. Now go on and read Departures in its entirety. I'm done.

# Thank You

Well now I understand how the winners feel when they receive their Oscars at the Academy Awards and other award recipients. They try to remember to thank everyone involved and don't want to forget a soul. It's tough. Thank God I am not on the spot like they are and I have time to think.

First, I must thank **God** for the blessing of *Departures* and for bestowing the will, inspiration, creativity, determination, and imagination in my very brain and soul. I thank him for the very words that he placed in my head and for allowing my fingers to work the magic that brings us *Departures*. He stepped in giving me words and ideas while I was driving, asleep, cooking, and always when I was "stumped."

One by one I will thank the people who read for me, gave me constructive criticism, encouraged me, and literally just pushed me on from 1996 when I started *Departures*. For additional information on my test readers, please refer to the full list of Thank Yous on my Web site www.bellamyadrienne.com.

LORETTA MILLBOURNE: Leo. She received a call from me in spring 1996. I told her I needed her to stop by. I needed a favor. She showed up and had plans for the day. However, they were altered and she spent most of that day at my dining room table reading the first few chapters.

MAX VIERRA AKA BARBARA THACKER GLANZMANN: Taurus. Is Ray going to write the screenplay? O.K. girl, it's over and done with. You've been pretty hard on Perry Shoreman. Now you can read the book in its entirety and see what Sheila ended up doing.

REGINA JOHNSON: I surely do not know where to start with this woman. When referring to her I call her the "recluse who lays around and reads novels." This is my Virgo cousin-in-law. She is tough on a book. A perfectionist. I let her know that I was writing a novel and she brushed me off. I bothered her until she surrendered and put a best seller down to pick up *Departures*. Well, Regina Johnson was up the entire night when she started. She could not put it down. Like the Whispers said "I only meant to wet my feet but you pulled me in where the waters run deep." That is what happened.

RALPH TRAVICK: My right-hand man. My only brother and the person who from November 2000 when he began taking it all seriously and decided to read *Departures* fell in love with it and decided the team of Adrienne Bellamy and Regina Bellamy Johnson had to include another partner, himself.

ALIA BELLAMY: Leo. This is my seventeen-year-old daughter and to be honest I do not know how we made it through this novel. The fights, Oh My God the fights. My begging her to read and fix the blasted computer. I thought I would either kill her or have a heart attack. She got so mad at me in October she cut up my disks. Luckily I had it on hard drive in other places. This child is alive and because of that I know God is in my heart. We had some rough days. If anybody wants a beautiful seventeen-year-old that knows everything, please call me. I'm willing to send food and money.

SUSIE SNELLENBURG: Aries. This woman, this sweet caring woman who had read a letter that I had composed for my daughter demanded that I write a novel. She threatened me. She told me she would not talk to me until I wrote for a living. She read for me and gave me constructive criticism. She believed in me early on.

WENDELL SAWYER: Aquarius. At first, you just read the chapters that sounded like you, huh? So, then you got roped into the Pisces chapter and Lucy reeled you in and took you on a trip. That's what you get for starting out being selfish.

AMY MYERS: Leo. Thank God we are sometimes unsure of ourselves and have to go to others for advice and information. Well, I was trying to ensure that *Departures* would rest on the capable shelves of Barnes and Noble Booksellers. So, I began making calls and asking questions at Barnes and Noble in Abington, Pennsylvania. I was shifted from one person to another and finally told I had to deal with Amy Myers, Manager, Community Relations. During our conversation I was given advice by Mrs. Myers and at the end, she asked to meet me and review the novel. I immediately took her a synopsis, which she read. Loved it. She began reading the entire manuscript right away, stopping on three occasions during her reading to call me screaming in delight. Thank you Amy for your encouragement, hard work, advice, and for dragging me away from "the vultures." It's nice to know that *Departures* will debut her "events" at your store.

ALAN EVANS: Gemini. One of my six bosses. Well, Chapter 28 got you huh? And then you got lured to Reba and the trash. Enjoy the other 41 chapters and it sure was great listening to that hearty laugh outside my office. Thanks for always being so positive, for offering to do whatever you think I need, and for always coming to my rescue. You and Jayne.

SHADIYAH: Sagittarius. Thanks for reading and loving it and helping me along the way with the editing. Write that book girl, the world is waiting for you too. Don't let *Departures* show you up. Come on out and fight like a good Muslim sister.

T. RONCALLI: Cancer. Well, she listened, read a little, and helped me to find a reader that did not know me so I could get an honest opinion about my book. I had to consult T. many times when I was deciding Paula's fate.

TEDD HALL: Libra. Well, how does it feel knowing I finally did something creative and stuck with it? Feels good doesn't it? Thanks for reading for me and not badgering me for more. Thanks for waiting and for so much encouragement. I really do enjoy our fights. Here it is and you'll love it. Sheila is really your girl, isn't she?

FRANK ALTOMARE: Cancer. This one and me have been hanging for fourteen years. You know how close we get to our hair stylists. I gave him two chapters of *Departures* and could not shut him up. His words to me after reading those chapters were "I want the whole book. I have to have it."

EVANS (SOLOMON) ROEBUCK: Leo. Thank you for the encouragement. You read too slow. You are too busy. I love you. You are one of the best people who have happened to me. I know how proud you are of me and I feel splendid about that.

ARLENE SACKS: Libra: *Departures* found me a new friend in the spring of 2001. I really like this friend. You know how sweet and dependable Libras are. So, I am truly blessed. And, of course she is an avid reader and very honest. Yep, she read it in a weekend. Called me and told me she even took it to the bathroom with her.

JERRY MURPHY, M.D.: Aquarius. Well, life is wonderful knowing you have someone of the sun sign representing the smartest people in the zodiac reading for you, contributing, watching over you, saving your life, and doing what they do best—teaching as they pull you along. This one is a perfectionist, a snob, and much too modest. *Departures* took her first trip out of the country with him to keep him company. I refuse to go on and on about you Jerry Murphy, but I will make sure you and everyone else knows how comfortable and relaxed I am, knowing you always have me covered. Thanks for your interest in *Departures* and for adding the creativity of your "dream" by sharing a portion of it in Chapter 20. I made out like a fat rat big time when we stumbled upon each other.

HARRY MORRISON, NORMAN STROBEL, JAMES CARR, ALAN EVANS, FRED HOPKE, AND CHARLES PARKER: (Capricorn, Virgo, Scorpio, Gemini, Aquarius, and Pisces. Just tell me what I would do without you? These guys are my six wonderful bosses who have put up with *Departures* and me.

TO MY EDITOR:
Thank you, Janete, for your patience, our long talks, the battles, your corrections, and our laughter. I appreciate your honesty and the fact that

you are meticulous. Your hard work and guidance have not gone unnoticed, for I recognize you not only put your sweat into *Departures*—but inside of me. You have made me a better thinker and a better writer. Thank God I was your "project." I'm going up, baby, soaring not only with you as a brilliant copilot, but also as a friend and confidante. You know I don't make promises I can't keep and I'm promising to make you very proud of me. Thanks also for working holidays and nights on *Departures* and me, and for loving the words I so enjoyed writing.

Luv ya!!
Adrienne

*Spring, spring, spring is here*
*Everything is nice and clear*
*The birds are blue and some are new*
*So what is spring to you?*

ADRIENNE BELLAMY, AGE SIX

# Departures

# Chapter One

# Amber

From what I hear, Lance and Grandma had a thing going. Yeah, I can believe it because you know what they say about Pisces women—they are sneaky, though they act innocent. They can have the morals of an alley cat, and you'd never believe they were cheating. Grandma Fannie, my mother's mother, was indeed a Pisces. Grandpa, Oscar Porter, worked hard at the gas station and brought all his money home to Grandma. Grandpa was fine, and younger than Grandma by about fourteen years. He couldn't read or write. I can't remember where he met her, but he fell for her, and she's been running over him ever since. I loved Grandpa. I mean I really loved him. I was his favorite thing in the whole world. He came home with Juicy Fruit gum for me every day and most of the time had a dime for me to spend. He loved his other grandchildren, too, but not like he loved me. He took the splinters out of my feet from the old wood floors, patted my head, and smiled at me all the time. He saved me from eating vegetables at the dinner table. He was also my favorite thing in the whole world.

My mother, Paula, worked in a department store downtown for a couple of years. I've never referred to her as Mom, Mommy, Mother, or anything close to that. She was simply "Paula" to us, because she wasn't the nurturing type, and she sure didn't treat her children in a motherly manner. Grandpa (who was actually my step grandfather) took care of my sister, Sydni, and me while Paula worked. There was no real daddy around. I don't know who Sydni's father was, but Paula said his name was Roy. I've never seen him in my life, and I don't recall her ever seeing or talking to him. Sydni is two years older than me and moody and stingy like our mother. They said my daddy was Lance Resnick.

Well, let's get the scoop on how they say I got here—I mean how I arrived in this world. Lance Resnick would come by to see Grandma. You know, they had a thing going on. One day Paula answered the door and, finding Lance on her doorstep, informed him that Grandma wasn't home. Paula was nineteen and hot. Lance was twenty-nine and eager? She asked him if he'd like to leave Grandma a note, and he said yes. She went to get a pencil and paper while he waited at the door. She came out and handed the paper to him and then stuffed the pencil down her bra. She told him if he needed the pencil he had to go for it. Lance went for it and went back a whole lot of times for more pencils and more visits with Grandma, too. She, of course, was unaware of the entire situation. I arrived about a year later. Deep, isn't it? Real fucking deep.

So . . . Paula was labeled a tramp during the pregnancy. Lance wasn't sure whether or not I was really his because of Paula's promiscuity. So, he started igoring her. Grandma was furious when she found out Paula was pregnant and had hidden it until she was almost seven months. Let's not forget that I'm number two coming out of her womb, because Sydni is bouncing around with no father either. Lance's family couldn't stand that tramp Paula and didn't believe he was my father. When I was born, everybody looked at me funny. Lance's family always stared at me when I was around, but I had to see the Resnicks because Grandma and their family were friends and all hung out together.

When I was little, I somehow got worms. I recall being in the shed kitchen with panties down to my ankles, crapping on the floor with worms coming out. Grandma Fannie tried to tell me where they came from, but I really didn't care; I just wanted them out of me. I was smart and perceptive, a little hustler who didn't have time for worms and shit to be slowing me down from things I enjoyed like reading all the labels on the packages and cans and jars of food in our cupboards. I dreamed of having beautiful dresses and exquisite things, yearning for Easter and Christmas because they brought new clothes and presents. I knew that some day I'd be rich and off the streets of Philadelphia. I'd live in the suburbs. I'd have one of those credit cards that you go into the department store with and just sign your name and walk away with the prize. I wouldn't be around pigeons or stray dogs. I'd swim in my own pool because I didn't trust the one at the playground. People peed in it.

Lance Resnick's older sister Libby had a daughter named Denise who was my age, so we had to play together. I referred to her as my "cousin" because that's what my family told me she was. But every time I did, Libby and her family looked at me funny and didn't say anything. They always referred to me as "Fannie's granddaughter." If someone asked who I was, they never, ever said "Lance's daughter." They never even acknowledged Paula. I felt awkward, but I never knew what they were thinking. It would be years before I found out the truth—I mean why I was looked at so oddly by Lance's family and why they always seemed to be staring at me. I found out when I was twenty-three years old. Libby actually explained the "pencil thing" to me when I grew up. I just didn't resemble the Resnicks. I was small and underweight. When I entered the first grade, I weighed only forty pounds. I had a medium brown complexion and thin dark hair that I usually wore in two long braids in back and one on top that reached down to my chin. I didn't have a lot of clothes, so I wore dungarees and overalls most of the time. I used to wear a red-and-white striped shirt a lot with the beige overalls. I was nicknamed "Dennis the Menace" because I was always doing something devilish. I had large dark brown eyes and a tiny mouth. All the Resnicks were very light-skinned with thick reddish brown hair. They had big eyes, too. The people in their family were chunky.

It seemed like card games went on every night, but actually it was only weekends—tonk, poker, cooncan, or pitty pat. Sydni and I went with Grandma to Libby's house, where the games took place. Libby Resnick was well respected. She ran the family and had all the money. She took care of her adult brothers and sisters whether they had jobs or not because their parents were down South in Georgia. When Denise and I were seven, we were pretty tight because we'd have to play together while those marathon card games were going on. Sometimes Sydni came, too. We usually spent weekends together at each other's house, and even though the Resnicks merely tolerated Paula, they were still pretty tight with Fannie. I always envied Denise; she had everything, I mean everything. Dresses by the designer Cinderella, lots of toys and money, and a fine piano. Her clothes were really beautiful, and I loved for her to spend the night with me. Most of the time she forgot something, like a dress or a skirt, and I could wear what she left behind. I felt so good in those clothes.

Six years later Paula was at it with someone else, and Renee was born. Her father, Horace Alston, acknowledged her. Horace was something else. He was so fine. Tall, dark, and handsome with a Cadillac and what seemed like a million dollars. He gave out dollar bills! He gave them to Sydni and me whenever he came around. Eventually we left Grandma's house. Paula, Sydni, Renee, and I moved to a really nice neighborhood and into a big house with Horace. Sydni and I had twin beds, and there was a front yard and a driveway that we played in all the time. Everything was so clean. I loved that place.

Paula was the best cook ever. We had Ovaltine, Wheat Chex, or Rice Chex for breakfast, depending on which one we wanted. We always had the variety pack of cereal in case we didn't want the other stuff. We liked Horace. I don't remember how long we were there, maybe a year, and then for some reason we ended up back at Grandma's, all except Horace. A year later Horace was still coming around, giving Paula money for Renee and sometimes taking us girls out, and he still gave us dollars. He was crazy about Renee. She really was a cute little girl. He didn't stop dating Paula—or at least sleeping with her—from time to time. They were an item, and everyone knew it, but Paula continued to sneak off with other men. Horace didn't go for that and could be pretty mean. Paula and everyone knew if he ever caught her, he'd kick her butt.

Well, lo and behold, he caught her one night in some dude's car outside the Rockaway bar. Horace drove up in his black Cadillac and parked. He noticed Paula in a car with a guy, and her dress was pulled up damn near to her chest. Horace didn't know him, but it was Wilson Jenkins, who came to the Rockaway from time to time. He actually lived on the west side of town. Wilson had one of his hands stuck between her legs, and they were kissing. Horace knocked on the window and calmly motioned Paula to come out of the car. The next thing you know, both of Wilson's hands were on the steering wheel, and Paula was refusing to get out. Wilson never said a word to Horace. He was petrified and not about to fight him for Paula. He asked her to get out of his car. She said, "No," and locked the door.

Horace stood there, looking at them, beckoning Paula to come. She knew he was about to kill somebody and didn't think it would be Wilson Jenkins. Wilson continued shouting at Paula to get out, but she ignored him. He reached over her, trying to get to the lock, but Paula kept pushing him away, fighting him off. He stopped trying and just opened his door, jumped out, and ran. Horace quickly moved to the other side of the car and slid in. He beat Paula so badly that she eventually required stitches in her face. He dragged her to his car, punching her every step of the way. He threw her in and took her home.

Grandma had gone out. Grandpa was asleep, and so were us kids. When Horace found out Grandma wasn't there and Paula had left all of us with Grandpa, he beat her ass again and told her she better not ever leave his daughter alone with Grandpa, who was known to drink too much beer and pass out, because anything could happen. He told her he better not ever catch her with that nigger Wilson again, or he would kill her for sure.

About two weeks later, Wilson came by with a brown paper bag and left it with Grandma for Paula. Her panties were in it.

I loved school. I was so smart. I taught myself to read before I ever went there. When I was in second grade, I was good at everything except math, but I could count money without any trouble. I had quite a personality and was known as the class clown, always demanding attention. The teachers liked me. I liked reading and writing and singing and making money. I felt I just had to be rich one day.

About twice a year, the school had a cookie drive, and all the kids sold cookies door-to-door and store-to-store. I did okay but didn't get the prize. A couple of months after the drive was over, I got myself a bunch of empty soda bottles and took them to the store for the refund. I'd been collecting them from all the neighbors, so I had a whole wagonload amounting to about eight dollars. I cashed them in and bought twenty-six boxes of chocolate circle cookies at twenty-nine cents a box. I put them in the wagon and began going door-to-door, telling the neighbors I was selling cookies for the school, and they cost fifty cents. All the neighbors bought at least one box. Many of them made comments like, "Gee, I didn't know the school was even having a sale. Amber, you're the first one to come here. I guess I have to buy from you." "None of the other kids have been around yet. Did the drive just begin today?" "Well, it looks like you got a head start on the others. You sure are a go-getter, baby. I know you'll win the prize for sure."

I made a killing and had spending money for the bus excursion to Wildwood that was coming up and movie money for quite a while. I also bought myself some shrimp from the seafood place near the school. I love shrimp.

One Saturday Curtis, another of Paula's boyfriends, came by and offered to take Paula, Sydni, and me to Atlantic City. He and Paula went to the bars while Sydni and I did the amusements on the boardwalk. I loved Atlantic City with its fresh air and cool ocean breeze. I liked the pretty hotels and the restaurants inside. I liked the large ladies' rooms in the hotels and how clean they always were. They had huge mirrors with lightbulbs around them like Hollywood dressing rooms. There was beautiful carpeting on the floors and bellhops dressed up neatly in uniforms, looking as if they belonged to a band. I admired the elegance of such fine establishments. We had fun on the boardwalk, especially at the Steel Pier with its diving horse. We ate salt-water taffy, corn on the cob, ice cream, and visited the wax museum. I loved those carts that carried you from one end of the boardwalk to the other. When I grew up and was rich, I wanted a fine car with a convertible top so the air could blow on me, through my hair, and I would be free, free to put my hands up if I liked.

I started playing games on the boardwalk. I won a game and selected a man's watch for the prize. It only cost me a dollar. I was ecstatic! The watch was beautiful—gold with a black face. It was shiny and had only four numbers on the face. "Amber, that watch must have cost those people thousands of dollars!" Sydni remarked when the man handed it to me. "You're so lucky to have won it." She assumed I'd give it to Grandpa, who would show off at the gas station when he wore it. All those white people there would think we'd struck it rich.

We had to meet Curtis and Paula in front of the Cartier Hotel at seven o'clock. When they picked us up, I showed them the watch. I was so proud of it, but wasn't quite sure what I would do with it.

"Amber," Paula said immediately, "why did you pick that prize, and who will you give it to?"

I knew how Paula was about pretty things. I didn't want her taking that watch and giving it to one of her boyfriends. I always thought she was stupid about money and people. I knew Grandma had more sense than Paula and really ran the show—the house and kids. In my eyes, Paula never seemed responsible enough to be the boss.

"I'll save it," I told Paula.

"Save it? For what? You won't ever be a man, and girls don't wear men's watches. You must be planning to give it to Oscar."

Paula called Grandpa "Oscar" because he was her stepfather. Paula's real father lived in Cincinnati. His name was Riley Gray. I was a Gray because of him, the grandfather I had never seen.

I said I was saving it until I got married, then I'd give it to my husband. That would keep her from bothering me about it.

I didn't know if I would give it to Grandpa or not—maybe yes, maybe no. I sat in the backseat of Curtis's car, riding home to Philadelphia staring at that watch. My mind was going a mile a minute trying to think of exactly what I wanted to do with it. I didn't want to just hand it over to

Grandpa, even though I really loved him and he gave me all that gum on a regular basis. I thought about all those dimes, and all those vegetables I never had to eat because of him, and, well, I knew he really did deserve the watch. Then I thought about Lance, my daddy Lance. He treated me nice even though his people looked at me funny most of the time. They looked right in my eyes, studied my face, and watched the way I walked. He often brought me new dresses or left money with Paula or Grandma to buy sneakers or shoes for me. He wasn't mad at me for anything; he was only mad with Paula. I could give the watch to Lance. Then I thought about Horace. He was nice to me, too, giving me money every time he saw me. He was good about taking me places with Renee, never mind that Sydni and I weren't his. But if I gave the watch to Horace because of that, then what about Curtis? I was riding in his car now, and he had taken me to Atlantic City. He had given Sydni and me three dollars each. Even though I had my own stash from the fake cookie sale, Curtis did help me out. If it weren't for him and his transportation, I wouldn't have made it to Atlantic City or won the watch. It was a hard choice to make, so I decided not to give it to any of them because I simply couldn't make up my mind. I didn't want to hurt anyone's feelings. Then I got the idea to sell it for twenty dollars. I didn't know where, but I was definitely going to make some money off of it.

The next day the older guys were on the corner. I showed one of them the watch. He was new in the neighborhood, and I didn't know his name. He liked it and wanted to buy it. I told him to give me a deposit of ten dollars, and he could get it when my mother got home from work because I needed her permission. He said okay, and I accepted the money. I waited a few hours and found Timmy Henry around the corner and showed the watch to him. I gave him the same story and took his ten dollars. After another couple of hours, I went into the local delicatessen, showing it to the owner. He loved it. I sold it to him for twenty dollars, collected the money, and gave him the watch. Paula arrived about nine o'clock that night. I was loaded with money but said nothing to her about the sale. When Timmy came for the watch, I tried to get rid of him but couldn't. He told Paula what I had done. She demanded I return the money, but I said I had left it at Denise's and would have to get it the next day. Meanwhile, I had to think of a way to avoid having to give it back. I wasn't worried about the new guy finding me. He didn't know where I lived, and that would buy me some time.

I had to face Timmy the following day in the street, and he wanted his money. I said I would get it from the house. I went inside and got a ten-dollar bill. I rubbed it all around between my legs and left it in my panties and returned outside. He asked again for the money. I reached down right in front of him and the other guys and pulled it out and smelled it. Before offering it to him, I made a face that indicated it stank. They all stared at me in disbelief. Then I tried to hand it to him, but he didn't want it after all. I got to keep it. Now I had to resolve things with the guy who didn't know where I lived. I was already thinking of what to do in order to keep that money.

It was New Year's Eve, with Paula and Grandma getting dressed to kill. Nina Penster was coming to babysit Sydni, Renee, and me. Renee was a little over a year old then. Nina's parents, Johnny and Reba Penster, had a big house around the corner from us. Mrs. Penster was a nice, quiet woman and a good mom. All she did was work and take care of the kids. One day a woman came to their door and asked for Johnny. Reba explained that he was sleeping. The woman told her to tell him that the two kids he had by her were hungry, and he'd better get some money to her for food. Reba said all right, closed the door, and simply went on with her housework, never waking Johnny.

Reba was exceptionally pretty, with skin the color of coffee with a lot of cream in it. She was tall and well built, but definitely no fashion plate in her long drab skirts and flat shoes. She was always wearing weird outfits that didn't match. People said she was color-blind. Whenever she had to dress up for a special occasion, the neighbors got together, lending her things and matching her clothes up. They loved Reba. She worked as a librarian at the city library. She didn't know how to cook, either, and whenever we stayed over there, dinner was colored red. Johnny Penster taught her to do that. It was always spaghetti or rice with tomatoes, and if she made something that wasn't red, she'd dump a can of tomatoes or a bottle of ketchup in it. Everybody had to eat it. We spent a lot of time at her house.

People said the kids' father was a dog. Most of the kids in the neighborhood were scared of Johnny. He looked so big and mean. Whenever he told us to do something, we did it quickly. We were always afraid he'd beat the tar out of us. He wasn't home a lot, but when he was, we were good. I don't know where he worked, but his kids told us he had a good job. We thought he was smart because he talked a lot about getting a good education. Whenever he took us for an outing, he piled us into his car, and, no matter where we went, we ended up in the library. He'd tell us to read and wait for Reba to bring us home. Grandma used to say that Johnny Penster married Reba when she was seventeen because she was so naïve, and he wanted to run around on her. To keep her from leaving, he had to be sure she didn't look attractive enough to get another man. To effectuate his plan, he made sure she didn't know how to dress. Because she didn't know how to cook, he taught her to dump tomatoes and ketchup into everything. If she couldn't feed a man properly and look good, she could never escape him. As it turned out, he was running with every woman in the neighborhood who would have him. Other kids wouldn't have known or suspected anything if they hadn't heard their own parents gossiping about it. They had looked up to him and respected him because they were afraid of him.

So, Grandma, Paula, their friends, and the gang that hung around with them were going to the Rockaway bar to ring in the New Year. Paula looked really sharp. She was thin and pretty and had on a tight-fitting black dress with fringes all over it that shook when she walked, plus black fishnet stockings and spike heels. She smelled like flowers and wore her reddish blond hair cut short and full of curls. She looked so pretty to me. Grandma was sharp as a tack, too, in a cream-colored chemise and sheer matching stockings and heels. She had waves in her hair and pearls around her neck.

Paula was meeting Jimmy Johnson at the party, and Grandma was meeting McNight, a friend of hers who came by the house sometimes. We never knew his first name. We just called him "McNight" because he was so black. Grandpa was asleep early. He had gotten drunk off beer and passed out, so Nina was hired to be in charge that night. We had plans of our own. I had just turned ten. Sydni was going on thirteen and Nina was fifteen.

Nina Penster lived down the street and had five brothers. Sydni and I used to spend the night at her house sometimes. I always peed in the bed. No matter where I went, I peed in the bed when I was asleep. When I stayed at the neighbors' houses, their kids often fed me gingersnaps until

I couldn't move. They thought that eating enough of them would stop me up so I wouldn't pee on them. Sometimes it worked; sometimes it didn't.

One particular night we were at Nina's house, and Mr. Johnny sat me down to tell me that if I wet the bed, I'd get a whipping. I prayed I wouldn't and did it anyway. I was sleeping in the bed with Sydni and Nina, and when I realized what I had done, I was terrified. I knew I'd better get it cleaned up and dry. I took off my panties and, very carefully, removed Sydni's as she slept. I put my wet ones on her and moved her over into the pee spot. Then I put on her panties and my clothes and headed home in the dark, scared to death. I banged on the front door, and Grandma let me in. It must have been after midnight. I told her I'd had a bad dream and wanted to be in my own bed.

The next day Sydni was in big trouble. She tried to explain to Mr. Johnny that she never wet the bed, and he didn't believe her at first. However, given my history and since I had left the scene of the crime, they figured it out. I never spent the night there again.

Once Nina got to our house and Grandma and Paula left for the New Year's party, we started to get into everything. First we took some clothes hangers and pulled them apart to make them straight. Then we stuck them into the light fixtures to create sparks, our own fireworks for the New Year. We mixed up all kinds of juice and ginger ale, trying to make Thunderbird wine. I had gotten a plastic doll baby for Christmas. She was really cute, even if she was white. I decided she should be brown like me. So I stuck her in the oven and began to bake her. The next thing we knew, the plastic was melted all over the oven, and the kitchen smelled awful.

After we got "drunk," we found a drill and went upstairs to the attic to bore holes in the floor. About eleven thirty, it was almost time to ring in the New Year. We dressed up in Grandma's and Paula's clothes. Wow! I had on a straight, red "wet-look" dress of slithery material with a belt tied at the waist. I put on stockings and low-heeled shoes, lipstick and rouge, and piled my hair on top of my head. Sydni hooked herself up in a long pleated skirt and a silver-beaded blouse that glittered. We had on bras with toilet paper stuffed in them, and Sydni found a pair of black T-strap heels. Nina wanted to be extra sexy and put on one of Grandma's long nightgowns with stockings and heels, but got scared she would fall and changed to boots. We got our coats, Nina wearing an ugly old fur of

Grandma's, and we left the house. Thank God Grandpa was sleeping like a rock. We walked three blocks to the white neighborhood and started to ring doorbells and run away laughing. It was freezing outside, but we didn't care. We were partying.

We got cold walking back toward home. When a man pulled up in a car, Nina asked for a ride, and he said to hop in. He asked us why we were on the street. Nina, the oldest and in charge, explained that we had been to a party and were on our way home. She told him we lived downtown, about eight blocks from there, and needed a ride. He agreed. I was in the front seat with him. Sydni and Nina were in back. For some reason, they began to tease him about his clothes and call him an old man. He had a Southern accent and Nina started to mock him. They kept on laughing and saying mean yet funny things. He began to get angry and sick of us. I couldn't understand why he didn't put us out of the car. Oh, they were carrying on and wouldn't shut up. They told him he had a lousy beat-up old car, and that did it. The man pulled over and ordered us all to get out.

I don't know what got into Nina. She reached over from the backseat and snatched the keys out of the ignition. She and Sydni jumped out and ran across the street, hollering for me to come. I had on a short-waisted jacket instead of a coat. That man grabbed the belt of my red wet-look dress before I could get the door open. The knot in the belt was so tight I couldn't get it undone. He yelled to them that he was going to keep me. Sydni and Nina stood across the street in shock.

Well, there I was, kicking and screaming on New Year's Eve, trying to get away from the madman whose car Nina suggested we get into. She and Sydni hollered at him to let me go. That crazy country dark-skinned man with a gold tooth, driving a big red Cadillac with fake leopard-skin seats, wearing white pants in December, a white shirt, a red sports jacket, white socks, red leather shoes, and a great big white hat with a giant red feather sticking out of it like the man on the cigar box, was holding me hostage!

That stupid nightgown Nina had on was blowing in the wind on Market Street in downtown Philadelphia. And those ugly brown boots of Grandma's were on her feet. The fur coat, either possum or rat, was hanging off her. Sydni's three-quarter-length jacket was loads too big for her and suddenly the silver glitter top she was wearing looked ridiculous. It was five minutes to two o'clock in the morning, and I knew Grandma and Paula should be home soon because the Rockaway closed at two.

I thought about that damn white doll baked in the oven, dripping plastic all over, holes in the attic floor, and glasses all over the kitchen. Renee was there with Grandpa, who had passed out. I thought, "If Horace is at the Rockaway and finds out about this, he may kill us, too."

I knew if the country animal in this car didn't cause my death first, Paula and Grandma would for sure. I was scared to death. By then Nina and Sydni were too frightened to come back to the car. I was being choked around the waist with that damn belt, and the dummies across the street couldn't figure out what to do. They shrieked for the police—they didn't have a dime for the phone. By then I was trying to bite that goon to get away from him. Ten whole long minutes went by that seemed an eternity. I was crying and the guy kept saying, "I've got you, and you'll stay with me until I get my keys."

Nina and Sydni were afraid to throw the keys to him for fear he wouldn't let me go. At five minutes after two, a police car came by. Sydni and Nina ran for it. They both talked at once and pointed to the car we were in. The goon got out, but the police told him to get back in and stay there. They put Sydni and Nina in the cop car, came over to rescue me, and called a wagon for the goon.

By 2:43 a.m. Rupert Taylor was in the wagon, crying about being charged with kidnapping. Sydni, Nina, and I were in the car with the cops, all of us bawling. They hauled us all into the station and sat us down. How were we going to get out of this mess?

The police took our names, addresses, and telephone numbers. Thank God we were minors. Nina told them that Rupert had abducted us. The cops noticed how we were dressed and shook their heads. Rupert's hat was all bent up from fighting with me. Nina in that nightgown was a hoot. At first she lied, saying Rupert broke into the house and got us out. By then I was so tired of the whole ordeal and scared to death that I just told the truth. The police called our parents. When they couldn't reach anyone at our house, they called Nina's dad. I would have gone to the electric chair right then and there rather than see Johnny Penster. Nina got diarrhea as soon as they got him on the phone and crapped on herself all the way to the bathroom. Sydni just sat and cried. She never said a word. In thirty-five minutes Johnny Penster arrived. When he took a look at Nina in that outfit and got a whiff how she smelled, I thought he'd slap her across the room. He couldn't find Paula or Grandma for us. It was after three o'clock, and they weren't home yet. The police wouldn't release Sydni and me to anyone other than Grandpa, Grandma, or Paula. They kept on calling home and getting no answer.

As scared as I was of Johnny Penster, I really didn't want him to abandon us at the police station. Nina was terrified, knowing her father was about to kill her. I felt sorry for her and was mad at her at the same time for getting us into this jam. She was the oldest, the babysitter, and was in charge. Maybe she deserved to get killed by Mr. Johnny. I had my own troubles to worry about.

After giving Rupert a lecture, the cops let him go. He had stopped crying and promised not to pick up any girls ever again. He tried to find a way back to his car. It was now after four o'clock in the morning.

Suddenly I figured that Grandma and Paula were probably at Libby's, or at least Grandma might be. Paula rarely went there because of the way they felt about her. I gave the police Libby's address, but I didn't know the telephone number. I was afraid to send them to our house for Grandpa because he would either have to leave Renee alone to pick us up or awaken her and bring her along. Either way, if Renee were involved, Horace would kill all of us for sure. The cops checking Libby's house was our best bet for getting out of jail and having some sort of a chance at survival, after being released to Grandma.

Well, I was right. Grandma was at Libby's, along with nineteen other people the police brought to jail for illegal gambling and selling liquor without a license. In an hour and fifteen minutes, four paddy wagons showed up. We had found our Grandma. Paula wasn't with them. Lucky Paula. Now my real daddy, Lance, was in jail along with my sister, Grandma, Libby, and me. It was like a family reunion. They even had McNight and seventy-nine-year-old Mrs. Dunlap in the paddy wagon. Sydni and I watched them file in. I started praying again for the electric chair. I didn't want to go home whenever they found Paula to come for us.

# Chapter Two

# *Sheila*

Perry and Sheila Shoreman and their four children lived around the corner from Grandma Fannie on Price Street. They had a small three-bedroom row house. They lacked a lot of things. Sheila was a strong, ambitious woman, but no matter what she tried to accomplish, it never seemed to work out. Her husband had a bad gambling habit and, smart as Sheila was, she couldn't get away from him. She was stuck trying to raise four children, constantly craving better things. She wanted a life that didn't consist of shut-off notices for utilities, her children wearing hand-me-down clothes, having to take in ironing for extra cash, and always wondering where her husband was or what time he would come home. She was sick of being broke, the fighting, and the arguments that occurred because of Perry's uncontrollable gambling. She was totally fed up with Perry, who had turned her into a violent, depressed, overweight woman with a faded dream of becoming a registered nurse. She had no college degree, but desperately wanted one. Sheila longed for a way out.

Perry Shoreman was in trouble with his bills again due to his gambling habits. He always messed up his money. One time he gambled from Thursday night until Monday afternoon, winning and losing and borrowing and paying back. Finally he was flat-out broke, and nobody would lend him another dime. He worried because Sheila, who weighed two hundred fifty pounds, was mad as hell that he'd been in the streets for five days. He had been sleeping at Libby's, waking up, and continuing to gamble. Sheila said she'd kill him when he got home.

Perry was so scared and broke that he stopped at Bobby Dixon's house, got a razor blade, and made a nasty cut above his eye. He let it bleed a while and headed for home. When he got in the door, Sheila was at the stove with one of the babies perched on her hip. She was stirring a pot with the other hand. She looked up and saw Perry as he leaned against the wall with blood running down the side of his face.

"Baby, baby," Perry said. "I was nearly killed by some jitterbug thugs on Uber Street. They robbed me and cut me. I am so glad to see you. I saw my whole life flash in front of me out there. I need to be with you, and I need my kids."

Sheila looked over at him, put little Gregory down in the playpen in the dining room, and didn't make a sound. She returned to the kitchen and picked up a box of Morton Salt. She snatched Perry by the collar, twisted it, bent his head back, and poured salt in both his eyes. She threw him down and jammed one foot on his neck. Reaching into the trash can, she pulled out two empty beer bottles and broke them over his head. Perry was screaming for God and begging Sheila to let him go. Blood was everywhere.

He only weighed a hundred forty-eight pounds. Sheila dragged him through the house right past the children to the front door. She dragged him down the steps to the street. He never stopped kicking and yelling until they reached the corner where she laid him down on the funeral parlor steps. She quietly told him that if he ever came back to her house broke after being out so long he'd be inside the funeral home waiting to be buried. She also told him he'd better find some money from somewhere. That day and Sheila's threat would later cost Perry his life.

Perry Shoreman had his head stitched up at the hospital. They also took care of his eyes. When he left there, he went to his mother's house, had a good meal, and watched the evening news. Then he called Sheila and asked if he could come home. He said that his father had given him enough money to buy groceries and make a payment on the electric bill. Sheila agreed.

For the next couple of months, Perry really laid low, got an additional job as a porter at the Rockaway bar, and tried to be a model husband. He hadn't even gambled for about six weeks—a record for him. Things were going okay.

Lo and behold, one Saturday night after the Rockaway closed, Perry got bored and lonely for that deck of cards and the poker game he knew was going on. So with his pay envelope in his pocket, he headed for Libby's.

There was a full house. It seemed like everybody was there, though only two games were going on. Libby was frying chicken and had collard greens and macaroni and cheese on the stove. At her card games, she collected a percentage on all the action and then made even more money by selling beer, liquor, and food. It was a hopping party. Libby knew how to make money. She owned a lot of real estate and rented properties out. She also wrote illegal numbers and employed her friends and family to take numbers over the telephone and call them in to her. Her bosses were the Italian numbers bankers. She also had a little grocery store. Everything she was involved in made it possible for her and her family to live well.

Libby's brother, Lance, was there when Perry arrived. Lance had won a good amount of money that night. Perry got himself a drink, ordered a platter, and went over to join Lance in the game. He lost close to forty dollars in the first two hands. Then he came up with a nice one, winning a hundred twenty-six dollars. Lucky Perry had aces back to back and caught another one on Fifth Street. He beat out Lance, Fannie, Jake Morgan with his two pair, and old Mrs. Dunlap, who was called the "five-card stud queen."

Perry was a happy man. He was victorious in the next hand with just a pair and was awarded almost eighty dollars while grinning like a Cheshire cat. He lost two more hands, folding early, and lost the next two going to Fifth Street, blowing ninety dollars on both of them. Now he was back and won four hands in a row. He started betting heavily and suddenly he was dead broke. Everything was gone. He borrowed two hundred fifty dollars from Lance and lost every last cent of it. It was now about seven thirty in the morning. Perry knew he had to go home, and he was petrified. He told Lance he was broke and had two bills to pay plus rent. He said they also needed food for the kids. He begged Lance to lend him another two hundred fifty to walk out the door with. When Lance declined, Perry started crying—crying real tears right there in Libby's kitchen! Lance whispered something to her, and Libby passed money to Lance, who passed it on to Perry.

"Man, I'll have it back to you, every dime, in a month," Perry told Lance.

Lance was a pretty decent and peaceful guy everybody liked and respected. He just nodded. "Okay, you keep your word, man, and I'll take care of Libby. So remember you owe me and not Libby—five hundred bucks. We understand each other? Now go on home to your wife and kids before she gets mad enough to kill you." Perry went home, handed Sheila the money, and had no problems.

Two months later Perry Shoreman still had not paid Lance. It was a shame because Lance was a nice guy and had done Perry a big favor. They'd seen each other quite a few times, but Perry always had a reason for not keeping his word. Lance quietly accepted the excuses. He didn't even curse Perry out, but let him know that he needed his money.

One night Lance ran into him at a poker game at Stanley Mason's house. Lance came in and Perry was playing. Lance hung around, bought a platter of food from Vivian, Stanley's wife, and had a drink. He didn't get into the card game. It was pretty interesting to him to watch because Perry was the man that night, winning almost every hand he played.

Paula had been giving Lance a hard time about money—child support for me—and she'd been on his case for the last few weeks. Lance wasn't having much luck with hitting the numbers or winning at cards, so he was being cool. He was tired of Paula's nagging. One day she got mad at him, packed me up, and left me at Libby's house. She told Lance if she could take care of me with no money then maybe he could too. So I ended up there for a few days until Libby took me home.

That night Perry won big at Stanley's game, and Lance asked him for the five hundred dollars. Perry started crying the blues again, but Lance was not interested in Perry's problems.

"Okay, if you don't have it all, give me part of it, and you can owe me the rest."

Perry didn't want to part with a penny. The reason he was gambling at Stanley's in the first place was that he didn't want to run into Lance. He couldn't gamble in peace at Libby's owing her brother so much. He refused to pay up, saying he had things to do with the money. Lance was still talking to him rather calmly, being owed five hundred dollars and all. That was no surprise—Lance was known for his gentle demeanor. He was the peacemaker not only in his family, but everywhere. However, he liked the ladies, and they liked him. No matter how nice a guy he was, he still banged both Paula and her mother. He didn't go after her, but Paula had her eye on him for a long time, and he was willing to oblige her.

The two men continued outside to discuss things. Lance tried to explain his own financial problems. Perry didn't want to hear any of it. He had been out all night again. Sheila would be furious and he'd better get his ass home.

Lance asked him politely again for the money. "Fuck you," Perry said. "I'm not giving you a fucking dime."

When Lance heard that he went over to his car and reached into the glove compartment, came back over to Perry, and shot him once in the neck and once in the chest. Lance replaced the revolver in the glove compartment and drove himself to the police station. He strolled in, told the police officer at the desk that he had just shot Perry Shoreman on the sidewalk of 2416 Beechwood Street, and left him lying there. He handed the officer the gun.

# Chapter Three

# Lucy

Lucy Noble lived across the street from Grandma and Grandpa. She was tall and slender and kept herself nicely dressed. She'd grown up in the neighborhood and was an only child. She was twenty-one years old.

She'd been engaged to marry a guy named Kenny Sharpton when she was nineteen. They had dated since their senior year in high school. When they graduated, Kenny went away to attend the University of Vermont and she enrolled at Beaver College in suburban Philadelphia. They corresponded regularly and got together during college breaks. She was extremely proud of the small diamond he had placed on her finger on her eighteenth birthday and was looking forward to a huge wedding after graduation. She planned to have a ton of kids. During their junior year, Kenny came home the day before Thanksgiving and broke the engagement.

It took Lucy fourteen months to get over him—but she did it. She missed him terribly and longed for his arms to be around her. She literally crossed days off the calendar when she would get through a day without picking up the phone to call him. She was truly heartbroken. She plunged into her studies and got a part-time job. She hooked up with her godmother, Peggy Kinard, a seamstress who lived on her block, and got a few modeling assignments. She also joined a dance class and learned everything from the waltz to the tango, as she had mastered all the black dances. She could really move her ass and feet on the dance floor. She finally graduated from college. She dated periodically and cautiously. She couldn't seem to find Mr. Right, the man who would be honest, shower her with love and affection, and give her those babies she so desperately wanted.

Two years later, Lucy would walk by the neighborhood all dressed up in the mornings and in the evenings going to work somewhere. She stayed sharp. Lucy loved wearing high heels and always smelled good. One day I ran up to her and asked her what made her smell so good.

"The Jean Nate I put on after my bath," she replied.

She always treated me well because I never teased her. The other kids were real brats and used to get on her nerves. I liked Lucy and definitely put Jean Nate on the list of things I was planned to buy when I was rich.

Lucy thought she was hot shit. I mean real hot. She had bright jewelry and wore wigs. All kinds of wigs, which intrigued us because they made her look different. Lucy was on the train one day during rush hour. She had her wig on and evidently didn't have it securely pinned. The car was crowded, and the woman sitting behind Lucy wanted to get off. When she grabbed the rail on the back of Lucy's seat, her watch got hooked on Lucy's wig and pulled it right off. The woman walked away unaware that Lucy's wig was dangling from her wrist. The minute Lucy realized her head felt cold, she went after the woman. Lucy touched her shoulder and whispered that she had her wig. The woman looked down and screamed.

"I was admiring all that pretty hair of yours as I sat behind you. Now I see that it isn't even real," she said to Lucy.

She untangled the wig from her watch and handed it back. Lucy quickly put it on in front of all the rush-hour people. She calmly returned to find a seat. The people on the train laughed hysterically. Lucy had never been so embarrassed in her life.

We thought she was a prostitute, but couldn't prove it. The other kids said things like "hooker" when she passed by, whistled, and did all kinds of devilish things. Lucy could not stand most of them, so she ignored them and switched on down the street.

As it turned out, Lucy Noble had a good job downtown. She wasn't a prostitute after all. She worked at a brokerage house and had a position as a stock liquidation clerk. She was levelheaded, had a gregarious personality, and people liked her. She and her family lived around the corner from us. Lucy was sharp, sensible, and had a bit of class. She was also very pretty.

Fifty-two-year-old widowed Peggy Kinard was a seamstress/designer who lived near us. She sewed for socialites in Philadelphia and was quite a social butterfly herself. She liked Lucy and almost everyone in the neighborhood. Having no kids, she kind of adopted the entire community as her family. She was especially fond of her godchild, Lucy. She used to let us all play in her beautiful dresses and wrap ourselves up in fine material. She often invited us to her shop in downtown Philadelphia for the day to watch her work and allowed us to make things for ourselves.

One year Peggy got a contract to do a fashion show in Norfolk, Virginia, and needed models for the show. She picked Lucy as one, who in return got a weekend trip. It was runway work for an entire weekend, all expenses paid, so Lucy was thrilled. They set a date for a photo shoot with a local photographer to take pictures of her wearing Peggy's designs. The slides would be shown on a big screen as Lucy came down the runway. She was excited and didn't care that she was only going to make twenty-five dollars for the whole weekend. She was just happy to be a part of it.

Since Reba Penster never went anywhere except to work and was always taking care of her own kids and others, Peggy decided to ask her along as a kind of wardrobe assistant. It didn't matter that she was color-blind and couldn't match her own clothing, because Peggy would have the outfits put together and labeled. Reba merely had to hand them to the models and help them dress. She was so quiet and shy and bored that Peggy thought it would be good for her to get away.

The bus left early one Friday afternoon with Peggy Kinard, Reba Penster, Lucy Noble, and about fifteen models hired by other seamstresses and designers in the area. When they arrived at the Château Hotel in Norfolk, they found the place absolutely gorgeous. Exquisite furniture graced the lobby; the dining room tables glittered. They were set with the finest china and glassware. The hotel boasted a splendid indoor swimming pool and two elegant bars. Reba and Lucy, roommates, thought they were in heaven. Neither had ever been outside of Philadelphia other than on a bus excursion to Wildwood, New Jersey, run by the neighborhood every summer. They had never seen a place as beautiful as this hotel. If Lucy hadn't thought she was hot shit before, she knew it for sure now.

Lucy and Reba had a ball unpacking and checking out each other's things. Reba pulled out her Ambush perfume, a new set of soaps, and some bath gels she had purchased for the trip. She also brought loads of Avon products with her.

"Hey, you want to try some of this? I've got everything."

Lucy sifted through the bottles and jars. "Yeah, you've got some nice stuff. Come take a look at what I brought." Lucy had the butter— Opium, Bijan, and Aromatics by Clinique. Reba tried them on and fell in love with all three fragrances.

"I'm throwing mine in the trash," she said, sort of pouting.

"Oh, come on. Don't feel like that. Let's switch for the weekend. Hell, I love Ambush. I ran out of it a couple of months ago and never got a chance to replace it," Lucy lied. She was being very careful with Reba because she knew she felt small and inadequate. Lucy intended to wear Ambush and Avon all weekend if it killed her.

"Let's put our clothes away," Lucy said.

Reba looked over at her suitcase and then at her friend's. "Let's go eat."

Lucy grabbed her hands and said softly, "Now let's go through this stuff you packed, little girl. Let's do nice, okay?"

Lucy began checking out the contents of the suitcase while Reba watched her expression. First she pulled out a red-and-black plaid skirt with gold running through it and a white blouse attached to it. A matching gold leather belt lay beneath it in the suitcase. Lucy looked at the outfit and put it on the bed. "Okay, what's next?"

Reba pulled out a blouse—olive green with hot pink polka dots. Attached was a mint green skirt and a black belt.

"Black goes with everything," Reba offered meekly. The third outfit was a navy blue tailored suit with a navy turtleneck.

"Can we talk?" Lucy said. "Look, I want to dress you this entire weekend. I'll also help you with your hair." She pointed to Reba's clothes. "All this shit stays in the suitcase. Don't show this stuff to anyone. You wear the same size as me, and I brought along loads of things. I'm going to hip you up this weekend. You can wear your things to work when you get home."

Lucy picked up the clothes on the bed and placed them back in the suitcase. Since Reba was already pretty, Lucy knew she would be gorgeous with the right clothes and makeup.

"We'll share the cosmetics," Lucy said. "Do we have a deal?"

"Okay, we got a deal. Shoes too? I wear a nine," Lucy said.

"I'm an eight—now what?" Reba said.

"Well, that means you go to Peggy's room and borrow shoes from her. *Comprende*?" Lucy said.

"*Comprende*." Reba smiled.

It was time for them to go to down for a late dinner. Peggy, who was more accustomed to places of this nature, went over the menu, which seemed extremely exotic to Lucy and Reba. She explained the entrees to them.

The company sponsoring the tour would pick up the expenses for the entire weekend, so they could have anything they wanted. Lucy chose Atlantic seafood and pasta, a mix of clams, mussels, shrimp, and scallops tossed with linguine in a basil-marinara sauce. Reba decided on roasted chicken marsala, which was sautéed chicken breast with mushrooms, wine, and roasted garlic served with wild rice and garden vegetables. Peggy ordered the three-nut crusted Chilean sea bass, pan seared with an almond, pecan, and walnut crust, served with wild rice and vegetables.

The food resembled something straight out of a gourmet magazine or the work of an artist. Everything was perfect until Reba asked the waiter for a bottle of ketchup. Lucy and Peggy had no idea why she wanted it. Although quite surprised at the request, the waiter quickly obliged. Reba doused every inch of her food, even the vegetables, with ketchup. Peggy Kinard nearly had a heart attack.

The waiter told them that there was a naval base in town, and if Lucy, Peggy, and Reba wanted a tour of the base, it could probably be arranged. They said they would probably do so before the weekend was out.

The fashion show was scheduled for Saturday night. It was now close to ten thirty, and Peggy and Lucy were about to retire. For some reason Reba wasn't tired. She was too excited about being away. She wanted to walk around for a while and finish checking the place out. Peggy and Lucy went to their rooms and left Reba in the lobby. She intended to take advantage of each and every minute of peace she had in this paradise so far away from the responsibilities of motherhood and marriage.

# Chapter Four

# *Sheila*

The ambulance arrived outside Stanley Mason's house. They quickly placed Perry Shoreman's body on a stretcher and proceeded to Holy Cross Hospital. He was bleeding profusely from the chest and neck. Sheila got the call from Stanley's wife, Vivian, and rushed to the hospital with her four children. On the way she thought about all the hard times she'd had with Perry since she met him in high school.

He always was a bunch of trouble. She couldn't understand how she'd been so stupid as to hook up with him in the first place. Sheila was smart in school and had aspirations. She made good grades and was well liked by teachers and students. She was a cheerleader at Roosevelt High. She was about five feet eight, and wore her hair in a becoming style. Her family didn't have much money, but Sheila was always presentable and looked nice.

Perry was on the track team at school. Skinny but kind of fine, he charmed Sheila into dating him. Even though he was fine, she really didn't want to go with him because he played hooky and didn't keep up with his work. He was always soliciting people to turn over their homework to him so he could copy it, and he cheated on tests. He shot craps with the older guys. When he did show up for school, he was usually late.

Perry liked Sheila, so he wouldn't leave her alone. He kept pestering her to give him a chance and to help him out with his work. He told her he'd straighten up. A few months into her junior year, Sheila started seeing him on a regular basis. They became a couple. He did a little better in school with Sheila's coaching.

A couple of months later Perry started to pressure her, but she kept saying no. Eventually after a few hot necking sessions and all that grinding he liked to do when her folks were at work, she gave up the crown jewels one afternoon when they were supposed to be studying.

Sheila was pregnant with Derek before the end of the school year and had him in October of what would have been her senior year. She never got a chance to return to school. On her eighteenth birthday in May of the next year, Perry and Sheila married. She was pregnant at the time with Dalton, who was born in December. After that came Margie and then Gregory, now almost two years old. Now twenty-seven with four kids, Sheila lived in a run-down shack and had a husband who stayed in the streets, gambled, drank, and blew their money. She no longer weighed one hundred fourteen pounds, but had ballooned to two hundred fifty pounds. Her hair was a wiry mess. Sheila was disgusted with herself.

She got to the hospital and parked her beat-up Chevy. She left the kids in the car and rushed inside to ask the nurse at the reception area about Perry. They took her right back to him. He lay there with tubes in him everywhere while they worked to save his life. He wasn't conscious. She stared at him for a moment as mixed emotions surged through her mind. First she was sorry for Perry, then she was scared for him, herself, and her kids. Would he live or die? If he did live, would he have learned a lesson or continue to be reckless and stupid for the rest of his life?

She pondered how they would make it and whether she could get a job. Who would help her out with the kids if she went to work? Gregory was two and was still in diapers. Every time she saw a nurse in a white uniform go by, she hated herself for being so hot in the ass and dumb back in high school. She hated Perry for robbing her of her dreams of being a nurse.

The doctor asked Sheila to leave the room. She did, and took a seat in the waiting room. She decided to get the kids out of the car in case they could see Perry. She got them settled down, bought cold drinks, and waited. She called Perry's mother and father and told them what had happened to Perry. Now they too were waiting anxiously. Perry was in surgery.

At one fifteen the doctor arrived to tell them that Perry had died on the operating table. Mr. and Mrs. Shoreman sobbed, along with ten-year-old Derek, but the other kids remained silent. Sheila didn't say a word. She picked up Gregory, told the rest of the kids to follow her, and abruptly left the hospital. She never even asked about the body or the particulars of what had gone on in the operating room. She didn't know if his heart had given out or if his lung was gone or if the anesthesia had killed him. After ten years Sheila simply did not give a damn and didn't want to know all the details concerning what had prevented Perry from not making it home to his family another night.

At least she'd been smart enough to have a life insurance policy on him. It was only for three thousand dollars, but it was more than she'd had in a long time. He was her husband, so she did have to use part of it to bury him. She let his mother handle the arrangements because she herself was still mad as hell at Perry and hadn't yet shed a tear. She gave the Shoremans five hundred dollars for funeral expenses. They could add more if they liked, but she was keeping the rest for herself and the kids. They were furious but accepted what she offered and tried to send Perry off decently to heaven or hell or wherever he was going.

Everyone from the neighborhood came to the funeral. Even though Lance shot Perry, Libby and her family came to offer their condolences. On that long pew up front sat Sheila and the kids, Mr. and Mrs. Shoreman, Perry's sister, Eileen, and her husband, Teddy. Their three kids sat behind the Shoremans. It turned out to be a pretty nice funeral, and the neighbors sent beautiful flowers. After the funeral director finished and all the words were spoken, they opened the casket for the final viewing. The congregation filed by, silent and solemn faced. Then came Eileen and her bunch, the Shoremans, Perry's kids, and, at the very end, came Sheila.

She went up to the casket alone and just stood there looking at Perry. Everyone figured she was about to break down and cry because she loved her husband and would miss him. Grief would finally hit her, and she was ready to let it all out. Everyone knows how wives act when they lose their husbands. Sheila hadn't shown any emotion since Perry's death. It had been a week, yet there was little or no response from Sheila. Many of us thought she had gone crazy or was in a trance or something.

"If she keeps all that grief locked up in her, she'll go crazy for sure," Grandma kept saying.

Sheila was still livid with Perry for all of this shit. The next thing we knew, Sheila suddenly started to choke Perry and smack him in the face, right there in the casket.

"You miserable low-life son of a bitch, you were always a pain in the ass. Always a problem. Your ass should be dead because you weren't worth anything alive. I ought to shoot you again right here," she shouted.

Friends ran up to stop her, but they couldn't pull her off. Sheila had him by the neck, dragging him out of the casket. His body fell on the floor and so did Sheila. Several people pulled Sheila's fat ass down the aisle, and others got Perry back into the casket. Mrs. Shoreman passed out. Sheila was kicking and hollering that she wasn't finished with Perry. She announced that she intended to dig him up after he was buried and finish beating the shit out of him. By then no one was paying much attention to what she was saying, because both Perry's shoes were missing from his feet, lost in the scuffle, and relatives and neighbors were searching for them. That funeral was something else!

After a month, the Shoremans were still irate at Sheila for attempting to kill their son all over again. Sheila didn't care what they thought. That no-good bastard had ruined her dreams and had almost cost them their home. She despised him for dying and not being around for his children and being a rotten example of a father. She'd hated it when thugs, people she had nothing to do with, knocked on the door, asked for him, and left messages that they wanted the money he owed them. He truly did ruin her life, and she felt stupid for ever bothering with him.

Since his death all she did was sit around feeling sorry for herself, eating uncontrollably and gaining weight. She was so filled with hatred and fury that she consulted a psychiatrist for anger management and was placed on tranquilizers. Her cousin Terri stopped by late one afternoon, and there was Sheila on the couch, staring into space with tears streaming down her face, a bottle of tranquilizers in her hand. Terri held and rocked her, and they both cried.

"Sheila, what can I do, what can we do for you?" Terri said. "You've got friends. Let us help. We're all worried sick about you." Sheila didn't answer. Finally Terri thought about what a fighter Sheila had always been. She felt sorry for her favorite cousin. Sheila needed to release something in order to get well, so Terri changed her tune from begging and pleading with Sheila. She stood up and yelled at her.

"Listen, bitch, we been hanging for a long time together through thick and thin, goddamn it! You better get yourself together and fight to stay alive! Now get your ass up! You've been talking about cursing that bastard Perry out and tonight you'll get your chance. Get your shit on and let's go. I'll make a couple of phone calls while you get ready. The first one will be to Pam Resnick to come babysit and the second will be to Wesley to round up his crew. We'll go to the fucking cemetery and dig his dead ass up! If that's what it takes to get you to come around, to come back, to get some closure, then that's what we're going to do!"

Sheila tried to say she could not, would not go. It didn't matter, and she didn't care.

"Bitch, I've known you since you were bald-headed and cockeyed," Terri replied. "You've never backed away from anything in your whole damn life. Let's go!"

Sheila wouldn't budge, so Terri shook her and pleaded, "Please, please, come with me." Terri was crying with frustration. At last Sheila obediently went to get ready. Pam Resnick showed up in a hurry, but they waited an hour and a half for Wesley and four of his friends.

"You owe me money and favors up the kazoo. I need a big one tonight. It will sound crazy, but we have to do this," Terri said when Wesley walked in the door.

"Do what?" asked Wesley.

"We have to go out to the cemetery and dig up Sheila's husband." Wesley looked petrified at first, and then he laughed.

"Your mind has gone, Terri, and so has your cousin's. You expect me to go out there and tell my boys this? You gotta be joking. What are the two of you on? Give me a hit of that shit."

"I'm serious, Wesley. Please," Terri pleaded.

"What the hell are we going to do with him once we dig him up— bring him back here? You guys getting back together or something?" He looked at Sheila. "Oh, no, Terri, I'm not carting his dead ass around. I don't owe you that much money. We'll all go to jail tonight."

"We ain't taking him anywhere. We're just going to fuck him up."

"He's already fucked up," said Wesley. "Shit, the man is dead. By the way, didn't your cousin fuck him up enough at the funeral? Shit, how many ass whippings does he have to take? Damn, the man already got shot, didn't survive the hospital, died, got his ass beaten at his own funeral, and now we got to dig him up and kick his ass again? I feel sorry for the poor guy. Jesus Christ, you two are hard on a brother. Remind me not to ever marry either one of you."

"Oh, shut up, Wesley," said Sheila, who had entered the room dressed to go. "We aren't going to jail. Let's just hurry and get it done before I change my mind."

Wesley stood still for a minute, shaking his head and laughing, then went out to his car. They didn't know if he'd come back or not, but in a few minutes he returned.

"How many shovels do you have?" he asked.

Terri, Sheila, and the three guys left with two shovels and gathered three more from the neighbors. They stopped to buy five decks of cards. On the way to the cemetery, Sheila announced that she wanted to stop at the hospital.

"What's the matter, you sick?" Terri said.

"I have to pick up something, I'll only be a minute."

"What, another dead body—did somebody else make you mad?" Wesley sarcastically asked.

Sheila came out twenty minutes later carrying a bag. At the cemetery they all dug until they got to the casket. They cranked it open, and Sheila took a long look at her dead husband. He stank like shit. She started telling him off.

"You got the nerve to be laying there all dressed up, you sack of shit. You still owe me for the clothes you're wearing. I should have been able to dress up, too, but I never got the chance to wear what I wanted to wear. I have it with me now though, goddamn it."

Sheila pulled a nurse's cap and a lab coat out of the bag and put them on. She cursed him out and cried for forty-five minutes. She hauled him out of the casket, kicked him a couple of times, smacked him around, and left him on the ground. She took out the five decks of cards, opened each pack, and spread them all over him—one deck for each of the kids and one for her. Then they left.

When Mr. and Mrs. Shoreman heard about it, they tried to file charges against Sheila, but they couldn't prove she had anything to do with it. After that night Sheila was fine and seemed ready to move on. She wasn't bitter anymore and decided to lose weight, get some help with the kids, go back to school, fix up her place, and be the finest nurse and mother in the world.

First, she had to find a babysitter. Gregory was almost two, and Margie was nearly five and would be attending kindergarten in the fall. She made inquiries and found that a woman by the name of Lenora Bush, who was about fifty-two, was looking for a housekeeping job. She also needed a place to stay. Since her husband had passed away, she was having a hard time making ends meet and was lonely. Sheila heard about her from Beverly Resnick, who was married to Bernard (Buzzy) Resnick, Lance's brother.

They had known each other for a long time and attended the same church. Beverly was a good, reliable person. Sheila trusted her judgment, so she set up an appointment for Mrs. Bush to meet with her.

Using some of the money from Perry's life insurance settlement, Sheila had fixed the place up nicely. The money helped to buy new carpet, beds for the kids, and new curtains. She also purchased a badly needed stove and refrigerator. Sheila was still on the County Assistance Program, but she did get an extra check from Perry's Social Security benefits. Thank God he had worked legitimately part of his life.

Sheila had all her plans in order. She was a smart girl and, with the seven hundred dollars left over, she planned to get herself through school and earn her degree as a registered nurse at last.

Mrs. Bush was due on Wednesday afternoon at two thirty. Sheila wanted her to come by a little before Dalton and Derek got home so they would have a quiet time to talk. She had put Margie and Gregory down for a nap. That way they had peace and quiet, and the woman would not be scared off with brats running all over the place.

Lenora Bush was a pretty, slender woman who in no way looked her age. She was dressed nicely in a light blue-and-white striped cotton dress, sheer stockings that made her legs look lovely, and navy blue shoes. Her hair was dark reddish brown and worn in a bun. "How did she keep so slender?" Sheila wondered. She had white gloves in her hand and carried a navy handbag with a gold clasp. Very classy. She had never had any children of her own but had taken care of kids almost all her life. Sheila liked her.

Sheila missed having her own parents around. They had moved to New Orleans seven years ago when Sheila's grandmother fell ill. Sheila was an only child now because her younger brother had died of pneumonia when he was eleven. Sheila described her situation to Mrs. Bush, showed her around the house, including the redecorated spare bedroom, and explained what her goals were. She was still on the diet she had started the day after she left the cemetery. She had lost nearly forty-three pounds but still had a way to go. It all was extremely important to her.

"Do you think you'd like to come to stay with us? I mean will you?" she asked Mrs. Bush. Sheila could only pay forty dollars a week, but would take care of all the bills and also feed Mrs. Bush. She told her that whatever money of her own she had coming in she could keep.

"Please help me get myself together. I do intend to get ahead, and I'll take care of you for the rest of your life."

Mrs. Bush looked into Sheila's eyes and saw she could trust her. She wanted to help.

They had chatted for about fifteen minutes when Derek and Dalton came in from school. They were polite kids and sat right down to talk with Mrs. Bush. Sheila went up to get Gregory and Margie to introduce them to "Auntie Len," as Lenora told everyone to call her. She could start next week, as soon as she got packed up.

Everything worked out fine. Sheila started taking adult education courses at the local college to earn her high school diploma. She worked hard at it and, in another six months, would be eligible to start nursing school. The kids adored Auntie Len, and she loved them back. Lenora knew how to keep them in line, too. Sheila was steadily losing weight on a steamed vegetable and fish diet and wouldn't even think about anything fattening. She was actually starting to look good. She exercised like a maniac and had a sharp new hairstyle.

Sheila loved having long talks with Lenora, and they became close friends. Lenora had taken over all the cooking as well as all the housework. She went out only on Sunday nights to play bingo.

A fur store in town needed a part-time accounts receivable clerk, and Sheila got the job. She worked five days a week from two o'clock until closing at six. Then she went home to help Auntie Len feed the kids and clean up the kitchen. She hustled to get their school clothes ready before heading to the gym until the place closed at ten o'clock. And that was where she met Leonard.

# Chapter Five

# *Amber*

Grandpa always woke up promptly at six thirty to get ready for work, but this was New Year's Day, and the station was closed. He got up anyway, ran his bath, and planned to have breakfast, which he usually made himself along with his morning coffee. It sure was quiet in the house. He noticed that Grandma hadn't made it home and had left their bedroom a complete mess, with clothing scattered all over and drawers pulled out. He thought she must have had a hard time trying to find something to wear and left in an awful rush. She was probably still gambling at Libby's.

He had his bath and washed that wonderful hair of his, slicking it down as usual, and got dressed. Grandpa was such an immaculate man. He was born April 12, an Aries. They are the cleanest men in the world. Neat, too. They like things in order. Grandpa took two baths each and every day and always smelled like a rose. He wouldn't even eat dinner when he returned from work until after his bath. I loved the way Grandpa smelled.

It was time to make breakfast. By seven fifteen he was wondering why Renee wasn't making any noise upstairs. He was used to her waking up around that time. Lazy, whorish Paula was probably knocked out upstairs. He went up to check on Renee. She was still asleep. Paula's bedroom resembled a disaster area, with clothes all over the place and everything out of the jewelry box strewn all over the bureau. Why in the world had Paula and Fannie torn the house up like this? Slick-ass Paula probably put Renee to bed later last night so she wouldn't wake up early. That way she could sleep off her booze a little longer or show up later if she picked up some good-for-nothing bum and let him screw her.

As Grandpa was checking on Renee, he decided to give his two angels, Sydni and me, a peek and a kiss. He was astonished that we weren't in our room and was immediately worried. He knew we had planned to stay home last night and that the sitter had come. What the hell was going on? Where was everybody?

"Now I know that Nina child was suppose to stay here all night," he said aloud to himself. He was sure we hadn't left the house to go down to Johnny Penster's late at night without waking him. Grandpa couldn't read or write and didn't have Libby's or the Pensters' telephone number. He had to sit and wait, because he wasn't about to wake Renee or leave her in the house asleep to go look for us.

Grandpa was really worried. He loved his family, even though Paula and Grandma really didn't treat him right. Grandma Fannie did whatever she wanted; she was only after his paycheck. She sure hadn't acted like that when he met her twelve years ago at Lauder's Tap Room on Hill Street. Back then Grandma was sweeter than sugar and gorgeous. Tall and lanky, she was forty and he was twenty-eight. Grandpa liked to drink his beer and stay out a little after work, but he was a good guy and a good provider. He helped her out with Paula as best he could. Grandma demanded he turn over his paycheck to her every week and gave him only enough money for the streetcar. He took his lunch to work. Grandma didn't drive and neither did Paula. Grandma had never worked a day in her life. She had moved to Philadelphia from Macon, Georgia, when she was eighteen.

Grandpa was raised in Lynchburg, Virginia. He had eight brothers and three sisters, and his entire family was still down South. He had no education because they were dirt poor and he had to work to help out, never getting a chance to go to school. He moved to Philadelphia when he was twenty-four and got a job delivering coal. It paid well, but Grandpa couldn't stay. He needed to drive, but unable to read or write, he couldn't get a license. He was able to stay on for a little while because there was a lot of work with such a cold winter. They used two guys on a truck. The other man drove, while Grandpa helped with the unloading. Eventually they had to let him go, but he got a job pumping gas. He had been living in a rooming house when Grandma snatched him up and married him.

Before marriage, he was having a ball. Nobody bothered him, and he had a pocket full of money most of the time. He had his beer and some clothes and looked good, a really attractive young man. After Grandma got a hold of him, he had to work harder and got pretty much nothing in return. He was also disrespected big-time by his wife. She cooked dinner for him, that was it. He washed his clothes on a washboard in the tub every night and ironed every piece himself. He couldn't afford to buy any new ones because she controlled all the money. She stayed sharp all the time and continuously complained that she didn't get enough to make ends meet.

Grandpa found enjoyment in the pride of his life—me—and drinking his beer. He'd grown uncaring about anything else. From time to time, Grandma obliged him with sex. He managed to keep a few dollars for himself from tips, occasionally hitting the numbers for a nickel or a dime and not letting Grandma know about it. He never suspected she was cheating on him, and she was doing it big-time.

Grandma sneaked men into the house during the day and met them at places at night. She was also stingy—tightfisted with everything, including food. One day she had cooked dinner and a plate of fried chicken was on the table. Grandpa wanted a second helping, and she actually smacked his hand away, telling him not to touch the food. Imagine that. The man bought all the damn food and paid all the bills and couldn't have anything more after she fixed his plate.

Grandpa decided to make some coffee and have a little breakfast while he waited for Renee to wake up and for Grandma and Paula to return or call. He couldn't believe the mess.

A funny smell polluted the air. He checked the refrigerator—nothing unusual. He started looking around the stove. Though there was a burnt smell, there were no charred pots in there or in the sink. Then he opened the oven door and found the burned-up baby doll had melted all over the oven racks. It was a horror. He could not figure out why it was there or who was responsible for such a thing. He closed the oven door and stood in the kitchen transfixed.

"What the shit is going on?" he yelled at the ceiling. "What is this place turning into? Fannie better get home and tell me something and put this goddamn place back in order!"

About eight o'clock on New Year's Day, the phone rang. It was Grandma calling from the police station. She told Grandpa to bring the fifty-five dollars she needed to get out of jail. He informed her that Sydni and I weren't home and he had no idea where we were. Did she know of our whereabouts? He also asked her why the house was such a wreck, with the doll cooked in the oven and all the rest. Grandma refused to answer any questions, but did tell him that she had Sydni and me with her and that he better come right away. She asked about Paula, but he had no idea where she was. Grandpa said he had no money. She asked him again, thinking he might be holding out on her. She suspected he secretly saved up tips or something. When she realized he really had no money or wasn't giving it up, she told him to take apart the light-switch plate in their bedroom and feel inside the wall for money. She instructed him to remove fifty-five dollars plus three dollars in carfare, making it exactly fifty-eight dollars he could use of her "house money." Then she told him to get Renee and come to the police station at Twentieth and Pennsylvania, which was about ten blocks away.

Grandpa couldn't stand Grandma, and today he was especially pissed at her. He woke Renee and washed and dressed her. She really was a cute little thing. Big brown eyes and jet-black curly hair. She was just as plump as a little hen, leading him to call her "chicken."

He got the money. There must have been over three hundred dollars in that wall! That bitch was always crying broke when she had all that! The rent was only sixty-five dollars a month, and she certainly didn't splurge on food.

"Man," he thought, "Fannie was ripping me off big time." He hadn't known how much she was up on gambling or where it was stashed.

Grandpa arrived at the police station a little after ten o'clock. He was surprised to see so many people he knew—even Mrs. Dunlap, who sat at the desk signing herself out. Her daughter, big fat Elsie Kendrick, had come to get her. Grandpa just stood there and gazed at them all. Many said hello and wished him a Happy New Year. He spotted Sydni and me at a desk in the corner looking scared to death. He noticed our weird clothing and our peculiar hairdos.

"Poor babies," he thought. "They were probably sleeping peacefully at Libby's when the place got raided, and all those police frightened them to pieces." He had told Grandma so many times she shouldn't have us kids over there when they were gambling. Now his babies were in jail. He was furious with her, so angry he felt like taking Sydni and me home and leaving Grandma's hardheaded ass in jail.

Paula—that tramp—where was she? She could never watch her own kids because she was always too busy running the streets. If Grandpa weren't afraid Horace would kill her, he'd let him know that his baby

Renee had been to the police station. That's all Horace needed to hear. He adored that child.

Grandpa came over and hugged us and told us he was so sorry we had gotten locked up with Grandma. He knew when he spotted Libby in the crowd that her place had been raided.

"That damn Libby," he thought. Why couldn't she just get a job and stop all of that speakeasy shit. Now she had gone and gotten his grand-kids arrested.

Grandma was led out of the cell and taken to the other side of the room. She was talking to McNight when she spotted Grandpa and Renee with us. They processed her out and told her she would receive papers in the mail about her hearing in a couple of weeks. Grandpa passed Renee over to her and scooped me up into his arms. He took Sydni by the hand, and we all went out and crossed the street to wait for the bus.

Grandpa hadn't asked Grandma a single question in the police station. Finally he turned and peered at her for a long time with a puzzled expression on his face.

"Fannie," he said, "I can understand your being late for your party and messing up the bedroom and rushing out. I guess Paula had the same problem and ended up turning her room upside down. I know what a no-good tramp she is, so I'm not surprised she didn't make it home. I guess you two probably had a few drinks before going out and left the kitchen a wreck. I can imagine how you and my grandkids ended up in jail. I'm just trying to understand why you have them dressed this way. I figure you got Halloween and New Year's Eve mixed up and that's why you did it."

He pointed to our clothing, touching Sydni's long pleated skirt and holding up my face with all the makeup on it.

"But please explain one thing I can't understand. Why the fuck did you bake that baby doll?"

"Oscar, please leave me alone until we get home."

Sydni and I looked at each other and then down at the ground. We absolutely did not want to go home. I wished I knew a magic trick to make us disappear.

# Chapter Six

# *Sheila*

Sheila looked down at the scale. It read one hundred ninety-eight pounds. She grinned from ear to ear.

"Oh Lord, please just take me on down this road to one hundred forty pounds," she prayed.

Things were going so well in Sheila's life these days that she couldn't believe it. The household situation was working out perfectly. The kids were happy and Auntie Len was doing a fine job.

Just last night Auntie Len had said, "I'm really happy we came across each other because your family has filled a void in my life. I'm so glad I can help all of you, too."

Sheila hugged her.

Leonard Toland was six feet two inches tall, with a beautiful brown complexion. He worked at Parson's Steel Mill in the suburb of Springfield, had a peaceful demeanor, and was single. He'd had his eye on Sheila for a few months, watching her work out at the gym, and she thought he was kind of cute, too. He was thirty-five years old and had been divorced for about two years. He had two children, a girl and a boy, who lived with their mother in town. Leonard lived on the west side of Philadelphia in a small house he rented.

He usually kept his children every other weekend, every other holiday, and one month in the summer. Sheila was happy to hear about Leonard's relationship with his children. Knowing he was a good father made her respect him. She liked that about a man. Leonard said that he liked to go fishing, that he was a health nut and watched his diet. He didn't care for playing cards or gambling. That was a load off her mind. Once in a while he even managed to attend church. She felt even better about him because of that.

After Leonard had been eyeing Sheila for a while, he went up to her and said, "Where's your husband?"

Whenever someone said "husband" to Sheila, and she thought about what a "husband" was really supposed to be and do, she would think about all the crap she had gone through to have a "husband" and would get real mad at Perry all over again. She thought about all the businesses she tried to start for him, all the ironing she'd taken in to make ends meet, all that money he'd gambled away. His lack of ambition and his irresponsibility had often terrified her.

So when Leonard asked, "Where's your husband?" Sheila politely looked dead into his eyes and said, "I don't know."

"What do you mean, you don't know?"

"Look, Mr. Newspaper, I don't know *exactly* where he is. The last time I saw him was when I went out to the cemetery and dug his grave up and beat the daylights out of him, because he made things real miserable for my children and me. I'm pissed off that he did not even have sense enough to keep himself alive. So I don't know where he is *exactly* because, after I dug him up, I just left him out of his coffin on the cemetery ground with five decks of cards thrown all over him. Cards are what he loved and cards are what got him killed. I figured since those cards meant so much to him in life, then he ought to have them in death. I didn't have time to put him back, so either he walked away, or somebody put him back, or he lay there and rotted away in the dirt. So that's why I can't say for sure where he is. Does that answer your question, Mr. Newspaper?"

Now Leonard thought she was not only cute but hilarious. When he stopped laughing, he said to Sheila, "Do you want to go out on a date? I don't play cards."

Leonard had asked Sheila on a date for three months, but she kept declining. She wanted to concentrate on school, her diet, and her family. She was reluctant to start a new relationship because she felt it would distract her from her goals. She thought about how she had rushed into things with Perry long ago. Now she basically wanted to take some time to get her life together without being responsible for a relationship. Also, she wanted to trim herself down before a man saw her with her clothes off, but she didn't tell Leonard that.

Leonard kept trying. Sheila was flattered and enjoyed his flirting. It made her feel good sometimes. He also called her "baby." It had been a long time since anyone had done that and it made her feel sexy. Sheila couldn't remember the last time she'd felt sexy. She'd been mad at Perry so much during the marriage that whenever they did have sex it was simply sex. Just going through the motions to bring themselves to an or-gasm. That's how it was—mad, automated sex—like robots.

One day, when Sheila was coming into the house from work, Auntie Len said to her, "Do you think we could make some new arrangements about my helping you and the kids? I would like to have Mondays off if we can swing it."

"What's the matter, are we driving you crazy? Or you just don't love us anymore?" Sheila replied, smiling.

"Oh, no, honey," Lenora said. "It's just that I met a friend at my bingo game and she's a widow, too. She lives around the corner from the bingo hall and invited me to stay there on Sunday nights because bingo is over so late. That way, I wouldn't have to take the streetcar back home and we could do some fun things on Mondays like movies or shopping. Some girl talk, you know? It just feels good being around someone your own age."

Sheila nodded. "Well, let's figure out how we can arrange it. I would have to get a sitter here by seven thirty in the morning when I leave for school. What time did you plan to be back on Monday?"

"Oh, I guess about six in the evening if that's okay."

"I'm all for it. Like I said, I just have to work out the details and find someone responsible to be here."

"Thanks, Sheila, I really appreciate it."

After dinner, Sheila called Beverly.

"Hi, Beverly, this is Sheila, how's it going?"

"Hey, Sheila, pretty good, how are you doing?"

"I'm doing fine, girl."

"How are you making out with Lenora?"

"She is a dream come true. That's why I'm calling you." Sheila went on to explain the situation.

"You know my daughter Pam, the seventeen-year-old?" Beverly said. "She's out of school now and hasn't found a job yet. She may attend Community College next year, but she's looking for something to do now and she might watch your kids. I wish she would, because all she does is stay around here all the time, eating all my food and having her friends in and out and feeding them too. Just having her and them out of my house one whole day would be a help to me. I'll ask her and call you back."

"That would be great if she will do it. Be sure to call me back."

"Hey, Sheila, when do you need her to start?"

"Next Monday if she can."

"Okay. Let's see what I can do."

Beverly called back the next night and told Sheila that she had a sitter. Pam got on the phone and said, "Miss Sheila, the only thing that bothers me about taking the job is that I'll have to get up so early to get over there by seven thirty in the morning. I have to shower and get dressed and take the bus there. Do you think I could stay over Sunday nights?"

Sheila thought about it for a moment. She knew she wouldn't be able to pick Pam up and Lenora's bed would be empty anyway.

"Okay, Pam, you be here every Sunday evening before eight o'clock and you'll leave Monday evening by six fifteen."

"Great."

"Will ten dollars for the day plus carfare and food be okay?" Sheila asked.

"Yes, that's fine."

The next Sunday, while Sheila was in the kitchen cooking dinner, Lenora dressed for the bingo game and packed her overnight bag. She rushed out with only a short good-bye. Pam arrived about eight o'clock. Sheila hadn't seen her in such a long time. She was cute and had those Resnick good looks and the thickest auburn hair in the world. She was built nice too, but just a tiny bit plump. Sheila could tell why by watching her eat. Pam seemed to love Sheila's cooking. Sheila laughed and said to her, "Pam, are you going to eat me out of house and home?"

"I'm sorry, Miss Sheila, but I haven't eaten since lunch, because me and my friends were at the movies. When I got home, I had to hurry to get over here."

After dinner, Sheila cleaned her kitchen and had the kids show Pam around the house and to Auntie Len's room where she would sleep. Pam sat down on the bed and admired the room. Lenora sure had it fixed up nicely. Her bedroom set was simply gorgeous. The drapes were a beautiful shade of green with a little navy and mauve running through them. Pam's family had a nice house, too, but she had never seen such a pretty room. Lenora had a French telephone that looked like brass, with an ivory receiver. Pam looked through the closet. There were some fine clothes in there and a beautiful mink jacket. The perfumes on the dresser smelled divine. Either this woman or Miss Sheila had to be rich, she thought. Somebody had some money around that house.

Then Pam went through Lenora's drawers and discovered some of the finest undergarments she had ever seen. Silks and satins that looked like the stuff in magazines. Beautiful hair clips in a silver jewelry case.

"Whew!" Pam whispered. By the bed stood an exquisite walnut table with one drawer. Pam opened it. Just some musty old papers and a couple of books. She spotted a small green plaid book marked "Philadelphia Savings Fund Society." She opened the book, flipped through, and saw pages of deposits. The current balance read $8,458.78.

"Wow!" exclaimed Pam, "this lady is rich!"

Downstairs the phone rang. Sheila answered.

"Whatcha doing, you warm, sexy, feisty, wonderful, beautiful, charming, independent woman?"

Sheila burst out laughing. "Leonard, what do you want?"

"What do I want? What do I want? Well, I want a million dollars, the best of health, a long life, a couple of strippers a few times a week who would come to my house and do a little dance for me, a chef, a chauffeur, and a sailboat. However, I'll pass all that stuff up for a date with Sheila who thinks she is too good for me."

Sheila started giggling again. Leonard told her about his day and his plans for the week. Sheila told him that Lenora was now off on Sunday nights and Mondays and they had a new sitter filling in for her.

"Since you have a sitter and you laugh when I flirt with you, can I take you for coffee or a cocktail at Bourbon's downtown next Sunday at seven o'clock?" Leonard said. "If you say no, I won't ask you out again. I am tired of being rejected."

"Hold on," Sheila said. "Pam!" she yelled into the living room. Pam didn't answer. Sheila put the phone down, walked to the stairs, and yelled again. "Pam!"

"Yes," Pam answered, and came toward the stairs.

"Can you be here at six thirty next Sunday?"

"Yes, Miss Sheila, no problem."

# Chapter Seven

# *Paula*

"Happy New Year," he said, rolling off her. Paula smiled. The smile turned into a grin and the grin became a chuckle that escalated into a laugh. She was extremely happy this New Year's Day because she had a fine new twenty-year-old man, and he seemed to be crazy about her. She had met him at the Rockaway bar last night. He was pretty good in bed and well hung, which pleased Paula immensely. He had a good job at the post office, a modest apartment, and all the latest music. He came from Detroit and had two sisters who lived over on Judson Street. He had been working since he was fourteen and had saved a lot of money. He was smart and a high school graduate, with no kids and a car. His name was Earl Frazier and he lived only two blocks from Paula. Best of all, he seemed like he'd want to screw all the time. They had done it three times since she got there at two thirty that morning. He was her kind of man, all right.

Paula wasn't worried about Horace looking for her. He'd gone to Florida for the holidays to see his parents. He'd bought all the kids' stuff for Christmas before he left and wasn't due back for two weeks. He also had business with some properties he owned down there. Things were pretty cool for her to get to know Earl a lot better without Horace being a hindrance.

Paula decided to keep Earl a secret. She intended to tell Earl to stay out of the Rockaway from now on. That way they would never be seen together. She made up her mind, too, that he couldn't pick her up or take her home, so no one could find out and tell Horace. Paula had it all figured out. Because he was so much younger and new in town, she could handle him. She only had to keep him happy in bed and find interesting things for him to do. She certainly could do that.

The next day after work, she went to buy some grapes to feed him in bed. Eventually she would train him with whipped cream and all. Sooner or later she'd get keys to his place and would be able to go there whenever she wanted. This way, she could monitor him and keep him from bringing other women there. She would make him her love slave and her banker and have some fun with him, too. Later on in the game, they'd take some trips on the weekends. It was going to be marvelous!

Earl started getting hungry, so he and Paula got up, put on some Sam Cooke and Aretha Franklin CDs, and began to fix breakfast. He had loads of stuff in the refrigerator. She made pancakes, home fries, which were her specialty, and scrambled eggs. He had a bottle of cheap champagne left over from last night, so Paula made mimosas. He was really impressed. After breakfast they took a nice warm shower. She taught him how to screw her standing up, letting the water run down on them. She had that young boy hollering for his mama. Paula was something else.

She began dressing, hating to leave, but she had better get home. Fannie and Oscar were sure to curse her out, but she didn't give a damn. Even if they beat her, they couldn't beat the fun out of her. She told Fannie last night when the Rockaway closed that she would walk since it was only three blocks. Fannie believed her, but Paula had already arranged with Earl to meet him around the corner.

Paula arrived home about two fifteen that afternoon. As soon as she put her key in the door, she heard Grandma's big mouth yelling. Paula thought, "Who did what? Why did I even bother to come back home? Here I am, back to reality. Reality stinks."

Sydni and I were at the kitchen table with our heads down when Paula came in.

"Where the hell have you been?" asked Grandma.

"Out," Paula replied. By then Grandma had told us to take baths, so we didn't have those crazy outfits on anymore.

"Sit the hell down and don't say a word," Grandma ordered. "Listen to me, and I mean it. If you say one word, I'll beat you half to death and I'll tell Horace when he comes back. So for once in your life, girl, you better listen up."

"Okay, but first tell me what stinks so bad in here," said Paula.

"Shut up," said Grandma. "I have been in jail most of the night. Libby's house was raided by the cops, and they took us all in. Her place was raided because someone sent the police there looking for me."

Paula's eyes grew big. Who would have wanted Grandma locked up?

Somebody's wife? Grandpa stood there listening to the whole thing and not uttering a word.

"The person who sent the cops for me was my ten-year-old grand-daughter, Amber Colette Gray, who's sitting at this table." Paula was totally bewildered by now. "My granddaughter sent for me because she and her sister were in jail. You know, the one right there." She pointed at Sydni. "And they had a friend with them—their babysitter, Nina Penster." Grandma took a breath and started pacing around the kitchen slowly as if she were a lawyer in court giving a summation to the jury.

"It seems the children were kidnapped. They decided after we left to get dressed up for New Year's and go out." Paula just sat there and shook her head in amazement.

"They hitchhiked with a man and told him they lived downtown. So he took them downtown. Then they decided to steal his car keys and run away with them, only Miss Amber didn't make it out of the car with her accomplices. The man wouldn't let her go. So the other two, Miss Sydni and Miss Nina, got the cops to assist them, and they all went to the police station.

"You, Miss Pain-in-the-ass Paula—who lied, telling me you were coming home and didn't show up—weren't here when the police tried to reach you to get your children. Soooo, since *your* children couldn't be released to Johnny Penster who, by the way, was at home to receive the news that his child was in jail, Miss Amber sent the police to Libby's house for me."

Grandma rested a moment. Paula looked scared to death.

"Not only did the police find me," Grandma went on, "they also found everybody we know except you and Horace and Oscar at Libby's house and arrested us all. And by the way, that stink you inquired about is the baby doll Horace bought Amber for Christmas. She decided to bake the damn doll because she wanted it to match her complexion! Your children were dressed like hookers when they left the house, wearing your clothes and mine. Nina Penster even had the nerve to put on one of my nightgowns and my fur coat!"

Flabbergasted, Paula rolled her eyes and sucked her teeth, avoiding Grandma's gaze.

"I cleaned this kitchen up because there were glasses and soda and juice everywhere. They were trying to make Thunderbird. They did do one good thing, they didn't drag little Renee out with them. They left her behind with Oscar."

Grandpa was hearing the story for the first time. When we had all arrived home, Grandma refused to say a word to him. She would only talk to us girls and help to clean up the mess. Now that he'd heard the whole story, he looked at Paula and Grandma. He looked at his two precious grandchildren and burst out laughing. He laughed so long and so hard that tears came out of his eyes, and he was banging his fists on the countertop.

Every time he looked back at Grandma, he burst out laughing again, and she was getting sick of it. She sure was pissed at him. She wanted to hit him so bad. Sydni and I looked at our grandfather strangely because we had never seen him this happy. Never. Not ever in our entire lives. We started to feel a little more comfortable and weren't so scared anymore.

That's when Grandma and Paula noticed us at the same time. Grandma swiveled her head around the way she did when she was real mad.

"Don't get too relaxed because you knooooow," and when Grandma said "know" and put the emphasis on the "o," her neck and head started to go around like an owl's and her eyes rolled around like a drunk. Her head went from side to side. Just when we expected her to do her power jig or dance or something of that nature, Grandpa stopped her dead in her tracks by holding his hand up, palm out.

"Hold it, lady," he sternly said. Grandpa never stood up to Grandma much or even Paula, but he did this time. He had the floor.

"If either of you two bitches touches these kids or attempts to punish them, I promise you I will do three things. First I'll beat the living shit out of you, Fannie, even if I have to go to jail for kicking your ass . . . you knooooow. . . ." Grandpa's head bobbed around as he imitated Grandma. "You won't be able to get a dime from me because I can't make any money in jail." He paused in front of Paula. He studied her hard and looked right in her eyes. "I'll not even begin to tell you what I think of you, but if you hurt Sydni or Amber, you better be prepared to find yourself some place else to live, and I will not let you take them with you." He paused again. "I also promise that if my grandkids shed one tear over the extravaganza that went on last night, I will personally see that Libby's house is raided every weekend. I'll call the cops on her myself."

For once in their lives, Paula and Grandma didn't talk back to

Grandpa. Not a peep came out of either of them. He told Sydni and me to come with him. We took another bus ride, and Grandpa explained to us how dangerous it was to leave the house at night alone and unsupervised by an adult. We were never to get into a stranger's car. He also let us know how wrong it was to take that man's keys and made us promise never to do anything like that again. We promised and we meant it. We went to Horn and Hardart's for lunch, then to the movies, and for ice cream afterwards. Grandma and Paula were absolutely livid. I loved every minute of it.

~

# Chapter Eight

# *Reba*

eba found herself at the hotel bar a little after midnight. She saw a gentleman sitting there, having a drink, and she took the stool beside him. He offered her one, and she accepted a glass of wine. It tasted good to her. His name was Doug Ransome and he was a patio furniture salesman. He was staying at the hotel on business for a few days. They continued their conversation while he ordered more drinks for both of them. She enjoyed his company. It had been a long time since she had a man to talk to. Johnny was either preoccupied, asleep, or gone when she was at home.

Doug was single, thirty-seven, and lived in Annapolis, Maryland. He was not a truly handsome man, but was tall, well built, and had a nice thick head of jet-black hair. He was of Spanish descent, with a trace of an accent that sounded cute. He had perfect teeth and a gleaming smile. She loved the sound of his soft voice; he was very articulate. Reba was halfway through her third glass of wine when it started to hit her. She hadn't had a drink in about two years—the last time she had wine was at her cousin Rhonda's wedding. She couldn't enjoy it or the reception because she had to keep an eye on the kids so they wouldn't tear up the place.

Reba had a nice buzz on. Doug looked better and better to her. Her six kids and Johnny became a dim memory. After a few more sips of wine, Reba undid her hair, letting it fall down onto her shoulders. It was beautiful—black and thick and just wavy enough to be lightly permed. As they chatted away about his work and his hobbies, Reba told him she was a thirty-two-year-old, unmarried wardrobe consultant in town for the weekend to do the fashion show. She made herself sound very important.

Her body temperature was rising. Her eyes moved down to Doug's crotch and her hand followed. Discreetly, she began to massage him slowly and gently so that even the bartender was unaware of what was going on. What she had in her hand immediately turned to steel. She looked straight into Doug's eyes and whispered, "Check, please."

Doug led Reba into the elevator. As it began to move, she took off her shoe and, leaning on the elevator wall, massaged his penis with the top of her foot. The smoothness of her silk stocking aroused him further. He was using every ounce of self-control to keep from throwing her down on the elevator floor. Finally the bell sounded and the doors opened. He led her to his room in silence as she held on tight to his arm.

Reba turned around in a circle, feeling a little woozy. She sat on the bed and giggled like a schoolgirl. Doug stared at her for a moment. He plopped down next to her and asked her if she was too intoxicated to know where she was or what she was doing.

"No, I'm fine, I'm fine," she replied.

She lay comfortably on the bed, telling him her real life story—how she had married Johnny Penster at eighteen. She apologized for lying to him at the bar and went on to say she had to cool things down for a while because she had to be honest with him about her life before anything happened. She told him about her five boys and one girl. She confessed she had never been with any other man—had never had any excitement in her life, never traveled. No hobbies. She only drank at social functions like weddings. She was a quiet person who worked at a quiet library and led a quiet life. She admitted to looking for some excitement in this new city with this new man. For once she wanted to do the unexpected. For tonight, she felt like losing the dreariness of her life. It was as simple as that. She let Doug know he could walk away, no strings attached. Would he do her a favor and let something happen for her tonight?

She fell silent, waiting for his reply. Doug looked at her, thinking, "I don't give a damn if this woman is a serial killer, Catwoman, or a ghost; I'm not sending her anywhere. If she's a killer, I'll die in pleasure."

Reba pulled back the bedspread on the other bed. She removed the sheet and took it into the bathroom with her. She never said a word. She took off all her clothes and wrapped the sheet around her naked body, tying the top in a knot just above her breasts. She did up her long mane of hair in a single braid and returned to the bed where Doug sat, still fully clothed. She was mysterious. She fascinated him.

Reba began kissing the top of his head, going down to his forehead and kissing each eyelid. His hands moved to hold her, but she wouldn't let him touch her body. Little did he know that she was experimenting on him. She was listening to see how he reacted. It was all new to her because she and Johnny had wham-bam-thank-you-ma'am nights, and she was never properly aroused. It was so bad that she kept a jar of Vaseline on her night table because he never took the time for the appropriate foreplay to moisten her before he entered.

Reba was in control now, though, and it felt good. She proceeded to kiss the tip of Doug's nose and cheeks and let her tongue flick his face. His ears needed some attention, and she nibbled on them gently in between kisses. Unbuttoning his shirt, she moved down toward his chest, took her hands from his and undressed him, kissing all the while. He tried to remove the sheet, but she stopped him. "Not yet."

When she had his shirt and jacket off, she ran her tongue across his chest and began to nibble and suck his nipples. He moaned and wanted desperately to yank the sheet away from her. She kissed him down to his navel and made him lie down. She undressed him completely without taking her lips from his body. Her hands roamed everywhere, and he wanted to be inside of her. He was panting. Once he was naked, she stared at his gorgeous skin, broad shoulders, and large erect penis. She thought for a moment about all those steamy romance novels she had read, trying to remember some of the scenes in order to give pleasure to this man.

She permitted him to remove the sheet. He kissed her and stroked her entire body until they were both damp. Reba definitely wanted to be the pursuer. She wanted to be in charge.

She placed her body on top of his for a moment before letting him take over. He made her feel unique, and she was totally captivated by him. He was at the wheel now, an excellent driver, speeding up when he had to, making all the curves safely and slowing down when the traffic got too heavy. By now Reba was praying to God, moaning and giggling. She came like Niagara Falls, with a rush. He followed quickly after, delighted.

"Thank you," she whispered, looking up at him. He was totally enchanted with the woman who lied to him at a bar and picked him up.

"The pleasure was mine."

The sun was shining in Norfolk. Light poured through the window into Lucy's beautiful hotel room. She stretched and moaned with delight. This had to be the life. "It just doesn't get any better than this," she thought. She looked over at the other bed to see if Reba was awake and was shocked to find her gone. Just waking up, Lucy didn't have her head together yet.

She thought maybe Reba was in the bathroom taking a bath and had re-made the bed already. She called her but got no answer. She then started toward the bathroom, calling again. No Reba.

Okay, maybe she went down to breakfast. Lucy glanced around the room. Reba's suitcases were on the floor just like they were when they left for dinner. Lucy couldn't find the purple skirt or the black knit wrap top she'd lent Reba. She decided to go down to the restaurant to search for her. Maybe Reba had been so happy with the new outfit that she put it right back on. Maybe she hadn't taken a shower. Lucy didn't see wet washcloths or any used towels in the bathroom.

Lucy washed what was necessary, doing the birdbath thing. She brushed her hair, threw on a pair of shoes, and rushed downstairs. No Reba. She peeked into the restaurants. She checked the coffee shop, the gift shop, and the restrooms. By that time Lucy was not only worried, she was frantic.

She went to the concierge desk where they had left Reba after dinner, but she didn't see the person who had been on duty when they left. She didn't bother to ask the new man—he wouldn't know her. It was time to call Peggy, but she thought for a minute. Reba could have stayed at Peggy's! Maybe she lost her room key and didn't want to disturb her, so she decided to wake Peggy up instead. Oh, hell. Lucy couldn't figure it out, but she ran to the house phone to call Peggy, praying they both would be there.

"Good morning," Lucy said. "By any chance is Reba with you, or have you seen her?"

"No, not since last night. What's the matter?"

"Her bed hasn't been slept in." Lucy told her the story. "I'm in the lobby right now, and I've checked everywhere. I can't find her and I'm scared."

"Come on up to my room," Peggy said.

When Lucy got off on their floor, she decided to double-check the room again in case Reba had come while she was out. She'd forgotten to check for messages. Nothing. She headed straight down the hall to Peggy's room and knocked on the door.

"Come on in, sweetie, and let's see if we can figure out how to find that child. I just wonder what's going on with her. Do you think that simple girl went for a tour of the naval base last night and got raped or kidnapped or something?"

Lucy just sat there shaking her head. "I'll tell you one thing, I'm not going over there to run around looking for Reba this morning. First of all, I'm starving. Now don't get me wrong—I'm worried about Reba, but right now she's a royal pain, and I can't figure anything out until I get some breakfast and some coffee. I wish she had brought her boring bored ass upstairs with us last night and went the hell to sleep like we did. We've got to find her because I can't deal with the police and Johnny Penster, too. I swear to God! Why is this happening to me when I'm about to have the time of my life? Rebecca Jocelyn Penster, if you are alive and well when I find you, I'll kick your stupid behind."

"Well, there's rehearsals at two thirty and at six. I have a meeting with the other designers at one. It's now eight forty. Let's get showered and dressed and have something to eat. Maybe she'll turn up while we're doing that. If not, we'll figure out what to do."

"Peggy, just two things." Lucy looked at Peggy as if she were going to cry. "Who will help me with the clothes and accessories backstage if we don't find her? You have to be out there with the designers and promoters. What are we supposed to do if something really bad has happened to Reba?"

At 11:17 A.M. the phone began ringing. Doug and Reba were asleep in each other's arms, exhausted after a night of lovemaking. They both sat up, startled. Reba looked at the clock and jumped out of the bed shouting, "Oh, my God, Lucy and Peggy must be having a fit. Jesus Christ, I hope they didn't call the police. I wonder if Johnny called."

"Calm down, baby, and let me answer the phone." Doug rubbed his hands briskly over his face and picked up the receiver.

"Good morning, Mr. Ransome, this is Alan Manning at the concierge desk. We seem to have a bit of a problem and hope you can assist us. We are trying to locate the wardrobe assistant of designer Peggy Kinard. We have contacted our night bartender at her request and he has said that Rebecca Penster was last seen having drinks with you. Can you give us any information as to her whereabouts?"

Lucy and Peggy stood right there at the desk, looking down Manning's throat and praying Doug had a lead on Reba. Doug didn't know what to say. Maybe Reba didn't want anyone to know she had been with him. He had to stall until he talked to her, and she was in the bathroom taking a shower.

"That nice woman is missing? I'm coming right down to help you in any way I can. Yes, I had a cocktail with her last night. Give me fifteen minutes to dress. It's terrible if indeed she's missing." He replaced the receiver.

"Rebecca," he yelled. "We've got a problem. The whole town is looking for you, gorgeous. There's an all-points bulletin out on you in the city of Norfolk. Come out of there with your hands up. You have to surrender to your boss, some Peggy person."

Getting out of bed, Doug stepped down on the floor and yelled out in pain. Blood began to gush from his foot.

"Oh, my God!" Doug screamed. A glass that Reba had brought into the room to put the hot water whammy on Doug had fallen off the night table while they were getting it on and he had just crushed it into his foot.

"Oh, shit, shit, shit," he moaned.

Reba came flying out of the bathroom and panicked at the sight of blood. Doug tried to tell her that Peggy was looking for her and the concierge was waiting for him. He said he'd better get down to the lobby because someone might think he killed her or something. His foot was bleeding badly and would require stitches for sure.

"Reba, what are we going to do?" She stood there naked as a jaybird. She realized they were in a crisis and had to think fast. Her two friends had to be very upset, and Johnny may have called. Doug looked so cute and so helpless sitting there, bleeding, that she started to think about what went on last night. He, too, was naked and at that very moment, all she wanted was to fuck him.

"Let's get that glass out of your foot," she said. Together they cleaned the wound and wrapped a wet towel tightly around the foot to stop the bleeding.

Looking at him with sexy eyes, she said, "I apologize for leaving that glass around where you could get hurt. I would never ever want to cause you pain."

Right after they finished making love, there was a knock at the door.

"Who is it?" Doug called.

"Hotel Security."

# Chapter Nine

# *Amber*

It was ten months after the New Year's Eve fiasco. Paula still couldn't stand Sydni and me, but she resented me the most. She didn't like me around and gave me a rough time, blaming me for what happened at Libby's because I sent the police. Paula couldn't beat me to death because she'd have to deal with Grandpa. At least I was safe from any whippings.

Paula was also pissed off because Grandma made her try to clean up all that mess in the oven. It wouldn't come off, so Paula had to pay for a new stove. That infuriated her.

Lance didn't come around much anymore, and Libby was still mad at me, too. I no longer went over there to play with Denise. Lance Edward Resnick had been indicted and charged with murder. Libby managed to get him bail even on the murder charge. She kept him out on appeals for two years, paying all the legal fees, but in the end, Lance received ten to twenty years for the murder of Perry Shoreman. He didn't see his family or me outside of prison until I was twenty years old. It seemed like everyone was splitting up and departing their normal lives.

Paula wasn't around much on weekends; she told everyone she had a job taking care of some old lady who lived way across town. Every other Friday she packed up and left. I was glad because I was tired of her rolling her eyes at me all the time. She acted being totally obnoxious whenever she could, not giving me any movie money or anything. I was convinced she truly hated me. It seemed that the only person who really paid attention to me was Grandpa. Nina Penster was no longer allowed to play with Sydni and me. Johnny Penster kept her grounded for two years for her role in our escapade. I was pretty bored.

I was also worried about running into the guy to whom I owed ten dollars for the watch. In my travels to the store and around the neighborhood, he continued to ask me for the money. I either ran away or gave him some lame excuse for not having it. I sure was sorry I did that deal. I didn't have any more money to pay him back. Neither Paula, Grandma, nor anyone else ever found out about him. I couldn't imagine why he hadn't tracked Paula down or discovered where I lived and come to the house. Maybe he didn't want the money that badly and asked for it when he ran into me merely to be saying something.

He was a cute guy, though, and kind of nice. I wondered what his name was. He never threatened me or anything like that. I decided that as soon as I got some money, I'd give it back because keeping it wasn't right. I had been thinking about the guy, the watch, and that bum deal and decided to ask Grandpa for the money. If he didn't have it, I'd ask Horace, or I could collect soda bottles and cash them in.

Even though I loved money and pulled off little schemes from time to time, I was basically sweet and didn't want to hurt anyone. A little devil sometimes got into me, and I wanted to be rich. I would help the neighbors out by going to the store for them and checking on them if they were sick. I babysat the three- and four-year-old kids in the neighborhood, making them sit on the steps to keep them from running into the street. I loved kids, especially little ones, and they liked me because I never yelled or hit them. I read to them. I could make them mind just by looking at them a certain way. I treated people well because I knew how it felt when Grandma and Paula hollered at me or smacked me.

I didn't like to clean up or wash dishes. I didn't like housework at all and swore I would have a maid when I grew up. Dirt and grease made my hands smelly and cleaning fluids made them dry and rough. I liked my skin to feel smooth. I didn't have lotion all the time, so I hated to have to put my hands in Ajax or Comet.

One day Sydni and I got home from school, and Grandma wasn't there to let us in. That was unusual. There wasn't even a note. Paula was at work and we wondered what was going on. We didn't have a key, so we sat outside for over an hour until Paula drove up in a cab. She was frantic, yelling at us as we sat by the door doing our homework.

"Get out of the way! Move, dammit, Amber, I'm trying to get in the house!" Paula yelled. Sydni and I scrambled out of her way. She opened the door and hustled up the stairs to Grandma's bedroom. We followed her. She started taking apart the light switch on the wall.

"What are you doing to Grandma's light?" I said. "She'll get mad at you."

"Shut up!"

I was quiet because otherwise she would probably hit me, and no one was there to protect me. She started grabbing money out of the wall.

Sydni's mouth was wide open—we had never seen that much money. Paula went through the bureau drawers looking for something. Amongst Grandma's underwear she found a book. She took it over to the telephone. She flipped through the pages and began to dial.

"Listen, McNight, this is Paula. I need you to get over to my house right away," she said into the receiver.

"For what, Paula, what's going on?" he asked.

"Fannie's in jail, and I have to get down there right away to get her out. The cops locked her up for writing numbers. Renee was here when they came for her, and they took her to some center or something."

McNight was there in fifteen minutes. He ran up the stairs, calling for Paula to come on.

"Stay here in this house until I come back and don't you dare get into anything."

She looked at me with a certain expression on her face, and I knew if I disobeyed, Grandpa or no Grandpa, she'd somehow get me. Paula and McNight ran out.

Just as they approached McNight's car, Horace pulled up. Paula tried to act like she didn't see him. She had her hand on the door handle when Horace came around to the car.

"Well, well, well. Hey, Paula, what are you doing home so early?" He suspected she was up to no good. McNight was thinking, "Oh, shit."

"We have a family emergency and I have to leave right away," Paula answered.

Horace did not believe anything Paula said and was determined to keep questioning her. "What kind of family emergency? Who do you think you are talking to? Do you think you're talking to someone who doesn't know you? You've been acting pretty mysterious the past few months with that new weekend job. You don't drive, but you never need a ride there or back. Nobody hears from you when you're there because you say the people don't want you to use the phone. You can't be making a whole hell of a lot of money because you claim you're strapped, and I have to pay for all Renee's stuff. What's going on, Paula?"

"Listen, I don't have time for this shit. My mama is in jail, and I have to go right this minute. Kindly move your ass out of the way so I can bail her out."

He looked surprised, but this time he believed her. Horace went on up to the house to visit Renee.

## Chapter Ten

# *Reba*

*R*eba jumped up, grabbed her clothes from all around the room, and ran into the bathroom. Lord, she didn't know what to do. Should she get dressed and talk to the people at the door to help Doug out of this mess, or hide and hope he could take care of it? Maybe, just maybe, they wouldn't search the place and find her. She started dressing as quietly as she could.

Doug jumped into his pants, telling the people at the door to wait a minute, he'd be right there. It took a long time because his foot was so sore that he couldn't put any weight on it. He finally hobbled to the door and opened it. A short white gentleman in a suit was standing there.

"Good afternoon, sir. I'm sorry to disturb you, but are you Douglas Ransome?"

"Yes, I am."

"The concierge desk has been waiting for you to speak with them about a missing woman by the name of Rebecca Penster. Would you accompany me to the lobby to tell them what time Ms. Penster left your company last night? They would also appreciate your letting them know if she told you where she was going when she left you. It seems she never returned to her room last night, and her employer is extremely concerned."

"I'd be happy to help in any way I can," Doug replied. "I was hurrying to speak to them after they telephoned me earlier this morning, but I accidentally cut myself on some glass in the bathroom." He raised his foot so the security officer could see the wound. As he examined it, he also peered around for any trace of Reba.

"Reba, you better be dressed and ready to run out of here when I get rid of this guy," Doug prayed.

"I am sorry about your accident. Can I help you to the infirmary or send someone up to you?" the officer said.

"I'd appreciate having a doctor take a look," Doug replied. "It may need some stitches."

"I'll have someone here shortly."

Doug closed the door, letting out a sigh of relief. Reba came out of the bathroom and was about to say something when he signaled for quiet. He opened the door and looked up and down the hall to be sure the officer was really gone. There was no one in sight.

"You'd better get to your room and think of something while I wait for the doctor," he told her.

"Thank God," she said, giving him a quick kiss. "I'll call you later." She put her hand on the doorknob but turned back to him, with a sexy look. "There's been a hot time in the old town last night and this morning thanks to you—what did you say your name was—Dexter? Can we do it again sometime—Dexter?"

"Get out of here and call me later . . . please," he said, laughing.

Twenty-five minutes later, the hotel nurse was at Doug's room. She examined his foot and recommended that he have it stitched at the local hospital's emergency room. The hotel arranged for a cab to take him there and requested he stop by the manager's office when he got back. When Doug returned on crutches, he was informed that Rebecca Penster was safe and sound. Doug went up to his room, ordered lunch, ate, and fell exhausted on the bed. As he drifted off to sleep, images of Reba flickered through his mind—and a huge grin spread on his face. It had been a divine night and an eventful day.

# Chapter Eleven

# Amber

The doorbell was ringing. Sydni looked out the window and saw Horace. We ran to let him in.

"What's going on, ladies?" he asked.

"Nothing. Hey, Horace, can I talk to you about a problem?"

He nodded at me and smiled. "Okay, Miss Amber, let's talk," he said.

"I did a pretty bad thing. I've been worrying about it, and I want to straighten it out." Horace looked surprised and told me to go on. "Well, I kind of cheated someone."

"Really, Amber, I'm disappointed in you. Who did you cheat?"

"I don't know his name, but I know what he looks like. He's a lot older than me."

"How did you cheat him?"

I confessed to Horace about the watch.

"So now you're in the jewelry business?" Horace said as he studied me for a moment.

"Not exactly."

I was tired of explaining and didn't want to give Horace too much information. If he found out about Curtis taking us to Atlantic City, he might be mad. Paula would hate me some more, and I'd be in a mess again and all.

"Know what, Horace, let's forget it; it's too much trouble." Horace was intrigued and questioned me further.

"Would you just give me the money—I mean loan me the money—until I get all my bottles together?"

"What bottles?" Horace was getting even more confused. Now I'd have to explain the bottle thing. I was so sorry I ever asked Horace for help.

"Never mind," I said.

"Oh, no, young lady. Come here, dear. We'll solve this problem right now. How much do you need?"

"Ten dollars."

He started to pace, looking from the ceiling to the floor and then back at me, analyzing the situation. "How will you pay me back?"

"I pick up all the soda bottles I can find and wash them out and take them to the store. I get a nickel refund for the fat bottles and two cents for the little ones. That's how I can pay you back."

"Okay, that should work."

I was relieved and figured everything was all right. I thought it was over until Horace asked where I got the watch. I looked up at him and spoke in a very grown-up manner.

"I don't want to tell you because you'd be mad. I didn't steal it or anything like that. I won it in a game." Horace sat there shaking his head, trying to figure it out. He seemed to believe my story so far.

"Amber, have you been gambling?"

"No," I promptly replied. I could tell he imagined me at Libby's playing cards. He knew I was bright enough to master poker. I looked like I was about to cry. He didn't want to upset me, so he stopped the questions.

"Now tell me again who you owe this money to?"

"I owe it to a guy who comes around here sometimes. I've owed it to him for a long time. Whenever I see him, he asks for it. I spent it and I need to get it back to him."

"Did he threaten you? Are you afraid of him?"

"No, but he just keeps asking me for it."

"Next time you see this guy, tell him you will pay him and that I'll bring you to him with the money. Don't forget to get his name and address. Then you call me. Agreed, Miss Amber?"

"Yes."

"I don't want you doing anything like that again, do you understand?"

"I won't," I promised. "Not ever."

"Since we have that all straightened out, I am here to take Renee off your and Sydni's hands," Horace said. "Paula had to go help Grandma with something. If you girls want to come for a ride with me, you can."

Speechless, Sydni and I looked at him. We were sure Renee was in jail.

"We can't go out because Paula told us to stay home," I answered.

"Okay, I'll go get Renee. She must be asleep," Horace said.

When Sydni walked out of the room without saying a word, Horace knew something was up.

"Come on, Amber, let's get Renee up," he said.

I put my head down and started to cry for real. Horace headed up the stairs. Now there would be trouble.

Horace came right back down and sat me on his lap. "Where is she?"

"I can't . . . I don't . . . Grandma Fannie . . . Paula . . . um . . . well . . . she wasn't. . . ." I didn't know how to tell him and was scared to death. He was getting mad now, but he didn't want to frighten me.

"Look, Amber, stop fooling around and tell me where Renee is. Don't be scared."

"She is in jail with Grandma or in a home or something."

# Chapter Twelve

# *Reba*

It was twelve forty-five p.m. when Lucy put the key into her hotel room door. She was sad, angry, and scared to death. Distressed about Reba, she worried about the show, too. Peggy was on her way to her meeting. Lucy walked in and found Reba curled up on her bed.

"I ought to kill you! I *want* to kill you! Where the goddamn hell have you been all night?" Lucy yelled at her. "Peggy and I have been looking all over for you! We've alerted the hotel and they're searching for you right now. You'd better tell me where you've been, or I'll kick your butt! Are you all right? Did somebody do something to you, or are you just plain crazy? I can't think of anything Peggy and I said to you to make you run away. Did you get sick from the food? You had no damn business putting all that ketchup on everything. I never saw anybody do that in my whole life. Were you in the hospital?"

Reba smiled and listened as Lucy asked a million questions without permitting her to answer. Lucy noticed the coy smile on her face and saw that she seemed fine and extremely relaxed.

"Reba, what's going on? Where have you been?"

"I've been to heaven," said Reba.

Lucy stared at her in amazement and sheer disbelief. She tried in vain to think of something more to ask but couldn't get a word out. Reba gazed at Lucy and just sat there grinning.

"You little boring-ass bitch," Lucy growled. "You sneaky once-in-a-lifetime tramp. You've been out fucking!" Reba cracked up. "Oh, my God!" shouted Lucy. "It's the truth, isn't it? Oh my God, oh my God, oh my God!"

"You sound like I did last night."

At that moment Lucy stood over Reba, gaping at her in astonishment. They both burst out laughing. Lucy grabbed a pillow and started hitting Reba in the head with it. Reba was still laughing. They stopped for a minute to regain their composure.

"Wait, shut up. I've got to make a telephone call," Reba said.

"Hotel Security, please. Good afternoon, this is Rebecca Penster. I'm a guest in room 427, and I understand that my employer, Miss Peggy Kinard, has been concerned about me. I spoke with the manager's office earlier and I am calling to let your department know that I am fine and back in my room. I'd appreciate your leaving a message for Miss Kinard indicating that I'll see her as soon as she's free. And thank you for your concern. I apologize if I caused you or your staff any inconvenience."

She hung up, and she and Lucy began laughing all over again.

Reba told Lucy all about her night with Doug. Lucy's mouth stayed open the entire time. She couldn't believe it. Not Reba. Not rag-doll Reba who no one ever heard a peep out of. Not quiet little Reba who simply went to work and did everything Johnny told her to do.

Reba finally said to Lucy, "Look, we've got a lot to do. First of all, I'm starving from all that fucking last night, I really am. Let's order some food up here. Are you hungry?"

"No, me and Peggy ate early this morning while we were trying to figure out where you were."

"Will you order me scrambled eggs and cheese on toast, some grits if they have them, and some grapefruit juice while I get dressed? If breakfast is over, then just order me a cheeseburger and some fries and a chocolate milkshake—and don't forget the ketchup. We've got that dry run for the show at two o'clock, right? By the way, did my wonderful husband Johnny call?"

"Yeah, and I told him you were somewhere getting your brains fucked out." They began laughing again, and Lucy got on the phone to order the food.

Peggy Kinard was a sharp lady. She had class and scruples and everyone in the neighborhood looked up to her. Her head was always held high, she had erect posture, and she knew how to strut. She had that fancy speaking voice and always used the right words and grammar. Her taste was impeccable. She wore the sheerest stockings and the most stylish high heels in the world.

It was two fifteen in the afternoon, and she had just left her meeting with the designers and promoters. She entered the hotel ballroom in a camel-colored wool suit and a beige silk blouse with a matching pillbox hat trimmed in leopard. The outfit closed with brown snakeskin shoes and a thick gold bracelet around her arm. She looked fantastic. She had made the outfit and hat herself. Peggy was indeed talented.

She waltzed through the ballroom, glancing at the myriad preparations for the fashion show. Hotel workers were busy setting up the runway and projection screen. She walked on to the area where the models were arranging tables for their makeup and accessories. Racks of stunning clothing marked with designers' and models' names surrounded them. Peggy spotted Lucy and Reba and quickly went over to them.

"Hello, ladies, how are you this afternoon?"

"Fine," Lucy and Reba responded at the same time.

Peggy looked at Reba. "It's nice to see you, sweetie. Are you making out okay with the garments?"

Reba's nerves quivered because she knew she had to deal with Peggy about the night before. "I'm fine. Everything will be in order."

"I'd like to go over some things with you around five o'clock at dinner. Can you meet me at Bello's in the hotel?" Peggy asked.

Though Reba knew what was coming, she appreciated the way Peggy handled it, not embarrassing her in front of everyone or firing her right on the spot.

"Yes, I'll be there. Is Lucy coming, too?"

Lucy looked at them both. The last place in the world she wanted to be was at that dinner.

"Of course Lucy is invited. I hope she doesn't have other plans."

"Sure, I'm going to dinner with you girls."

The rehearsal went well, no hitches at all. Lucy had to work carefully with Reba to make sure she had the garments together right. Lucy and Peggy both made sure Reba had the pieces of each outfit numbered so Lucy would know when to put on what. It worked out pretty well, and Reba seemed to be catching on. At four fifteen they were finished. Reba was glad, because she hadn't had a chance to check on Doug all day. She missed him and wanted to know how things went with the doctor and how he was feeling. The three of them left the ballroom together and headed for the elevators. Peggy went toward her room alone, saying to Reba, "I'll see you at five, honey, and don't you get lost." Reba merely nodded.

As soon as Peggy turned away, Reba and Lucy looked at each other.

"Honest to God, I don't feel like hearing shit at the dinner table,"

Reba said. "I don't even want to go to Bello's. I want to spend some time with Doug before the show."

"Look, Reba, show up for dinner and get reamed out. Hurry up and eat, then stop by Doug's on the way to the show," Lucy said. "You have to explain to Peggy sometime that you turned into a fucking whore overnight. Just get through it, okay?" They started laughing.

As soon as they got to the room, Reba ran to the phone.

"Room 714, please," she said, smiling to herself.

"Well, if it isn't the runaway. How are you?" asked Doug.

"I'm fine, I'm worried about you. I just got out of the rehearsal."

Doug explained what had happened to him. She felt bad and was really worried about him now. Hearing Reba's gasp, Lucy was dying to find out what had occurred. Reba ignored her, trying to listen to Doug.

"I'll be right there," Reba said.

"What happened?" Lucy asked. Reba explained the situation as she prepared to leave.

"Are you coming back?" Lucy watched Reba fix her hair, dab on lipstick, and brush off her clothes.

"I'll be at the show on time, but right now I don't know about dinner. I'll call you soon. Don't say anything about this to Peggy—I'll deal with her."

Doug opened the door for Reba. She wanted to cry when she saw him on crutches. They sat on the bed and began to talk.

"What can I do?" asked Reba.

"Spend the rest of the weekend with me."

Reba smiled and kissed him on the cheek. "Listen, in half an hour I have a dinner date with my boss and Lucy. Then I have to work at the show. I still have to take a quick shower and dress. I don't have much time. I miss you. You know what I mean? Why don't you do this—get dressed and meet me at Bello's at five thirty. By that time Peggy should be done bawling me out, and you can meet her and keep me company while we eat. If you can hobble around some more, come to the show."

Doug studied Reba. He really liked this young woman. He was enchanted with her; he was also afraid of her because she was married. Her children had been on his mind all afternoon. He didn't know what he was getting himself into.

Reba squeezed his hand. "Please."

"Okay, get out. I'll meet you there—hey, Reba," he said as she reached the door, "you know something? I think I really dig you."

Reba hurried back to her room where a surprised Lucy was getting ready.

"Thank God! I didn't think you'd come," she said.

"Look, Lucy, help me out. Get me an outfit together—either your stuff or mine, but do it as quickly as you can while I hop in the shower."

"What's up? How is Doug?"

"He's okay, he's meeting us for dinner."

"What!"

Reba was out of her clothes and about to get into the shower when Lucy ran up behind her. "Johnny called," she said.

"Johnny who?"

At ten minutes after five, Peggy was sitting at the table in Bello's with no Lucy and no Reba. She breathed a sigh of relief when she saw them come in. They sat down, and Peggy gazed at Reba.

"Mrs. Penster, there are menus for you and Lucy. Will you hurry so we can talk?" she said.

The waiter arrived and asked if they wanted drinks. They were about to order when Reba cut in. "Sir, can you switch our table quickly? We have a fourth person joining us."

Peggy looked shocked but remained silent. He moved them to another table. Peggy ordered a white wine, and Lucy and Reba ordered iced tea. They decided on dinner, and as soon as the waiter walked away, Peggy started in.

"What happened to you last night?"

"Well, here we go," Reba thought. "Listen, Peggy, I have to give this to you straight up because we don't have much time. Bear with me and let me have my say. Don't interrupt or ask me any questions until I finish. Then you can say what you want. Deal?"

"All right."

"First of all," Reba began, "I apologize for worrying you by not calling. It was thoughtless and inconsiderate. I'm sorry. I've been married to Johnny Penster for fourteen years, and I tried to be right with him. I was an eighteen-year-old baby when I married him. I didn't know anything about anything and all I'd done in my whole life was what my parents told me to do. So I married Johnny and started doing what he told me to do. You may think he's a nice guy, and he may be, sometimes to some people. He may even think he's nice to me, and maybe he is sometimes. But I've been miserable for a long time, ladies. I've been bored and lonely—yes, lonely, living in the same house with him. I've been neglected, overlooked, and forgotten by my husband. I've been a good and obedient wife. I've been a good mother. I took Johnny's shit and kept my mouth shut because I'd made a commitment. When I married him and had those kids, I felt I had to stick it out. So I got used to being put off by my husband. I thought the way he treated me was normal. I even stopped expecting my life to be any different. I've worked my ass off to make those seven people in my house happy. I can honestly say that I've tried to be the best I could be for all of them. I gave up my dreams before I even knew what they were. I concentrated on everyone except myself. I've ignored my husband's women, his late hours, and the times he never showed up at all. I have ignored the things I've heard he's done and closed my eyes to his indiscretions. I've gone without a lot.

"I'm here to tell you that his party is over and mine began last night. I met a man who has decorated my life these last seventeen hours with ornaments of humor, sensitivity, concern, acceptance, and passion. He's a guest here at the hotel. He's joining us for dinner. This is a decent man, and I'm not the least bit ashamed, sorry, or embarrassed about my behavior. I may be crazy, or overconfident, but I think he cares for me. I had a wonderful time with him, and I intend to keep seeing him . . . somehow, some way. If by chance I get on that bus tomorrow afternoon and say good-bye to him and never hear from him again—if he never wants to see me again—I can still smile about this weekend and honestly say that no matter what, he did me a big favor. I needed to know what time it was, and he was the alarm clock. It is time for Reba now, and anybody . . . *anybody* who does not like it, understand it, or approve of it, can kiss my ass, including Johnny Penster!"

Lucy was so proud of Reba she wanted to stand up and applaud. But Peggy was about to say something. When Reba fell silent, she was free to have her say. She sat and stared at Reba, impressed and overwhelmed. She thought about her own empty life and how she missed her husband, who had passed away seven years ago. At that moment, in a way, she envied Reba.

The waiter came with the food while Peggy was still staring at Reba.

She relaxed and said to Reba, "I have one request of you and one question to ask."

"Shoot."

"Please don't pour ketchup all over your food if your man is eating with us. It's a sign of no class, and I'm sure you want to impress him. Do you need a ticket for him to attend the fashion show?"

They all burst out laughing, and Lucy applauded.

# Chapter Thirteen

# *Paula*

ere it is, sir, a hundred and seventeen dollars and my identification. Now would you please release Fannie Porter to me? I'm her daughter, Paula Gray."

The clerk counted the money and told the guard to release Grandma. She came out of the dingy cell with her eyes all swollen up. She looked disgusted and couldn't believe the police had found out about her and locked her up. She was really surprised they had taken her to jail, especially since Renee was home with her. She couldn't believe they'd given Renee to an agency.

Paula rolled her eyes at Grandma, furious at her for getting into this mess, involving Renee and calling her off her job. Grandma was a pain in the ass.

As soon as Grandma saw Paula's face, she knew Paula was going to start up, and she already felt bad enough. Before Paula could say anything, Grandma told her to shut up.

"Where's my baby?" Paula demanded.

"They took her to County Care at Broad and Reed."

"You should have let me get her first. Why didn't you tell me everything on the phone?"

"I didn't have all the information then! Now shut up, and let's go get her."

They were walking toward McNight's car when Horace pulled up with Sydni and me. He was steaming. He jumped out and ran over to Paula and Grandma.

"The only reason I brought the kids here is because I knew I wouldn't slaughter you both in front of them." Sydni and I thought about that other time. Horace never found out about it.

"Where the hell is my baby, woman?" Horace said to Grandma.

"At County Care," she muttered with her head down. Horace was so mad he almost spit on Grandma right there in the street.

"Would somebody please tell me where in the world County Care is?"

"Broad and Reed," Grandma replied.

"Let's go," Horace said.

Paula didn't want to hear Horace's mouth all the way to South Philly and she couldn't curse us out in his presence for giving him the scoop on Renee. So she headed for McNight's vehicle.

"Get your ass in my car, I want to talk to you." Horace stopped her dead in her tracks.

He started up all over again, wanting to know why she was so sneaky and why she hadn't told him where his baby was when he had caught her in front of her house. Oh, he really carried on, and all Paula could think about was Earl and how different he was from Horace—how Earl never gave her any trouble and how much fun it was being with him. After a while she stopped hearing Horace's yakking and just concentrated on seeing Earl for the coming weekend. It would be a pleasure to be with him and not be bothered with Horace and all those fools in her family, especially her three brats. It was such a paradise at Earl's that she never even discussed her family with him. He knew that she had some kids and parents, but he didn't even know where she lived. Her life was a blast because she was seeing Curtis a couple of nights a week, too. And if he wasn't available she could always call Wilson, to pick her up. She needed to stay pretty tight with Horace because he was her only source of real income, but she had to be careful he didn't catch her doing anything.

So far, everything was working in Paula's favor. She was surely keeping her sex life alive and was getting money from everybody. Earl was falling in love and had created a haven for her. She was giving him enough bullshit and sex to keep him from even entertaining a thought about another woman. Hell, he even talked as if he wanted to marry her. She was staying sharp, dressed to kill all the time. Horace worked the eleven- to-seven shift, and she was rocking steady with someone at least three times a week. She had it made. They had some wild times in that apartment of Earl's!

Paula would screw him to death and then enter the bedroom with a basin of warm water to wash the boy up in bed. She kept the place supplied with whipping cream and fruit. She had X-rated magazines and tramp underwear with zippers on the crotch. She had taught him how to fuck on the toilet seat, in a kitchen chair, against the walls, and on the very edge of the bed. The kitchen table had become a favorite.

They had been to Atlantic City and stayed in a hotel quite a few times. One weekend Earl took her to New York. He felt bad for her with her "husband" in jail and all. He was giving her money because she couldn't take care of three kids with what she had. He'd be glad when Paula could see him more than every other weekend. He got lonely sometimes. She couldn't see him during the week because of the kids and helping with their schoolwork. He told her if she liked she could bring them by sometime, and they'd all go out. She explained that they were kind of shy and scared of people, so she didn't take them around anyone other than family. She never even told him their names. "Come on, don't spoil the mood. Let's enjoy each other," she'd say whenever he asked about them.

"Well, here we are," Horace said, when they got to the County Care office. Inside, Horace did all the talking, launching into the clerk.

"I am Horace Alston. My daughter is Renee Alston, and she's two years old. She was brought here today when her grandmother, Fannie Porter, was arrested for writing illegal numbers in her home. This woman right here is Fannie Porter, who has just been released from jail. I had no knowledge that Mrs. Porter was involved in illegal acts, or I wouldn't have allowed her to babysit my child. I'd appreciate your bringing my child to me right away so I may take her to my home. I promise you nothing like this will ever happen again."

Grandma stood there embarrassed as Horace went on and on about her lousy morals and his own innocence. He must have memorized that speech on the way there. Why in the world didn't he pass out from talking so much without taking a breath? She wanted to kill him.

They brought out little Renee, and Horace took her in his arms. On the street in front of the County Care office, Horace turned to glare at Paula.

"I'm getting you an apartment tomorrow. You're moving, and you will take care of these children yourself. I'll pay your bills. Since you want to work, find a suitable sitter and pay her. Get a responsible woman who doesn't drink, write numbers, gamble, abuse kids, or fuck around them." He looked at Grandma.

"Fannie, I don't care what you do for a living—it's none of my business. But if my child is ever taken away again, I'll blow your brains out, what little you have. I hope you trust me and understand that I'm not threatening—I'm promising. I'll keep Renee until I get an apartment for Paula."

# Chapter Fourteen

## Amber

I hated that apartment, and I was starting to hate Paula. I missed Grandpa so much since we weren't living with him anymore. Sometimes on weekends when Paula went to work, Grandpa came to babysit us. The other weekends, Sydni and I stayed with Grandpa and Grandma, but it wasn't the same as seeing Grandpa every day.

I had to change schools and didn't have any friends. Sydni took the bus to the junior high. Horace came over to visit sometimes, and I liked that. He was always nice to me. Whenever he wasn't there, Paula started her stuff and brought someone to the apartment.

It was only a one-bedroom, so Horace wouldn't ever stay over. But when he wasn't around, Paula brought someone in and put me in the crib to sleep with Renee. I hated that crib, because I was too big. I was ten years old and had to sleep with my knees up almost to my chest, trying not to smother Renee. Sydni slept in a twin bed on the other side of the room. Paula naturally slept in her bed with the man. If there wasn't a man there, I could sleep with Sydni and be a lot more comfortable. Paula wouldn't permit me to sleep with Sydni if she had company, figuring I could listen and spy on them easier. I hated it when the men came because I had to listen to the funny noises and the crying and the bed would be shaking. It was just awful. I hated Paula for that.

One night when she arrived with a man, I rebelled.

"You shouldn't come here to make noise and keep me up and make me sleep in that crib. Just get out of my house!" I said to him.

Paula was shocked and looked as if she could kill me. She told the guy to sit down and ordered me into the bathroom. She got an extension cord out of the kitchen drawer and beat me with it a long time. I crawled under the sink by the pipes, so she dragged me out by my feet, still beating me and cursing. Sydni couldn't get her to stop. She and Renee were both horrified and crying along with me. The guy finally pulled Paula off me and said he was leaving. When he went to the door, she ran after him, but he just got into his car and left.

Paula said that if I ever tried to stop her from doing anything again, she'd kill me. She went on about how I had messed up her life just by being born.

I was hurt so badly, I cried all night. The next morning I had bruises and welts all over my body. I found some witch hazel in the bathroom cabinet and put it on them. I wanted to call Grandpa, but we didn't have a phone and I didn't have any money.

I was scared that if I told anyone, Paula would kill me for sure. From then on, she made me clean the bathroom with Ajax and wash all the dishes every day. She checked every night to be sure it was done, and if it wasn't I'd get beat again.

After that, I started doing a little babysitting for the lady upstairs who had a boy of four and a girl of three. Natalie couldn't pay me, but I got some peace and time away from Paula. Natalie let me eat with them, and I spent the night during the week sometimes. I tried to stay there whenever Paula had company so I wouldn't hear the bedroom sounds she and her boyfriends made.

About two months after the beating, I was at Grandma's for the weekend because Paula was at work. I was playing around the corner on Friday around five thirty, when I saw the guy I owed the money to. I was excited because, at last, I was able to pay him. I went up to him and just stood there, playing with that long braid that hung down to my chin, twirling the tip of it around my finger.

"Guess what?" I said with a smile on my face.

"What, you little con artist?"

"I have your money," I sang.

"You've got to be kidding!"

"I don't have it on me but I can get it pretty soon, I think. Tell me where you live and I'll bring it to you. Could you write down your address and your telephone number for me?" He smiled at me and scribbled down his name and address and gave it to me. He was surprised and really impressed with such a cute little lady.

"It was wrong to cheat me, but what you're doing now is very good. Your folks should be proud of you."

"We'll probably give you the money tonight, okay? Will you be home?"

"Yes, I'll be there. See you later."

I ran back to Grandma's and went into her underwear drawer to look for Horace's telephone number. I dialed and Horace answered.

"Hey, Horace, this is Amber. You okay today? I'm at Grandma's because Paula has to work this weekend. I called you because I saw the guy I owe the money to. I told him I could pay him tonight."

Horace liked me—I was always so polite and sweet with him. He also thought I was charming and didn't have a mean bone in my body.

"Amber, I'm okay, how are you?"

"I'm fine."

"Okay, baby, what do you want me to do?" he said.

"Will you drive me over there so I can pay him tonight?"

"Yeah, I can do that, sweetie, but I can't come until around eight o'clock. Will that do, Miss Amber?"

"That's fine."

"Good, we've got a date."

"Horace," I said with hesitation, "thank you for helping me out. I promise again to pay you back when I get all the bottles together and cash them in."

# Chapter Fifteen

# *Paula*

Jesus, these fish are pretty!" Paula exclaimed as she studied them swimming in the big tank in Earl's living room. The tropical fish flashed shades of coral, blue, dark orange, and yellow. Earl had decorated the tank with lush plants, rocks, and glittering stones. It was magnificent, and sometimes when she and Earl were getting it on, Paula would glance over at all those beautiful fish. The room glowed in the light of the aquarium. She was certain she was in paradise. That's what she had nicknamed Earl's apartment—Paradise Alley.

It was ten minutes after five, Friday night. Paula had left work earlier than usual and he was in the shower when she arrived. She sure felt independent and in control now that she had the keys to his place. She had to pick up some ingredients to make a cake from scratch. She knew she had to do special little things to keep him from missing his mother and going back to Detroit, or moving in with his sister. The weekend before last, she'd made an entire Thanksgiving dinner on Saturday night, and Thanksgiving was nowhere in sight. Then she fed it to him in bed.

Tonight Paula was tired, but she knew she had to keep things going because she only saw Earl every other weekend and he was getting a little tired of that. He grew lonely when she wasn't there, and he'd been complaining. She had to do something to keep him occupied at least some of the weeknights. She'd conjured up a plan and intended to spring it on him tonight.

Paula really didn't like where she was living. The place was just too small. Horace wouldn't get her a two-bedroom because he was afraid she would have too much room and maybe sneak someone into the apartment. She knew that was why he had gotten so small a place. It was deliberate, because one thing about Horace, he was not cheap. He just knew Paula too well. Well, she figured she had it coming not to be trusted by Horace because, after all, he did catch her in his own house with Freddie Morris when she and the kids were living there. He had come home early from Florida, and there she and Freddie were, asleep in each other's arms. That seemed like an eternity ago.

Paula really did like Earl. He was a nice guy and he dug Paula too. But she could not let herself go. He would cost her Horace, and Earl didn't have even half of what Horace had. Horace was well established here and in Florida with property. She knew he had a nice stash in the bank and kept a decent car. Earl would also cost her freedom if she really hooked up with him and lived with him.

But he was fun, even though he was young, and Paula was trying to mold him into exactly what she wanted. She was going to tell Earl tonight that she thought it would be a good idea, since he was so smart and all, for him to enroll in the local college. He should take some night courses. This way, he would stop bugging her about coming over during the week. God, he had even suggested one time that she could bring her kids over to meet him. So, tonight, it would be a good dinner of broiled porterhouse steaks, creamed potatoes and spinach, and fresh lemonade. Paula had even baked a coconut pound cake from scratch. Since she had planned such a family-style, old-fashioned dinner, the rest of the evening had to be the other extreme—wild.

Paula got dinner ready, and they sat down to eat. Over dinner she said to Earl, "You are so smart, baby, did you ever think about taking some classes at Community College?"

"Not really, I have to work and all and I'm really not even sure what I'm going to do. I mean in terms of a profession. I haven't thought much about that lately."

"Well," said Paula, "why don't you think about it over the next couple of weeks and when I come back, maybe you'll have decided to become a doctor or a lawyer or an Indian chief."

After dinner, Paula normally took a shower and put on something really sexy for Earl. Then they would cuddle up, listen to records, and then make love. Tonight she had other plans. She went into the bathroom and took off all her clothes. When she returned she went over to Earl, who was in his robe and underwear bent over looking at the fish in the tank.

Paula, naked in just red high heels and swinging a pair of handcuffs, shouted at Earl, "Take everything off—now!"

Earl looked shocked. "Paula . . . what . . . ?"

"Take the goddamn shit off now, motherfucker!" she screamed.

Earl obeyed her, stripping down to nothing. He was a little scared now. He realized he didn't really know Paula that well. She might be one hinge short of a nuthouse door. After all, he had only been dating her for about seven months.

"Now lie on the floor."

Earl got down on the floor. Paula stood over him with her legs wide apart. She pointed to the couch and said, "Lie over there on the floor."

She put a foot on his thigh, careful that the heel of her shoe didn't stick him. She nudged him toward the couch. He obeyed by crawling on his hands and knees to the designated spot.

"Mr. Frazier, you are under arrest."

When she said "arrest," she bent down on the floor and got on top of him, squatting with the front of her body facing him. She handcuffed his wrist to the leg of the couch.

Her next words were, "You have the right to remain silent." When she said "silent," she pushed one of her breasts in his face and shoved her nipple in his mouth.

Then it was, "Anything you say can be used against you in a court of law."

Then she said, "You have the right to an attorney." On the word "attorney," she began to massage his penis, bringing it to an erection. "If you cannot afford an attorney, one will be appointed for you free of charge." Her tongue circled his ear. On the word "charge" she shoved his penis between her legs and up into her vagina.

Earl was no longer afraid; in fact, he helped her out by using his one free hand to hold onto her hip in an attempt to help her maneuver her body to fit his penis comfortably inside her. She began riding him like a jockey, her back erect as she sat on top of him, her head straight up to the ceiling of that living room. She had her hands behind her neck, both elbows extending out, and her ass vibrated like a machine. She needed something to hold her concentration and keep her momentum, so she dropped her head backwards, her face up to the ceiling, and imagined that she was an African native doing a tribal dance. Her hips and ass had to move back and forth and around and around as fast as possible in order to outdance her competitors. Then she'd be crowned queen of the tribe.

Earl was screaming like a maniac. When it was over, he lay exhausted on the floor, grinning like a fool.

"Do you understand these rights as they have been read to you?"

# Chapter Sixteen

# Amber

"Hi, Amber," Horace said as he walked in. He nodded to Grandpa, who was sitting at the kitchen table. Grandma was playing with Renee in the living room. Renee jumped up and down when she saw Horace. She really loved her daddy.

I ran over to Horace and said, "Are you ready to go?"

"Hold on, honey, let me play with the baby for a minute."

He sat on the couch swinging Renee up and down in the air. She squealed with delight. Sydni was on the hallway floor, playing jacks. Horace noticed her and called out, "Aren't you speaking to me? What's wrong, you mad at me?"

"Hi, Horace, I'm not mad at you."

"I have a date with Miss Amber tonight for a little while," Horace said to Grandpa and Grandma. "If she doesn't mind, I'll take her sisters with us." He winked at me, and I shook my head up and down. "What do you two old people think? Can you do without them for a couple of hours?"

Grandma, who wasn't angry anymore with Horace over the County Care incident, looked at all of us. "You can take them, but try to get back before eleven o'clock."

"No problem." Horace yelled to Sydni to come on as he scooped up Renee and took her to the bathroom.

We all piled into the car. Horace said to me, "Amber, do you have the guy's address?"

"Yes. Do you have the money?"

He grinned at me, shook his head back and forth, and started up the car. He asked me to read the address to him. We were there in about ten minutes. He parked the car and got us out. We walked across the street to the house. Horace had Renee in his arms and me by the hand. Sydni followed closely behind.

We rang the doorbell and, in about two minutes, the watch guy came to the door.

"Hi," I said.

He looked surprised. He had probably forgotten all about me.

"Hi," he said, and looked at all of us. Then he looked at me and said, "This must be your family."

"Yes. This is my big sister Sydni and my little sister Renee and this is Horace." I paused, looking up at Horace. "Horace is Renee's daddy and part our daddy, too."

The watch guy thought that was cute, and Horace was flattered. Horace extended his hand. "How you doing, man? It's nice to meet you."

"Likewise," the watch guy said.

"Amber has been worried about what she did to you, and I'm here to make the situation right. I beg your pardon regarding what happened, and Amber would like to formally apologize."

I looked up at the watch guy. "I'm sorry I cheated you, sir, and I won't ever do it again."

Horace went to pass Renee to Sydni so he could get his wallet out. The watch guy stopped him. "May I?" He reached for Renee and took her from Horace's arms.

"She sure is a pretty thing and she certainly does favor her daddy."

Horace grinned as he handed me a ten-dollar bill. I gave it to the watch guy and extended my hand to shake his. He shook my hand and, as he was doing so, said, "I'm glad I finally know your name. Amber— that is a beautiful name."

"Thank you." I realized I still didn't know the watch guy's name.

Sydni peered into the hallway of his apartment curiously. The watch guy said to her, "You are really cute, too, and very quiet I see."

She smiled and blushed.

"Do you like fish?" he asked Sydni.

"Yes, porgies mostly."

He laughed. "No, I mean fish in a tank, like an aquarium?"

"Well, I've never seen an aquarium, but we had goldfish in a bowl un- til they died because Amber fed them Cheerios."

"I have a nice tank, do you want to see my fish?"

Sydni and I looked up at Horace for his approval.

"Oh, man, you don't have to do that, we don't want to bother you," Horace said.

"It's no trouble—and I also have some good coconut cake. Come on up."

"Well, okay," said Horace, and we all went inside the apartment.

The watch guy led the way up the stairs. I was almost running behind him, foot to foot, with Sydni scurrying behind me. When he reached the top of the stairs, he yelled out, "Baby, we've got a little company, put something on and come on out. I promised them cake."

Sydni, Renee, and I ran over to the tank in the living room to look at the fish and tapped the glass to make them swim around. Horace looked around.

"You have a nice place. You know, I'm sorry, I don't think I caught your name."

"Sorry, man. It's Earl. Yeah, this is a great place, I lucked out finding it. I haven't been in Philly long, I just moved from Detroit." Earl glanced over Horace's shoulder. "And here's my baby." We all turned around at once and saw—Paula!

Sydni screamed, "Paula!" Renee lunged for Paula, trying to get out of Horace's arms. Horace was totally speechless. I looked at Paula in amazement and said, "You work here?"

"Paula, you know these people?" Earl asked.

Paula did not open her mouth. She was backing up toward the bedroom and looking strange.

"Earl, come here," she said.

"What's the matter with you, Paula?"

He was about to walk toward the bedroom when Horace abruptly put Renee down and went after Paula. He had a real mean look on his face.

Earl was confused. "What's going on? What's happening?"

Horace held his hand up and said to Earl, "Man, you seem like a nice guy and I have no beef with you. Paula is the mother of these children, and I thought she was my woman. She better get her ass out of here because she has a lot of explaining to do."

"When did you get out of jail?" Earl asked Horace. "Were you released today or something?"

"What? What jail?"

Horace and Earl both looked at Paula at the same time. Sydni and I stood there with our mouths open. I cut in to try to explain.

"Oh, no, Earl, you're mixed up. My *real* daddy's in jail. You've got Lance mixed up with Horace."

Earl looked at Paula and said, "Get out."

Paula tried to get to the bedroom for her clothes, but Horace followed her, almost running.

"Don't make me tear this boy's place up. Get your shit and get out of here."

Earl noticed Renee in the kitchen reaching for the cake on the table and sticking her fingers in the icing. She was trying to climb on the kitchen chair to get closer to it. He went over and picked her up. Horace came out of the bedroom, collected us, and stood by the stairs waiting for Paula. He did not trust her and thought she might try to jump out of a window. He was not leaving without her. She saw that she had no way out, so she put her clothes on and grabbed her handbag. She left the other belongings that she kept there. As she emerged from the bedroom, Earl grabbed the coconut cake and smashed it into Paula's face. He rubbed it into her hair before she could make it to the steps. He grabbed her by the wrist and said, "I cannot believe you are such a lying, conniving . . . bitch. Don't you ever, as long as you live, come anywhere near me or this apartment. I never want to see you again."

Paula didn't reply. She was trying to remove the icing from her eyes so she could see her way down the stairs.

Earl looked at Horace and said, "I'm sorry, man, I didn't know she belonged to anyone."

"No problem. In fact, as of right now, she doesn't belong to me. We've just got a score to settle." We all walked down the steps and out of Earl's apartment.

Earl sat down on the living room couch and put his face in his hands. He felt like a fool, a complete jerk. He had been seeing this girl for nearly nine months. He couldn't believe all the lies she had told him. How could he have been so gullible? He sat there and reflected on all the time he had spent with her, all the money he had given her and spent on her. He wondered how he could lie in someone's arms so many times and sleep and eat with her and not know who the hell she really was. He hated himself for being so naïve and stupid. He thought about all the times he had kept her away from those cute little girls, and he felt ashamed.

When Horace got us all into the car, he headed for Grandma's house. He took us all into the house, including Paula. Grandpa asked, startled, "Aren't you working this weekend? Paula, what are you doing here? And what's all the cake and icing doing all over you? Girl, are you working at a bakery?"

Paula did not answer. She walked out of the room and started toward her bedroom, stopping off at the bathroom to grab one of the guest towels off the rack.

Grandma gave Horace a puzzled look. "What happened?"

"Nothing I care to talk about," said Horace.

Grandma ran after Paula. "Did Horace do that? Why aren't you at work? What happened?"

Paula was wiping her face with the towel, trying to get the icing and shredded coconut out of her hair and eyelashes. Horace entered the room and said to Grandma, "Fannie, can we have some privacy for a minute?"

Grandma looked at Horace, pleading with her eyes for him not to hurt Paula. She turned and walked out of the room and down the steps to the living room.

When she entered the living room, she overheard Grandpa saying to Sydni and me, "You girls been to the bakery?"

I disappeared. Sydni stayed perched on Grandpa's lap.

Horace told Paula to come with him. She refused. He kept telling her and she kept refusing. He was mad enough to kill her. I hid outside her room and peeked in, watching and listening to everything. I clutched a brown paper bag in my hand. Paula refused one last time to go with Horace, and then he grabbed her. He got her in an armlock. She screamed at him to leave her alone and let her go. He refused and dragged her down the steps. Grandma came to the steps and told Horace to stop, to let Paula go and leave.

Horace looked at Grandma and said, "Fannie, do me a favor please, so me and you won't have a problem. Stay out of this, it's too big for you."

Grandpa never said a word. He just sat there shaking his head as he watched Paula going down the stairs. He figured Horace had caught Paula in a bakery with some guy and thought that it was about time.

Horace pushed Paula on down the stairs. She was taking one step at a time, trying not to go, but Horace stuck with her. I was right behind Horace. When he got outside the front door with Paula, he put her in the car, locked her in, and just stood by the car, leaning on the door, tired, trying to collect himself. I came over, handed the paper bag to him, and walked back toward the house. Horace looked into the bag. Inside was an extension cord.

—

# Chapter Seventeen

# *Sheila*

*I*t was five fifteen when Lenora said good-bye to Sheila and the children. They wished her luck at the bingo game. Lenora walked down the street holding her brown leather overnight bag. She hailed a cab about a block away and said to the driver, "729 Essex Avenue." The driver sped off.

When Lenora arrived at the big white house with the black shutters and manicured lawn, she entered with a key. She walked into the parlor and placed her bag on the floor. "Hello, Lizzie. How's it going?"

The young woman replied, "It's going okay. We have three upstairs on the third floor who came last night and one due about nine thirty this evening. The other one is due around eleven o'clock tonight."

"How are the three upstairs feeling?"

"Okay, just pretty nervous."

"How are you on supplies?" asked Lenora.

"Well," said Lizzie, "I think we can make it until next weekend and then I have to call Joanie."

"Did you pay Joanie this week?" Lenora asked over her shoulder as she headed up the stairs.

"Yes."

"I'm here now, I'll start soon."

At six fifteen when Sheila heard the doorbell ring, she thought, "Thank God nothing happened and Pam showed up on time." Sheila was excited about her date tonight. She and Leonard had been talking on the telephone all week and having a ball getting to know each other better. She lost three more pounds. Tonight she looked sharp in a black double-breasted coatdress with brass buttons, sheer black stockings, and black suede pumps. Her hair was frosted with a little red in it and the back of it was cut close. She had borrowed a pair of gold earrings and a gold bracelet from Lenora. Sheila was very pleased and felt good about herself.

Pam ran up the stairs to speak to Sheila and asked, "Did you cook dinner?"

"Meat loaf, broccoli, and mashed potatoes, plus I made Jell-O."

"Can I eat?"

"Yes, of course. I'll be leaving shortly and I'll be back before eleven o'clock."

"Okay," Pam said.

Pam ran down the stairs, ate dinner, and straightened up the kitchen for Sheila. When the doorbell rang, Pam answered and let Leonard in. They exchanged greetings and Pam called Sheila down. Sheila introduced Leonard to her kids and to Pam, and they left.

As soon as they got into the car, Leonard took a look at Sheila and said, "You look ravishing."

"So do you in your new sports jacket."

"How do you know this is new? What makes you think I got that dressed up for you?"

"Because you have the price tag sticking out of it."

They both laughed. Sheila pulled the tag off of his jacket and handed it to him.

"So, what kind of place are we are going to?" she asked.

"A small coffee shop with health food cuisine and not all that fattening stuff other restaurants have," Leonard explained. "I'm watching my weight, too, and trying to stay away from things that would take me off track. The place also has a little jazz band, and it's not too noisy. The music's usually good, too."

Sheila smiled. It had been a long time since she had been out. Leonard was a real gentleman. When they arrived and parked the car, he opened her door, helped her out, and held her hand until they were seated—"The works," Sheila thought. He looked good all dressed up. She felt very relaxed with him. The place was nicely done in fine wicker patio furniture with glass-topped tables, candles on every table, and plants all around the room. Sheila complimented Leonard on choosing such a nice spot for a first date. They both ordered lemonades and alternated between listening to the music and chatting about their plans and their kids.

Sheila was very curious as to why Leonard was divorced because he seemed like such a nice guy and a good father and all. She couldn't imagine why anyone would want to divorce him or not want to be with him. But what? He seemed like a great guy. She just couldn't figure it out.

As much as they had talked over the past few months, and even during their phone conversations the past week, she had never tried to pry. She wondered why he never brought it up, and it crossed her mind that maybe talking about it was too painful. Maybe since they were not that tight and weren't talking about seriously hooking up with each other, he didn't feel a need to explain. She thought she'd play this by ear and maybe he'd discuss it soon. After all, this was just their first date. She didn't know where this thing was going. She also wondered why he was chasing an overweight widow, with four children to boot, who had dug up her husband's grave. But, for right now, she wasn't going to question him about that either.

After the jazz set ended, Leonard asked her if she wanted to take a drive and she agreed. They drove along the Delaware River and then out to East Falls, a beautiful scenic area. He stopped the car. It was dark and Sheila was a bit nervous now because, after all, this was the park and she really didn't know him that well. He kept the radio on. The music was soft and relaxing. He took her hand and began to talk. He explained that he really thought a lot of her and was very interested in having a relationship with her. He asked if she wanted to continue to date him. She said she wanted to, but he had to understand that she didn't have a lot of time she could spend with him because of school, work, and children. If he could deal with that, then it would be fine. He said it would be. Then he tilted his head and kissed her, first on the cheek and on her lips. She kissed him back. His lips felt good.

The kiss ended, and he squeezed her hand. "I've had a nice evening, and I know it's time to get you back home."

As soon as Sheila had left the house for her date, Pam called her boyfriend. He begged her to let him come over.

"Vernon," she said, "I don't want to start that. I just started working here and Miss Sheila would probably have a fit if you came over. Also, you know she isn't home now and I didn't ask if I could have any company."

She paused and listened to him explain how much he wanted to see her and that it would probably be fine. She could tell the kids not to mention that he had come by. She said, "Oh yeah, and they'll probably tell her anyway and then there may be trouble."

They talked a little while longer and hung up. Pam searched around the kitchen looking for something to munch on, found some potato chips and cheese, and perched herself on the couch to watch television.

Lenora took her things upstairs and put them in the second floor rear bedroom. Then she proceeded to the third floor, where there were four bedrooms. She went into the three that were occupied to say hello and that she would be right back. She went into the bathroom and gathered alcohol, catheters, hangers, and plastic bags from the closet. She went back into the rooms and asked the women to come out. They all filed into the third floor front bedroom, and Lenora told them to find seats.

Lenora showed the three girls the materials collected and demonstrated the procedure she would perform. She estimated how long the procedure would take and told them what she would do and what would eventually happen. Then she picked up a notepad and took information from the women about their ages, how far along they were, and when their last menstrual period had been.

She asked whether they had ever had a baby or an abortion. Then she explained what they should feel during the procedure and what to expect after it was over. "You'll stay until Monday morning," she said. "I want to keep an eye on you." She collected her fee of one hundred fifty dollars from each woman.

"Well, Tracey, let's start with you. Let's go back to your room."

Lenora told the other two girls that she should be back in about fifteen minutes. Then she and Tracey left the room.

As Lenora was preparing Tracey, she asked, "By the way, Tracey, where did you tell your parents you were going to be tonight?"

"I'm supposed to be roller-skating with my friend Rosie and spending the night at her house. I told my parents I'd be with Rosie because she doesn't have a phone and my folks can't check on me."

"Who is picking you up tomorrow?"

"My boyfriend and his brother."

"Did you tell them that they were to meet you at the corner of Morris and Eighteenth Street instead of here?"

"Yes, I did."

"Good. So Lizzie will order you a cab for eleven o'clock tomorrow morning to take you to meet your boyfriend."

"Okay," murmured Tracey.

Tracey lay on the bed trembling. She was sixteen years old and two and a half months pregnant. She was a pretty Puerto Rican girl, built small. Lenora straightened out the coat hanger and put it on the bed. She put gel on the vaginal speculum and inserted it into Tracey's vagina. Tracey jumped, and Lenora told her she had to relax and be still. After the speculum was in place, Lenora could see the opening of Tracey's cervix. She took some more gel, coated the catheter with it, and inserted the hanger, which had been sterilized with alcohol, into the catheter. Then she slid the catheter into Tracey's cervix, advancing it slowly as far as she could, then removing it. She continued this process until she saw a bloody discharge.

Lenora instructed Tracey to stay in bed, to lie still, and to anticipate cramping in her stomach. "You tell me when those cramps start," she said. "I'll be right down the hall. Everything will be just fine—don't you worry."

Lenora left the room, picked up some fresh supplies, yelled down the hall, "Next," and went into another room.

# Chapter Eighteen

# *Lucy*

oug arrived at Bello's on time with both his crutches. Reba rushed over to him, kissed him on the cheek, and helped him to their table. She introduced him to Peggy and Lucy. Peggy studied him a bit. They all made small talk, and Doug ordered something light to eat and iced tea.

"Doug, what happened to you?" asked Peggy.

Reba looked at him and blushed.

"I cut my foot on a glass that I didn't realize had fallen on the floor in my hotel room today."

"Good Lord. What's the extent of the damage?" asked Peggy.

"Just a nasty gash that has been stitched up. I'll be fine."

"How long do you plan to be here in Norfolk?"

"I have one more meeting on Monday and then I'm on my way back to Annapolis on Tuesday."

"My, however are you going to drive home? I can see that it's your right foot that's injured."

"I don't know, I'll have to figure that one out."

By then everyone except Doug had finished eating. Peggy and Lucy were about to excuse themselves when Reba said, "Peggy, please don't forget to leave a ticket at the main door for Doug to attend the fashion show."

"Yes, I would love to attend if they allow handicapped people," Doug said.

Everyone smiled. Then Doug said, "How much is the ticket?"

"It is complimentary to you," Peggy replied.

"No, Mrs. Kinard, I insist on paying for it."

"Please, allow me," Peggy said.

"Okay, thank you. I'll see you there."

After the others left the table, Doug grabbed Reba's hand and blew her a kiss. She blew one back to him and reached down to place his injured leg across her lap. She reached under the table and put her hand in his crotch and massaged his penis.

"I see you're at it again. That's what got us into this mess in the first place."

"I'm rather fond of the mess I've gotten myself into," she said sweetly.

Doug glanced at his watch. "It's twenty after six and the show starts at seven. We'd better get going, lady."

"I bet you breakfast tomorrow morning I can turn your world upside down and be at that show by seven o'clock," Reba whispered.

Doug looked at her, grinned, and shook his head. "You're on." They left the restaurant and headed for his room.

Lucy walked into the ballroom at 6:50. She thought, "Can I do this thing right? I sure hope everything works out okay." She looked around for Reba. She didn't see her, so she began to walk around, looking at how lovely the ballroom was. She stood at the end of the runway, thinking that in less than an hour she'd be coming out there all dressed up, looking like a million dollars.

She ran into the back room to check out her dressing station. Everything was in order. A few models were around in the back area and more were entering the ballroom. Guests were starting to arrive, too. Lucy was beginning to get excited. She was walking toward the front of the ballroom to check for Peggy or Reba when a very pretty girl stopped her. Lucy had seen her before around the hotel and at the rehearsal, but she hadn't been on the bus with them. She was tall, about five feet eight, with short brown hair and deep brown eyes. She had white skin that seemed glazed in honey, and she looked like a mulatto. She wore a clinging olive green knit midcalf skirt that fell softly against her streamlined legs. The skirt had a thin teasing horizontal slit from thigh to thigh. The matching sweater was also slit at one shoulder, exposing just enough to imagine how sexy she really was. Very exotic.

"Hi, I'm Angie, how you doin'?" she greeted Lucy.

"Hi, I'm Lucy Noble, and I think I'm a nervous wreck."

Angie laughed and said, "I saw you at rehearsal, girl, struttin' your stuff, and you're gonna do just fine."

"Thanks, I needed that."

They began to talk. Lucy hadn't expected this beauty to have such a personality. She expected her to be uppity and reserved, and instead she was charming and bubbly. Lucy liked her right away.

It was now exactly seven o'clock, and Reba rushed in alone. Lucy walked toward her.

"Where's Doug?" Lucy asked.

"He's coming—you know it takes him a little longer than me." Reba smiled coyly.

They hurried into the back room to Lucy's station. Lucy introduced Reba to Angie.

Angie said to them both, "I'm from D.C.—where are you two from?"

"Philly," Lucy replied.

"We went over to the base today for a tour," Angie said.

"Was it nice?" asked Lucy.

"Yeah, they were nice, all fucking six hundred of them."

Lucy laughed and walked back toward Angie's station.

"Lucy, are you down here with your husband or man or anyone you sleep with?"

"No, I just came down with Reba and Peggy Kinard, the designer and my godmother."

Angie said, "Well, I see your friend Reba brought her man down here, so why didn't you bring yours?"

"Nothing is mine in Philly to bring."

Angie laughed. "Listen, we told every man we saw over there today to come to the show. Maybe we can hang out later?"

"That would be great. So, who else went over to the base?"

"Chillie, the Puerto Rican girl—she went over there dressed to kill in a black pantsuit. Girl, the pants were at her waist on one side and the other side was cut low to the hip. They fit her like she was poured into them. They were straight-legged and had a tiny flare at the bottom. The jacket was a midriff that opened a little more on one side of the chest than the other, exposing a little of one breast. The sleeves to the jacket were long to her wrists. It snapped at the bottom in the middle, just under the breast, so girlfriend's navel, stomach, and back were showing, but just a little, nothing vulgar. She wore a black scarf around her neck and it hung down the back, flowing when she walked. Oh, my God, it was the baddest thing I ever saw, and she looked fine last night. Her hair was slicked back in an updo. She should have worn that shit in the show.

Bonita went, too—you know, the tall girl with the red hair—and the one over at station six, and Rochelle Wagner, at station eleven. Oh, let me tell you! You know the white model with the short blond hair? She wears it off her face?" Lucy looked puzzled, not remembering the model.

"You know," said Angie, "she wears her hair slicked down in the front and pulled to the side? Come on, Lucy, the one with those big full African American lips, carefully painted with red lipstick. She's modeling that black denim pantsuit with the black suede knee-high boots. She went with us, too. We had those guys going crazy. I'll bet you they bring their asses here tonight."

Lucy said, "Let's hope so. I've been through the wringer and would love to meet Mr. Right."

"Well," continued Angie, "all of us went over there and had a ball flirting with the guys. Some of them are really fine, too. Shit, we hated to leave. I just know some of them will show up. They'd better, so I don't have to go looking for them in the dark after the show. Look, I want to party so bad I just might start banging on barrack doors and snatching their asses out of there in their underwear. So listen up—wait for me after the show. Try to check the crowd out while you're waiting your turn and when you're on the runway. Just don't look too hard because I'd hate for you to fall on your ass on that damn runway."

They both laughed and reported to their stations to get made up and ready for the show. Peggy arrived at 7:10 and went directly to Lucy's station to check on her and Reba.

"How are things going?

Both girls smiled and said, "Great."

"Reba, I like your friend, he's very nice," Peggy said.

"You know what? I think so too." Reba was getting a little worried. "Did you see him outside when you came in?"

"No."

Reba and Peggy began Lucy's makeup. They had her first outfit ready to go. Lucy would be the fourth model out, in olive green silk lounging pajamas. Her next outfit would be a red glitter V-necked gown. Peggy had done a terrific job on them. Lucy could not wait to get out there! By now models were running around nervous and naked or in their underwear. Lucy looked over at Angie, who was number seven going out. Her assistant had just finished doing her makeup and was starting on her hair.

Peggy announced that it was time for Lucy to get outside and, giving them a wink, said, "Good luck."

When Peggy got out into the ballroom, she noticed Doug sitting alone with a glass of wine. She went over to him, said hello again, and told him the show would start in about ten minutes. Then she said, "Reba was wondering if you had arrived, and, by the way, she's doing just fine backstage."

Doug was glad Peggy was treating him so nicely. He sat there thinking about himself and Reba, really wondering what in the hell the two of them were getting themselves into. He was dating two women at home, but wasn't serious about either of them. Reba was a problem. Jesus Christ! Was he falling in love with a married woman with six kids? He wondered what the fuck he was going to do with six kids. Or was he going to do nothing with them and break it off tomorrow? Was he going to sneak around with her and start a "long distance telephone" thing and a "meet you somewhere in between Annapolis and Philly" thing. He wondered how he would correspond with her. Would it be the "I sent it to your friend's house" thing? "Oh shit," he thought, "I just cannot get involved with my personal life tonight. It's much too complicated."

Then he started to relive the little quickie they'd had before the show. She came to the hotel room after they had left Bello's. Before he could put his crutches against the wall, she said, "Sit down. I don't have time to take everything off. Here, let me help you to the chair."

Then she lifted her skirt, removed her panties, unzipped his pants, taken his penis in both her hands, and massaged it to erection. She got down on her knees and looked up at him and said, "I want a Popsicle, Daddy," just like a little kid.

Then she jumped up, grabbed his hotel key off the table, and ran out the door. He had no idea where she was going and called after her, "Come back here, woman!"

Just as he was thinking, "What the hell is going on now?" she had returned. She knelt between his legs, resumed massaging him, and then put his penis in her mouth. He moaned with joy. She took her free hand, which contained a few pieces of ice, and began to rub the ice up and down his penis. He started to scream. She replaced him into her mouth and pretended she had a Popsicle. Periodically, she would remove herself from him and replace the ice again, repeating the process. Then she stood up and sat on top of him in the chair, inserted his penis into her vagina, and eased down on him.

She moved vigorously, whispering in his ear, "I really used to be a hula dancer and I'm from Hawaii, hanging out in Norfolk having the time of my life."

When they both were satisfied, she eased off of him, walked over to the wall, collected his crutches, and handed them to him. She stepped over her panties lying on the floor and said to him, "See you at the show, Dexter."

Doug ordered another wine, relaxed, and waited for the show to start. He decided that Reba just might be worth all the trouble the relationship would cause him.

Lucy said to Reba, "Okay, I'm set." She stood up at her station, dressed, and was ready to go out on the runway. She noticed Angie, who looked beautiful in a black, cream, and mauve oriental print robe.

"See the one in the print robe? She really is an attractive girl, isn't she?"

Reba agreed and asked, "What's she about?"

"Well, remember, she's from D.C. She's single and likes to party. I don't know anything else. She asked me to go out with her and her friends after the show."

"Go where?" Reba responded protectively.

"Well, they'd been over to the base earlier and found some men. Angie's all excited and wants to try to hook up with some of them tonight. She thinks some of them may show up here."

"Are you going?"

"I really don't know. Let's go, partner, this is me."

Lucy got up from the station and took her place to go out onto the runway. She was nervous, but she wanted this moment more than ever. The commentator called her name and number and she stepped out. Reba tried to get a decent spot so she could watch, but the entranceway was a little crowded with all the models. Lucy was out on that runway now, grinning and strutting and doing a little switching. She was a perfect size four, five feet six, and she looked good out there in Peggy's design. Lucy remembered what Angie had asked her to do, but she was too excited to look for anyone.

This was her moment. "Let them look for me—I'm it tonight," she thought. When she walked back into the dressing room to her station, she was beaming. Reba looked as proud as a peacock, and all the other models gave her the "thumbs up," saying "Good job." She rushed to get into her next outfit.

The show ran full swing until nine thirty. Everybody was in a jovial mood, and Lucy was on cloud nine all by herself. Peggy congratulated both her girls on a job well done. Reba announced she wanted to get out to Doug. Peggy reminded her that the garments had to be held in the security area to be picked up the next day. They had to be labeled and put back in order, and security had to be notified to come for them. She also reminded Reba that the bus back to Philly would leave at two o'clock the next day, and then she left the room.

Reba didn't want to hear anything about Philly. She didn't want to be bothered with all the garments or the phone call to security. She just wanted to get back to Doug. So she quickly made sure everything was in order, ran over to the house phone in the ballroom to call security, and returned to the station.

Lucy offered to help, but Reba said, "It's done. Listen, you just get yourself together and think about having some fun, too. I'm on my way to Doug. Don't get alarmed if I'm not in the bed next to you in the morning." She added, "Hey, Lucy, do me a favor and lay out an outfit for me before you go to sleep, because I'll be rushing in the morning to have breakfast with Doug. He doesn't know I haven't a clue how to dress."

Lucy spotted Angie and gave her a wave. Angie came over and said, "Well, do you think you want to hang out after all that hard work?"

"I don't know. Did any of the guys you met last night show up?"

"Yep, they're here. I don't know who, but there are men in the house tonight! Should I count you in?"

Lucy looked at Reba and thought about what a blast she seemed to be having with Doug. "Count me in."

# Chapter Nineteen

# *Paula*

*P*aula sat in Horace's car trying to figure out what happened—how Horace had found her and why Earl had invited him and the girls to the apartment. She was completely baffled.

Horace remained silent during the drive. He was heading straight to Paula's apartment, but didn't know what he was going to do when he got there. He kept rehashing everything in his mind from the day he met Paula. He thought about all the things he had done to change her, to make her a better person and a better mother. He thought about his child and how much he loved that little girl. He knew Paula was definitely a bad influence on all her children. He remembered how he had brought them to live with him, provided for them, and how home life went down the drain because Paula just couldn't be trusted. He looked over at her and wondered if she wanted anything decent out of life.

Paula sat still and quiet. No tears—just a bewildered look. He pulled up to her apartment and said, "Let's go."

Paula sat for a moment contemplating whether she should get out of the car. Then she got out and walked past Horace, up the steps. He followed her to the apartment. Paula went straight to the bedroom and sat on one of the twin beds. Horace sat on the other one and just looked at her.

"What are you going to do, Horace, kill me?"

"You know what, I would very much like to at this moment, but too much would be at stake. I have a daughter to raise."

"*We* have a daughter to raise," she corrected him.

"Paula, what is your problem? I mean, are you some kind of nymphomaniac or something? Does one man just not satisfy you? Is it that I don't satisfy you and you're pretending when we're in bed? Can you answer these questions for me? Because I would really like some answers."

"I just like excitement, and I like it with different people. I like a good time all the time. It has nothing to do with you sexually, and it has nothing to do with you as a person. There's nothing wrong with you."

"You are creating a horrible moral example for your three daughters. You're a liar and a cheat. You use people. You hurt people and you damage their souls. I don't know Earl very well, but I believe he is a decent guy, and I don't believe you really give a damn about him either. I also believe that if you continue on the course you're on, someone is going to kill you one day."

"Tell me something," Paula said. "Tell me how you found out about Earl and why you had to come to his apartment to create that scene."

"I won't answer that question, but I will let you know that I did not come there to cause a scene. I will also tell you that you are on your own now. I'm not going to hit you or kick your ass because, frankly, it won't change a damn thing and it won't change you. But I am going to take your ass to court. I'm not paying you another dime. I'll shop for Renee and bring her clothes to you. That will be my form of support. As soon as I retain an attorney, I will file papers to get custody of Renee."

"I don't believe you," Paula said.

"Paula, I am very serious. I am going to try to get custody of my child. I do not want any type of relationship with you, because if I continue with you, I will be the one to kill you and end up in jail. That leaves Renee left without parents. So I'm going to go about it the legal way and beat you with paper."

"Listen, Horace, I can change. Just give me a chance. Just one last chance."

"Paula, you have had more chances than anybody has ever known, heard about, or read about. You aren't about change, you're just totally fucked up. I will not stand by and let you ruin Renee's life, or neglect her, and bring every Tom, Dick (he's your main problem), and Harry around and let her witness your 'excitement.' Be prepared to have your rent money the first of the month. Since you have a weekend job, you ought to be able to handle that. Now, I'd like to keep Renee until this thing is over with the court. Can I do that without a fight?"

Paula knew Horace was dead serious. She wondered how she could possibly pull off paying the rent *and* a sitter. There was no more Earl, and Curtis didn't give her much. She said to Horace, "Take her, and you know what, you don't have to bother taking me to court. I'll sign her over to you."

Horace looked at her and shook his head. He removed Renee's things, all the pretty things he had bought her, from the dresser drawers. He had gotten what he wanted, but he felt pretty low.

Horace left the apartment and drove around, wondering what he was going to do. He needed a sitter who could stay overnight with Renee while he worked. He thought about how Renee would miss her mother and wondered how she would make that adjustment. He wondered how he would manage his own life and thought about Sydni and me, feeling sorry for us. He had been careful not to let Paula know that I was the key to him finding out about her and Earl.

Horace wondered how Earl was making out. He still thought Earl was a decent guy, a nice young dude just caught up in Paula's bullshit. He decided to go back by Earl's place to talk. He could imagine how Earl must be feeling and remembered the expression on his face when they left. Horace thought, "The two of us ought to get together and beat the shit out of Paula."

He drove over to Earl's place and saw lights. He rang the bell. Earl was shocked to see Horace and said, "She ain't here, man."

"I know, I came to see you. Are you okay?"

"Do you want to come up?"

"No, I want to take you out for a beer. No hard feelings on my part."

"Let me grab some shoes and a shirt. I'll be a couple of minutes."

They rode over to Jasmine's, a nice spot not far from Earl's place, and ordered beers.

Horace said, "Man, I have been dealing with that chick for about five years. I was taking real good care of her, and that baby of mine wants for nothing. Paula is just a trifling bitch. It's as simple as that. I knew I should have stopped dealing with her when I caught her wrong in my own spot. But instead, I just threw her out and kept right on seeing her."

Earl's eyes lit up. "You caught her on your own turf?"

Horace nodded.

"Well, man, what's wrong with her? I mean, what exactly is she looking for? She said her husband was in jail and all the kids were his. Damn, I was a moron—I didn't even know where she lived and I'd never even seen the kids or found out their names. I've been seeing her for over eight months." He took a swig of beer. "So, what's up with the guy in jail? Was she ever married to him, do you know?"

"Man, Paula has never been married to anyone. The guy in jail is a pretty cool dude named Lance Resnick who went up for blowing somebody away over some money. From what I hear, the guy he shot had it coming to him. Concerning him and Paula, the way I heard it, Lance was banging Paula's mom. He came by one day and her mom wasn't home, so Paula gave him some. Didn't want it to be a wasted trip. From then on, she gave him some more, and some more. Mom didn't know what was going on, so she was still banging him, too. Then Amber came popping out."

They both sat there shaking their heads.

Earl said, "You know what, man, can we talk? I mean, can you handle some things I want to say man to man, or are you still fucked up about her and would rather I not go in that direction?"

"No, man, the shit is over with now—come on with it."

Earl smiled and said, "You've gotta know she is really something else—between the sheets and on the floor and on the kitchen table and in the shower and in the park."

Horace shook his head and laughed. "Yeah, she told me when I was firing her tonight that she liked excitement." Horace summoned the bartender. "Give us two more and also bring me a Dewar's on the rocks, water back." Earl asked for a Hennessy straight up.

Horace continued, "Man, that's what got me into this shit. That thing between her legs ain't nothing but an oven cooking everything well done." They both laughed.

"Let me tell you something," said Horace. "When I first started dealing with her, she came on my job at break time one night. Now, I work eleven-to-seven down at the Navy Yard. That bitch came down there one night around three o'clock in the morning—my lunchtime. She didn't even tell me she was coming. I saw her walk up and I was shocked. She had on a bad trench coat and high heels—dressed up like she was going somewhere. Hair and everything was done. She found me eating lunch, kissed me on the cheek, and said, 'I brought you some lunch. Can we go somewhere and eat it privately?'

"Now, I didn't have any place to be private on the dock and eat with her. This wasn't some fancy restaurant, you know what I mean? This was the fucking dirty-ass, muddy-ass, wet-ass dock. I got up and started walking around with her. Other guys were out there, too. We walked by the bathroom and she said, 'I gotta pee.' She went into the men's room and I waited outside. Then she calls out to me, 'Come in here, I've got a problem,' and she sounds scared. I go in there and this bitch is butt naked with her ass in the sink. The trench coat was on the toilet. She had strawberry jam and whipped cream all over her snatch. She said to me, 'Here's dessert.'

"Before I knew it, that bitch shoved my head down between her legs and I thought I was in one of those pie-eating contests at a county fair. I was in that fucking bathroom for over an hour because she took me from the sink to the toilet to the sink to the toilet. I was so dizzy, tired, fucked up, and fucked out when that shit was over that I had to leave early from work. Now tell me what the fuck she pulled on you. I know it had to be something, the way you looked when you found out about her."

When Earl stopped laughing, he called the bartender back and ordered another round.

"Horace, she took me to a graveyard. She actually fucked me beside a grave that was dug for somebody."

"What? You gotta be lying."

"Oh, no. I guess the funeral was going to be the next day or something. I know this was an empty grave. She came over my house one Friday night, and after we had eaten, she wanted to go for a ride. The next thing I know, we're at the fucking graveyard! I was scared to death, but I was trying to be a man and, shit, I didn't want her to think I was a punk. I thought maybe a relative of hers was buried there, and she'd been thinking about them and decided to go out there to talk to them. So, we go walking through this damn graveyard and she stops in front of this grave. Then she starts to mess with me right out there—you know, massaging my Johnson—and then she took my pants down. I said, 'Look, Paula, I ain't about this out here.' Horace, honest to God, the woman tried to get me to jump in that fucking hole. I tried to leave, but I couldn't move very fast because my pants were down to my ankles. She grabbed me by the legs and I fell. I just lay there. That bitch got on top of me and proceeded to fuck my natural brains out. I was enjoying the shit and scared to death at the same time. Yeah, man, she did that shit. She also fucked me one night at the YMCA playground. She put me in one of the big swings and got on top of me, and you know what, she knew how to fuck me and make the swing go at the same time. Damn, that bitch is wild!"

They drank for a while and Horace said, "Come on, let's get out of here. I want to make one stop and then I have to head in. I'm getting my baby Renee for good in a couple of days and I have a lot of arrangements to make. I just have to stop at the Rockaway and pick up some money that a pal of mine owes me. You wanna come with me or do you want me to drop you off now?"

"Let's hit it, man."

They left Jasmine's and headed for the Rockaway. Horace spotted his friend. He also saw Paula in the corner sitting on some dude's lap.

He went back over to Earl and said, "Come here, man, I want to show you something. We've got company."

Earl walked over and looked Paula up and down. She looked up at both of them standing there together, and her jaw fell open.

Horace said to her, "I see you decided to go back to work."

# Chapter Twenty

# *Lucy*

The ballroom was packed after the show. Lucy, Angie, Rochelle, and Bonita searched through the crowd, looking for guys to party with. They headed for the bar. Lucy spotted Doug and Reba at a table and went over to them. "Hello, folks! Well, Doug, how did you like the show?"

"I thought the show was spectacular and the designs were superb. You really did a fantastic job, Lucy, and Peggy's clothes look really good on you. You should think about going into this modeling thing. It suits you."

Lucy blushed. "Thanks, Doug, that is really a nice compliment."

Reba was smiling. "You want to join us? Come on and have some wine."

"No, thanks, I don't feel like being a third wheel even for a minute. Can't you see all these men in here? I'd like to meet someone and have some fun tonight, or at least get a chance to talk to someone."

"We understand," Doug said.

"Bye," said Lucy. As she walked away, Reba ran over to her. "Lucy, please don't forget to leave me some clothes out for the morning. I don't want Doug to know about my problem. You'll be doing me a big favor."

Lucy replied with a kiss on the cheek, then headed toward the bar looking for Rochelle, Angie, and Bonita.

"And how many more of those lines do you have, sweetie, because I've got time," Lucy overheard Angie saying as she walked up to the crowded bar. Angie was surrounded by a couple of the models and about six gentlemen. She called, "Hey, Lucy, come on in here and join us." They shifted to make room for Lucy. Angie said, "You've got to meet Rochelle Simpson, from Queens, New York, Bonita Hilliard from Baltimore, and these are some of the guys from the base. Now, gentlemen, introduce yourselves to our friend Lucy from Philadelphia."

"Hi, everybody, nice to meet you," Lucy said.

"Hey, Lucy, I'm Kevin Graham."

"Hello, I'm Roger Travis."

The rest of the guys blurted out their names. "Hello"s and "nice to meet you"s were exchanged all over the place. Lastly it was, "Hello, Miss Philadelphia, I'm Bernie Shaw and I think you're stunning."

Angie cut in. "Lucy, what are you drinking?"

"Let me think a minute . . . um, I don't know. I think I'll try a Bloody Mary, light on the vodka and make it spicy."

While Lucy waited for her drink, she checked out the crowd. It sure was a lively party. Everybody seemed to be having a great time.

"So, Lucy, have you been having fun?" asked Rochelle.

"It's been kind of hectic, and I was a total nervous wreck before the show. I haven't seen any of Norfolk. It's good just being away from Philly. How about you? What do you think of your weekend so far?"

Rochelle said, "I've had a pretty nice time. We had a ball running all over that base. I think the show was dynamite and I hate to go back to Queens and my dreary old job."

"What do you do?"

"I'm an RN. I do private duty for a woman with cancer. It's very depressing."

"Sounds like it. I guess you're ready for a party."

"Yes, I really am. I do get to go out in Queens on my days off and I go into Manhattan sometimes, but there's nothing like seeing new places and meeting new people. You know, just getting away from your normal life for a moment can really make you feel better."

Angie said, "Hey, Lucy, here's your drink. Try it out. If it's not right, we'll just tie the bartender up and steal his job."

Everybody laughed. Angie went for her purse, but Bernie objected. "We've got that, just enjoy."

Drinks kept coming. It was a swinging crowd, Lucy thought. Angie was definitely the center of the group. She ordered the drinks, read Harold's palm, and put quite a dent in her Tequila Sunrises. Lucy began to chat with Bonita, who told her she had been living in Baltimore for about eight months. She had lived most of her life in Atlanta and, now, was working in the city government in Baltimore. She was a clerk but was looking for something a lot more interesting. Lucy shared that she worked at the stock exchange as a clerk and was bored as hell, too, but it paid pretty well and the benefits were good. It took her only fifteen minutes to get to work, and she was off every weekend, so she guessed it was better to stay.

Bonita asked Lucy if she was married or had a steady man. Lucy said, "I don't have a soul at the moment."

"Same here."

Lucy turned to the rest of the group. "Can I get in this conversation?" she said, looking at one of the guys. "Well, um, now you are . . . don't tell me . . . you're Bernie."

Bernie turned around and said, "You lookin' for me, Lucy?"

She laughed. "Oops, wrong one. Look, I'm getting mixed up with the names. There's just so many of you. Hell, there aren't this many men in Philadelphia." Everybody laughed.

"Remember me? I'd like to get in the conversation too. I'm Roger."

Roger was slender and about six feet two. He had wavy black hair, dark brown eyes, and the creamiest complexion Lucy had ever seen. She looked at him and said, "Feel free to join in. I was just telling Bonita what my world is about. So, Roger, it's your turn. What are you about and who are you for real?"

When Lucy said "for real," she and Bonita grinned at each other and then looked back at him for the answer. Bernie jumped in. "Roger's a hit man." A dozen people turned around and looked at Roger, who was blushing.

Kevin yelled out, "He blows women away, so Lucy, Bonita, get out of the way!"

By now the entire crowd was laughing. Rochelle summoned the bartender. "Can you give the hit man a drink on me? Hey, hit man, what are you drinking?"

"A slammer, baby," Roger replied sexily.

"Ooooo," hooted everyone in the crowd.

By now Lucy was giggling and really having a ball. The drinks kept flowing and the music sounded so good they started dancing. This party was on! The reception ended at eleven, but everybody had a nice buzz and didn't want to go in for the night. They sat at the bar and tried to think of someplace else to go. No one was really paired up, and there were six guys in their group. Kevin said, "There are some clubs downtown. We could do them until two o'clock when they close."

"Listen, guys," the bartender said, "we have our in-house astrologer here tonight. She's really great—sitting over there in the Blue Room. She's a lot of fun for twenty-five bucks."

"What!" screamed Angie. "I love that stuff. I'm going." She grabbed her purse.

"Hold up, Angie," Roger shouted, "I'm with you." They all ran to the Blue Room and crowded around the table, blurting out their signs and asking the woman to tell them about themselves.

"I'm about to close. I can only do one of you. Who's it going to be?" she asked.

Kevin, Angie, Roger, and Rochelle screamed at the same time, "Me!"

They all looked at each other. Kevin immediately threw his money on the table before anyone else had a chance. "Money talks, bullshit walks. Step aside, all of you." Lucy had been checking cute Kevin out at the bar and was definitely attracted to him. She was proud he'd taken over and was ready to hear this reading. This way, she would learn some things about him without interrogating him.

"I'm a Sagittarian, born December fifteenth. Lay it on me, baby," Kevin said enticingly to the reader. "And, by the way, what's your name?" The crowd started hooting. Lucy loved his seductive tone.

"I'm Bridgette," the reader answered, taken aback by the handsome Kevin. She looked at the others bunched up in the room. Coolly, she asked Kevin, "I gather this is not a private reading?"

Lucy thought Bridgette was flirting with Kevin. She found herself feeling a little jealous. She immediately emerged from the back of the crowd. "No, it's not. We're *together*." Then she looked directly at Kevin and said, "Let's hear all about this gentlemen. Tell us who he really is." The rest of the crowd started to hoot again.

Kevin blushed and announced to everyone, "Just keep your mouths shut or I'll have you all thrown out. Come on Bridgette baby, do your thing."

"Okay, Kevin, here we go. Hmm—a Sagittarius—aka Honest John. Well, you're a wonderful asset to a crowd. You're an exceptionally friendly guy. You're a fire sign, an extrovert, talkative and forward. There's not a shy bone in your body. You are extremely witty—quite a jokester.

"Sagittarians are brave. They rarely make a plea for help. There's no running away on your part. You're also a very clever person. You're warm and generous and you hate stingy tippers. You like helping people— especially your mother. You're a good son. You're lovable and likable. You love sports, but your clumsiness makes you accident-prone.

"You are a very optimistic person. You believe that the future will definitely be better than the past and today is very interesting to you. You need to stop trusting everybody—you'll get into trouble. You're so damn honest that you are downright blunt. You'll make a lot of people mad because of this trait, but there's no malice in your heart. You don't mean all those things you say to people that make them crazy. You're simply too direct, thoughtless, and have no tact, buddy. And, guess what, you're totally oblivious to your problem, so you don't mean to offend anyone.

"You're a person who sets his standards high. Sagittarians love to drive cars. They are usually good, safe drivers. They love all forms of travel. You're raring to go because you hate to be still. You love sharing ideas and moving fast. You like fast things like roller-coasters and you are a daredevil. You fear nothing—in fact many of you are attracted to danger in your occupations, hobbies, and sports. You also adore animals.

"Risks and challenges excite you. You will take a chance. You are terrific at counseling people. You're basically a happy person, but your temper will fly if someone pushes you around or tries to abuse your friendliness and good nature. One should never accuse you of dishonesty. You have integrity and no one should ever go against that. If you are ever moody, it won't be for too long. You bounce back quickly.

"Most Sagittarians love gambling. That's because you are such risk takers. Be careful on the tables at the casinos, horse races, playing numbers, and the stock market. You could easily blow a fortune even though you are incredibly lucky. You're also lucky with love, and if a relationship does shatter, you'll recover quickly.

"Sagittarians look for the value of a person and way past external beauty. You're definitely a flirt, but you're looking for more than sex in a relationship. You'll plunge into romance, but will be hesitant on marriage. A girl can snag you into marriage—but she's got to have the right trick. Your woman should give you lots of freedom and should not be jealous or suspicious. You can't handle a Scorpio, Mr. Sagittarius. The woman after your heart should also understand that your suitcase stays packed. Remember—you're the traveler.

"Because you are so honest, you cannot tolerate any form of deception. You Sagittarians love a hearty meal and have a tendency to eat too much food. Be careful, Kevin, you don't want to get fat. An unpleasant trait of the Sagittarian is having violent tempers. They tend to go off on tangents. You aren't able to keep a secret and Sagittarians are very unsuccessful liars. Sagittarians are curious and inquisitive by nature—they ask a lot of questions. Your heart and your mind will guide your train of thought and your decisions, so sometimes you'll be foolishly courageous.

"Everyone you get involved with—be it a lover, friend, or colleague—should be aware that they should only ask you for the truth if they can stand it.

"In these cards, I see that you're going to come across a Pisces. Be careful of this fish. I'll give you some warnings. Listen up, my trusting Sagittarian.

"Pisces—be sure you can handle it, gang. Any Pisces in the house? Can you take the truth?" Bridgette asked. The crowd started to look around at one another, hooting.

"And what is the truth?" Rochelle asked. "I'm a Pisces. Let's have it."

"Pisces people are very unsuspecting. I mean, they're conniving and you never know when they're up to no good. They play the innocence game extremely well. They're very bright and clever people. They are the sign of the fishes. Brain stuff. The females are exceptionally intelligent. These upper-level people usually have multiple professions. All Pisces are whorish, but the women are far worse than the men. They're treacherous. They are capable of fooling around on their men, who never suspect a thing. If a man has a Pisces wife and works at night, you better believe she has her other man right there in her own house fucking her, and hubby never guesses. Pisces people are capable of pulling all kinds of dirty deeds on a person. I never trust them."

Lucy's eyes lit up. She was enjoying herself.

"I'm just giving you some advice," Bridgette went on. "If you even so much as smell a Pisces around you, beware. I'm not saying that every Pisces in the world is ruthless, but I am letting you know their capabilities.

"I also believe that if Pisces females have planets in their charts that are Aquarius, Libra, or Sagittarius, there is hope for them, or should I say hope for the people they are hooked up with, because those signs have a lot of compassion. You see, Aquarians are great humanitarians; Libras are about fairness. They have a conscience. They want to do the right thing. They have class and scruples. So Pisces with a little Aquarius, Sag, and some Libra in their charts can be reckoned with, and maybe saved. They can behave more compassionately toward people.

"Pisces are unlike the Scorpios who are ruthless, too, and can do some horrible things to people. They're vindictive, but they attack *after* someone has betrayed them. That's kind of normal. People can understand and justify revenge. It's a reflex with Scorps. Pisces set out to do their dirt without any reason. Now Pisces with some Leo, Aries, and Capricorn in their charts will screw you over big-time. Pisces people basically just have it in them to do you in. They are the sign of the fish, cold-blooded.

"Pisces people are born late February through the middle of March. Remember that, guys, and beware. You heard it here first. It all fascinates me, so now I am an astrology nut. I really know my subject."

"Miss, may I have a card to call you? Do you do this over the phone?" Lucy was intrigued. The woman passed her a business card.

"I can't believe I was the first one over here and I couldn't get read. Give me a card, too," Angie demanded pouting. "So, Rochelle, you've turned out to be a whore. Humph." The crowd started to hoot. Everyone reached out for cards.

Bernie asked, "Well, is anybody hungry?" They all declined food at the same time.

Angie said, "I wanna do something devilish. I want to be out of control. I want to do something different."

"Ooooo," the guys and girls chorused.

"Look, let's just get in the cars, head downtown, and see what we come up with," Roger suggested.

"I'm not riding with Roger the hit man," Rochelle said.

"Good—he's cute. I'll ride with him," Angie said. The laughing started again. The guys paid the tab and everyone went out to the hotel parking lot.

"Ten people going downtown half high. Oh, boy. All right," continued Bonita, "how are we riding and who's driving?"

They decided to take two cars, Kevin's and Bernie's. Kevin, Lucy, Angie, Bernie, and Roger piled in Kevin's car, with Lucy at the wheel. The rest piled in Bernie's car.

"Which way?" Lucy asked.

Kevin directed her downtown from the front passenger seat. Angie, Bernie, and Roger were telling jokes and horsing around in the backseat. Kevin said to Lucy, "It's going to take about twenty minutes to get downtown. There's a pretty nice disco spot called Hannibal's on Fifth and Canal. That's where we're going. The others already know."

"What's the place like? Are we dressed for it? And will they let these drunks in?" She pointed to the gang in the back.

"It's a pretty decent spot. They don't sell food, but the music is good. There's usually no riffraff."

"Is there a cover charge?"

"Yes, it's ten bucks and you don't get a drink."

Angie cut in. "Ten bucks and no drink! This place better be swinging!"

After a moment, Kevin said to Lucy "So, you're single, from Philly, work for the stock exchange, and you're a good model. That's all right."

"So you overheard everything at that noisy bar and you paid attention to the show, too? I'm impressed." They both laughed.

Loud honking interrupted Lucy. The other car sped by, its occupants shouting and waving. Lucy looked at Kevin, a little embarrassed. "I don't drive fast."

"You don't have to kill me to get me to a party—I can wait. You're doing just fine."

"Kevin, where are you from?" Angie yelled.

"A little town in California called San Jose. I grew up there and then joined the Navy. I'm making a career of it."

"You gotta girlfriend?" Angie asked. Everybody laughed.

"You got a boyfriend?" Kevin shot back.

"Oooooo," cooed Lucy, Bernie, and Roger.

"Nope—no boyfriend. I'm hanging loose," Angie responded.

Lucy was laughing so hard that she said to Kevin, "Where can I pull over? I gotta pee."

Kevin looked around and pointed. "Just down the road a bit."

Lucy pulled the car over, jumped out, and ran into some bushes.

They pulled into Hannibal's parking lot where the rest of the gang stood waiting, and stumbled out of the car. The guys paid the cover charges and they entered the club. There were two bars, a nice long one and a cozier circular one with about fifteen seats. They all headed to the smaller bar. The bartender was pretty cute. She eyed the girls, trying to figure out who was with whom. Since everybody was talking to one another, she had a hard time.

Angie ordered a Tequila Sunrise for herself and ran through a list of drinks for the others.

The music sounded super. Lucy said to Kevin, "Marvin Gaye says we 'Got to Give It Up.' Let's get out there, man."

One thing about Lucy, she could dance. Kevin was not as good, but he kept up with her. Pretty soon the whole gang was out on the floor. After that endless record the lights began to flash before they could sit down, and the DJ blasted Parliament Funkadelic's "Flashlight." Angie and Roger immediately escaped the bar and hit the dance floor again. The Château Crew was burning the floor up.

Everybody was having a ball, and it was a nice scene. None of the guys got fresh or obscene. They were real gentlemen. Lucy kept her eyes on Kevin and thought she just might dig him. She also liked Harold's body—he had cute dimples and a nice smile.

After about an hour and half, they were ready to hit another spot.

"Let's just get in the cars and ride around. We'll find something," Bernie suggested.

Roger and Kevin drove. They spotted a neon flashing sign downtown— LIVE STRIPPERS.

Angie yelled, "That's the place, let's go there. I've never seen a peep show!"

Kevin obeyed and pulled over, and Roger followed. Roger got out of his car and walked over to Kevin. "Man, I know you aren't doing this one."

"Angie wants in. Go find out if your gang is down with this."

Roger came back and said, "I guess this is the spot."

The place was small and smoky, with inky blue walls. It had a wide bar and several curtained-off rooms. Small booths lined one side. Everybody ran around, checking the place out. Only twenty patrons sat at scattered tables. The Château Crew finally sat down and ordered drinks. Roger put some money in the jukebox. Angela Bofill came out strong singing "People Make the World Go Round." Roger and Lucy started to sing it together: "Trash Man didn't get my trash today / Oh, why? Because they want more pay."

The duet between Roger and Lucy was short-lived, because the floor show was about to begin. A tall white girl came out onto the floor. She was made up heavily and had long blond hair. She wore a turquoise silk robe and high heels. The bartender shut off the jukebox and put on a record. She began dancing seductively to Tina Turner's "What's Love Got to Do with It." She immediately took her robe off and put it on a chair near the small stage. She had a skimpy bra and a G-string on. The dance floor had poles, and she began to slide up and down them. She rubbed her body against the men who were stuffing money into the sides of the G-string. She moved around, came over to the guys, and rubbed her body against them. Then she lay down on the floor and dropped her legs open.

Lucy didn't think she was that hot.

The crowd yelled, "Take it off. Come on, give us our dollar's worth."

The gang was on their second round of drinks. By now Angie was plastered and still had a drink in her hand. They decided to call it a night.

"Let's get out of here," Angie yelled over her shoulder. "I'm hungry, take me to food."

The guys paid the tab and the gang left. Angie passed out in Kevin's car. The Château Crew stopped at a pizza place, ordered six pizzas to go, and returned to the hotel.

# Chapter Twenty-one

# *Reba*

fter Reba and Doug left the reception, they decided to take a drive. "I hate to see tomorrow come, Miss Reba, baby," Doug sighed.

"Me, too. I hate to even think about it. Do we have to discuss it now? I'm not ready to face reality."

They drove down to the river and lay in each other's arms in the car. It felt good.

"What's your life in Annapolis like?" Reba asked.

"Slow. I'm pretty low-key. I travel a lot for my company. I have a twin home in the suburbs and the grass grows, the wind blows, and I just go with the flow."

"I didn't know you were a poet."

They both laughed. Reba continued, "Who's in your life?"

"I usually date a girl named Joyce, and I also go out from time to time with Maria."

"Oh, so you have two of them?"

"Yes, two lightweight relationships. Just dating, neither one is serious."

"Why? You don't like monogamy?"

"It's not that, it's just that neither of these relationships is the right thing. Neither really clicks. What about you and your husband?"

"He makes me lonely."

"What?"

"He makes me feel alone most of the time. I feel like a robot. There's no spontaneity or excitement. He fools around and I just ignore it. He neglects me and I overlook it. I kind of live for my kids and dream of something for me later when they are grown. Other than you and Johnny, I've never been with another man in my life."

"Well, you've given me plenty of excitement this weekend. Are you that way with Johnny?"

"No."

"You sure? Those six kids came from some heavy nights, I would imagine."

"Those kids came from an overabundance of wham-bam-thank-you-ma'ams. That's where they came from."

"Well, then, tell me, where did you learn all those little tricks you threw on me? At the library?"

Reba laughed. "You're on the right track. I read a lot and I have a hell of a lot of fantasies. You were my guinea pig this weekend. Did I do okay?"

"You scored big-time." Doug lifted her chin and gave her a passionate kiss. "To be perfectly honest, you are the best and most exciting thing that has happened to me. I am so glad you chose me to make your fantasies a reality. I don't know what we are going to do, because I know I really dig you. I think I've found the missing click."

Reba started up the car and drove back to the hotel. They got back into the room and she began to help him undress.

"Want a bath?" she asked.

"You want one with me?" he asked.

"Yes."

She helped him into the tub and then got herself undressed. The water was nice and warm. Doug told her how good it felt. She was careful getting in not to upset his foot, which hung out of the tub so water would not get into the stitches. She gently washed his body. She took the warm washcloth and patted his face with it. Then she carefully cleaned his ears and neck and chest. Periodically, she would squeeze the washcloth, full of water, over his body. Each time, he sighed with contentment. She picked up the foot that was in the water and washed each toe separately. Then she put his big toe in her mouth and sucked it. A smile spread across his face. His eyes were shut. She noticed his erection and turned her body around, so he entered her from behind. She used her hand to hold down the leg that was outside the tub, and they moved together. He held her around the chest and squeezed her breasts. Her body was arched backward, and he gently ran his fingers through the hairs on her pelvic area.

She said to him, "I need to scream, baby, I want to scream."

Doug replied, "Scream," and she did.

\* \* \*

They awoke the next morning to a glorious, sunny day.

Doug looked at her. "I had a nice time last night."

"Me too. Remember, you owe me breakfast."

Doug smiled.

"I need to go to my room and get dressed, and then I can come back for you. I'll help you get dressed when I get back, okay?"

"Okay, but what time does your bus leave?"

"Two o'clock."

Reba was shocked to see people sleeping all over her room. She counted bodies. "What the hell went on here?" she muttered.

Two of the models and two guys were asleep with their clothes on. Angie, wearing only panties and a bra, lay sprawled across the bed with a guy. Lucy was out like a light with a guy crashed next to her. Another model lay on the floor with covers from one of the beds on her. Takeout food bags, paper plates, and forks littered the place. Reba looked around to see if Lucy had left any clothes out for her and saw nothing. She thought, "Oh shit, Doug is about to see the real me, Miss All Fucked Up."

She went into the bathroom to take a shower, but there was a guy asleep in the tub with a few slices of pizza next to him and one piece, eaten almost down to the crust, on his chest. Hanging on the shower rail was a set of clothes, and a pair of women's shoes were perched on top of the sink. Reba left the bathroom, went over to Lucy, and kissed her on her forehead. Lucy didn't move. Reba quickly grabbed the outfit and shoes and found a comb and brush. She took her overnight bag from the closet, then tiptoed around the room gathering soap, underwear, perfume, a toothbrush and lotion. She zipped the bag shut and fled to Doug's room, laughing all the way.

Reba let herself into the room and helped Doug get showered and dressed. As she was getting herself together, he began to wonder exactly how he felt about himself and Reba. He hated to see two o'clock come. As they headed down to the hotel dining room, they avoided each other's eyes. Things were pretty quiet in the elevator.

They ordered breakfast. Doug looked at Reba. "Well, I guess I'm going to lose you in about three and a half hours."

She didn't answer. The waiter brought coffee and she added cream and sugar, stirring it like she was in a trance.

Then she looked up at Doug and smiled.

"You know, I feel like somebody else. I feel this thing between you and me has removed me from something, unleashed me—you know what I mean?"

"No, I don't know what you mean, but I know my life is confusing right now, because of you."

Reba looked at his injured foot and smiled, suppressing laughter. "You've certainly gone through a lot for me this weekend. You've even become a cripple."

Doug smiled. "Yes, you have certainly done me in, these last forty-eight hours."

The waiter brought their food. Reluctantly, Reba skipped the ketchup, remembering what Peggy had said.

"You're leaving on Tuesday?"

"Yes," said Doug.

"How are you going to drive? Do you have any other appointments scheduled this week?"

"I have to be in Atlanta on Friday for four days. Can I ask you something straight up?" he said.

"Sure."

"Can you drive?"

"Yes."

There was silence. Then Doug said, "Would you like to see Annapolis and my home? Can you stand to be in this hotel for another two days?"

Reba's mind raced. She saw herself not getting on that bus to Philadelphia. She looked at her man—her real new man—and knew she was about to give Johnny the shock of his life. She just did not know how she was going to arrange it. What about the kids? What about work?

The two of them left the restaurant and went back to Doug's room. They sat on the bed and stared at each other. Reba was feeling guilty about the kids. Doug didn't know what to say because he knew he was asking a lot of her.

Reba moved closer to Doug and kissed him on the cheek. "I am moving too fast. This is why I can't figure out what to do. I want to stay. I really do want to stay here with you. I've had fun and I've been real. This has been the best sex of my life, and I like you. You're funny and cute and warm and I'm thoroughly impressed with you. I've had a wonderful weekend.

"But I just cannot do this. Not this way. We have to plan a little better.

I have to go home. I have to think at home. I have to see if this thing is for real. I have to see about my kids. I have business to take care of in my marriage—in my life. If you really care for me, give me time. Let me figure it out. Trust what you feel for me and what you think of me. Let's give each other some room. If it's real, it won't go away, and I'll have to come back to you. If I do something more serious than this weekend with you, I want it to be for keeps. I want you to understand the responsibility of being with me, because I have six children. Six children, Doug, who need me. I cannot be running back and forth for escapades. You better think about what you may be getting into with me. Think about how easy your life is. So simple. I'm not going to be one of your dates. I'm complicated."

Doug tried, but he couldn't really digest what she was saying because he didn't want to hear it. He didn't want her to leave. He knew he was being selfish and she was being real and right. He couldn't handle it.

"I see you have your mind made up and I know you're right. I just don't like the words. I hate the truth right now and I despise reality and the separation. But I understand. I will give you space and time—my home address and every number I have so you can reach me."

He wrote a note on the pad of paper on the night table and handed it to Reba with one of his business cards from his wallet. "You get your business straight in Philadelphia. If your husband and your children continue to take precedence over this—this thing between you and me—then I have to accept and deal with that. Just know that you never were a one- or a two-night stand and that I have very serious feelings for you. I will miss you. Don't make love to me before you leave because if you do, I won't let you leave. Give me a kiss and get out. I hope I hear from you soon."

Reba kissed him, gathered her things, and left him sitting on the bed.

# Chapter Twenty-two

# *Sheila*

*a*untie Len walked in the door promptly at six o'clock. Sheila and the kids were glad to see her. They had missed her.

"Hi!" everyone shouted.

"Well, hello, everyone. How are all of you?"

Margie ran up to Lenora and hugged her. Sheila stood in the kitchen doorway, smiling, happy that Lenora was back and glad she had gotten some time off.

"Well," said Sheila, "did we win at bingo last night?"

"As a matter of fact I did, I won thirty-five dollars. I got the 'cover all.' "

"That's the way to do it—get some time off from the family and your luck changes."

Lenora just smiled. The kids grabbed her bag and raced upstairs with it. Lenora turned to Sheila. "Well, miss, how did your date go?" Sheila grinned, so Lenora said, "Looks to me like it went just fine."

"You know, I really think I like Leonard," Sheila confided. "He's a gentleman, he took me to a really nice place in town and then for a drive. He kept the conversation going and he treated me fine—like a lady. He didn't try to stuff his hands anywhere they didn't belong, and he didn't have any alcohol. There wasn't a deck of cards in sight, and he held my hand. That is what I liked most of all—he held my hand. He held my hand from the time we parked the car, all the way across the street, and into the restaurant until we got seated. It made me feel good."

Lenora smiled and hugged her. "So I guess there's going to be a second date and the phone is going to stay busy."

"You are exactly right. I think I have me a man. A real man with a real job and a real personality. And let's not forget that he's responsible, too. Leonard's going to be around for a while if I have anything to do with it."

"What's for dinner?" asked Lenora.

"Pigs in a blanket—the kids have been begging for them—and French fries. Salad for me. Sound good?"

"Just fine. I'm hungry, so let's get started."

Ten minutes later Beverly Resnick called to find out what time Pam had left.

"She left here at about five o'clock," said Sheila. "The bus may be late or something. She didn't mention that she was stopping anywhere."

"Okay. I just have to go over to my sister-in-law Libby's, and I was trying to wait for Pam to get home so I wouldn't have to take the kids. I guess she'll be here soon."

"Hey, Beverly," said Sheila, "I've got a new man."

"What, who is he? How long you been seeing him?"

"Well, I met him a while ago at the gym. His name is Leonard Toland. He's divorced. It's nothing serious, we've only been on one date. I'm taking it slow, but I like him a lot and, best of all, he doesn't play cards."

"Speaking of cards," said Beverly, "Sheila Shoreman, I swear I've got to ask you something. Now this may be a bold-faced lie, but somebody told Buzzy that you dug Perry up, beat him, and put decks of cards all over him. Sheila, every time I think about it, I die laughing. Buzzy came home one night and told me, and he had tears coming out of his eyes he was laughing so hard. Girl, did you really do it?"

"Beverly, your information is most accurate. I dug his dead ass up all right. You know I am still pissed at him. I don't even want to start talking about that asshole—might ruin my day. He's probably in hell right now playing cards with the devil, and as bad as Perry's luck is, the devil is probably winning. Yeah, I bet he even owes the damn devil money. He is probably screwing up the devil's finances. God knows he kept me in the red."

"Look, Vernon," said Pam, "we have to do something. My mom and dad are going to kill us."

"How far along are you?"

"I've missed three periods. If we don't do something, I'll be showing soon."

"Look, I don't have any money saved for a baby, for marriage, or for an abortion. Now what in the world are we going to do?"

"Well, I just don't know," Pam said, her eyes welling up with tears. "I only make ten dollars a week babysitting. The only person I know with money is Aunt Libby, and she'll tell everybody in my family if I go to her. You and I are in trouble. Vernon, can't you borrow money from somewhere to get this taken care of?"

"Pam, do you want to keep the baby? I mean, can't we just go to our parents and tell them? Hell, they aren't going to kill us. They'll raise a lot of hell, but then you'll have the baby and they'll think it's cute and all, and everything will work out."

"What about money?" demanded Pam. "How are you going to take care of it? Are you going to quit going to Community College and get a job and take care of this baby? And me, I'm supposed to start college at least by next year. My parents are already on my case."

They were sitting in Fairmount Park near Lemon Hill. The grass and trees were pretty, so quiet and peaceful, unlike Pam's or Sheila's house. No kids running around making noise. Pam did not need a baby. She shouldn't have been so hot and careless. She sure was sorry that Uncle Lance was in jail, because he would have covered her. He would have given her the money to get rid of the baby, just to keep the peace in the family, and wouldn't have said a word to anyone.

Pam wondered if she could tell Sheila. No, she really couldn't trust Sheila with something like that, because sometimes Sheila talked to her mom. Pam wondered whether any of her girlfriends had a health card so that maybe she could have it done in a clinic using their name. She was eighteen, so there was a chance the hospital wouldn't say anything to her parents. But most of her girlfriends had just graduated and were in college, not working full-time. She had to come up with something. She certainly didn't want to change shitty diapers and carry a whining baby on her hip. No more beach. No more freedom. She was pissed at Vernon. He had no answers, but he was still making out with her every chance he got. As soon as he got out of school, he was at her house. As soon as Beverly left to run an errand, his fingers started traveling through her clothes. He could get her hot quick, slide his fingers up her vagina, and next thing they were stealing a quickie on the couch or in the basement. That's what got them into this mess, and lately, since she was knocked up, seems he couldn't get enough. She was afraid that if she wouldn't give him any, she'd lose him. And they did it real well together. Vernon was good.

They had done it many times in Fairmount Park in the bushes. Pam didn't know why, but the quickies always felt the best. Maybe it was the excitement of the risk of getting caught. Once some teenagers came by and saw them. Pam was petrified. She had taken her pants and panties off and laid them on the grass. The teenagers grabbed her clothes and ran away with them. Vernon had to chase them and beg to get the clothes back. After that, no more quickies in the park. That was probably the only reason Vernon wasn't trying to get some right now.

# Chapter Twenty-three

# *Paula*

It was Saturday morning, and Horace lay in bed trying to figure out what he was going to do about Renee. He needed a sitter, a routine, and some help to raise his child. He thought about how he had really cared for Paula and about all the things he had tried to do to make things work out for them. He thought about Sydni and Amber and knew they would continue to catch hell. He had to look out for them, too. He reached over to his night table and picked up his address book. He saw the names of all the women he used to date and wondered why he had been dumb enough to get hooked up with the worst one of all, Paula Gray.

Horace didn't have any family in Philadelphia. His mom and dad were in Florida, and they wouldn't move to help him out with Renee. They loved her and looked forward to her visits, but they wouldn't come there to stay, and he wasn't prepared to go down to Florida to live. He had a good job, and he liked Philadelphia and his home. He kept looking through his book for someone who could keep Renee while he worked. Under no circumstances did he want to use Fannie full-time. He came up with nothing.

He thought about Earl. Earl was pretty cool. He knew they were going to be friends. They had exchanged telephone numbers, and the next time Horace went on a fishing trip, he planned to invite Earl. He wished he knew some decent young girl to introduce Earl to.

There were no acceptable people in the book to watch Renee. He would have to call his job on Monday and say he needed a week off for a family emergency. He would use the week to find a sitter and get started with Renee. Renee was going to love being in this house with its big backyard. He wanted to get her a tricycle, some toys, and fix her room up. He would also have to fix up the spare room because he would get the other girls sometimes. Renee loved her sisters and Horace didn't want them all to be away from each other too much.

He had already decided to remodel the basement, which was quite large. He would have a bathroom put in so a sitter could stay with some privacy. When he went to work at night, the sitter could sleep in the second floor rear bedroom. Horace would have the front bedroom, Renee would be in the middle one, and the sitter and the girls could use the rear bedroom until the basement was done.

Horace had always been a good planner and organizer. In junior high school, he had a job at a toy store after school. When he started he was making twenty-five cents an hour stocking shelves. Then, it was on to waiting on customers. During the summers of eighth and ninth grade, he worked full-time and saved money for clothes and outings. His parents were proud of him because he was smart and a hard worker and never got into any trouble.

He liked the ladies, too, and they had to be pretty. Horace didn't like ugly people; he never had. His mother told him that, when he was a baby, if an ugly person picked him up or even tried to talk to him, he would scream until they got away from him. So his dates were always exceptionally attractive, well dressed, with their hair in order. He was good to those girls. If he took them to the movies, he took them out for dinner or to his home for a meal. If he took them to the beach, he had round-trip bus tickets to Atlantic City. They got on the rides, walked on the boardwalk, and had nice lunches and dinners.

But Horace always had a temper. If someone did something he felt was unfair, and he had done everything right in the situation he would turn into a wild man. He would fight if he had to. But he didn't get into too many squabbles, because most people treated him well and respected him as a decent guy.

Horace didn't believe in used cars, doggie bags, run-down shoes, or anything out of style. At sixteen he was making his own car payments to his parents for their shiny blue Cadillac convertible with white leather interior. He was a junior at Boys' Catholic High and worked at night at the Navy Yard. He knew how to save and how to spend.

At twenty he bought his first home, and then every few years he bought a piece of property in Miami and rented it out.

By the time he was thirty-three, he owned seven properties in Florida and two in Philadelphia. He had his thing together. The only mistake he felt he had made in life was hooking up with Paula. But every time he looked at Renee, he couldn't be entirely sorry about their relationship.

Paula had taught him one thing: how to be real mean. Sometimes, no matter how hard you try to do the right thing, some women will beg you to kick their asses. You could be going in an entirely different direction, on a positive road, and some women will back you up and put you on the negative. Maybe some of them like it like that. He couldn't understand it.

Horace got up, showered, dressed, and made his favorite breakfast of salmon croquettes and grits. It was now lunchtime, but he enjoyed the meal. He called Grandma.

"Hi, Fannie, this is Horace, how's my baby?"

"She's fine."

"What are the other two up to?"

"Amber is out collecting bottles and Sydni is glued to the television set."

"Well, Fannie, I didn't kill Paula last night, so you don't have to worry."

"Thank you, Horace. Is she at work now?"

"I don't know where Paula is, but I'm calling to tell you I'll pick Renee up tomorrow night and keep her for good."

"What?"

"Yes, I talked to Paula last night and she isn't putting up a fight. She's letting me have my daughter. Renee will come to my house to live, and I'll also get Sydni and Amber sometimes. I'm not going into details, but that's the way it is. I'm looking for a sitter next week while I'm off from work."

"Jesus, Paula must have really torn her ass with you. What did she do?"

"Well, first of all, your daughter is a liar and a whore. She doesn't have a weekend job and never did. She'd been shacking up with a real nice boy every other weekend while you were babysitting. I'm through with her. I just want my daughter."

Grandma was silent. Horace continued, "I'll be by today to see Renee for a while and I'll pick her up about six o'clock tomorrow night. See you then."

As soon as he hung up, the phone rang. "Hey, buddy, this is Earl. How are you making out this morning? Are you hung over?"

"No, not at all, I'm up and dressed. I have to find a sitter to keep my baby while I work. She's coming to live with me tomorrow."

"You're really serious, aren't you, man?"

"As serious as a heart attack. If I let Paula keep Renee, I'll end up in jail, and Paula just ain't worth that. But seriously, I have to find a sitter in a week. I don't know a soul at the moment."

"My sister Emily doesn't live far from me and she's not working at night. She may do it. You want me to check with her? She's pretty good with kids. She lives with my sister Regina and helps with her kids all the time."

"How old is she and what's the deal with her?"

"Emily is twenty-two and single. She's pretty cool and she can cook. She's been up here for two years. She's not seeing anyone at the moment, so you don't have to worry about guys being around the baby and all."

"Can you give her a call and call me back? If it's cool, I'd like to take my Renee to meet her."

"Okay, let me see what I can do. Horace, man, thanks for last night, I mean for looking out for me and for being a real cool dude under the circumstances. I think you're all right."

"Right back atcha, man."


Paula looked over at Floyd sprawled over her bed. "So, sugar, you really ain't got a man?" asked Floyd.

"No, not at the moment."

"Where are your kids?"

"Oh, at my mother's. They'll be home tomorrow."

Paula rolled over and picked up her pack of cigarettes from the floor. Floyd grabbed a handful of her ass and squeezed it.

"You are something else under them sheets, sugar. I could get real used to you."

She lit a cigarette and exhaled. She turned on her side, checking Floyd out as he lay next to her. He was not as tall as she liked them—only about five feet nine. He was dark complexioned and had a few pimples on his face. Nice teeth and a small mouth. Nice lips. He could fuck real good, so she thought, but she'd had a few too many last night and wasn't entirely sure.

"Where did you say you worked, Floyd?"

"I'm an orderly at St. John's Hospital," he responded proudly, showing every tooth in his head. "You know, over on Palmer Avenue. I've got a real good job and I've been there for eleven years."

Paula thought, "An orderly. Oh, my God, he hasn't got a dime."

She not only had to train him, but she had to talk him into getting a part-time job or something so he could give her some money. She sure was sorry now that she had screwed up with Earl and Horace. She couldn't remember much of what Floyd had told her last night—she had quite a few drinks after Earl and Horace had left the bar.

Floyd told her all about his job—how important it was and how everybody at the hospital looked up to him. The damn place couldn't run without him. Floyd explained about the patients and their illnesses and how he always got his patients where they had to be. "I'm always, always on time when I have to get a patient to surgery or anywhere, sugar. They depend on me and know I'm coming through. I always check their wrists to make sure I have the right one, and I also read their chart and ask their name. And I push them real slow down the hall so they don't get scared. I feel like they must be nervous being in the hospital and all, so I'm real careful with them. Sometimes I even take them by the snack bar or the gift shop in case they want to pick up something. And I chat with them. Chatting is important because sometimes the patients are lonely or nervous about a procedure they have to go through.

I had a patient last year—a real pretty white woman about thirty years old—named Robyn. She was tall and thin with long red hair and gorgeous hazel eyes. She was eight and a half months pregnant, but she was really beautiful, and every time I looked at her, I wondered why she wasn't in the movies or something. Her husband was a lawyer downtown and a sharp dude, too. They had two kids. Her husband and those kids came to that hospital twice a day every day to see her. They really fretted and made a fuss over her. I could tell how much they loved her and how worried they were about her. Her husband would put a ten spot in my hand each and every time he saw me and tell me to make sure she had whatever she needed and wanted, and please be sure I was kind to her.

"She was in the psychiatric ward—one day she had just gone crazy. She had parked her car in a place where it shouldn't have been parked, near a bank. As she was walking into the bank, the security guard there told her she had to move the car. She told the guard she didn't feel well, that it was ninety-two degrees, and she just wanted to get in and out of the bank and get home. He told her she had to move the car. She promised she wouldn't be long and asked him to leave her alone. She would be right back to move the car. He refused and kept insisting it be moved immediately. She told him again that she would hurry and he told her again to move the car. He said if she did not move the car that he would call to have it towed away. She ignored him and just went on into the bank. While she was in the line waiting for the teller, she noticed him on the telephone. When she was finished, he was still on the phone. She went up behind the guard and heard him give the person on the line information about her car. All of a sudden she took her big leather handbag and began beating the shit out of him. He fell to the floor. She continued hitting him in the head and kicking him and screaming. By the time the bank people and the customers realized what was going on, she was sitting on top of the guy, choking him and biting him. Blood was squirting out of the side of his face and he was yelling and screaming. She was screaming, too, and started having trouble breathing.

"They both ended up in the hospital. He was released, but they had to keep her in the psychiatric ward for two weeks. She kept mumbling, 'I'm just sick and tired of people fucking with me. I've had enough.' They gave her all kinds of tests to see how crazy she was and to make sure her baby was okay. I used to take her to a lot of the procedures and she told me the story. She told me that the next time somebody fucked with her when it was ninety-two degrees and she was pregnant, she was going to kill them. From what I hear, the guard got a few stitches and told the nurse in the emergency room that he was getting a new job because he never wanted to see that bank again."

"He ain't got much money," Paula thought to herself.

She finished the cigarette and lit up the last one in the pack. She pulled the sheet off of her to expose her body. She looked around at her one-bedroom apartment and wondered how the hell she was going to manage to afford this place now that Horace was gone. Then she looked at Floyd again. She really couldn't stand him. He was too country for her. He wasn't sharp or hip. He lacked coolness. He was too nice. She'd never walk into a room with him and see people look at her with envy. He damn sure couldn't pay her bills and take care of her like Horace, Earl, or Curtis could. After all, he was just an orderly. An orderly rolling crazy-ass people around in the hospital. "Yuk," she thought, looking at him. The more she thought about him in that white uniform and those big white ugly shoes with all those wheelchairs around him, the more she couldn't stand him. He was too obedient. He complimented her too much. He was so damn nice, always smiling at her, showing all those teeth. He must have over a hundred teeth in his mouth, all pearly white. She began to loathe him as she gazed at him in her bed. Why did she ever pick up this country fool anyway? She must have needed a man real bad last night, or she was drunk as hell. She was convinced he was stupid. He reminded her of a grownup Buckwheat.

Paula caressed Floyd's face gently. Softly, she stroked his small thin lips with her index finger. Then she said to him, "Get into the closet."

"What for?"

"Just do what I told you."

"I want to know why you want me to go in there."

"We're going to play a game."

"What kind of game?"

"A sex game. Just take your naked ass into the closet and stay there until I tell you what else to do."

Floyd went over to the closet and stared at the door. Then he turned around and stared at Paula.

"Go on into the damn closet, Floyd."

The closet was stuffed with clothes, the floor littered with shoes. He looked back at Paula. "There's too much stuff for me to fit in here. I don't want to go in this closet. I don't want to play this freaky game with you."

"It's only hide-and-go-seek, Floyd. Jesus Christ, you are such a baby. Don't you want to have some fun? Just move the clothes around and get in the damn closet."

"How long will it be before you come in with me?"

"I'll just be a couple of minutes. I just want to freshen up. Go on in, baby, it'll be fun. Something different, you know," she smiled sexily at him and winked.

Floyd made some room and went into the closet, leaving the door open for Paula. She came to the door, and he smiled—he thought she had changed her mind about freshening up and was relieved she was joining him. Paula quickly closed and locked the closet door.

After Floyd was securely locked inside, Paula walked across the room and looked back at the closet door. "What a stupid son of a bitch," she thought. She walked down the hall to the kitchen, ignoring Floyd's calls from the closet. She sat down at the kitchen table and didn't give a damn if the idiot yelled for her all morning. She got up and headed back to the bedroom for her cigarettes. When Floyd heard her enter the room, he said, "Sugar, are you coming in now?"

She answered, "I'm almost ready. Just relax. I'm coming. Be a good boy and just be quiet. I'll be there soon." Grabbing her pack of cigarettes, she remembered she had smoked the last one. "Shit," she said.

"What's the matter, sugar?" yelled Floyd. "Are you okay?"

"Fine, I'm fine, I just got a run in my stocking. I'm getting all dressed up for you."

"Okay, sugar, don't worry about the stockings, just hurry up. It's lonely in here."

Paula snatched a pair of pants and a top from her drawer and ran to the kitchen, where she threw them on. On the coffee table in the living room were Floyd's car keys, which she grabbed, along with her black handbag. She had no driver's license and few driving skills, but she decided to take the fool's old Mercury Cougar anyway. So what if she wrecked his ride. She started the car and tried to adjust the mirrors. "This big old boat," she thought. "Oh, my God, I sure can pick 'em when I've had too much of the sauce." She pulled out of the parking space and headed toward the supermarket. She got there in one piece, and pulled into a slot and parked. She ran into the market, grabbed some packaged boiled ham and American cheese from the deli area, and got in line to pay. She asked the cashier for two packs of Newports. She paid for everything and started toward the door but was stopped by a security guard.

"Miss, please do not go through the door. Please come with me. Just step to the side."

"What do you want with me?"

"I want to check your handbag."

"Check my handbag for what? Here's my bag and receipt. I've paid for my items. Why are you bothering me?"

"Miss, please move to the side and come with me."

"No, I'm not going with you."

"Give me the handbag. I'll check it. If you have nothing you can go."

"No, I will not give you my handbag. I haven't stolen a damn thing and I'm leaving."

By this time patrons behind Paula were attempting to leave the store, but she and the security guard were blocking the way. Paula decided to leave. The guard grabbed her, put her arm behind her back, and pulled his revolver out, placing it at her head. He dragged her down the aisle kicking and screaming.

"Let me go, motherfucker! You don't know who you are messing with. You better let me go."

"You're not going anywhere, you little thief. You're going to jail after I get our merchandise out of your pocketbook."

Paula continued to kick and scream. The customers stood frozen in astonishment. Paula's wiry legs were going all over the place, but the guard still had her in the armlock, with the gun pressed against her neck. He took her into a large room full of all kinds of fresh produce. Paula looked around in amazement. She didn't know supermarkets had these big rooms in the back. The guard sat her down in a chair. He stood over her with the gun and ordered, "Give me the handbag."

"Nope."

"Look, miss, if you give me the handbag so I can get our merchandise back, I may let you go without sending you to jail."

"Nope, I have no merchandise besides what I paid for." Paula clutched the handbag at her chest with her arms wrapped around herself. "When you find out who I am and the mistake you've made, you'll be sorry."

"When you get out of jail in twenty years, you'll be sorry. Give me the handbag."

"Nope."

This went on for two and a half hours. Finally, a white gentleman entered the room reporting to work. He observed Paula and the guard when he entered.

"Good afternoon, I'm Gerald Carr, the produce manager. You must be new, what is your name?" he asked the security guard.

"I'm Tyrone Miles, sir, this is my first day on the job. And guess what? I've already nabbed a shoplifter."

"Oh, you have? What has she stolen? And why is she back here instead of with the police?"

"Well, I'm still trying to get our stuff from her. She just refuses to give it to me. It's in her pocketbook."

"You saw her place it in her pocketbook? What was it?"

"Well, Mr. Carr, I didn't actually see her put it in her purse, but I know she has something in there."

"What makes you think she has something, Mr. Miles?"

"Well, she just looks like a shoplifter, so I stopped her. You know, she just has that look. Don't you worry, Mr. Carr, I'll get that handbag from her and we'll get our stuff."

Mr. Carr motioned the guard to come over to the other side of the room. Paula thought, "Floyd must be having a fit for real now." How was she going to get out of this shit with him?

"Miles," Mr. Carr said, "are you telling me you have detained this woman back here and you have no proof that she stole anything?"

"I'll have the proof when I get the bag. I'll get it soon because she's getting tired. I can tell. We've been back here almost three hours. She'll break, she'll give up."

"Miles, I am letting this woman go. I'll talk to you after she leaves."

"Mr. Carr, you shouldn't let this woman go, she's got something, and I just know it. We've got to get our stuff back."

"Miles, I am letting this woman go, right now. Do you understand?" At that point Mr. Carr went over to Paula. "I am very sorry, ma'am. You are free to go."

Paula stood up and picked up her bag with her lunch meat and cheese and an unopened pack of Newports. She reached for the other cigarette pack on the table, which was missing the eleven cigarettes she had smoked through the last two and a half hours. Then she looked at the simple security guard and thought about the stupid orderly she had at home locked in her closet. She thought about the story Floyd told her about the security guard at the bank and his patient. She sized them all up as people who were upset with themselves because they had to guard things and wait for something to happen. They had to depend on people doing something to break the monotony of their boring jobs. Tyrone Miles, assigned to guard food. Fucking food. Suddenly, she dumped her handbag upside down, allowing lipstick, Fashion Fair liquid makeup, suntan lotion, one Chap Stick, a mascara wand, Doublemint gum, three condoms, a pack of Kleenex, Floyd's car keys, her apartment keys, her red leather wallet, and three Tampax to fall onto the table. She shook the bag so that the security guard and Mr. Carr could see that it was empty, and sat back down again. "Mr. Carr, you are welcome to go through these items."

She sat silently, awaiting his examination of the contents of her purse. The security guard looked at the things from the bag and sputtered, "No way. I know she had something." He checked the items to see if they had been used. The gum was open, tissues were missing from the Kleenex pack, and the Chap Stick was rubbed down to a small nub. He looked down on the floor beside her chair to see if she had put anything there. He scanned the room for items she could have kicked or slid into a corner. He was absolutely livid. He knew he hadn't taken his eyes off Paula long enough for her to get rid of anything. He knew he had made a mistake.

As he was going through the stuff, Paula opened her legs and placed them one at a time on the table. She never took her eyes off Miles. They were both pissed, but Paula had the upper hand. She was just sorry she hadn't worn a skirt to the store.

Mr. Carr came over to the table and looked down at the items. "I apologize, miss. I never did get your name."

"Miss Paula Gray."

"Well, Miss Gray, I apologize for your being detained and suspected of shoplifting. You are free to go." Paula gathered her belongings, put everything in her handbag, and sashayed out of the store.

Paula prayed to God she could get the car back to her apartment without wrecking it. All she could think about was that dizzy Floyd in the closet all this time. He had probably either fallen asleep or was screaming like a country maniac. She couldn't even remember whether he had to go to work. Trying desperately to keep the car straight so she wouldn't hit anything or anybody, she forgot to pay attention to the route to her house. She turned down Ringgold Street, which was one way. She couldn't back the car up—she had never driven in reverse. She kept going. At the end of the street, she noticed a police car at the corner. "This is it," she thought, "I am going to jail for sure now." The police officer watched as the car approached the corner. He never got out of his patrol car. Paula stopped Floyd's car, briefly looked at the officer, closed her eyes for a second, and stepped out of the car. She walked over to the patrol car, met the officer's gaze, and recited, "I'm all mixed up. I'm a nervous wreck. I've got a lot of problems and I would like to have a ticket. I need to have a ticket because I've made a mistake and come down this one-way street. I apologize. I'll just wait here for my ticket. What I did was wrong and I deserve a ticket."

The officer looked up at Paula. "What are your problems, miss?"

"I have been held against my will in the supermarket for the last four hours because they thought I was shoplifting and I was not. They kept me a long time, then realized I didn't steal the ham and cheese and cigarettes that I had a receipt for. They made a mistake." She didn't stop to take a breath. "Then I dumped my pocketbook out and they saw none of their merchandise, so they let me go. I haven't been home for four hours and I left my boyfriend locked in the closet."

The officer looked at her as if she were indeed crazy. "Your boyfriend has been locked in the closet for four hours?"

"Yes."

"Why was he in the closet in the first place?"

"He was in there because of a game. You know, just a game, but I had to go to the store and, well, I hadn't let him out, and he can't get out without me. So, if I can have the ticket I deserve, I'll take it, leave, and let my boyfriend out of the closet."

"What's your name, miss?"

"Paula, Paula Gray." Now Paula realized she had no driver's license. She knew what was next, but instead the officer said, "Look, Miss Gray, turn yourself around, get back into your vehicle, and go home. I'll follow you in case your boyfriend is dead from suffocation due to being locked in the closet for four hours. How was he supposed to get any air? If he's dead, I'll arrest you and take you in and charge you with manslaughter. If he's alive, we'll forget about this little meeting and you won't drive down one-way streets again bumping into me. You got that?"

"Yes, sir, you can follow me home."

This was all very amusing to the police officer, and he wanted to get a look at the nut who would stay in a closet for four hours. There was also something about Paula that piqued the officer's interest. He decided he was going to have a little fun with his most current moving violator. The boyfriend couldn't be dead from being in that closet, but he wasn't going to let her know it.

Paula walked back to the car and prayed to God she could steer it home and that stupid-ass Floyd was not dead in the closet. She made a right turn with the officer behind her. She wondered how the hell she was going to park the damn boat once she got home. In two and a half minutes they were outside her apartment. She stopped the car in the street and got out, saying, "I'll run inside and check on my boyfriend. I'll come back out to let you know how he is, okay?"

"No, Miss Gray, I'm coming in with you."

Paula grimaced. "Okay, follow me in." She started toward the steps, but the officer stopped her. "Pull your car into that parking space so you don't hold up traffic."

She looked at him and then at the space. She couldn't park in that space. "Listen, officer, please let me run into the house and see about my boyfriend. I need to make sure he's okay. Here are the keys—can you park it to help the traffic out? Then come on in. I've got to run."

The officer looked at her, shook his head, and held out his hand for the keys. "I'll see you in a minute. Go check on your boyfriend."

# Chapter Twenty-four

# *Reba and Lucy*

Peggy came by the room at one fifteen to check on Lucy and Reba. They were packing.

"Hi, girls," Peggy said cheerfully.

"Hi," came their subdued answers.

"Well, glory be—you both act like you're going to a funeral instead of home to your families."

Reba shook her head. Lucy seemed kind of pissed off.

"What's going on with you two?" Peggy sat down on the bed.

"I don't want to leave Doug. I don't want to see Johnny. I don't want to return to Philadelphia," Reba answered.

Peggy understood. She remembered how she felt about her husband. She thought about the comfort of his strong arms, the way he had caressed her face and kissed her forehead so many times. For a moment she relived the passion they had shared over so many days and nights. She missed him. His sickness and death had stolen the love of her life and had robbed her of so much joy. Benson Kinard, gone too soon.

Reba zipped up her bag, hating herself for leaving. She wished something magical could happen so her life would be with Doug. No obligations of motherhood or marriage. How could she ever let Johnny touch her again? She watched Lucy get the rest of her things together.

Knowing she couldn't cheer either of them up, Peggy said, "I'll see you both at the bus at two o'clock." She went off to her room to pack and have security put her designs on the bus. She hoped Reba would feel better.

The phone rang, and the two of them just stared at it. Reba knew it would be Johnny and let it ring. Finally Lucy picked it up.

"Hey, Miss Philly," said the voice on the other end, "I called you to say good-bye or so long or something, and to thank you for being so nice to me—chauffeuring me around and allowing me to spend the night in your room."

"Kevin! Hey, how are you? Where are you, at the base?"

"Yeah, I got back and showered. I really wanted to talk to you before you left."

"I am so glad you called. I had a ball last night. I'd love for you to come to Philly some time before you die. I hope we stay in touch when I get back home."

"Really?"

"Yes, really."

Kevin sighed. "It's a shame you have to leave today. I just wish you had more time—I mean, I wish I had more time to spend with you because you are pretty cute and pretty cool and pretty together, and I like your company. Do you still have my address, telephone number, and everything?"

"Yes, I have it all."

Reba listened and smiled, happy for Lucy. She glanced at her suitcases, looked at Lucy, who was still on the phone, and walked out. She went to Doug's room to tell him good-bye again, but decided against it. She headed for the lobby bar where her dream had begun.

Lucy and Kevin remained on the phone. It was now 1:40. Kevin said, "Can't you get a couple of days off or something? Do you have to go back today?"

Reba ordered a white wine. Peggy was already in the lobby, and the bus had pulled in. She paid for the wine, picked up the glass, and went to the bell station.

"Please get the bags from room 427 and load them on the bus for Philadelphia."

She headed for her room and walked in, sipping the wine. Lucy was lying back on the bed staring at the ceiling.

"Reba, I'm not going back to Philly today. I'm just not going," Lucy said.

Reba looked at Lucy, gleaming with pride and happiness for her.

"You know what? Me either!"

"Let's go find Peggy," Lucy said.

Laughing, they scrambled out the door and raced for the elevator. They met the bellman and told him they weren't checking out after all. The three of them rode down to the lobby in silence. Reba was thinking about what she'd tell Johnny and how Peggy would take their decision. How happy Doug would be to hear she was staying. What a wonderful surprise he'd have.

Lucy was ecstatic and couldn't wait to tell Kevin. She planned to call her job first thing in the morning to get a few days off. Would she sleep with Kevin that night or was she rushing things? They'd had a wonderful time the night before. Was this finally "Mr. Right"?

"Whatever, I intend to do this. If it doesn't work out—tough. Like they say in the poker games, I'm all in."

When they reached the lobby, they saw Peggy and broke the news to her. Reba stood there silently. She felt guilty but looked at Peggy very casually so she wouldn't start lecturing her.

"What are you doing?" Peggy demanded, astonished. "How are you getting home? When are you coming home? Reba, what am I supposed to tell Johnny? Have you spoken to him?"

"Tell him I didn't make the bus, and I'll call him. That's all. Don't get involved."

Both girls raced away, leaving a bewildered Peggy. She went out to board the bus with the other models and designers. Johnny Penster would have a bird!

"Listen, Lucy," Reba said, "let's go back to the room. We have to talk." When they got into the room, they both headed for the beds and sat down. "What in the hell am I going to tell Johnny? I've got to figure out something quick."

"Yes, you're right, Reba, you have some thinking to do. I want to call Kevin right now, but I am going to wait and help you out.

"Let's take first things first," Lucy continued. "I have to talk to Kevin about the next few days. There's our room and it has to be paid for. It's not like I can stay on the base with him. I've got to count my money. See, I don't know how this thing is going to go down because nothing has happened between us. I mean, he was quite a gentleman. He may not want to stay here with me—it might be awkward."

"How much money do you have?" asked Reba. "For the room and food, so you don't have to obligate the man?" Lucy got her handbag from the dresser and started to count her money.

"Ninety-three dollars, and I know that won't go far."

"Let me check my money," Reba said. "I haven't spent much since I've been here."

She came up with fifty-four dollars, and threw it on the bed before taking out her American Express card.

"That will keep you here and feed you for a few days. We'll have to talk to the desk about keeping the room. Let's think of something to tell my ever-loving, faithful husband."

"Shit, let's tell him the truth, and it goes like this: I cannot come home right now because I met a real man who feeds me and takes care of me and does it to me so good. He also talks softly, and the guy has blown my natural mind and I don't want to know your ass anymore." They both laughed hysterically.

"Come on, Lucy, we gotta do better than that."

"Look, I'm sick of figuring out shit, I want to call Kevin. Oh, hell, that's what you get for marrying the sorry-ass nigger. You should go home and poison his ass. Put something in his ketchup. Get some fucking arsenic and mix it up in some of that red shit you make and just kill his ass. It's a wonder he didn't die from your cooking a long time ago. Just think, if you kill him and they have to open his ass up, they'll see all that red slime from fourteen years back. That's a whole lot of tomatoes, Reba."

"Look, you better stop playing and get things straight. Now, what are we going to tell Johnny?"

"Okay," said Lucy, lying down on the bed, "let's think."

Reba paced the room. "We can't tell him I was in a car accident or anything like that because he might haul his ass down here. Peggy will be back on time, so he'll know she didn't have a problem with anything. Shit, I don't know what the hell to say."

"And guess what else," said Lucy, "you have to call your job in the morning. And what about the kids? When were you planning to go home?"

"I wish I could send for my kids at the end of the week and never have to see another soul in Philly." After another twenty minutes she spoke up. "Fuck it. I won't call. I just won't say anything until I can think of something that will make sense. I'm calling Doug right now to tell him I'm not on that bus headed back to Drearyville."

"No, let me call Kevin first before he goes out or something. He doesn't know I stayed. You can get hold of Doug easier than I can Kevin because he's crippled and has a meeting here tomorrow."

"Right, call him."

Holding the receiver to her ear, Lucy was getting nervous. Kevin's phone rang three times before he answered.

"This is Miss Philly calling."

"Are you at a rest stop already? What's the matter, you had to pee in the bushes again?"

"Not exactly, Mr. San Jose. I missed my bus and I'm stranded in Norfolk."

Kevin gave a yelp of joy.

"I'm on my way! Where exactly are you?"

"In the room where you woke up."

"Hour, tops. See you then." They hung up, and Reba grabbed the phone.

"Hey, Dexter, you okay?" Doug laughed. He loved it when Reba called him that. It made him feel totally sexy and let him know that he was more than adequate in bed. Black women referred to good sex partners as "Dexter." He said, "I think I lost someone, but I'm trying to manage."

"Well," Reba sighed, "I thought I talked a good game in that room with you about an hour and a half ago, but it wouldn't fly. If you think you lost me, you are delightfully mistaken because I'm on the fourth floor of this hotel. I let the bus leave without me. I don't know what I'm doing because you've made me crazy. In two days I've become a drunk, a whore, and an unfaithful wife. I have deserted my children, and I probably have Peggy Kinard in more trouble than she has ever been in her entire life. Maybe when you get your foot checked out, the doctor can refer me to a shrink who can explain how I went from a mild-mannered, quiet housewife to a full-fledged maniac. Even Lucy has gone wild. She's still here too, and Kevin's on his way."

Doug laughed again.

"Oh, so it's funny? Let's just see how amusing it is when those six brats of mine show up on your doorstep in suburban Annapolis or wherever you live. What I'm doing is completely insane and irresponsible, but I know I want to spend some more time with you. I have things to work out. Maybe we can do that together over the next few days, if you'll have me. And by the way, Johnny Penster doesn't know a thing yet. Poor man thinks I'm on the bus."

"Reba, you're amazing! You are crazy and sweet and utterly fascinating. How soon can you get to me?"

"Let me call and have the bellman bring my things to your room, and we'll play it by ear from there. How does that sound?"

"Great. Hey, Reba—thanks. You've made my day."

Reba handed Lucy half her cash and told her to have her things sent to Doug's room. She strutted to the door, but looked back at Lucy who was staring off into space. She went back, kissed her on the forehead, and held out her hand to give her five. Lucy slapped her hand as hard as she could.

"I'll call you later," Reba said, and switched out of the room.

"Sergeant Henzler, please, Kevin Graham calling."

"Kevin, I'm surprised to hear from you on Sunday. Is everything okay?"

"I'm sorry to disturb you at home, but I have a favor to ask, and it's sort of an emergency."

Vince Henzler liked Kevin a lot. He was the best in his squad, the type of guy who always went the extra mile. Kevin had favors stored up with Henzler. He willingly worked on his days off if they needed him. If there was an emergency, Henzler could always count on him. Kevin had sometimes worked doubles. He also did personal favors for Henzler, such as helping to build a championship go-cart for his son. Kevin was a fine Navy man. Henzler hoped his own son would turn out like Kevin.

"Okay, Kevin, let's have it."

"I need four days off starting tomorrow. I have the time. It's not a family emergency. May I be open?"

"Relax, Kevin."

"I met a very nice young lady last night. I'm really impressed with her. She's from out of town and I want to show her around. I have some special plans that could take me out of the city for a few days."

Vince was shaking his head on the other end of the phone. "Well, well, well. Congratulations on your newfound friend. I wish it were me. I can't possibly say no because of the points you've racked up. You've got a green light, son. Take care of yourself. I'll expect you back on the base by Friday. I'll make a couple of calls to clear you today and process your papers tomorrow when I get to the office."

Kevin quickly checked his cash and bank balance before he called Lucy.

"Hi, Miss Philly. I have a question."

Lucy tensed, figuring things were about to get complicated.

"Shoot, San Jose," she said.

"How many days will you be in Norfolk? Or shall I say how many days can you be here?"

Lucy wasn't sure if he was trying to get rid of her. "I can leave tomorrow."

"Can you stay till Friday? I got some time off."

Lucy squeezed her eyes shut, not believing this was happening to her. She wanted to scream with joy. She wanted to shout into the phone, "I don't ever have to go back!" But she was cool. "I can probably get time off, too. I'll call in tomorrow."

"Okay, plan on being here until Friday if you can work it out, and give me an hour and a half. I'm on to something, and I'll get to you then." They hung up. Lucy jumped up and down, she was so thrilled and happy. She wished Reba were here so they could share this moment. She felt like a princess, like Cinderella. Peggy Kinard had turned out to be her fairy godmother, Kevin was most definitely the prince, and Norfolk was the palace!

# Chapter Twenty-five

# *Reba*

Peggy peered out of the window as the bus pulled up. There were a lot of cars waiting to meet the models and designers. She gathered her belongings and stepped off the bus as the driver unloaded her luggage. She looked around for her best friend, Esther Kayer, who was supposed to help her get everything home. She saw her and waved.

"Hi, thanks for coming. Let's load up—get me home quickly. I'm really exhausted."

Peggy wanted to get away fast, without running into Johnny Penster. But before they could leave, he pulled up.

"I can't help you," she quickly said to Esther. "I've got to get in the car. One of the models didn't come back, and I see her husband." Peggy hopped in the passenger's side and scrunched down to watch Johnny. He went right to the bus, looking for Reba. Peggy put her head down on the seat. She felt pretty guilty leaving Esther with the rest of the luggage, but had to avoid Johnny at any cost.

After carefully watching the last passengers get off the bus, Johnny looked around outside for Reba. He saw Esther working alone and walked over to help, and noticed the name PEGGY KINARD on the luggage tags.

"You're with Peggy Kinard?" he said to Esther.

"Yes."

"Where is she?"

"In the car with a terrible headache."

Johnny went to the door of the driver's side and opened it. "Hi, Peggy, how did things go? Where is Reba? I can't seem to find her."

Peggy sat up and was silent for a moment before getting out of the car.

"Johnny, we had a problem—well, Reba must have had some sort of a problem—because she didn't make the bus. We tried to wait for her, but she never showed up. I can't imagine what happened. I'm sorry, but I don't have any more information."

"Where is she? Did anything happen to her while you all were down there? I called and she never called me back, so I just assumed she was real busy."

"The show went pretty well, and she did fine. There were a lot of models from here and other cities, and they were together a lot. I don't know if any of them missed their buses. I didn't hear that there had been any accidents. I just can't imagine what happened to Reba. Lucy Noble didn't come back either. Reba will probably call you soon if she hasn't already."

"I guess I'd better get back to the house and call the hotel to see if I can find out what is going on." Johnny shook his head, looking bewildered and worried. "Peggy, do you know if Reba had enough money to get home on a regular bus?"

"She never seemed to have any money problems during the weekend, and I'm sure if she ran short of money, Lucy probably had some. Or if she needs anything, she'll call you. They may even be on another bus bound for Philadelphia right now. I wouldn't worry too much if I were you. Reba can take care of herself. No news is always good news. You should go on home and wait for her to come or call."

"Yeah, I guess. No, I think I'll call the hotel right away to see if they know anything."

"Well, Johnny, I've got to run. I'm sure everything will be fine." Esther sped off, and Peggy was thankful to be away from Johnny Penster. She wondered when Reba would call him, and what she'd say.

"What's that all about?" Esther asked. She was such a good friend. She and her husband, Roland, had looked out for Peggy since Benson's death. When Benson was alive, the four of them spent a lot of time together during holidays and took some vacations together. Esther was like a sister to Peggy.

"Like I said, Reba and my goddaughter, Lucy, did not make the bus. They were out having a good time last night, and I guess they decided to continue the fun. I am sure they'll be back by tomorrow."

Peggy would never dare expose Reba's personal business to anyone. She was glad Lucy hadn't come home, because it made things look better for Reba. However, Peggy prayed that Reba would show up soon.

"So how did the show go?" Esther asked as she parked the car in front of Peggy's house.

"Oh, I was very pleased. It was a success and I am sure I made some good contacts. I enjoyed the hotel and everything. It was a pretty place and I met a lot of nice people. My designs went over well. I wish you could have been there. How is Roland, and how was the weekend for you two?"

"As usual, we were in church this morning, but as of now, we're finding another church."

"You two quit Carver Light Temple? For what? What the heck happened? Wait a minute with the luggage—it can wait. What happened at church to make you quit? We've been members there so long."

"Chile, Reverend Ross has lost his mind, lost his ever-loving mind."

"How, Esther?"

"Well, you know we've all been going along with him being separated from Alberta and all. You know, we all just figured they were having problems like a lot of married couples do, and they'd work things out. We thought this was kind of a lightweight thing that would blow over."

"Yes," Peggy said, "I thought so too. I mean, I haven't seen Alberta at church for a while, but I just assumed she'd be back anytime."

"Oh, no, Peggy. Let me tell you what that snake did. He has taken up with that young girl, Barbara Allen."

"Barbara Allen!" screeched Peggy. "No! You've got to be mistaken, Esther!"

"No, I ain't mistaken, Peggy. You listen to this: He moved in with her."

"What!"

"Yes, honey, that's what happened."

"Reverend Ross is nearly fifty-five years old. Barbara is about twenty-seven, isn't she?" asked Peggy.

"They tell me twenty-six."

"How did you find out?"

"Just before service was over, he stood in the pulpit and announced that the church had a new 'mother.' We just sat there. It didn't really sink in because it had been a long service, and we were tired and hungry. I wasn't real alert. For a minute I thought he was talking about *his* mother. Then he said that oftentimes things don't work out the way we plan, but God is at work all the time."

"You have got to be kidding! I can't believe it."

"Wait now, Peggy. Then he went on about how happy he was because God sent Barbara Allen to him and to us. Now Peggy, hold on, 'cause this will blow you away."

"Come on, Esther."

"Then he said, 'Let me introduce you to my newfound happiness sent

straight from the Lord—Barbara Allen, the new mother of our church!'
Peggy, the entire congregation was in shock! When Barbara walked up to
the pulpit, my mouth fell wide open. That skunk had the nerve to say
they were engaged! He isn't even divorced from Alberta. Can you believe
it? He made a speech saying we should share in his happiness and if we
truly wanted to be saved and blessed, each and every one of us had to
come to the altar. There was a large gold bucket up there. He told us that
each and every member of the congregation had to put twenty-five dollars into it as an engagement offering to the happy couple, and we would
receive extra blessings."

"Has he lost his mind?" Peggy was fuming.

"You tell me, Peggy, has the man lost his ever-loving mind, or does he
simply think *we're* crazy? After that he kept going on and on, standing
there drooling over Barbara. She was grinning from ear to ear. She was so
happy she was crying real tears. Boo-hooing. Do you know that over half
the people in the church went up there to put money and checks in that
bucket? I had a fit! Roland and I wanted to smack him off that pulpit.
You should have seen old lady Bryson pulling money out of that change
purse of hers.

"But guess what? You know old Mrs. Dunlap who plays poker every
weekend, the one they call the 'five-card stud queen'? She told his behind
off in front of the whole congregation! She stood up in front of the
church, facing him, and said, 'You got a lot of nerve trying to lead us,
you scoundrel. You know you got a wife at home and grown kids, and
you got the nerve to disrespect her. And if that ain't bad enough, you're
doing it in the church. You ought to be ashamed of yourself, using God
in this mess that you know is not right and trying to drag us into it with
you! So now it is evident you are just playing with my Lord. I wish I
would give you one cent of my hard-earned money for an engagement
present to you and that baby tramp you found. And believe me, *you* are
the one that found her because *God* didn't find her for you. You are a
low-down, dirty, conniving con artist, that's what you are! And if these
dummies want to help you out, that's their business. Believe me, that
young chick will probably give you a heart attack and kill you if God
don't step to you sooner and do it himself. And another thing, I have a
record of every dime I put in the collection here, and I'll call you with the
total tomorrow morning at your house, or the tramp's if you're not
home. You better also believe that if you don't come up with my money,

I'm going to my lawyer on Tuesday morning and sue your black, stinking, lying behind. You'll give me my money back, every penny of it! I've been coming here for seven years. Do you know how much money that is, Ross? I'll include everything I paid into the Building Fund, the Missionary Fund, the Pastor's Aid Fund, and the Fuel Rally Fund. So don't think I only want what I have been throwing into the collection plate all these years. I want it *all* back. You got that, Ross? Now it will be me, you, my Lord, and my lawyer all sitting at the same table together. Just like the Last Supper. The only difference is there will be fewer people, and I'll get everything." Then she sat down on the floor beside the pulpit, took a small calculator out of her purse, and started putting in numbers.

"Peggy, everybody in the church started hollering and screaming. People came running up to take their money back. Mrs. Dunlap never moved from her spot—everyone stepped right over her. Reverend Ross was calling for order, but nobody paid him any attention. He went to grab the bucket back, to save whatever was left in it, I guess. Minnie Kershaw tried to scoop her money out, but he wouldn't let it go. He was shielding Barbara with his other arm because Sally Fredericks was calling her a tramp and a home wrecker and hitting her with one of the collection plates. Roland went up to help Minnie get the big gold bucket, and they got it. Roland turned it upside down, and all the money fell out. Everyone else came up and scrambled on the floor for their money. It was a mess! So me and Roland quit the church."


"Room 427, please." Johnny waited impatiently while the hotel rang his wife's room.

"Sorry, sir, there is no answer. Would you like to leave a message?"

"Yes. Please leave word for Rebecca Penster that her husband called and to please call home."

"Certainly, sir."

He wondered where Reba could be. He looked up the telephone numbers for Greyhound and Trailways and called them both. There were no buses scheduled to arrive in Philadelphia from Norfolk before the next evening. He went to the children's bedrooms and told them that their mama had missed her bus and would be home tomorrow. They seemed a little disappointed, but not upset. Johnny was really worried by then and felt guilty because he'd been away from home most of the weekend, lying up in Geraldine Royer's bed. He had left Nina with the kids and checked on them every five or six hours. He did manage to get in before ten o'clock in the morning both Saturday and Sunday, telling the kids he had worked the weekend to fill in for another man. Geraldine had a boy and a girl by Johnny—the boy was four years old. Reba didn't know about that, and Geraldine never bothered Johnny at home.

He figured Reba probably fell asleep and missed her bus and that Lucy stayed to keep her company. He sure would be glad when she returned because he was tired of checking on the kids, and they were sick of his cooking. He and Nina were even worse cooks than Reba. "Everything will soon be back to normal," Johnny decided. He got undressed and went to bed.

Reba and Doug found a nice, plain diner in Norfolk. They kept looking at each other and giggling like kids throughout the meal.

"What is up for tonight?" Reba asked.

"What do you feel like doing?"

"Let's find a movie."

"Okay, we'll need a local paper and some directions. Let's get out of here and do that," Doug said.

They left the diner, rode by the hotel, and stopped at the lobby for a paper and directions to the theater. When Reba arrived at the desk, she was handed a message. She looked at it and put it in her purse. Doug was waiting in the car. She got the paper and directions, and walked out of the hotel.

"Sorry, Johnny, not just yet."

# Chapter Twenty-six

# *Lucy*

Kevin arrived at the hotel at about five fifteen and went straight up to Lucy's room. By this time she had taken a bubble bath, had on fresh makeup, a mustard yellow pantsuit, and a black top. Every curl of her short hair was in place. She glowed.

"Who is it?" she asked when he knocked on the door.

"San Jose." He walked in and hugged her. It seemed a good sign, so she hugged him back. "I don't know if you've made anyone else happy today, but you have surely taken care of it for me. I am so glad you decided to stay. I'll do my best to give you a great time."

"If things go anything like last night, I won't regret my decision." She thought for a moment about how they had talked, lying across her bed until they both fell asleep. He had told her all about his childhood, which sounded like a great one, about his family—his parents owned a small supermarket in San Jose and his two sisters, one younger and one older, still lived there. The family dog, Casey, was a collie who Kevin claimed was smarter than anyone in the family. Kevin had been captain of the track team in high school and loved to play basketball. He really enjoyed the Navy.

Kevin was a handsome guy—chocolate skin, gorgeous brown eyes, and a gleaming smile. Not a tooth out of place. He had the cutest butt, and Lucy was dying to grab it. His dark hair was neatly trimmed. He reminded her of Blair Underwood. He looked pretty sharp, dressed in khaki pants, a navy button-down shirt, and slip-on loafers.

They sat down on her bed. He took a long look at her and told her how beautiful she was.

"You should stay in that color; it becomes you," he said. He gently kissed her on the cheek.

"Well, what's on your agenda for this good time?"

"Is there anything in particular you want to do this evening, or shall I call the shots?"

"It's your town, you decide," replied Lucy.

"How about taking a drive and stopping at a nice place for dinner? We have to be up early tomorrow morning so you can call your job and all. Tomorrow I need to stop at the bank, and if it's okay with you, there are some friends I want you to meet. I'd also like to take you to a very nice restaurant on the water. Does that sound like a good plan?"

"Sounds great to me."

"Do you think your boss will give you any trouble about the time off?"

"No, I'll be okay. Should we get going?"

Kevin took a scenic route and acted as tour guide, telling Lucy all about Norfolk. He pulled into a quaint café with a piano player. The menu featured seafood, so Kevin ordered grilled snapper and white wine for them both. They shared a huge salad. Lucy was ecstatically happy. Kevin was an affectionate gentleman, squeezing her hand and feeding her bites of food.

"Who's the man in Philly?"

"My father."

Kevin laughed. "Come on, Philly, who's the man I'm keeping you from?"

"My boss."

"So the man in your life is your boss?"

"No, Kevin. I am totally unattached."

"Why?"

"I was very much in love with a guy I dated in high school and college. We were engaged—ring and all. He damn near left me at the altar. He met someone else while at college and broke things off with me when we met at home for a Thanksgiving break. He came home with the chick. He turned out to be quite a turkey. That was two years ago and I've been hanging pretty loose since then," Lucy said.

"Wow. That had to blow your mind. How hard a time did you have with the breakup?" Kevin asked.

"Well, to be perfectly honest, I cried my eyes out and threw myself into my schoolwork. I got into a dance class, worked part-time, and did every damn thing I could to keep my mind occupied. I also hit the therapist's office. I was pretty screwed up. He was all I knew, you know? I'd depended on him for my happiness. I learned you can't do that in relationships. I've grown up some since that. I think I have my head on straight now. Okay. Now, you tell me who lights up your life in Norfolk, or is she waiting in San Jose?"

"Her name was Debbie and she lived in San Jose. When I was sent here three years ago, I didn't like being away from her. She came up and got an apartment and a job. My commanding officer thinks I'm the best man he has, so he keeps me here. Debbie hated Norfolk and got bored. She said she wanted to get married and wanted me to get a transfer. She stuck it out about four months and has been gone for five. I wasn't ready for marriage, but I wasn't messing around on her. To make a long story short, she started going out a lot without me. Checking the place out, so she said. She met someone, hooked up with him, and I got a 'Dear John' letter. They split for New York. That's my story, baby. Since then I've been solo too. I've had some dates, but no one I was impressed with."

"What impressed you about me?" asked Lucy.

"You're light and cool. You go with the flow. You're fun and funny, but a responsible person. You're impulsive but not fast. You're cute, your heart is warm, and I like you. Now, let's change the subject. How did Angie make out? She is really a wild chick."

"Yeah," said Lucy. "She's a piece of work, but I like her. We exchanged numbers, and I plan to call her when I get home. I may go to see her sometime."

"Yeah," said Kevin, "Angie can keep you laughing. I think Roger has his eye on her." They finished dinner and left the restaurant for a drive.

"I want to pay your hotel bill tomorrow," Kevin said.

"That's not necessary—Reba and I have it covered."

"Isn't Reba staying with her friend?"

"Yes, she's with Doug."

"When is she going home?"

"I have no idea. He's supposed to leave on Tuesday for Annapolis."

"You mean he didn't come down here with her—he's not from Philly?"

"He's from Annapolis, but let's not get into that."

"Right," Kevin said, "but I'm paying the hotel bill. I insist."

"Because you are staying there with me?"

"Do you want me to?"

"I have two beds."

"What if I am afraid to sleep alone in a strange hotel?"

"Then you'll do what you did last night."

"That worked out, didn't it?" Kevin laughed.

When they got back to the room, Lucy pulled a crossword puzzle out

of her suitcase, threw it on the bed, and sat down. "Here's our entertainment for the evening."

They had been at it for about fifteen minutes when Kevin threw the
book on the floor, grabbed Lucy, and kissed her passionately. He was certainly a good kisser, no doubt about it. He looked at her and said, "I'm
going to leave and go back to the base, but I'll be here for you about ten
o'clock. I'll call you when I get there."

"No."

"What do you mean, no?"

"I mean no, like you can't leave, like I don't want you to leave, like I
want you to stay with me."

"Okay, Miss Philly, you have a gentleman from San Jose to stay here
with you all night and protect you. All you have to do is go downstairs
early tomorrow morning and buy him a toothbrush. Your gentleman will
sleep in his clothes. You'll get under the covers and I'll lie on top of them.
I promise not to do anything a gentleman shouldn't do. Agreed?"

"That's fine."

Kevin removed his shirt and shoes and took the covers from the other
bed. Lucy snuggled under the blankets. He turned off the lights and settled himself.

"Will he make a move?" Lucy wondered. She really wanted him to,
but she wasn't about to take the initiative. She lay in his arms, but he
made no passes at her and they fell asleep that way.

They awoke to a ringing phone.

"Lucy, this is Johnny Penster. May I speak with Reba?"

"Oh shit," thought Lucy. Kevin was awake and looking at her, asking
with his eyes who it was.

"Johnny, how are you doing? How are the kids?"

"We're all fine. Are you two okay?"

"Sure, but Reba got up about an hour ago and went downstairs to
have breakfast before she called you and her job."

"Why weren't you two on the bus yesterday?"

"Johnny, things got so messed up. The models and assistants were invited to a party after the show, and we went. We ended up staying across
town at a model's house. We were up pretty late and slept in. We couldn't
make it back to the bus on time. A lot of us stayed over."

"What time are you getting out of there?"

"I don't know. Reba is probably finding that out now and will call you soon. As soon as I see her, I'll have her call you."

"I've called before, and she never called back."

"It was so hectic with the show and all. Reba worked like a dog, and then there was the party."

"Does she have money to get home?"

"Yes, she does. Look, Johnny, I'm in a rush. Are you going to work today or will you be home?"

"Tell her to call me at work."

Kevin looked up at Lucy, shaking his head and smiling. He started that "Ooooo" stuff from the night before. "Good morning and shut up," Lucy said. She dressed quickly, ran down to the lobby, and bought a toothbrush. While she was down there she used the phone.

"Doug, put Reba on. Sorry if I woke you up."

"We're up, Lucy. Here's Reba."

"Hey, I'm in the lobby. Johnny just called. He wants you to call him at work."

"What did you tell him?" Reba asked. Lucy repeated her tale.

"Good girl, Luce."

"Look, Reba, you better call that man, you hear me?"

"Okay, I will. How are you making out with Kevin?"

"He's upstairs."

"Oh, a passionate night, huh, girl?"

"No, a perfect gentleman."

"That's no fun. What are you going to do today?"

Lucy explained their plans.

"It sounds nice. Call me later."

"Are you cool with your clothes for the day, Reba? I matched you up two outfits. Put them on the way I arranged them. You can wear the low-heeled black shoes with both outfits. Put your hair in a French braid, and spray a little perfume on your wrists and neck. Dab a little on your knees and thighs. Not too much, though, you don't want to smell like a prostitute. You got that?"

"Thank you, sweetie."

Lucy returned to her room. Kevin was in the bathroom getting ready to go. "Why don't you come along with me?" he asked.

He had a nice place. She headed straight for the stereo to start some music. Kevin got a large briefcase. He stuffed a toothbrush and some personal items in it while Lucy used the phone.

"Hi, Miss Cantor. I'm calling to say I won't be there today. I have a family emergency and can't come in until next Monday. Please deduct the time from my vacation."

"What kind of emergency, Lucy?"

"My cousin in the Navy has heart trouble. I'll be with him until the doctors are finished with his tests and release him."

Kevin shook his head, laughing.

"Okay, Lucy, I guess Rosemary can cover for you. I hope your cousin will be all right."

"Good-bye, Miss Cantor."

Then Lucy called her mother and told her she was having a great time, had met some nice people, and wouldn't be home until Friday. She said she was fine and would call in a couple of days.

Once she was off the phone, Kevin said, "Lucy, you have to meet my best friend David. He's my main man. He's a really smart doctor, too. We shoot hoops together, do a little fishing from time to time, and hang out sometimes. We may stay over at his house tonight. He also has a really cool girlfriend, Sonja, who lives with him. It's fun over there and you'll love their baby, Tokay. He's an Irish setter. I thought I'd ask them to go out with us tonight. Do you mind?"

"Sounds like fun to me," Lucy said.

"Okay, great. They'd have a fit if I didn't bring you by. We're pretty tight. We'll stop by the hotel sometime today, pick up your things, and take them over there."

After stopping at the bank, they went to breakfast and stuffed their faces with pancakes, home fries, ham, juice, and coffee. Then they headed to the Sigmund Forrester Art Museum.

Lucy found the art museum fascinating. It had been a long time since she'd been somewhere like that. Kevin knew all about paintings by Picasso and Rembrandt. He educated her as they strolled around, and both chose the works they liked best.

They went to the hotel to pick up Lucy's stuff and, after a short drive, arrived at David and Sonja's. They were a white couple who lived in a beautiful, three-story colonial house on two acres of land. The house featured a big screened-in porch, elegantly furnished, with a view of a placid pond. Tokay greeted them at the car. David was tall and blond with arresting blue eyes and long hair in a ponytail. Lucy saw why he and Kevin played ball together—they were both tall and so athletic looking.

Sonja was a pleasant, slightly plump redhead about five feet six. She and David seemed happy together. "Let me show you around," Sonja offered. She gave Lucy a leisurely tour. There was a great fireplace, a gigantic family room with all kinds of stereo equipment and gadgets, as well as a finished basement with a pool table. The guys shot pool while Sonja finished preparing a nice lunch to have on the porch.

Lucy was a little uneasy because she had never stayed with a white couple. She had never even been in a house as big as theirs. Sonja invited her to her bedroom and put on Teena Marie's album *Wild and Peaceful*. "So, Lucy, where did you and Kevin meet?"

"I came down here on a weekend modeling assignment."

"Oh, you're a model?"

"No, but I've had a few gigs. The designer is my godmother. I'm really a stock liquidation clerk for a broker in Philly."

"So, how did you and the big K hook up?"

"He was part of the 'after party' at the hotel. We went out with a bunch of his pals and had a blast. Here I am, not back in Philly, not at work, and not giving a hoot about home right now."

"Do you like Norfolk?"

"I haven't seen much. It was dark when we went out, and yours is the only home I've seen. By the way, it is lovely—so peaceful and serene here. You lucked out on the good life."

"Dave and I have been together for almost three years. We have our ups and downs like every other couple, but we basically get along pretty well. We don't stab or shoot each other."

Lucy laughed. "How did the two of them meet?"

"At the go-cart races a year and a half ago. Dave is a Big Brother to a kid and built him a go-cart for the race. Kevin was also there, sponsoring his boss's son."

"I heard Dave was a doctor," Lucy said.

"He's a neuropsychologist."

Lucy's head tilted to one side. "A neuro what? Sounds like an astronaut or something."

"A neuropsychologist," Sonja repeated. "That's a doctor who treats people with head injuries such as concussions, or maybe someone with a blood clot in the brain. He analyzes people and gives brain tests, too."

They take about six hours and are sort of like games. Some use cartoon cards that tell stories the patient has to put together by lining the cards up in order. He also does memory tests giving a person about fifteen items to remember; then he goes on to something else. After a while he'll ask the patient to recall as many of the items as he can. There's a test in which someone is blindfolded and has to place objects in the correct slots with one hand. He has to feel his way. Then he has to do it again with the other hand. Stuff like that. He can tell from the tests how smart you are and how smart you used to be before the injury. He also hypnotizes people. He teaches organizational skills because most of the patients are all mixed up from the trauma. They lose, forget, and misplace their belongings. One man lost 27 pairs of eyeglasses in less than a year. Brain trauma is deep shit."

"Does Dave ever try to play head games with you?"

"I don't know for sure but sometimes I think so. I find myself listening very carefully to everything he says when we are talking about something serious. I don't trust him, because he's always reading peoples' minds. It's a trip sometimes."

Sonja paused and put on another album. "You like Phoebe Snow?"

"Yeah, she's cool, but I only know a few of her cuts: 'Love Makes a Woman,' 'No Regrets,' and 'Never Letting Go'."

"I've got them all, here she goes."

"Yeah, I dig Phoebe." Lucy relaxed and listened. When "Love Makes a Woman" came on, Lucy started to dance.

"You can dance a little bit, huh, Lucy?"

"A little bit? Girl, I can jam. I put them all to shame Saturday night. We had a ball."

"You really like dancing, Lucy?"

"I love to dance. I wish I could have been a dancer."

"So why aren't you?"

"I don't know. I never seriously pursued it."

"Hey, do yourself a favor—and this is on the serious side—chase your dreams. If you want to dance, girl, go for it. Life is much too short not to be doing what pleases you."

"And Sonja, what do you do?" Lucy asked.

"Legal work part-time for a local criminal attorney. I also do a radio talk show from seven until midnight during the week. I'm off on weekends. I play music and talk a lot of crap on the air. People call in with their problems. It's a fun job but doesn't pay a lot of money, but there's absolutely no stress. I give my callers advice, even though I have no degree."

"Yeah, that sounds like a fun job," said Lucy.

"Yeah, sometimes—it's a gig, you know, pays the bills."

Sonja glanced at her watch. "Look at the time! We better eat lunch before we all faint from hunger."

Lucy wasn't very hungry, but she ate a little of Sonja's salad to be polite. At two thirty, Dave announced they had to drop Tokay off at the vet and would be right back. Kevin said he would take Lucy for a short drive while they were gone. They planned to meet back at the house at four.

Kevin drove Lucy around for about fifteen minutes and then pulled a bandana out of his pocket.

"This is the surprise I planned, and you have to be blindfolded."

"No way! You aren't blindfolding me!"

"Look, Miss Philly, you're messing up my thing. Put the blindfold on."

"Okay, but you're crazy."

Kevin sped to the airport, where he double-parked. He picked up Lucy's handbag and took tickets out of the glove compartment, then helped Lucy out of the car. "Where are we? What's going on?" she demanded.

Dave and Sonja drove up behind them. Kevin had left a set of keys in his car so they could drive it back. He guided Lucy into the airport.

"Come on, Kevin, what's going on?"

People stared at them. Kevin sat Lucy down on a bench and told her to stay put, not to remove the blindfold or speak to anyone. By now Lucy realized that they were at the airport. Kevin checked in for the flight and went back for Lucy, who looked silly sitting on the bench, blindfolded.

"Come on, Miss Philly," he said as he helped her up.

"Kevin, I hear flights being called and planes taking off."

"Let's go." He escorted her to the gate where they sat down, waiting for the flight to be called.

"Do you want anything to drink or eat? Are you all right?"

"I want to know what the hell you're up to."

Kevin walked her to the sign indicating their destination and removed the blindfold. "See that—it says Freeport, Bahamas. We're spending the next four days there."

Lucy squinted. She was beyond being shocked. She was grinning, blushing, and full of questions.

"Here's your handbag. Have you ever been to the Bahamas?"

"No, sir. And I've never met a man like you, never been this surprised, never, never, never!" She hugged him. "Kevin, how did you do it? You are something else! Wonderful!" She paused. "What about my clothes?"

"Your bags are checked in. Anything else you need I'll buy when we arrive. And by the way, I checked you out of the hotel and paid your bill. You and I are about to have a blast!"

Doug and Reba went down for breakfast and returned to the room. Reba called the library to say she would be out at least until Wednesday because she was not feeling well. No problem. Now it was time to call Johnny.

"John Penster, please. This is his wife calling."

"Hold on, Mrs. Penster," said the woman on the phone. In a few seconds she heard Johnny's voice.

"Reba, what is going on, why didn't you come home? When are you coming home? How did you manage to miss the bus? Don't you know the kids are having a fit wondering why you're not here? Don't you think I'm sick of watching them? Do you have any money to get home? What time are you getting the bus? What time does the bus get you to Philadelphia? Why didn't you call me back when I called you? Why didn't you call me at home before you left the hotel room this morning? The toilet overflowed. You'd better get your ass back here. Craig lost one of his sneakers. The kids hate Nina's cooking."

He never came up for air. Reba hung up.

~

# Chapter Twenty-seven

# *Sheila*

Four weeks had passed since Leonard and Sheila started dating. Her life with him seemed to have grown easy and comfortable. They had gone to a concert and deep-sea fishing; he was teaching her how to play chess, and they enjoyed shopping for clothes together. Leonard still hadn't spent any time with her kids—she was holding off on that until things looked a little more permanent. She had stayed at his house the last two Sunday nights. They'd had sex twice and were still pretty nervous and shy with each other, but Sheila felt they would relax in time. She didn't much mind about the sex because she wanted a relationship based more on friendship and companionship.

Leonard was so shy that he didn't like walking around nude in front of her. When he took his shower, he emerged with a towel around him, or in his pajamas. His underclothes usually came off in the bed. Sheila wasn't embarrassed anymore about her weight. She had lost another fifteen pounds and was down to one eighty-three. She had bought a couple of nice nighties despite being overweight. She felt sexy. She was pretty relaxed at Leonard's house when she stayed over. She had to be up early to fix breakfast for the kids and get them off to school, but didn't really mind because at least she had some quiet time and some privacy with her man.

Leonard had a nice place, a four-bedroom house with a third floor, exercise room, and a high-tech stereo system. They enjoyed working out together. They both liked to cook, so when she stayed over they fixed their Sunday night meal together. They usually started about seven o'clock, after Leonard dropped his kids back with their mother. Sheila hadn't met them yet, but they spent every other weekend with him. He seemed to be a good father.

Things were going well with Auntie Len. She enjoyed her time off from Sunday afternoon to Monday night. Sheila was glad Lenora had a friend and was having some fun shopping and playing bingo. Lenora looked forward to that bingo game every Sunday, and when four o'clock came, she was out the door in a hurry, bags and all.

Pam, too, was good with the babysitting, and the kids liked her. The girl sure did eat a lot, though. Sheila told her that if she kept it up, she'd be spending a lot of time at the gym. Pam was too cute to let herself get fat.

Leonard's birthday was in two weeks and fell on a Saturday night. Sheila had arranged to be with him from that night until Monday morning. The kids would stay over at Pam's so Beverly could help out with them. Sheila was excited about his birthday and had been shopping for gifts. She decided on three different colognes, a nice set of towels—the masculine kind, thick and expensive—and a nice book. She had the weekend all planned. First, the Dockside Theater to see the Miracles and Gladys Knight and the Pips that evening. On Sunday, lunch at the Claremont Hotel and swimming later at the hotel pool. After dinner Sunday night, they would attend a revival at Leonard's church.

She was truly excited. The only thing bothering her about Leonard was that an old girlfriend had called a couple of times the last Sunday she stayed over. It made her uncomfortable. Leonard said he had stopped dating her about three months before he met Sheila, but from time to time she still called. Leonard was up-front with her and explained in Sheila's presence that he was seeing someone and had company.

The next time the phone rang, Leonard was in the shower and Sheila answered it. She was extremely polite to the woman under the circumstances and said she would give Leonard the message that she had called. Sheila let him know that the girl wanted him to call back, but he opted not to. The third time she called, Leonard answered.

"Look, Bea, this is kind of getting out of hand. Please stop calling. You're disturbing me. Good-bye." She called again, and this time Sheila answered, with Leonard next to her in bed, and handed the phone to him.

"How bad is your problem, Bea? You know, the comprehension difficulties."

Sheila could hear a shrill voice carrying on. Leonard hung up. After that they let the phone ring. She continued to call until they took the phone off the hook.

The next two weeks sailed by. She and Leonard attended two church concerts during the week and a play at the Merriam Theater. They were falling in love, having a lot of long talks, and definitely becoming more comfortable sexually.

Tonight was the big night—Leonard's birthday. Sheila had on the baddest dress in Philadelphia, black silk and ankle-length. She borrowed a beautiful gold necklace and earrings from Lenora, and her hairdresser had done her hair perfectly. She wore a leopard-patterned, three-quarter-length silk jacket to go with the dress. She completed her outfit with black suede pumps and a small clutch. She looked like a million bucks. With her overnight bag packed, they headed out the door.

"Giving up is so hard to do when you really love someone," sang Gladys, and the Pips chimed in, doing their smooth thing. Smokey Robinson and the Miracles tore the place up singing "Shop Around" and "I Like It Like That."

Sheila and Leonard were grooving. She could tell he was proud of her. When they got home, she rushed upstairs to put on the fancy red nightie she had bought just for his birthday. She was retrieving his hidden birthday gifts when the phone started ringing. Leonard was downstairs and she could hear him answer the phone and quickly hang up, muttering. This happened several more times. When it rang the fifth time, she picked up the phone. "Can I help you?"

"Bitch, put him on the phone!" said the voice on the other end in a very nasty tone.

"Hold on," Sheila said sweetly.

Leonard had just stepped into the room with a tray of cocktails. Sheila held the phone out to him. He set the drinks down on the night table and took the receiver.

"Bea, I want you to stop this. It doesn't make sense and it's getting on my nerves. First thing Monday, I'm changing my number.

"Sheila, I apologize," Leonard said after hanging up. "That girl used to call me periodically, just to talk, but since I told her about us, she's getting crazy."

Sheila looked around the room at the gifts so nicely wrapped. She felt sexy and beautiful. She reminded herself that this nice man was celebrating his birthday and decided to continue the evening in a positive way. She told Leonard to get undressed so he could open his presents. He looked around at them, smiled, and hugged Sheila. He changed into a pair of silk pajamas, and they sat down on the bed. She gave him a big kiss. "Happy birthday," she said. She handed him the gifts one by one. He loved them all. Then they fell into each other's arms and fondled and caressed each other. She kissed him, letting the tip of her tongue circle his and taking little sucks so she wouldn't take over the kiss. Without being obvious about it, there were things she wanted to teach him about relaxing and letting go. She knew things would heat up from there, and she wanted him to have full confidence. She gently kissed his earlobes and ran her fingers through his hair. Now, lying on top of her, he was ready, no doubt about that. Sheila spread her legs and he entered her. They looked at each other with pleasure. It was nothing fancy, nothing wild— just straight sex that was very, very good.

The doorbell rang less than an hour later. Leonard looked out of the window and saw a car double-parked. "That's Bea's car! I can't believe she came here!"

Leonard was royally pissed. He hurried into his pajamas and went downstairs. Bea was banging on the door and ringing the bell. Sheila straightened up the bed, grabbed a magazine, and lay back as if she were on the beach. She deliberately did not put any panties on, and the nightie was pretty short, just covering her ass. She was ready.

Leonard was cursing Bea out and telling her to leave.

"Look," Bea said. "We're supposed to be together. You belong to me. I was giving you time so we could get our thing back. I don't care who you're hooked up with—we're going to get back together one way or the other." She stormed up the stairs yelling, "Where's the bitch?"

As the two of them entered the bedroom, Sheila was lying on her back, pretending to be engrossed in the magazine. She never looked up. Leonard was behind Bea, telling her to get out of his house. "Bitch, what are you doing here?" Bea said to Sheila.

Sheila let her legs fall open, exposing herself. She looked up at Bea and all but purred, "Now, honey, since there are no windows or doors broken, this nice man must have invited me, so I guess that's what I'm doing here."

"You've got to leave. Me and Leonard have a situation." Sheila ignored her. "Leonard, tell her to leave," Bea said.

"You're the one who has to go."

Bea looked around the room at the glasses of wine and the gifts and wrappings on the floor. She looked at the bed, a platform type with no box spring. She had given it to Leonard as a housewarming present when he moved in. She thought about the time and money she'd spent searching for it, and all the times that they had made love in that bed. And there was Sheila, lying in the middle of it.

Bea blurted out, "I bought this bed." Sheila continued to read, never looking up. Bea dragged the mattress off the bed and slid it on the floor with Sheila still on it. Sheila never said a word. When it hit the floor, she politely repositioned herself with the magazine and let her legs flop open, both knees bent, vagina facing Bea. Leonard couldn't believe how cool she was. Was this the same woman who dug her husband out of his grave and beat him up?

Bea began to knock things around. Glasses, records, and books were flying off the shelves. Sheila kept right on reading as Leonard struggled to get Bea out.

Then Sheila got up and walked by them both. "I'm thirsty. I'll be right back," she said, and went down to the kitchen. She poured herself some fruit juice and headed back to her mattress. As she was coming up the stairs, she heard Bea ask Leonard, "Why can't you just tell her to leave? What's your problem?" Before Leonard could answer, Sheila returned to the room.

"Honey, you want to know what his problem is? It's this right here." She lifted up the nightie and pointed to her pubic area. Leonard was shocked and so was Bea. By now, Bea was begging Leonard to get Sheila out of there. She reminded him of how long they'd been together and gave him reasons why they ought to stay together. Sheila had gone back to her post, her mattress and magazine. Bea went back to wrecking the place, and Sheila finally had enough of it.

"Look, honey, you are upset, you have got to calm down. Now if you really don't want to leave, you stay here with us. Why don't we both get in your bed together and fuck him? Then you won't feel left out. Hell, I don't mind sharing. After all, it is his birthday; let's give him something to make him really happy. But I will tell you this. If you aren't going to stay, you'd better leave now, because we are tired. I am tired from going at it all evening, and I need some sleep. Now, if you get your clothes off and get in bed with us, I'll oblige him one more time and call it a night. Otherwise, get your ass out of here before I call the police department to come and remove you. Really, sweetheart, I will call the law."

Bea looked at Sheila as if she wanted to kill her. She kicked Leonard in the leg, kicked the mattress, and stomped out of the house. When Sheila heard the door slam she looked at Leonard.

"Now you know I should have hit that bitch, but I spared her because it's your birthday. If she comes by here next Sunday with some shit, I'm going to put her next to Perry's grave."

# Chapter Twenty-eight

# *Amber*

aula went into the house calling for Floyd. No answer. In the bedroom the closet door lay half on the floor and half on the bed. There was no sign of Floyd. While she was trying to figure out where he'd gone and how, the officer entered.

"Where's the boyfriend?"

"I don't know," Paula said. "You see the door is busted open. He got out." The officer looked around the place suspiciously.

"Why don't you give me his name, address, and telephone number, and I'll try to track him down for you? Just to make sure he's okay."

"Look, I don't know. He has to be okay. I mean, he's gone and all. I need help with fixing the door. Will you do it?"

"I'm not a handyman or a carpenter, I'm a police officer."

"When you are not a police officer, I mean when your shift is over, can you help me with the door?"

"Why? So you can lock up another law-abiding citizen?"

"Do you want to be the one?" Paula said.

"You're right about being all mixed up, Miss Gray. I'm the officer, I do the locking up. Now, I'm going to forget about all the stories you've told me this afternoon and the one-way street and the missing or nonexistent boyfriend. If I hear anything about a Floyd missing or dead, I'll be looking for you. *Comprende?*"

He smiled and left. In his squad car, he had to admit that he was intrigued with Paula. He had a feeling it wasn't their last encounter.

"St. John's Hospital," the operator answered.

"Whatever department orderlies work in, I'd like to speak with Floyd Morse. This is his mother calling, and we have a family emergency."

"Hold the line, Mrs. Morse."

Paula waited impatiently, praying Floyd would answer. "I'm sorry, ma'am, I can't reach him. May I take a message?"

"Is he working today?"

"I'm not sure, no one in the department has picked up."

"My telephone number is 784-6513. Please have him call right away."

"Sure, Mrs. Morse, I will track him down, and someone will be back to you shortly."

In thirty-five minutes Paula's phone rang. It was Floyd.

"Why did you steal my car and my keys, and why did you lock me in the closet?"

"I am very upset, Floyd. I almost went to jail and I can't explain it all right now. I intended to play the game with you, but I wanted some cigarettes, and I just felt like fooling around and driving the car. A lot of things happened. Listen, I'm too tired to get into it all. Things were so bad. I was in such a terrible way that the police have been here. Oh, Floyd, I've had an awful day!"

"I don't want to be friends with you anymore, Paula. You play too many games. You messed with my job. I like my work and I don't like being late. It was hot in that closet. I got tired of it. I had to take the bus straight to the hospital and shower here. I'm wearing dirty underwear because I would have been late if I had gone home. I'm mad, and you have to find someone else to play games with. I'm coming for my car on my lunch break at nine tonight, and I'm through with you." He hung up.

Paula was exhausted from all the madness. She decided to take a bath and a nap and deal with Floyd when he arrived. She ran the water and added Neutrogena's Citrus Marine Scented Rainbath. It smelled delicious. She lit up a Newport as she waited for the tub to fill. She wondered how she could calm Floyd's ass down and keep him until she found someone else. "Problems, problems, problems," she sighed. She put the cigarette out and oozed down into the hot bubbles in the big, old-fashioned tub. After a long soak, a glorious lathering, and rolling around in the water and suds, she stepped out, dried off, and put on a beautiful cream-colored negligee with beading on the bodice. She backed the closet door against the wall so it would be out of the way. She put on sheer brown stockings and stepped into a pair of clear plastic mules with gold heels. Her hair was now brown and straight with blond streaks, and she brushed it all the way back off her face to accent her eyes and lips. She took drags from a Newport as she worked on her makeup, mixing berry and deep brown lipsticks together and using gold eye shadow highlighted with cream on the brow bone.

It was time for the flowing jacket that matched the negligee, with beading down the lapels. She looked into the full-length mirror for approval—perfect for blowing Floyd's mind and making him forget about spending half a day in the closet. It was now ten minutes to seven. She began to disrobe to take a quick nap before he arrived. She intended to sleep as straight as she could, flat on her back, negligee off. She carefully stepped out of the heels, removed the jacket, and laid it on the chair beside the bed. Just as she was about to lie down, the doorbell rang. "Oh, boy, here we go," she thought. He couldn't wait until lunchtime to break up or start some shit, whichever he came to do—maybe both. She quickly sprayed a little Red Door behind her ears and on her wrists and thighs. She put the entire ensemble back on and checked herself in the mirror before answering the door. The negligee and jacket flowed as she walked.

"Just a minute," she called out. She opened the door with a smile, ready for Floyd—but the face she saw wasn't Floyd's.

"I'm a handyman and carpenter," the man said, "and I hear you have a problem with a door." He was out of uniform and had a gleaming smile. She was shocked. Completely outdone. She moved back so he could enter. Playing it cool, she turned away from him and walked down the hall to the kitchen. He followed her. She opened a drawer and paused, looking back at him. He stood against the wall, checking her out. He had an unusual complexion—not white-white, maybe Puerto Rican, but she didn't think so. Maybe he had been away and had a little tan. He had dark brown hair cut short and deep brown eyebrows. His lips were fuller than the average white guy's. He looked like a cute boy, but had wonderful short sideburns that made his face sexy. The cop/fix-it man was a rare one. Images ran through her head of showing up at the Rockaway bar with this fine thing on her arm.

And he was white. Oh, shit. White and fine and a cop. She was getting ready to make everybody mad. The men would have a fit, and the sisters would be green with envy. She saw it all in her mind—Paula with a gorgeous white cop. She would get some respect then. Damn. It was the coolest thing that ever happened to her. She had some shit for Horace now—better than Earl. She was almost on her way back to paradise with a white guide.

She hadn't said a word to him since opening the door. She wanted to blow his mind, to be mysterious. She pulled a hammer out of the drawer, held it up, and looked into his eyes.

"I suppose you have some nails or screws? I can't provide everything," she said.

He held up a toolbox. "I come packed." He went to the bedroom and straight to the door lying against the wall. She watched him align it with the hinges and completely restore it, doorknob and all. When he was done he looked her up and down. She was still holding the hammer in her hand.

"Now I see why he went into the closet, especially if you looked as ravishing as you do right now. He must have busted out to go looking for you, baby. I'm glad the supermarket didn't call me to arrest you."

"Officer, may I have your name and badge number?"

"I'm not an officer right now, I'm a handyman. Don't you see my tools? I don't know any cops tonight. I'm Terrance Nesman."

At that point the doorbell rang. Paula had completely forgotten about Floyd. Damn! She wanted to kill him.

Her face said it all. "You can walk me to the door and let your company in." He picked up his toolbox.

Floyd was standing at the door looking mean and mad. When he saw Terrance he looked meaner and madder. Terrance pushed by the two of them and left.

"Who was that?"

"That was the carpenter who fixed the door you busted out of. Let me get your keys. I know you have to get back to work."

Floyd headed down the hall to verify that the closet door actually was fixed. He was surprised. Apparently she wasn't lying. And she looked so damn good. He realized seeing Terrance had made him jealous. He thought he'd better try to work it out between them, because Terrance might become someone significant in her life and he really didn't want to be without her. After all, she hadn't really mistreated him. He was only stuck in the closet for a few hours. She was feeling a little low—and at least she was going to play a sex game with him to give him a little extra fun. He'd never had anybody who made him feel like she did in bed. You name it, and he was trying to think it up to stay with Paula. The more he looked at her, keeping her seemed like less of a problem.

"Didn't you say you had to get back to work?" Paula tapped her foot impatiently.

"I'm sorry about the door, Paula, and I'll pay for it. I just had to get out. Don't you want to talk?"

"Listen, Floyd, it's been a long day. I'll talk to you tomorrow."

"I need to use the phone."

"Use the phone. I'm going to bed."

"This is Floyd Morse," he said into the receiver. "Something's come up, and I won't be back tonight."

I hated living with Paula and I missed Renee so much. Paula seemed to be getting meaner and meaner, and the only peace I had was at school and whenever else I was away from her. I really liked the school and Miss Peterson. She was a good teacher and a nice person and thought I was smart as a whip. I still babysat for the couple upstairs from time to time. But Paula still beat me on a regular basis for anything and everything.

One evening I came into the apartment about eight o'clock, returning from babysitting for Natalie. I headed toward the bedroom at the end of the hall and heard voices. It was Paula moaning. The door was open, and I walked in to find her in bed with a big black guy. Her legs gaped open, and he was on top of her. I watched her and listened a little and then decided to go out on the front steps to wait for it to be over. I hated Paula during those times.

Sydni had gone to a movie with a friend from school and came walking up about an hour later.

"Don't go into the house right now. Paula has company." Sydni said nothing, just plopped down on the steps and waited with me.

"I sure am hungry," I said.

"Is anything here for dinner?"

"I don't know. I came right back out after I saw Paula and her boyfriend in bed."

After about half an hour, the guy walked out of the apartment and ran down the steps. This was a new one. We had never seen him before. He got in his car and sped away. I went into the house with Sydni behind me, heading for the kitchen to look for dinner. In the refrigerator were a jug of water, Kool-Aid in a pitcher, bacon, and a pot of spaghetti Paula had made a couple of nights ago. I grabbed the bacon and began pulling off and eating the lean parts.

Sydni was at the bedroom door. Paula was in the bed asleep, so I shook her awake.

"Can you get us something to eat? We're hungry."

"Didn't you have something to eat?"

"No, I only had some bacon. It's raw, but I ate it anyway. I want some dinner."

Paula sat up, angry at being disturbed. Sydni hadn't moved and was looking at the two of us.

"What the hell are you eating raw bacon for? There has to be something else in that refrigerator!" she snapped at me.

She got up, still naked, and stomped past us. We were both scared to death. Sydni ran into the living room, and Paula marched me by the shoulder down the hall to the kitchen. She opened the refrigerator door and shoved my head inside.

"Do you see that pot of spaghetti? Why didn't you eat that? Why are you bothering me? You had to see this spaghetti in here, so why would you eat raw bacon?"

I just stared at her, too frightened to answer. She grabbed the pot out of the refrigerator. She took the top off and pushed me toward it.

"This is your dinner, you little bitch. Now since you are stupid enough to eat raw bacon, eat this shit." Paula turned around as if she were looking for a plate or something, but then just turned the pot upside down and dumped it on the floor. She knocked me down to the floor and shouted at me, "Since you're so hungry, eat it all, and eat it right there!" She began to kick me.

I was astonished and crying.

"Paula, don't make Amber eat off the floor," Sydni cried. Paula slapped her down to the floor, too.

"Since you're so worried about Amber, you eat with her!"

I stared at the mess, remembering the nights Sydni and I played "Exterminator" because we had so many roaches. I thought about how we took slices of bread and left them on the counter and floor and turned the lights off. We'd wait about half an hour to come back armed with shoes in each of our hands and on our feet. We'd turn the lights on and the roaches would be everywhere. Then we would stomp the ones on the floor and smash the ones on the counter. I couldn't bear to eat off that floor.

"Eat it, dammit, eat it all, or I'll kill you."

Sydni and I ate. Paula pushed the spaghetti around with her bare feet, kicking it across the floor so we had to go after it. We were yowling as hard as we could.

"It better be gone by the time I wake up, and don't bother me for food when there's plenty in my refrigerator," Paula said. She returned to the bedroom and went to sleep.

I ate as much of it as I could stand. I got the rest up with the broom, put it in the trash can, and went to bed. Paula woke up about two o'clock in the morning and went to the kitchen. The spaghetti was gone, but she noticed the broom with sauce on it. She was furious and looked in the trash can. She woke me up and dragged me into the kitchen. She stuffed my head into the trash can.

"Didn't I tell you to eat it all? Didn't you tell me you were hungry? Why did you lie to me?" I tried to get away from her, but she wouldn't let go. She dragged me down the hall to her bedroom. She disconnected the television and took the extension cord from the socket. She beat me with it for about fifteen minutes. I screamed in pain and prayed for the beating to be over. Sydni never said a word and never moved from the couch.

I waited until Paula was asleep. Then I fled the apartment in my pajamas. I ran down the street and kept running. I spotted a cab and hopped in it. I was crying and told the driver to take me to Grandma's house. When he pulled up at the corner, I went to Peggy Kinard's house instead of going to Grandma's. I rang the bell and banged on the door.

"Amber, what are you doing out this time of night?"

I was choking with tears, the driver standing beside me.

"I brought her from Germantown, and she's been beaten pretty badly. The fare is seven dollars," he said.

Peggy ran inside for the money, paid the driver, and pulled me in with her. I had welts all over me. Peggy called Grandma to come over. They applied witch hazel to my wounds. Peggy ran a warm bath and put me in the tub. I asked Peggy if I could stay because I knew Paula would find me at Grandma's the next day and probably kill me. She agreed, and Grandma said she would get me in a day or so. She couldn't call Paula because the phone wasn't working. She hadn't paid the bill. Peggy laid my battered body in her bed and snuggled next to me while I cried silently. She held me in her arms until I fell asleep, and Peggy wondered how someone could do this to her own child.

In the morning, Grandma arrived with clothes for me. She told me to get dressed and that she'd take me home with her. She promised to straighten Paula out.

"Now she'll kill me for sure," I thought.

Grandma called Paula at work and told her she had me. Paula just hung up on her. The day went by and Paula never came. That night Grandma took me back to Paula's. She answered the door, and Grandma pushed her way in.

"Bitch, if you ever touch this child again, I'll kick your ass and turn you in to the police myself. Did anybody ever beat you this way? Look at this child. Are you crazy? I am ashamed of you! I'm leaving her here with you, and you'd better take care of her. You'd better see that she's in school tomorrow, and if you think I am kidding, try me, just try me, Paula! I swear I'll have you locked up!"

I started to scream and cry, "Please Grandma, don't leave me here!"

"Look, Amber, I am sorry about this, but you have to stay here so you can get to school," Grandma quieted me. "Paula won't hurt you again, I promise. Get some sleep and go to school tomorrow. You can come to my house for the weekend." I obeyed and went into the bedroom, still crying. Sydni came over and hugged me.

"I'm sorry, Amber, sleep next to me real close."

I cried myself to sleep and begged God to get me away from Paula. Things were a little better for a while, and I did my best to stay out of Paula's way and keep my mouth shut.

About three months after that, I sat in the emergency room, watching doctors and nurses moving about. The little boy seated next to me had his foot wrapped in a towel with ice on it. He looked about four years old.

"What happened to him?" I asked his mother, who was holding the towel in place.

"I was straightening my daughter's hair with the electric hot comb. It was plugged in on the floor and my other daughter distracted me when she fell out of a chair. Simon was playing around in the kitchen and stepped on it and burned his foot."

"Don't worry, you'll be okay," I said to Simon.

"I'm Kathy." The woman smiled. "Why are you here?"

I turned in my chair to let her see my back. She gasped at the blood on my blouse.

"What happened to you?"

"I got bitten," I said.

"A dog bit you?"

I looked into her eyes. "My mother bit me."

"Your mother! Your mother bit you like that? For what? Where is she?"

"Right now, I don't know where she is, but she got angry with me because I wasn't nice enough to one of her friends. So she bit me."

"Who brought you here?"

"I'm alone. I took the bus."

"Honey, hold this towel on Simon's foot until I come back—and tell me your name."

"My name is Amber Gray."

She stepped up to the desk and talked to the receptionist. I couldn't hear what she was saying. I wondered what was going on. I hoped the nice lady would take me home and I'd never have to see Paula again. I thought about how it all happened, how I had come home from school and heard noises in the bedroom. I walked in and found the big black burly man naked in the bed. Paula was lying across him, rubbing him, and he had his hands all over her.

"Get it, get it," she was saying.

I stood in the room and shouted at him, "Get out of my house!" I shouted over and over. Paula hollered at me to get out before she killed me. I ran into the kitchen. I was angry. As soon as he left, Paula came for me. I was sitting on the radiator looking out the window.

"I ought to throw you right out of that window," she said.

She smacked me around the kitchen. I lost my balance and fell. She grabbed at me while I was squirming away and caught me by my blouse. She dragged me back to her, sat on my legs, and gathered the flesh on my back between her teeth and bit down. When she tasted blood, she let go. I nearly fainted.

She rolled over me and looked me right in the face.

"If you ever disrespect another one of my friends, I'll kill you."

I hobbled to the bathroom. I perched myself on the sink, pulled my blouse up, and turned so I could see the wound in the mirror. Blood was still trickling out of it. Then I went to the coffee can hidden behind the leg of the bathtub. It had a dollar from the money I was saving to pay Horace. I crept out of the apartment and ran down the street to wait on the corner for the bus. I knew how to get to the hospital.

\* \* \*

A doctor followed the nice lady back to the waiting room. He came over to me and smiled.

"Honey, you come with me, and I'll see about that bite you have." I let go of the towel on Simon's foot and followed him. He took me by the hand and sat me on an examining table.

"We have no consent form," the nurse said.

"I'm treating her anyway."

He told me to take my blouse off and lie on my stomach. I had quite a gash. It hurt, and I cried. The doctor swabbed it with something that stung and put stitches in it while the nurse held me. After it was over, she sat me up on the table.

"Amber, please talk to me so I can help you. You need to tell me where you live and your mother's name. I want to help you so nothing like this ever happens again."

"She'll kill me if I tell, and if she doesn't kill me, I'll have to go to a home or a jail or someplace like that to live. I'll be okay, just let me go home."

The doctor tried to persuade me to talk to him, but the phone rang and he had to take the call. I slipped off the table and left. I headed for Horace's house. I would need him, because the doctor said the stitches had to come out in a few days and I would have to return to the hospital for that. It was close to nine thirty at night. I waited impatiently for the bus, hoping to get there before he left for work. I wished I had enough money to call Grandma to get his telephone number, but I only had enough for the bus. I stood there, trying to think of what else I could do.

I decided to go back to the hospital and ask Simon's mother to help me. I looked around but didn't see Kathy or Simon in the waiting room. I slipped past the receptionist and spotted Kathy with the doctor, who was examining Simon's foot. I walked over to them and said to the doctor, "I'm sorry I left before you could talk to me, but I have to go home. I want to get to my other daddy's house, and I need help calling him." I looked at Simon's mother. "Can you help me? Can you give me money for the telephone?"

"Sit here with the doctor, Simon. I'll be right back." She took me by the hand to the pay phone. "What is the number, Amber?"

"I don't know."

"What is his name?"

"Horace Alston."

"Where does he live, Amber? Do you know his address?"

"He lives on Van Kirk Street. I don't know his address."

The woman got Horace's number from Information. After three rings, he answered.

"Mr. Alston, my name is Kathy Sanders. I have your daughter, Amber, with me at Fitzpatrick Mercy Hospital, Northern, and she needs to talk to you." She handed me the phone.

"Can you come get me? I'm scared to go home."

"What are you doing at the hospital this late at night, and where's Paula?"

"I am in trouble, Horace. I got bitten and stitched up. I need you to come over here. Please come." I started to cry again.

"Amber, put the woman back on the phone."

Kathy took the phone, listened to Horace, and hung up.

"What did he say?"

"Come with me, Amber. I'll take you to the waiting room, and you stay there. I have to be with Simon until the doctors finish with him. You wait here for Horace. He's coming for you." I breathed a sigh of relief.

At ten fifteen he came through the doors. He spotted me and ran over to scoop me up.

"What happened, baby? You were bitten by a dog? Where is Paula?" I just started crying.

By this time, Kathy came out carrying Simon, whose foot was bandaged up. She came over and introduced herself to Horace. He thanked her for her kindness.

"Your daughter really needs help. Talk to her." She wrote down her name and phone number and gave it to me. "You call and let me know how you're doing, okay?"

"Thank you." I smiled as I took the piece of paper.

Horace took me by the hand, and we went outside. He saw Kathy and her son heading for the bus stop and called out to offer her a lift, which she accepted. He helped Kathy into her house, carrying Simon. It was ten minutes to eleven, and Horace had decided he was not going to work.

Emily sat on the couch in Horace's living room folding Renee's clothes and watching Alfred Hitchcock. She liked taking care of Renee the nights Horace worked. The child was so cute and sweet. Horace was a good boss and paid her well. His house was nice. He respected her, making no passes at her. She was also glad she didn't have to be at her sister's house as often, with her nieces and nephews making such a constant racket.

Emily was a pretty girl with a mahogany complexion and fine, naturally curly brown hair, highlighted with a few red streaks. She was tall and thin, without an ounce of fat on her body. Her big brown eyes were set off by perfect eyebrows. People told her she should do lipstick ads because her mouth was so pretty. She wore her hair in a ponytail most of the time—no bangs to overshadow her beautiful features.

Emily had a day job as an accounts payable/receivable clerk. She'd had it for the past two months and was grateful, because she was fired from her last job for setting her desk on fire. Emily was a smoker, but her first office job forbade smoking. Her boss, an older man named Sam, explained that when he hired her. But Emily basically did her job well and ignored everything else Sam said.

One day she felt a warm sensation around her feet. She ignored it, thinking it was the heating system. When it became even hotter, she rolled her chair away and looked underneath the desk. Flames were shooting out of the wastebasket. She tried to grab it, but it was too hot. She ran toward the end of the gigantic warehouse, screaming for Sam and yelling "Fire!" She grabbed some fabric to wrap around the basket, and Sam raced back to help. By the time he got there the desk itself was on fire. The office burned until the fire department arrived and put it out. It took her four months to find another job—and she quit smoking.

Emily was surprised to see us.

"Hi," I said.

"Hi, and who might you be?" Emily looked up at me.

"This is Renee's sister, Amber," Horace cut in. "She's spending the night."

"Where's Renee?" I said.

"Amber, this is Emily. She babysits Renee, and Earl is her brother," Horace explained to me.

"Oh, I know Earl. I like him. He's got some pretty fish at his house."

"I've got to call my job. I'll be right back," Horace said. I sat down next to Emily.

"So, what brings you here tonight? It's kind of late. Don't you have school tomorrow?"

"I got bitten and I was at the hospital. Horace had to come get me." I turned around and lifted my blouse so Emily could see the bandage.

"You got bitten by a dog, baby? That's a shame."

Horace walked into the room and told me to come upstairs with him. On the way he said, "Are you hungry or thirsty or anything? Have you had any dinner?"

"I am hungry. I want some home fries. Do you have any Kool-Aid or soda? Can I take a bath? What am I going to do about some pajamas? You have to take me back to the hospital in some days to get the stitches out. Can I sleep with Renee?"

Horace looked at me, smiling and shaking his head. He really did love me. "Emily, do me a favor," he yelled down the stairs. "I'm not going to work. Can you cook Amber some home fries and a grilled cheese sandwich while I talk to her and let her get bathed?"

"Sure," Emily yelled back.

"Well, Miss Amber, let's have it. What happened? Whose dog bit you and where is Paula?" I didn't say a word. He lifted me onto his lap. "Tell me what happened."

I was thinking what to say because I knew he would get Paula, and if he did, she would get me for it sooner or later.

"Hey, Horace, can we skip it and you just take me back to the hospital in some days?"

Horace knew me too well and suspected something wild had occurred. "No, no skip. Let's have it."

I started to cry.

"Come on, sweetie, tell me."

I told him everything, spaghetti and all. Horace's face tightened as I talked. "I'll fix it, and I'll see that you get back to the doctor," he said when I was finished.

He went into the bathroom and ran water in the tub. He told me to be careful not to get the dressing wet. Then I could eat. He went downstairs and asked Emily to please find something for me to sleep in, give me some aspirin, fix my plate, and put me to bed in his room after dinner. He said he had to go out.

Horace sat in his car for an hour. He was absolutely livid. He drove across town to his pal Benny Slator's house. It was almost one o'clock in the morning, but Horace leaned on the bell. Finally he heard Benny yelling as he came down the stairs, complaining about the time of night it was. "Who is it?" he shouted. "I'm coming, already, I'm coming."

"Benny, open the door, it's Horace."

"Man, what are you doing here this time of night? What the hell is going on? I thought you worked nights."

Horace told him. Benny was in shock. "Benny, I need a favor."

"What is it, man?"

"I want to borrow Killer."

Killer was Benny's mutt, part German shepherd and part whatever. But whatever he was or wasn't, he was big, with the hugest head in the world and a zillion teeth in his mouth. Even Horace was scared of him.

"Horace, what are you going to do with Killer?"

"I got a job for him," Horace said.

Benny looked at him and started to laugh. "No way, man. You're not about to do what I think you're gonna do, are you?" Benny could see Horace was serious. He didn't even know why he bothered to ask.

"Look, man, she needs a lesson, she really does. Now what do I say to that animal of yours to get him to bite that bitch?"

"Look, Horace, I guess I'm getting ready to go to jail, because Killer will only attack if I tell him to. So I guess we'll both go over to that wench's house, and you'd better leave bail money somewhere so I can get out of jail."

"Everything's going to be cool," Horace replied. "Come on, now, and let's go."

"I'm not budging until you make some arrangement about the money. If I get locked up—I mean if *we* get locked up—I want to know my ass is getting out of jail. I mean it, man."

"All right. Let's stop by my house. I've got some money there."

I woke up as soon as Horace came into the bedroom and said, "You finally got back. I was trying to wait up for you. The bite isn't hurting as much."

"Hey, baby, I just came to pick something up. I'll be back in about an hour. You'd better get to sleep."

Horace went into his closet and pulled out a metal box. He unlocked it with a key he kept on top of his medicine cabinet. I was following him around. He placed the box on the bed, counted out some cash, and locked the box. He put the key away, kissed me, and went downstairs where Emily was watching television.

"Listen, Emily. This is eight hundred dollars. Hold it. If I call and say I need it, I want you to bring it to me, okay? If you have to bring it to me, please take Amber and Renee over to your sister's house and leave them there while you're out. That's all I can tell you. Do you understand what to do?"

"You getting in a poker game or something?"

"Yes."

"Okay, I'll come if you need me."

"Thanks, Emily."

Horace and Benny sped away. Their first stop was Benny's place, to fetch Killer. He barked at Horace for a few minutes until Benny quieted him down.

"Man, don't you think we need a muzzle for him in the car? I don't want him to eat me up before we get there," Horace said.

"Aw, come on, you old punk. You'll survive."

"Hey, Benny, what do you say to him to get him to attack someone?"

"Give me a pen and a piece of paper and I'll write it down. If he hears it, he will bite you." Benny snatched an old envelope from the glove compartment and wrote. When they stopped at a red light, Benny handed it to Horace. Horace laughed and shook his head.

At 2:10 in the morning Horace, Benny, and Killer arrived at Paula's apartment. Horace told Benny to get out of the car by himself and ring the doorbell. Benny obeyed, leaving Killer in the car with Horace. Horace looked over at the dog and smiled. He was praying the creature wouldn't get upset and bite his head off. Paula had never met Benny. Her bedroom light came on, and in a few seconds she was at the door.

"Something has happened at your mom's, and they sent me to tell you since your phone isn't working," Benny recited. Paula glanced at the phone off the hook and believed him. As soon as she fully opened the door, Horace jumped out of the car and ran inside.

"You are the worst bitch tramp I ever met in my life!" he yelled.

"What are you doing here?" Paula shouted back. "Why are you bothering me? Who is this with you? You'd better get out of here!"

Sydni ran into the room and stared at them all. She was scared.

"Take Sydni out to the car and bring our friend in," Horace said to Benny.

"Get off of my daughter! You ain't taking her nowhere!" Paula yelled at Benny.

"Take her out, man!"

Benny left with Sydni. At that point Floyd, who was spending the night, emerged from Paula's room. "Who the hell are you? You'd better get out of here."

"Man, you better stay out of this before you get hurt," Horace said to Floyd.

Floyd lunged for Paula, but Horace pushed him away. At that moment Benny arrived with Killer. When the dog saw them, he started barking, scaring Floyd and Paula shitless.

"Back off, man, before you really get hurt," Horace warned. He had Paula in an armlock. He pushed her into the kitchen. Benny and Killer kept an eye on Floyd, who was standing in the kitchen doorway, petrified, clad only in his underwear. Paula was in a robe. Horace noticed a couple of pots on the stove and, with his free hand, lifted the tops off the pots, one by one. He smacked his lips.

"Mmm, pork chops smothered in gravy, macaroni and cheese, and what's this, baby? Oh, you cooked my favorite vegetable, spinach. By any chance did you make any spaghetti?" Paula didn't answer. Horace twisted her wrist. She screamed in pain. "I said did you cook any spaghetti?"

"I don't have any spaghetti!"

"That's too bad, Paula, because I was really looking forward to some spaghetti tonight, but I guess all this stuff will have to do." He grabbed the pots one at a time and turned them upside down, dumping the food onto the floor. "I really am sorry there's no spaghetti."

Paula looked at him as if he were crazy. She tried to dodge him, but instead he pushed her down on the floor and shoved her face into the macaroni and cheese.

"Now, bitch, eat your fucking dinner!"

Paula squirmed and gagged. Horace had his foot on her neck. Killer was barking like crazy and lunging for the food. Horace reached over and opened the refrigerator door. He found two steaks in a package. He tore it open and threw the meat down to the dog.

"Eat that stuff or the dog will eat your naked ass!" Paula began to eat along with Killer. Like her dinner guest, Paula was on all fours. Her robe no longer covered her behind, so she was exposed to the three men and the dog. Horace took a large spoon from the drain board and mixed the food on the floor. Paula's face was full of gravy. She was the one crying now.

After she had been eating for about fifteen minutes, her face, hands, and knees were full of glop.

"Tell Killer," Horace said to Benny. Benny froze. Horace looked at him, demanding with his eyes. "Do it, man."

Benny moved Killer closer to Paula. He pointed his finger at her. "Killer, get the motherfucker."

"Oh no, please, man, oh no!" Floyd screamed.

Killer lunged at Paula, biting her on the shoulder and going for her neck. Blood ran from the wound, and she yelped in pain. Floyd moaned and begged Horace to stop the dog. When Killer started to bite her on the neck, Horace motioned for Benny to stop him.

"Killer, no, come to Daddy," Benny ordered. The dog let go.

Paula lay on the floor wailing for God. Horace knelt down and yanked her up by her hair. He looked deep into her eyes.

"If you ever touch Amber again, if you ever do anything inhumane to her or Sydni again, I will personally finish you off. If you tell the police about this little dinner party we had tonight, I will take Amber to the Department of Human Services and get your ass locked up. Do you understand me, bitch?"

"Yes," Paula whimpered.

They left the house. Horace went over to the car window and told Sydni to roll it down.

"You're coming home with me," he said. "Amber is already there. My friend will put his dog in the car, and you don't have to be scared, because he won't bite you, okay?"

Horace signaled Benny to get into the car with Killer, and they drove off.

# Chapter Twenty-nine

# *Reba*

*I*t was seven twenty in the evening when Reba and Doug pulled up at Doug's door. Reba was tired. It had been a long drive from Norfolk. They had chatted, told jokes, stopped for food, and wondered how Lucy and Kevin were making out or if they were "making out." They had avoided the business of what they were going to do about each other. They didn't want to blow the nice moments they had right now.

Doug's house was red brick with shutters at the windows and the cutest porch on the side. Two large trees in the front yard had tires hanging from them. Reba walked around admiring the place. It was quiet and peaceful and such a contrast from the city life she was used to. Doug was managing better now and walked slowly up the three steps and unlocked the door to his home.

The living room walls were the palest shade of light green, as if cream had been added to olive. Very soothing. Reba liked it a lot.

"Get comfortable—look around and unwind," Doug said.

Reba walked through the first level, admiring everything. She noticed pictures on his mantel—photos of himself, another man, children, and a woman.

"Who are these people?" asked Reba.

"My sister, her husband, and their two kids."

"Oh, so that explains the tire swings outside."

Doug nodded. He told Reba to take a look upstairs while he got the bags out of the car.

"You can't carry that stuff in."

"I know. I'll get it out of the trunk and you can give me a hand getting it inside."

"Okay."

Reba wandered through each of the three bedrooms. One was set up as an office with a desk and stacks of furniture catalogs. A spare room held twin beds. Doug's room was attractively done with a cherry bedroom set and charming bamboo shades at the windows. He really had a lovely place.

She headed outside to bring the bags in. When everything was inside, the two of them sat on the couch. Doug picked up her hand and held it in his.

"Well, I've got four questions," he said.

"Shoot," she said.

"Are you hungry or thirsty? Do you want to freshen up? Do you want to call home to speak with Johnny? What the hell are we going to do?"

Reba grinned and shook her head. "Well, I am not hungry. I am thirsty and I am going to get us something to drink in a minute. If you are hungry, we need to talk about the fact that I am the worst cook in the world. I plan to take a hot bath shortly and relax. I am not going to call home. I am savoring these moments with you because tomorrow I am returning to Philadelphia. And we can talk more about that later, okay?" She reached over and planted a kiss on Doug's lips. "I like your place." She checked out the kitchen, made some lemonade, and returned with two glasses. "I found some lemons, and I see you like chocolate milk. I threw it out, it's bad."

"So are you. However, I'm not throwing you out," said Doug.

They chuckled, and Reba finished the lemonade.

"I'm going to get the bags upstairs and run a bath. You want one first—or a shower? Or do you just want to sit here for a while and relax?" Reba said.

"I'll watch some TV while you spend some time with yourself. I know you have things on your mind. Go on up, I'm okay."

Reba lay back in the tub. This life was so peaceful, so perfect. She hated to leave it in less than twenty-four hours. She relived the last five days in her mind, wondering about the kids. She knew Johnny Penster was having a fit. She hadn't called him back since hanging up on him and imagined he had worried the staff at the hotel to death, as well as Peggy Kinard. She wished she could just snap her fingers, get her kids to Annapolis, and never see Johnny again, but it wouldn't be that simple. She could certainly use Lucy here to help her figure out what she was going to tell Johnny. She wondered how things were going with Kevin and Lucy, when she would be returning to Philly—or if she was ever going back.

As soon as she saw Johnny he would have a million questions. He would be shouting, pointing, threatening, and she dreaded the whole ordeal to come. She also had some explaining to do to her children. Damn, her life was a mess.

Then she thought about her man downstairs. She adored that man, and she had to figure out some way to hold on to this. She was different now. She had "come out." She felt like a butterfly that had finally emerged from its dull, ugly cocoon. There was no turning back. She couldn't imagine ever letting Johnny touch her again.

She got out of the tub, dried off, and went into Doug's bedroom to find something to put on. She sat on the bed naked, just looking around. She went into his closet and got one of his shirts. She let her hair down from the ponytail, and it fell against the light blue, crisply ironed shirt. Her feet were cold, so she looked through his drawers for a pair of socks. Then she went downstairs and found Doug asleep on the couch with a newspaper on his chest.

She gathered their belongings from the living room floor and brought them upstairs. She unpacked Doug's things and put them away as best she could. When she returned to the living room, she went over to the couch and, as gently as she could, lay down with him and placed her head on his chest. She didn't want to disturb him, but she needed to be with him. She needed this peace with him. Doug stirred when he felt her body touch his and welcomed her by putting his arms around her.

They both slept for a few hours. It was a little after midnight when they headed up the stairs together to his bedroom. Doug undressed and Reba curled up on his bed. She was deep in thought. "This is our last night—what's it going to be?"

Doug disappeared into the bathroom and Reba heard the shower running. Her attention was drawn to the large, dark wooden dresser. It was beautiful and had an enchanting mirror behind it. In a few minutes he returned, wearing only a towel around his waist. He stopped for a moment. She certainly did look sexy to him lying there in his shirt and socks. Doug sat on the bed and unwrapped the towel. He reached toward a drawer for underwear.

Reba stopped him. "No." She got up from the bed and led him toward the mirrored dresser. She eased up on the edge of the dresser, holding both his hands.

"How's the sore foot?"

"It's okay."

"Can you place any weight on it?"

"Maybe," he said, kissing her ear.

Reba opened her legs, let go of his hands, and put one hand around his waist, pulling him closer to her. With her other hand, she massaged his penis while they shared a passionate kiss. Drops of water from Doug's hair trickled down his neck and onto his chest. Reba sucked the water off of him. Then she eased his penis into her vagina. They started to move together. The pleasure was relentless.

Reba had his buttocks in her hands, massaging them and pulling him more inside her. They were running a race to ecstasy. The mirror began to shake, but they couldn't stop. All of a sudden the mirror fell onto the dresser, just missing them. Swiftly, Doug scooped Reba up, remaining inside her. They clutched each other and prayed his penis would not come out. He hobbled to the bed and leaned back, and she was still with him. She thought, "This has to be the work of the Lord."

They continued to move within each other, and Reba thanked God that Doug's penis had stayed there for her. The orgasm that followed seemed to come from heaven. She melted and waited for her man to come.

It was nearly nine in the morning when they awoke in each other's arms. They got the mirror up and back in place. "Hey, Reba," said Doug, "what did you say about not knowing how to cook?"

"I never said I didn't know how to cook, I said I was a bad cook."

"Okay, what does a bad cook do about breakfast?"

"Her man either cooks it or takes her out to eat."

Doug laughed. "Get dressed so we can go for breakfast."

They showered together, got dressed, and left. They didn't talk to each other about her leaving. When they returned from breakfast, she asked for the phone book to check the bus companies. While she was doing that, Doug said, "I've never been so confused in my life."

"What are you confused about?" asked Reba.

"I feel serious about you. It's scary—especially with the kids. If I continue this, it means a lot of responsibility. I'll be responsible for seven additional people. It's a load, you know."

"You want out—you've got out, baby. This is not prison. You can walk away."

"What scares me is I don't want to walk away. It's a challenge. You mean that much to me. I just have to get this right, you know. I said, I'm serious. Kids. Humph. The closest I've come to that is my nieces spending weeks at a time with me," Doug said.

"You're going to have some time to think and so will I. Let's slow things up for a moment. Let's breathe away from each other," Reba said.

She packed, went outside, and got into the tire swing. She stayed in that swing nearly an hour, crying, swinging, and thinking. Then she came back into the house, got her things, and called a cab. Doug gave her eighty dollars to cover her ticket and a little extra in case she needed it when she got home. When the cab arrived, she kissed him on the forehead and walked out the door. She never said good-bye.

It was a pleasant bus ride, and Reba had a lot of time to think. She was ready for a change, and she believed Doug was the one.

She closed the door behind her and heard noises in the kitchen. She dropped her bags and went in. Four of the kids were at the table. The oven was on. They looked up at Reba.

"Hey, Mom! Hey, Mom, you're home!" They ran to her, pushing each other aside to be the first to hug and kiss her. "What happened to you, you missed the bus?" seven-year-old Andrew said. "You've been gone a long time. Daddy's been mad. Oh, man, Mom, he has been so mad!"

"What's going on, guys?" asked Reba. "How are you all doing? I think you missed me. Well, give me some more kisses." They all surrounded her, kissing and hugging her again.

"Where are the other two nuts? And I guess your daddy didn't get home from work yet, huh? What are you guys cooking?"

"We're making pizza," said Craig.

"Mmm, smells good. Where's Nina?"

"Nina went to the library with Anita Hayes and is supposed to be back by six o'clock. Aaron went to the market with Daddy to get some more food," said Rudy.

"Okay. Can you guys take my stuff upstairs for me?"

They scrambled for her bags and ran up the stairs with them. Reba looked around the house. It was the usual, a mess. She took off her shoes, found some sneakers, hung up her coat, and went to work on the house. She peeked in the oven at the "pizza," and it looked like a disaster. If her kids ate this it would kill them.

Rudy came down and said, "So, Mom, how did you do on the job with Mrs. Kinard? Did you like it?"

"Yes, Rudy, I had a good time and it was a nice trip. I met a lot of people and you know what, I had fun down there. But I did miss you guys a lot."

Reba got the kitchen cleaned up and her things put away and then heard someone come in. "Who's that?" she yelled from the second floor.

"Mom, you're here?" yelled Nina. Nina ran up the steps and hugged Reba. "Mom, I'm so glad you are home, I missed you. Those boys are crazy. We should have them put away. Did you have a good time, Mom? Tell me all about it. How did Lucy do?"

Reba hugged her. Nina was growing up to be quite a lady. Reba had missed her and started to feel a little guilty. Reba sat on the bed and told Nina all about the beautiful hotel and the food and how well Lucy did in the show. Nina lapped up every detail. Then she said, "Daddy wasn't here most of the time at night, and he was gone a lot Saturday and Sunday during the day. You know him." Reba just nodded her head.

"When you didn't come home, he was calling all over the place, and he was angry at Mrs. Kinard, too. I did most of the cooking and babysitting. Guess what, Mom? Craig went out to the park with a bunch of kids and they were playing on the railroad track out there. Somehow his foot got stuck as the train was coming. It was his shoestring or something, or the hole in his sneaker. Anyway, they had to get him away before the train came, and he left his sneaker out there. Daddy had a fit. Also, Craig and those Saunders boys all got together and went into the trash at that alcoholic hospital around the corner. They all got needles out of the trash. They played doctor on those adopted kids around the corner. Well, they gave them vaccinations and took the needles to school on Monday to give out polio shots to the kids. They got in trouble at school and the adopted kids' parents, you know, Mr. and Mrs. Stover, are having a fit. The kids were crying because the needles hurt. Also, Mom, Andrew has been eating a million sugar sandwiches since you left."

The door opened again. Reba and Nina looked at each other. It was Johnny for sure. Reba went down the stairs and said to Johnny, "I heard you ran out of sugar."

Johnny stood in the middle of the living room with two bags in his hands, just staring at Reba. He put the bags down in the kitchen and returned to the living room. Reba thought, "Here we go, this is the moment I have *not* been waiting for." She told the kids to go upstairs and sat down on the couch in silence.

Johnny stood in the middle of the floor, looking at her as if she were a ghost. Finally he said, "Reba, have you lost your mind? I mean, are you really crazy? Where have you been for three days? Why are you just now bringing your ass back here? Don't you know you have a family? This place has been a wreck."

Reba looked at him. She saw Doug one minute, Johnny the next. She thought about the bubbles in Doug's tub and the pizza she had taken out of her oven. She looked around at the house she was in and thought about Doug's home. She thought about her bed upstairs and about Doug's dresser. She thought about last Mother's Day when she was on her hands and knees scrubbing the kitchen floor and Johnny was in the street. She thought about Valentine's Day and all of her birthdays when little or no mention was made. She thought about the woman who had come to her door. She thought about the clothes she'd washed and ironed and the children she'd borne.

Suddenly Johnny shouted, "Reba, are you asleep with your eyes open? I'm talking to you, woman. What the hell is wrong with you? You'd better answer me. I have been here for five days with your kids. Where have you been? You think you're going to be gone for five days and just sashay your ass in here and stare at me and the walls? You better talk to me, woman!"

Reba stood up, stretched, and ran her hands through her hair. She had to get this right.

"I've been in Norfolk, Virginia, working and having fun for once in my life. That answers one of your questions. I am not crazy, and that answers another. Now, I want you to listen to me. Have a fucking seat, Johnny."

Johnny was shocked. He had never heard Reba say "fuck." Not even in bed.

"Johnny, I am sick of Philadelphia, this house, my life, and you. Are you hearing me, Johnny Penster? I am sick of sharing every damn thing, including my soul, with you. I am sick of who you are. I do not like you. Do you understand that? Are you hearing me, Johnny Penster? Do you want to know something else? You're not so hot in the sack either, buddy." Johnny got up to raise his hand and Reba stopped him. "Now I know about the other woman you have. Tamara. Yes, Tamara, the one with the two kids. I met them. I don't want you inconvenienced anymore by having to keep your clothes one place and fuck around somewhere else. I don't want you to have to go to that much trouble. So, why don't you do me a favor, a big favor, and get out of my house and my life? I may not have known it before, but I know it now, and what I know is that I can make it without your sorry ass! It took me five days to realize that I have been fucked up, fucked over, ignored, and mistreated for fourteen years, but better late than never. I emptied my suitcases and you can have them to pack your shit. It's time *you* took a trip. And another thing, if you bought any ketchup or tomatoes when you went to the market, take that shit with you because that food isn't part of my diet anymore!"

Johnny was shocked. He could not believe that mild, passive Reba was standing there ranting and raving and giving him orders. He wondered if she was drunk or on some kind of medication. Maybe she had gone crazy. How the hell did she know he wasn't so hot in bed? After all, who would want her? She couldn't even match up her clothes or cook—he had personally seen to that. He was dying to know who had gotten hold of his wife. Who had been talking to her and turned her all around? He wondered if she had really been with another man or if she had seen some movie. Knowing Reba, it was a movie. Or could those models down there have filled her head with those crazy notions? Whatever it was, he had to get her back in line, and back to normal. She was definitely out of control.

He didn't quite know what approach to take. Should he accuse her of things and try to threaten or scare her? Should he just try to talk to this crazy woman? Maybe he should leave for a few days and she'd come to her senses. Or should he try to make up with her by getting her into bed and working her over really good? Could he put his specialty, "double whammy do it to her on the washing machine when it was on the spin dry cycle," the way Tamara liked it, on Reba? He'd never given it to her that way. That just might work. Yeah, just fuck her brains out with the assistance of the washing machine, and he'd have control again. Maybe he also needed to think of some new moves to help himself out with her.

Reba walked to the kitchen and began to put the groceries away, literally throwing the items into the refrigerator and cabinets. She was making sure she made noise and acted crazy so Johnny would know she had changed and she meant what she had said to him. She put all the bottles of ketchup and tomatoes aside on the counter so Johnny could take them with him. She hoped he would leave. She had made up her mind that she would do everything she could to make him confused and crazy if he decided to stay with her. After she put the food away, she went toward the living room where Johnny still sat on the couch like a block of ice. After all, it had only been ten minutes since she had basically told him to go to hell. Reba looked at him, rolled her eyes, and headed to the stairs. When she got to the top, she yelled for the children.

"Kids, everybody, come downstairs to the kitchen right now. I want to talk to all of you. I want every last one of you right now!"

Reba really didn't want to scare them, but it was all in line with the new her. The up-to-date, "I'm not taking any mess" Reba. And she wanted to keep Johnny on his toes every minute. If he heard her speaking to the kids that way, it would help her plan.

The kids ran downstairs. It was a three-story, six-bedroom house, so they came from the third floor down and out of almost every room. Reba came down the stairs and walked past Johnny again. He was shocked she was handling the kids this way. She was usually so submissive, slow, lenient, and understanding. Dad was always the one to crack down on them. Johnny thought that Reba had done a complete turn around or maybe she really was on some medication or had read a book on the bus that changed her.

When the kids arrived in the kitchen, they looked frightened. "Everyone sit down at the table," Reba ordered. "I want all of you to be quiet and listen to me. When I am finished talking, you can ask questions that I will try to answer for you. Or you can make a comment about what I said. Do all of you understand me?"

Their eyes were wide open and they looked scared, but they knew they had to obey.

"First of all," Reba began, "I want all of you to know that I love you very much. However, your mother has not been happy for a long time. Your mother has not been happy because she has six children who have not been very good most of the time. They have gotten into trouble and disobeyed her, and they have not done their best in school. They have not helped her around the house. Your mother is tired. Your mother wants to feel better about her children and herself. Your mother needs help from you.

"Today is the day that we all, all of us in this house, begin to grow up.

I am growing up, too. In order to grow up right, you need responsibilities and you have to learn to do things correctly. All of you will have duties in this house, even you, Andrew. I realize you are only seven, but you have to share in the responsibility of being a member of this household and this family. All of you have responsibilities to each other as well. Now, first, we are going to start with your behavior. I am going to run through these things once today, and when I get time I am going to type them up and give each one of you a set of rules and regulations that you will follow as long as you live in my house. Anyone who does not follow the rules will have to deal with me.

"So, if you disobey me and I find out about it, I will tell you that I know about you. Then you will know that you should be careful eating your meals in this house because you won't know whether or not there is poison in your plate, bowl of food, or, in your lunch that you take to school. Now, poison comes in all forms, liquid, crystals, and pills I can crush up, and medication. There are poisons I can put in your food that can make it seem like you died from a natural cause, you know, something regular like a heart attack or pneumonia."

"So all of you had better watch it. If I choose to tell you I have decided to poison you, you will have the option to refuse to eat. Then you will starve to death. If you don't die from starvation, I will have you put in a home. I am serious. I am not taking any crap from anyone anymore.

"Now, I have heard about some things that happened while I was away. I know about the needles and the train tracks and all the sugar sandwiches. I know about the sneaker, too."

Johnny, who had moved from the living room to the dining room to hear this conversation, was now convinced that somebody had gotten to Reba and turned her all around. He couldn't believe this was her talking. He couldn't wait to talk to Lucy Noble and Peggy Kinard. Somebody was going to tell him something. He wanted to run upstairs and go through her things while she was talking, to see if he could find any drugs or books to explain her behavior, but he didn't want to miss any of the conversation. He thought he might learn something by just staying there. He also wanted to stick around to see if she was going to tell the kids that he would be moving out of the house.

"Now, these are the rules: Everyone will be up at six in the morning and you'll make your beds before leaving for school. You'll all be responsible for cleaning your rooms and doing your laundry. Homework will be done as soon as you get in this house after school. It will be checked by the brother or sister older than you, but closest to you in age. For instance, Craig will check Andrew's homework. It will be the responsibility of the older brother or sister to see that your homework is correct. I'll check Nina's homework since she is the oldest. If you are having a problem in a subject and you need extra help, come see me. I will fix it. Otherwise, I will hold the older brother or sister responsible if the work is not completely and correctly done and turned in to the teacher on time. Everyone got that? Does anyone not understand?"

The kids nodded in unison.

"Now, these are the good things that will happen for you. You earn points by doing your schoolwork and chores efficiently. Efficiently means correct. You can earn up to twenty-five points per day each. Your schoolwork is worth fifteen points and your housework is worth ten points. Points are worth a penny each, so at the end of a seven-day week you could earn up to one dollar and fifty cents.

"Think about using that money for the circus in June, the Atlantic City boardwalk, the annual fair at the hospital, day camp, or the movies. I will keep a record of all of the points. I'll be watching you, and you guys better be watching each other. Understand?"

By this time the kids were ecstatic. They buzzed around the kitchen, making plans. Johnny was still hiding out in the dining room. He couldn't believe what he'd just heard. What the hell had gotten into Reba?

"Okay," said Reba, "we start next Sunday. Sunday starts the week. All teams are assigned on Saturday nights. For the next three days, you will be in training. I am going to show you how to do everything. Then, on Saturday, we pick the three teams, Kitchen, Laundry, and House. Got that?"

The kids chorused, "Yes."

"Good. Saturdays you also get a special treat. You can pick whatever you want to do after your work is done. Just let me know by Wednesday of each week what your plans are and I'll help you work it out. On Sundays, everyone attends Sunday school and church. When you get home from church, we are going to do something very different. I am not perfect. I do not do everything well and I understand that. I am a terrible cook, but I want us all to learn. So I am going to buy a couple of cookbooks and the seven of us are going to start having cooking lessons every Sunday between three and five thirty. Everyone must be present. We will make the complete dinner, dessert and all. Everyone participates, even you, Andrew. When I get the cookbooks, everyone will share in reading them. They will be kept in the kitchen. Each week one of us will choose the entire meal and dessert and all of us will make it. A new person gets to choose the meal every week. Let me know on Tuesday of each week what you are choosing so I have time to buy all the ingredients we need. Another thing. We are finished making everything red. Aren't you tired of eating so much red stuff? No more pouring ketchup and tomatoes all over everything. That's over. Ketchup goes on french fries, hot dogs, hamburgers and sometimes eggs. It does not go on mashed potatoes, cabbage, cereal, or a million other things we've been using it for."

Reba could tell by the "ohhs" and "ahhs" that the kids were delighted with this idea.

"Are there any questions? If there are questions, raise your hand."

Rudy's hand went up. "When do we get paid for our regular points, you know, the work and the school?"

"You get paid every Saturday night, just before the names are picked for the following week. Next."

There were no more questions. The kids were hyped up and excited. Reba was proud of herself. Johnny was still in the dining room trying to figure out who this new Reba was and how she got that way.

"Training begins tomorrow at seven sharp, in the evening, in this kitchen. Everyone be here—it will be right after dinner. Training for the Laundry team will be Friday night at eight thirty, and the House team training will be Saturday morning at eleven. Now, all you little brats get out of my kitchen. I'll call you for dinner soon."

The kids ran out of the kitchen and up the stairs, chattering. Reba had a plan. She was going to shape these kids up so they would know how to live in Annapolis with her and Doug. They were going to be the neatest, nicest, smartest, most responsible kids in Maryland.

As for Johnny, she didn't think he was going anywhere. It wasn't going to be that easy. From time to time she planned to run down to Annapolis to see Doug, so she had to make sure the kids could run the house when she was away. Eventually, she'd move herself and the kids to Annapolis. They would need a bigger house. She'd start to put some money away to make that possible, saving for the future. She would have to spend some money she had not expected with her new venture with the kids, but it would keep them busy and teach them how to get along and work together. It would also teach them some responsibility, make them try harder in school, and give her some help. Reba was even going to learn to cook. It was perfect!

Reba walked out of the kitchen and tried to get through the dining room. Johnny grabbed her arm. "I need to talk to you."

Reba sat down at the dining room table. "What is it, Johnny?"

"You're not acting like yourself. You go away for five days, leaving me with these kids, I don't hear from you, you don't come back on time, and now you walk in the door like a drill sergeant. You imply that I have some sexual problems on top of everything else. Then, to beat all, you tell me I have to leave my house and accuse me of having affairs and other children. What's the deal, Reba? What's going on with you? I think you have lost your mind."

Reba looked at him and thought he was pitiful. She was so sick of him, and so tired. "Johnny, you've been running around on me for a long time and, yes, I know about your other kids. So look, don't waste my time by lying about it. A man would own up to it. But whatever is or isn't or happened or didn't happen, there is nothing happening between you and me anymore. I just want out. That's all, plain and simple. No more questions asked, no fight, no argument, no sorry, no anger, no crying over spilled milk, I just want out."

"Reba," Johnny insisted, "I have not, never, cheated on you and I do not have any other kids. I don't know what someone has told you, or why they lied, but the times I've been away I was either with the ball team or out with the boys or something. I never cheated on you."

Reba thought about the "black books" she had kept on Johnny all these years. She had a record of every time he had stayed out all night, with dates, the times of his return, and the excuses he had given her. She had the names and some addresses of women he was seeing over the years. She had pictures of kids, and one of the women had even sent her a picture and a birth certificate. She had the date and time when the woman came to the door asking for Johnny. She had never said a word to Johnny about the evidence she had collected over the years. She had never discussed anything with anyone, and only shared part of it with Peggy and Lucy when they were away. Now she had to listen to his lies. She wanted to puke on Johnny, she was that sick of him.

"Listen, Johnny, like I said, it doesn't matter because I'm not the same anymore. We're not right for each other. It's time to stop."

"Reba, I'm sorry. Let's get it together." He reached for Reba and put his hand to her face.

"Don't do that, Johnny." Reba flinched.

Then Johnny got mad. He felt certain she was involved with someone now. It was all adding up. He stood over her and shouted, "What's the matter—you can't stand for me to touch you because you've been laying up with someone for the past five days? So that's it. Some dude fucked your brains out and that's why you're acting crazy. What's the matter, Reba? Did you leave your brains in Norfolk in somebody's bed? Is that what the real problem is here? Is that why I've got to leave home, Reba? I mean, things have been the same around here for the last fourteen years and you haven't complained. Now, all of a sudden, my kids have got to get up at six o'clock in the morning and work like slaves and I've got to get out altogether. What did he shove up you, Reba, a fucking cannon?"

Reba didn't answer. The more Johnny looked at Reba, the more he thought maybe she *hadn't* been with a man. He couldn't dream of anyone else really wanting her and couldn't imagine her cheating. She wasn't the type. But he did believe that someone had given her a book or she had seen a movie or one of those models had gotten to her. She got up and walked away. Johnny grabbed her again and stopped her.

"Take your hands off me, Johnny."

"I don't have to take my hands off you because you're mine. My wife, my kids' mother, and my woman. That there thing between your legs is mine, too." He grabbed her crotch and squeezed it for a second. He released her and said, "You got that? I ain't going nowhere. I'm staying right here with you for the rest of my life. When you finish playing drill sergeant with the kids, when you're done for the night, your man will be waiting in his bed for you. You wanna boss me around between them sheets tonight, baby? Now you better make up with me. I apologize for what I said or if I did something that made you mad at me. I know you weren't fucking around, knowing what you got here."

Reba concentrated for a second. Then she took Johnny by the hand and walked him over to the couch and sat him down. She sat on his lap. She held both his hands, letting their fingers interlock. Johnny was feeling pretty good about this. He felt like they were going to get it on right there, in the living room, and he was excited. She nuzzled against his face and spoke softly in his ear. He was getting aroused. He liked this—Reba initiating this shit at seven thirty at night in the living room with the kids upstairs. He liked the idea of sneaking a piece in his own house with his own wife. He was fired up.

"Hey, Johnny," said Reba. "Listen to me, baby."

"Um-hum, I'm listening, baby, and I'm real sorry about the things I said." He began trying to free his hands from hers so he could touch her thighs. Reba would not unlock his hands. He was getting hotter. She had him pinned down.

"You don't have to apologize, Johnny. That's not necessary."

He started to grin. He knew he had her then.

"We all make mistakes," she said.

"I know, baby," Johnny sighed.

"I made some mistakes in my life too, Johnny." Reba breathed hard in his ear. He wanted her bad. She would not let go of his hands, and she was still straddled on his lap.

"I forgive you, I forgive you," murmured Johnny.

"You forgive me, Johnny?"

"Yeah, baby, Reba, yeah, I forgive you." By now he was trying to squirm out of the lock in which she had him. He had an erection.

"What do you forgive me for, Johnny?" she whispered in his ear.

"I forgive you for everything, everything you did, you know, whatever you think you did."

"Hey, Johnny," said Reba.

"Yeah, baby, yes, yes, yes, baby, what is it? Please let me go. Let's get this on. Come on, Reba, stop playing around. Oh shit, what, baby?"

"Can you forgive me for fucking my new man all weekend from Friday to this morning? Can you forgive me for leaving your ass to go back to him as soon as I can get my business straight here in Philadelphia? Can you forgive me for that, motherfucker? And by the way, yes, it was a cannon."

With that she jumped off his lap and strutted upstairs. She yelled to the kids to order a pizza. She wasn't cooking tonight.

# Chapter Thirty

# *Lucy*

Lucy had never seen a palm tree before in her life. The sun was shining and the weather was gorgeous. The cab pulled up at the breathtaking La Miracalle Hotel. The huge lobby boasted rattan tables and chairs, and a band was playing salsa music. A punch bowl was set up for serving drinks while guests checked in. Beyond the lobby was an intimate bar and a stunning open-air restaurant.

Kevin and Lucy had no reservations and very little luggage. "We'd like a room for two for three nights," said Kevin. Lucy leaned against him and rested her head on his shoulder. He squeezed her hand in acknowledgment.

She whispered, "This place is fantastic. Take a look at the pool over there—it has a waterfall."

"Baby, why don't you take a real good look around while I do this? I'll meet you over at the pool bar when I'm through here. By that time our bags should be upstairs, too."

"Okay." She kissed him on the cheek and walked through the lobby. She noticed that the hotel shops sold everything from bathing suits to jewelry. She also spotted a casino. She went through another exit and emerged at the pool. It was shaped like a giant kidney, with sparkling aqua water. The pool wasn't crowded because it was the dinner hour, but a few people sat around holding colored drinks with fresh fruit garnishes. Everyone certainly seemed happy and relaxed.

Signs pointed the way to the tennis courts and golf course. She thought, "We're going to have a ball." She took a seat at the bar and the bartender appeared instantly.

"Hello, miss, what can I get you?"

"Suggest something that tastes good and looks pretty and won't get me too bombed."

Lucy was surprised; the bartender didn't look like an African. She had never been to the islands, but just assumed that black men from the islands resembled the natives in Africa. She expected to see dark-complexioned men with short nappy hair and giant lips. This guy was altogether different—tall, nicely built, with a beautiful brown complexion and wavy hair.

"I'd like to suggest a Chocolate Banana or a Bahama Mama. Both are great, but made from very different ingredients."

"Tell me about them both," said Lucy.

At that moment, Kevin walked up, sat down next to Lucy, and kissed her on the cheek. "Yes, man, tell us both about them."

"Good evening, sir," said the bartender.

"Oh, no," replied Kevin. "I am definitely not 'sir.' Call me Kevin, and this young lady, the cutest thing sitting here, is—let me think, what's your name?"

Lucy laughed, and the bartender was smiling at them.

"My name is Lucy."

The bartender interrupted. "Lucy, Kevin, let me tell you about the drinks."

"What's your name?" Kevin asked the bartender.

"I'm Clifford."

Kevin extended his hand. "It's a pleasure to meet you, Clifford."

"Okay," said Clifford, "the Chocolate Banana has dark crème de cacao, banana liqueur, milk, and a fresh banana blended together with crushed ice. The Bahama Mama has pineapple, orange and lemon juice, sugar, and light and dark rum blended together with crushed ice. Both are delicious."

Kevin looked at Lucy, sizing her up.

"I'll take the Bahama Mama. Lana, what'll it be for you?"

Lucy smiled, shaking her head. She thought about them having sex later and coolly said, "I'll go for the Chocolate Banana."

Clifford began to make their drinks and asked them, "Where are you two from?"

"Lucy is Miss Philadelphia," said Kevin. "We're from Philly."

Clifford set the drinks down in front of them. Lucy made a toast. She got up and twirled around with her arms stretched out. "To Peggy Kinard who made all this possible." Then she took her seat and tasted her drink. "You did better than all right, Clifford—it's delicious."

"How about you, Kevin? Do you like that Bahama Mama?"

"I like it just fine."

Clifford left to serve the other customers, and Kevin and Lucy began to talk.

"You really are crazy," Lucy said. "You've got a lot of imagination and you are so much fun. On the serious side, I am really glad we met."

"So you liked my little blindfold kidnap trick?"

"Yes, I loved it. Are we all checked in?"

Kevin took the keys out of his pocket and dangled them in front of her. "All right, Miss Philly, are you tired or hungry or can I do anything for you?"

"Nope, I'm fine."

"Do you want to pee in the bushes? They've got a lot of bushes around here."

Lucy was cool. "Nope, no peeing in the bushes."

Clifford appeared and Kevin ordered another round of drinks.

"After this we'd better head to the room. It really has been a long day. We can decide what we're going to do tonight."

"You know, they have a casino, some shops, tennis, and golf," said Lucy.

"Okay, how about this? Let's finish the drinks he's making. We can take our time—there's no need to rush. Then we'll go back to the room, unpack, unwind, and decide about dinner. After dinner we'll check out the casino and win a few bucks. How does that sound?"

"Sounds good to me," said Lucy, "but I want to check the beach out, too."

"Okay, you're on."

Lucy and Kevin liked the smoothness of the "no pressure thing" that had developed between them. They were totally relaxed with each other. They were happy together in the Bahamas, away from the cold weather, highways, and hustle-bustle of everyday life. Everything was going good.

They finished their drinks. Kevin signed the bill and grabbed Lucy by the hand.

"Come on, Lana, let me show you to your new digs for the next three days."

They walked hand in hand through the lobby. It was getting late and people, dressed for dinner, were milling around while the band played. On the elevator, Kevin lifted Lucy's face up and kissed her. By the time they got to the fifteenth floor, they were engrossed in a passionate kiss.

The room had bright yellow print drapes with a matching spread, and honey-colored rattan furniture. The huge bathroom boasted marble floors and plush towels in pink and mauve.

"They've done a nice job here. I really like this room. As you can see, there's one bed—who's sleeping on the floor?" said Kevin.

Lucy giggled.

"What's so funny?" asked Kevin.

Lucy laughed hysterically.

"Come on, tell me, what's so funny?"

Kevin began to laugh with her. He picked up a pillow and hit her with it. She grabbed him and threw him on the bed.

"You're attacking me, you're attacking me!" screamed Kevin. Kevin grabbed Lucy's foot and kissed it. He pulled her sandal off and rubbed her foot. Next her toes got the works—he massaged every one of them.

"Jesus," moaned Lucy. Kevin's lips and tongue traveled up Lucy's legs, kissing and sucking her flesh. He unzipped her pants and gently pulled them off, looking into her eyes. She lay still and lethargic. She was going to let him do his work.

When he got her pants off, he bent down to kiss her on the lips. Then his face disappeared. She felt him begin to kiss her gently between her legs.

Kevin was very gentle and patient. He gave her a lot of small kisses, as she was fragile down there. He came up for air and blew on her, hoping it felt like the Caribbean trade winds. The air cooled her hot body momentarily. Lucy began to move her butt in slow circles. He had ignited her and she couldn't take much more of this.

She was whimpering and moaning—she wanted him bad. Kevin made her feel so good she got mixed up. She couldn't decide whether she wanted him to stay down there or move inside her. She told him to stop and come on and then she would push him back down. Finally, she wrestled his pants off him, grabbed his penis, and sucked his cute little nipples.

Soon she was on top of him and had eased him into her. She could feel him, unlike the last guy she had, who told her he was an Indian and turned out to be Chief Little Dick. Kevin had backup. Extra force. Lucy didn't have any wild tricks for him because she was pretty inexperienced. Kevin was hip to her. He could tell she had not been around, but he liked the fact that she didn't know everything and wasn't too aggressive. He knew then that she hadn't been used up. He liked this girl.

* * *

It was a beautiful night. They arrived at the Cotillion Restaurant. Kevin had made reservations earlier. When Lucy walked in, she was taken aback. She had thought that Bello's in Norfolk was the loveliest place on the planet, but now here she was, outdone again. She squeezed Kevin's hand and kissed him on the cheek. The maître d' escorted them to a candlelit table in the dim room and handed them giant menus. Everything sounded divine. They settled on their appetizers and entrees and selected a bottle of wine.

Lucy said, "Do you treat all your first dates like this?"

"No, just the ones who pee in bushes. I just have a thing for a girl who does that. It turns me on."

Lucy chuckled. "You know," she said slowly, "I can't get over you—I'm really impressed. I mean, not just all of this, but the coolness of you, your organization. You have a lot going for you, Kevin."

The waiter arrived with their appetizers and the two of them began to nibble on the food. Kevin said, "Tell me something."

"What?"

"Tell me your fantasies. The sexual ones."

Lucy blushed. "How do you know I have any?"

"You have to have some—everybody does. You can trust me. I promise not to tell anyone. What turns you on in a man, Lucy? What gets you all riled up, baby?" Kevin growled softly. They both laughed, but Lucy didn't answer. "Scared, huh? Scared to tell me after I went to all this trouble." Kevin waved his hand around the room. "Shit, you weren't too embarrassed to pee in the bushes while all four of us waited for you. Why are you so bashful now?"

Lucy sighed. "Kevin, you are a pain in the ass. Eat your food, please."

"Okay, Philly, since you won't tell me what you like, I might—well—do some dull, mundane stuff in bed, just to pass the time."

Lucy picked up the bottle of wine.

Kevin said, "I'll pour it for you, baby. Was everything okay up there with me this afternoon? I mean, did I do the right things the right way, or are you going to flag me and tell your friends about me? I know how you women have those hen parties and all you talk about is sex."

Lucy blushed and took another sip of wine. She stuck her finger into her glass and sucked it.

"Okay, listen up, buddy."

Kevin eased back in his chair and smiled. "Bring it on, baby."

Lucy said, "Now, I am no expert at this, so I just have to explain the way it is one thing at a time. If you laugh at me, I will discontinue the conversation. Do you understand, Kevin?"

"I understand."

"Now, no matter how ridiculous or freaky my stuff sounds, you better not even chuckle. You got that?"

Kevin replied, "Yes, ma'am," and took a sip of wine. He reached for the bottle of wine and filled her glass. "You might need that, baby," he said.

"Okay. I like men's feet. I like a man who wears slip-on shoes and no socks. Preferably lizard, ostrich, alligator, or snakeskin shoes. Slip-on shoes and no socks turn me on big-time. They get me started—you know. I think that's sexy."

She looked at Kevin and waited for him to laugh. He kept a serious face and sipped his wine.

"Go on," he said.

"I like doing it in different places. My favorite fantasy is to do it in a car. I would love to do it in a car."

"Why? What is it about a car?"

"I don't know. It just seems like there won't be enough room, it would be a hassle, and you might get into trouble for doing it in a car. You know—maybe with the police. That's exciting. Like sneaking some. It's like getting away with something."

Kevin smiled. He liked this girl. They both took a sip of wine.

Lucy continued. "Well, it just seems like it would be a good piece be-cause . . ." She took a gulp of wine. "Well, everything would be in the way, and we would have to try harder for it. Whenever you have to work harder for something, it of does something to you. Makes you want it more. That's the best I can explain it."

Kevin nodded. "You're doing good, baby."

The waiter brought their entrees and Kevin ordered another bottle of wine.

"Lucy, do you have any other fantasies or any instructions for me?"

Lucy was totally relaxed by now.

"Well, I like foreplay with my clothes entirely on. There's some-thing about rubbing up against a man with my clothes on. It excites me, especially here." Lucy pointed to her lap. "I believe it's a combination of the fabric and the man's hands. Hell, I don't know. I just know it feels good to me. It excites the shit out of me." She finished her glass of wine and Kevin filled it halfway again.

"Also, when you mess around with your clothes on, it's more spontaneous." She waved her hand in the air. "Just let the shit come off wherever it may. Start in the kitchen on top of the goddamn counter."

Kevin felt an urge to laugh, but he remembered his promise. So he kept a straight face, shaking his head.

"Okay, baby," he said seriously. "Anything else?"

"Yes."

First, he couldn't get her to fess up to anything and, now, he couldn't shut her up. Shit, Lucy probably had an entire laundry list of things to tell him about.

"Let's hear it, Miss Philly."

"I'd like to show up at a bar or a restaurant in a coat and high heels with little or nothing underneath. I would be meeting a date there. I'd see him at the bar, but we'd act like strangers. He'd pick me up. You know, like I'm a hooker or a tramp."

"What else do you like, Lucy?"

"Okay. Let me think. I like it when my nipples are gently bitten. I really love that."

"Is that it?"

"No. I like it when I step out of the shower and the water trickles down my back, just below my shoulders, and my man kisses the water off. That's what I like." She finished the glass of wine in a long gulp. "I'm done."

Kevin applauded, reached for her hand, and kissed it.

After dinner they went to the casino and lost a few bucks. It was fun. They took a stroll on the beach, but they were pretty high from all the wine, so Kevin suggested they call it a night. He stopped to talk to the bellman. Lucy couldn't hear what they said, but she saw the bellman pointing and explaining something. Then Kevin took Lucy's hand and they continued to walk.

"Where are we going? I'm tired," said Lucy.

"We're going for a walk, baby. I've got something for you. I want to give it to you in a special place."

"Aw, come on, Kevin, you're starting tricks again, and I've had too much wine and I'm tired. Let's go to the room."

"Aw, come on, Philly, be a sport. You can hang."

Lucy followed him to the hotel parking lot. Kevin walked up to a small car. "Get your ass in, it's fantasy fulfillment time."

Lucy squealed. "Kevin—" She almost said, "I love you," but she managed to stop herself. She didn't want to scare him. "I appreciate every single thing you do for me, sir."

He laughed and threw her in the car.

# Chapter Thirty-one

# *Sheila*

*S*ix weeks had flashed by and Sheila and Leonard were still dating. She had lost another nine pounds and was loving herself. Everything was under control with the kids and school. Sheila was particularly excited this morning because she and Leonard had a big night planned, to see a singing group from her neighborhood. They would be performing at a hall near the University of Pennsylvania. It was going to be a threesome tonight because they were taking along Sheila's best buddy, Emily.

Emily carefully laid out the tightest black knit pants she had, black high heels, and a silver and black wrap top. She applied her makeup and worked extra hard on her lips. She had the biggest, prettiest lips in the world. She was excited about going to the show tonight.

Horace had planned to go to work late that night, at three a.m. That would give Emily enough time to have a few drinks after the show before she came home to stay with Renee. Emily wished she could find herself a man like Horace. He was a good boss, a good man, and an excellent father.

Sheila and Leonard picked Emily up a little before nine and drove to the Dynasty Room where the Knightcaps were performing. Emily had never seen them before; they were Sheila's buddies. When they arrived, the place was packed and the group was already singing on the stage.

Sheila wanted the group to see she had come, so she inched up to the front with Leonard and Emily and started to wave. Emily looked at the Knightcaps, checking each of them out. "Shit, all these guys are fine," she thought. She wasn't moving from her spot. The group wore black turtleneck sweaters, red sports jackets, black pants and shoes, and black derby hats. They looked sophisticated and smooth. She noticed one guy with a beautiful brown complexion, like the caramel inside of a Milky Way. He had dimples and nice eyes. She stared at him as he moved and sang. She could not take her eyes off him. She was totally captivated even without knowing who the hell he was. Something had truly come over her.

"Who's that one—do you know him?" she asked Sheila.

"Yes, that's Jared." Sheila looked at Emily. "What's up, girlfriend?"

"I'm in love with him," Emily replied, never taking her eyes off Jared.

Sheila laughed and kept grooving and swaying to the music.

During the intermission, Emily asked Sheila to introduce her to the group, particularly Jared. They made their way through the crowd of people trying to get to the group. Sheila introduced Leonard and Emily to Damon, Lee, Rodney, and Kelly. Then she took Emily by the hand and walked her over to where Jared sat. Leonard followed.

"Hey, baby," said Sheila. "How the hell is it going? I haven't seen you since Kelly's barbecue. You've done pretty well for yourself, I see."

Jared smiled and hugged her. "You look good, Sheila, with your skinny self."

Emily waited for Sheila to introduce them. It seemed like it took forever. Finally Sheila turned to her and Leonard.

"Listen, you've got to meet my new man. I think he's cuter than you. Leonard, this is Jared, we go way back."

They shook hands. "Nice to meet you, Leonard. Do you play cards?"

Leonard laughed. "No, man, I'm scared of cards."

Jared laughed. "Sheila, you have got to give me a call. I heard about you. That's all I am saying."

"All right, you got that. Start busting on me right here. That's what you gonna do, huh? Well, in that case I just may not introduce you to my best pal Emily."

Jared switched his attention to Emily. Sheila said, "Emily, this is Jared."

Jared took Emily's hand and gently kissed it. "Any friend of Sheila's is a friend of mine. After all, when I die, I don't want to be dug up."

They all laughed. Sheila moved out of the way so Emily could make her move.

Emily said to Jared, "Can I sit down?"

Jared politely gave her his seat and leaned against the table. She sat down and crossed her legs. She was in this for the long haul no matter what he felt. She could feel in her bones that he would be hers—by hook or crook, exhaustion of her pride—whatever it took. She looked straight into his eyes and asked, "Do you have a girlfriend?" Jared was thrown off guard by her bluntness. Smiling, he said, "Yes."

"You've got to get rid of her, baby, because I am in love with you."

He blushed, surprised and tickled by her confidence. He thought she was cute and was fascinated by her boldness. They chatted a bit and Emily told him she couldn't leave without his telephone number. He gave it to her and she left but returned in less than five minutes.

"Oh, just one more thing, Jared."

Now he was getting irritated with her. "What do you need, Emily?"

"I also cannot leave here without you. I'll be at this table when you finish your next show. Can you make arrangements not to leave the premises without me?" Jared gave a noncommittal shrug and walked away toward the stage.

Emily stared at him for the next thirty-five minutes. He had it all! A beautiful voice, looks to kill, and goddamn dimples to boot! Shit, he was better than hitting the number. She wondered if she were under some sort of spell. She couldn't imagine what had come over her. Was she on the right track or just chasing a rainbow? Whatever it was, she had to look him up if he didn't leave with her that night.

Leonard and Sheila were having a ball. Sheila was extremely proud of the Knightcaps because she had watched them grow up. She knew they were going to make it. They already had a record deal.

When the show was over, Emily told Sheila to hang around the door. She was going back to the table to see if Jared would meet her. She told Sheila she wanted to leave with him.

Emily got her wish—and that fine thing came and got her from the table when it was time to leave. Sheila and Leonard left.

# Chapter Thirty-two

# *Emily and Jared*

ow, what's up? Where are we going? Can I take you for a drink to get to know you, since you are already in love with me? You can also explain to me how you expect me to get rid of my girlfriend." Jared inspected Emily carefully. "You don't have any weapons with you, do you?"

Emily smiled. "No weapons." She stood up, lifted her arms, and spread her legs. "Do you want to search me? Shall I assume the position?"

Jared shook his head. She was tough. It was going to be a wild night.

She studied him for a moment. There was something so sweet about him. Something she had never seen in any other guy. He was different. She didn't give a damn what she had to do, she was going to have him.

"Are you driving? Because I'm not."

"Nope," said Emily, "I can't drive and I have no car."

"This one's going to be a pain," he thought. "Where do you live, Emily?"

"I live with my boss. I'm a nanny and take care of a little girl. Where do you live, Jared? Do you have your own place?"

Jared sighed and said firmly, "I live at home with my mother, sister, and brothers."

Emily needed to figure this out. She couldn't take him to Horace's house. She was reluctant to suggest a hotel. They only had a few hours before Horace had to go to work.

"Okay, baby," said Jared. "What am I going to do with you?"

Emily squinted. "Can you take me home to your mother?"

Jared looked at her as if she were crazy. She was something else. He led her outside, put her in the limousine with the rest of the group, and took her home.

When they got to his house, they went straight to his basement. He put some music on and offered her something to eat and drink. The quickest thing he could come up with was Cheerios and milk, and she ate it.

He asked her a million questions and laughed a lot because she was amusing. He was surprised that she didn't interrogate him about his business, relationship expectations, and women. None of that seemed to matter to her. At two o'clock she called Horace to say she was sorry but she would not be home.

The two of them chatted and were curled up in each other's arms on the couch. It was strange. He was sexy, and she was excited by him, but she didn't want sex. She just needed to be in his arms with her head on his shoulder. She felt secure with him, this stranger. Jared held her like that until they fell asleep. Emily got up the next morning and left.

She called him later that day to thank him and asked if she could see him that evening. He had plans, but she asked him to cancel them. He said he couldn't. Emily got dressed and went there anyway. He was shocked to see her at his door, but he let her in. It was quiet and no one was else was there. He took her upstairs without saying a word. His sister's bedroom was the first one they encountered. He led her in and gently pushed her down on the twin bed. He knew what she wanted. He undressed her and fucked her natural brains out. It was the first time she had ever had her legs on a guy's shoulders. It was the best sex she had ever had.

Over the following three months Emily had made up her mind to latch herself onto Jared. She found herself hopelessly in love with him. She also felt a special bond with him, magnetic yet controlled. It wasn't all sex, even though she had an insatiable desire for him. He was a great kisser. She could lose her tongue in his mouth. Foreplay was his forte, and by the time his penis was inside Emily, she was extremely grateful to have it. In fact, she thanked God for it. Sexually, he was unselfish and a true concentrator. He seemed to calculate his every move and capitalize on her every move. Oh yes—he gave Emily the sweetest workout she'd ever received.

She loved his calmness; he never raised his voice and he always tried to teach her things. He read the Bible and often went over verses and chapters with her. They played around with words, attempting to write songs together, and they read poetry to each other. Sex was not their main form of entertainment.

Emily often dreamed of Jared, of images of danger encroaching upon him. They instilled fear in Emily. She became protective of Jared. She had only been in two relationships before, and she had never experienced these feelings with either of them. Her strong feelings compelled her to attend all of the Knightcaps' local shows.

His girlfriend, Stephanie, also attended most of the shows, so Jared couldn't leave with Emily. She didn't care—she wasn't mad or jealous—she just dealt with it. She was very much in love with Jared, and something in her mind told her not to worry about Stephanie. There was no doubt that Stephanie was on borrowed time.

Jared had been with Stephanie for a few years. If he were seen too much with Emily, all hell would break loose because it would get back to Stephanie. Emily wasn't on a mission to hurt Stephanie—it wasn't about that. She understood Stephanie's love and need for Jared. He was quite a catch. He was born under the sign of Aquarius, the smartest sign in the zodiac. She knew how appealing his demeanor was to a woman. He was polite, organized, articulate, well dressed, well raised, and not foul-mouthed. People liked him, and his smooth coolness was a sexual attraction that could rope any woman in nothing flat.

Jared really did care for Stephanie, but Emily made his shit look real good. Another thing she always did was let everybody around know how much she liked Jared and how he kept her turned on and tuned up. He loved that. Emily was fine, tall, thin, and had something "electric" about her. She was spontaneous and daring. Unlike Stephanie, Emily would walk into the dressing room at intermission and do things to make Jared horny as hell—setting him on fire. Emily had no pride about the way she felt about Jared. She remained persistent and relentless. She didn't give a shit who found out, except Stephanie. Emily was always cordial and pleasant to Stephanie. Despite her feelings, she respected the fact that Jared and Stephanie were a couple, so she never made a scene. She didn't want to officially break them up or hurt Stephanie's feelings. After all, it wasn't Stephanie's fault that Emily had to have Jared. But she did not want to get Jared that way. She wanted him to come to her because he had made the choice completely on his own.

Emily could get Jared going on his own many times at the shows. She would show up looking like a million dollars with some "date" she had found to drive her to the show, one of her friends' brothers, a plumber a handyman or an uncle—anybody she didn't give a damn about.

One night she even hitchhiked to the club and talked the driver into being her date. She could always charm her way into front-row seats with no tickets and cheer loudly for the Knightcaps. She would dance and shake her ass so Jared could see her. Later, Jared would always call her in the middle of the night or early in the morning and she'd be back in his arms again. She could work him.

Over the past three months, the time she had shared with Jared was beginning to make her feel they were true soul mates. It wasn't a fly-by-night fling, they weren't two people just fucking around in their spare time. Their union was not a mere coincidence. It was real, planned, and destined to be. The two of them belonged together.

Stephanie didn't know who the hell Emily was or why she was always there. She couldn't determine whether Emily was dating someone in the band, someone in the Knightcaps, or just a groupie. None of the other guys' girlfriends ever discussed Emily with Stephanie. They would never dime Jared out. Everyone loved it when Emily came around. They envied Jared and nicknamed Emily "the package." It was the code they used to warn Jared when Stephanie and Emily were in a club at the same time. Emily and Jared were also meeting secretly at Jared's after shows, or on his days off. Sometimes Jared would take Emily on a weekend show date. He enjoyed being with her, and she always managed to get time in with him one way or another.

Emily had personality. She was funny and had made friends with everybody in the band. She showed up at the concerts with things they liked—a little pot, champagne for everyone. She told dirty jokes and funny stories. She was one of the boys, but she had impeccable taste and was always getting attention and compliments from everyone. She knew exactly when to be quiet, charming, reserved, and cool when Jared was in business transactions. He never had to cue her.

Jared let things go on with Emily because he trusted her. People had fears—of snakes, illness, dying, mice, or poverty. Jared was petrified of sexually transmitted diseases. His worst fear was of catching something from a woman, so he was careful. He was always reading up on sexually transmitted diseases, their symptoms, and treatment. He was careful on toilets in public places, carried Lysol Disinfectant Spray on the road, and sprayed every toilet he used.

He rarely got tangled up sexually with chicks on the road, and if he did they had to be pretty damn special. If he couldn't resist his desire and they landed in his bed, he took all kinds of precautions to protect himself no matter how hot and rushed things got. This included using condoms, jumping up after it was all over for a shower, and dragging the strange woman with him to make sure she stayed clean. She was not going to fuck him and lie around and talk about how good and wonderful it was and then fall asleep in his arms. She unromantically hit the shower—pronto. When he was at home he dealt only with Stephanie and Emily. They were clean, and he trusted that they were not sleeping with anyone other than himself. He never used condoms with them.

Jimmy, one of the band members, once told them how he had caught the clap. He walked into the doctor's office crying and placed his sick, limp Johnson on the doctor's desk begging for help. Jared was the last person who needed to hear that story. Everyone else was laughing; Jared was terrified.

Jared's mother, Connie, had always liked Stephanie, but she adored the charming Emily and looked forward to her visits. Emily also made it a point to stop by to see Connie when Jared was out of town or rehearsing. Emily never questioned Connie about whether Jared had any other women and she never mentioned Stephanie. Connie thought a lot of Emily just because of that. Sometimes Jared would come home from the road surprised to find Emily watching television with his mother. She would be curled up on the couch with a pillow from his bed. He had a sense he wouldn't be able to get rid of her even if he wanted to.

One freezing Friday night in February, the Knightcaps were away doing a four-nighter in Toronto. Emily and Jared had been together the night before the group left. He had given her a nice evening, complete with a limousine, dinner at her favorite restaurant, plenty of sex, a couple of bottles of fine wine he had brought back from the Napa Valley, and a few bucks to have some fun with while he was away performing.

They were getting dressed to leave the hotel when Jared said, "Are you okay? Is everything okay? Can I go to work in peace now?"

Emily looked up at him and said, "Yeah, I'm all right. I'll just miss you. I'll see you when you get home. By the way, when do you get back?"

"I'll be home Tuesday afternoon. I'll call you from Toronto. I'm leaving you three hundred dollars so you can have some fun and buy yourself something."

"You're leaving me money in a hotel room like I'm a hooker?"

He smiled. "You are a hooker, baby—let's go."

He smacked her on the ass. They grabbed a cab, and he dropped her off at Horace's house.

Jared got home and called Stephanie to tell her he had a late rehearsal and was tired. Stephanie complained and was pissed because she wouldn't see him before he left. She wanted to come over right then. Jared pacified her by promising he would spend some real time with her when he got home and would pick up a nice surprise for her while in Toronto. He got into bed, passed out, and left for Toronto when he woke up.

Emily awakened that morning with an uneasy feeling. She had dreamed of someone holding a gun to Jared's head, near his left ear. He hadn't called yet. She was worried and apprehensive, and these emotions continued throughout the morning. By late afternoon, she was getting frantic. She called his office and spoke with his secretary, Astrid, who really liked Emily a lot.

"Astrid, girl, give me the name and telephone number of the hotel in Toronto where the Knightcaps are booked. I've got to talk to my baby."

"Come on, Emily, you know I can't do that.".

"Oh, yes, you can. Just do it. Hell, there are so many people in and out of that office they'll never know who gave it to me. You know I'll cover you. Come on. Shit, I'm having a bird. Give it up, sweetie pie."

What the hell, she thought, if Jared gave her any shit about it she'd threaten to tell Stephanie everything, lose her job, and go on unemployment. She needed a rest, anyway, from the madness of all the women constantly coming in the office to look for the Knightcaps, and the telephone ringing every two seconds.

"It's the Hilton downtown, and here's the telephone number. The room number is 1707. Remember, Emily, you didn't get it here."

"Okay—just one more thing—what is the name and address of the club where they are playing? If you have the number, I need it."

Astrid blurted out the information and said, "Bye."

"I love you, girl," said Emily.

Emily wrote down the information and stared at it for over an hour. Finally she picked up the telephone and called American Airlines. She booked herself on American's flight 4949 departing from Philly at 10:20 that night. She checked her wallet for the money Jared had left her, as well as her own. The ticket was four hundred and eighteen dollars one way. She had that amount and a few hundred dollars she had saved. She was going to blow Jared's mind for three whole days!

She called her sister Regina and said, "Do me a favor—make yourself available to Horace to babysit tonight and Monday night. Be here by eleven tonight. Don't fail me. I'll lose my job. I've got to split for a few days. Give Horace a call this evening to confirm."

She hung up before her sister could answer, then called her brother Earl at work, told him the same thing, and hung up. She took the phone off the hook, so they couldn't call back to refuse, or to interrogate her. She grabbed a suitcase out of the basement, ran up to her room, and started to pack. She threw the suitcase underneath her bed in case Horace came in and dashed out to take the bus downtown to purchase two new nightgowns.

Jared was finishing up dinner in the hotel dining room with the rest of the group. He checked his watch. It was almost seven. He thought about calling Stephanie and Emily. He paid his check and went up to his room.

He and Lee were roommates as usual. Lee was like a brother and had lived at home with him since he was a teenager. Jared and Lee were the same age and attended school together. They had always been best friends. Lee's parents had been killed in an automobile accident when he was twelve years old. Connie didn't legally adopt Lee, but she took him as her son and raised him. Lee's older sister in Philadelphia actually had legal custody of him, but Lee preferred to stay at Connie's home. Now he was in the Knightcaps, the group Jared had formed. Jared's younger brother Rodney was also a member of the group.

Lee was sharp and a real heartthrob. He always looked as if he had just stepped out of *GQ*. He had that Leo charisma and charm. The women loved him and the Knightcaps were now making money hand over fist. He could have gotten his own spot, but he liked being at Connie's with Jared and Rodney. They were doing so much traveling—being around strangers, staying in hotels, and eating in restaurants—that they liked coming home to Connie and finding pots on the stove and pies and cakes in the oven. Connie took care of her three boys.

Jared sat down on his bed in the hotel and dialed Emily's number. It was busy. He called Stephanie and let her know he had arrived safely, chatted with her a bit, and told her he missed her and would see her on Tuesday. He felt guilty about cheating on her. She was so quiet and boring most of the time, but she was a nice girl and really cared for him. She had no pizzazz, no bitch in her. She was predictable. She would never do the wild stuff Emily did. Stephanie was a guppy and Emily was a piranha. That turned Jared on. The two women were exact opposites and Jared enjoyed being with both of them, depending on his mood.

Jared showered and dressed for work. The Knightcaps were going to give these French Canadian honeys a fit. They had to be at the club for a sound check at eight thirty and had shows scheduled for eleven p.m. and one thirty a.m.

The first show was a sellout—a great crowd that loved their music. At the intermission, Damon brought three fine girls back to the dressing room. Some of the group were exchanging numbers and chatting, but Jared had had a rough night with Emily before he left and was tired. He wasn't up for a party tonight.

The Knightcaps captivated the audience at the last performance. Jared was bushed. As they were preparing to leave the club at around three, Jared saw Lee engrossed in a conversation with a beautiful Asian girl, hair down to her butt. He called Lee over and said, "If it's party time for you tonight, get another room, I can't take it."

"Okay, that's cool," Lee replied.

Jared grabbed a cab to the hotel. In spite of what he said, Lee arrived about twenty minutes later with two chicks and four bottles of wine the club owner had given him. They were ready to get fired up, and Jared was in bed. Jared tried to be polite to Roslyn, who was winking at him and offering to give him a massage. She spoke French with English mixed in, but he didn't understand a word. He couldn't keep his eyes open long enough to figure out anything more than that she was white with red hair. He wished they would all go away.

Lee became the bartender. Melina was trying to get Lee to give her a shirt of his to put on so she would be more "comfortable." Roslyn attempted to get more friendly but Jared just nodded and drifted in and out of sleep. Suddenly, the phone rang and startled everyone at about four-thirty a.m. Jared reached over Roslyn and answered, "Hello."

"It's me. You miss me?" Emily said.

"Yeah."

"Don't fret, baby, I miss you too. That's why I'm downstairs on the house phone. You've got ten minutes to clean up."

"You're lying, Emily. You're in Philly."

"You're busted, Jared. You're in 1707. See you in eight minutes."

Emily ran to the elevator and pushed the button. She hoped it would take a few minutes because she wanted to give Jared a full eight minutes.

But it came in a few seconds and she hopped on. When she got off at the seventeenth floor, he had six and a half minutes. She checked her watch and when there was one minute left, she started toward their room. She listened at the door, but didn't hear any voices. She knocked and Jared appeared.

"Hi, it's me," she said.

Jared stepped into the hall and closed the door behind him. She looked puzzled, but kept her cool. Jared gave her a quick kiss and said, "I've got to talk to you before we go in."

"Okay."

He walked a few steps down the hall and she followed. "Listen, baby, there are a couple of women in the room."

"Are they housekeeping or room service, sweetie?"

Jared paused. Emily was tough. "Neither. They are sort of friends Lee met and brought back from the club."

"Oh, yeah? That sweet Lee. It was mighty generous of him to bring something back for you."

"Emily, you aren't going to believe this, but I didn't have anything to do with this and they are his friends. You got that? Now what's it going to be? Are you going to turn this place out?"

"Me? Turn it out? I've got class, baby. Let's hit it. I'm tired. I had a long flight."

Jared stood in the hall afraid to move. He didn't need this shit tonight. He had never encountered this type of situation with Emily. He didn't know how she was going to act. He studied her. He didn't know whether she would put them out or curse them out. He was worried, but he didn't want Emily to know. He tried to be cool, hoping she wouldn't test him by acting a fool once she got in the room.

"Okay, Emily, let's go. Just remember, I'm being honest with you and I didn't arrange any of this."

Emily said, "Okay," and they walked back down the hall. Jared opened the door with his key, let Emily in, and picked up her bags. She came in all smiles. Melina and Lee were sitting on Lee's bed and Roslyn was in the chair.

"Hello, folks! Here I am live in living color, freezing my ass off in Toronto! How are you guys? Hey, Lee, give me a hug, baby! How are you doing? And who are these two beautiful ladies?" Emily said, smiling at them both.

Lee got up and hugged Emily. The two chicks looked like they had seen a ghost. They weren't prepared for this. Emily walked up to Melina and shook her hand and said, "I'm Emily, a friend of the Knightcaps. You're about as cute as they come. Look at all this long pretty hair. What's your name, sweetie?"

"I'm Melina." Melina looked over at Roslyn. "This is my friend Roslyn."

Emily moved over to Roslyn. She extended her hand and then hugged her. Emily stepped back and looked long and hard at them both. Lee and Jared were scared shitless. They were all puzzled and uneasy as she stared at the two women.

"I'm in quite a bit of a dilemma here." She paused. Her silence was killing the four of them. Finally, she spoke.

"I'm just trying to figure out who is the prettiest."

Jared stood against the wall in amazement. Emily was something else. This was showtime for her and he knew it. She took her coat off and buzzed around the room, looking at the décor, opening drawers, and checking out the bathroom. She was quite bubbly, talking the entire time, making a big fuss over how nice the place was. No one else said a word. She picked her suitcase off the floor and opened it.

"I knew how cold it was here, and so I brought some tea with me. I don't want my friends catching a cold. Here's the good stuff, baby." She threw the box of herbal tea on the bed to Lee. "I brought you a box, too, Jared. I didn't know you guys were having company, or I would have brought some down for Melina and Roslyn."

She was glad she remembered the names. She added, "If room service isn't open now, we'll get some hot water when we wake up." They all looked at each other.

Finally Jared said, "How was your flight?"

"Oh, honey, it was fine. I just had to change planes in some city—I can't even remember which. But I'm here now. Damn, it is cold here! Melina, Roslyn, how do you stand it? It's such a good thing you guys made friends with Jared and Lee, and I'm so proud that they were hospitable enough to have you two spend the night. It is much too cold to be traveling late at night. You know, we Philadelphians live in the City of Brotherly Love and we don't turn our backs on anyone."

Jared wanted to gag. Emily was really working the room.

She began to unpack, hanging things up and putting clothes away in the drawers. Jared lay across the bed, watching. He couldn't believe her. Lee was in shock, too. Emily was the only one talking. As she unpacked, she showed her things to Melina and Roslyn. She pulled out her new makeup and discussed the colors with them.

She told Melina, "I can't get over all that pretty hair you have. You've got to let me play in it tomorrow. What are you guys planning to do tomorrow? Maybe we can go shopping or something. How about that? What time are you planning to get up? I just need a few hours sleep to get my second wind."

Jared put the pillow over his face to keep from laughing out loud. He thought Emily was a trip.

"Roslyn, has the cat got your tongue? What about us doing a little shopping tomorrow?" Roslyn started to speak her French-accented English and Emily said, "Go slower, baby, I think we have a language barrier. Just talk slower and take your time." Emily was now holding her hands.

"I can try to go to shopping with you," Roslyn replied.

"Isn't that cute?" said Emily. "She is going to try to go *to* shopping with me. You are just too cute, Roslyn." She pinched Roslyn's cheek.

"Well, listen, folks, I have to take a quick shower. I've been flying since about ten thirty this evening. I probably smell and all." She lifted her armpits and sniffed them. "Let me get my shower, and when I get out we'll talk some more, order some food if room service will oblige us, and really concentrate on getting to know each other. Hell, maybe you two fine things can go back to Philly with us when the Knightcaps leave this freezing place. How about that?"

With that, she dashed into the bathroom and ran the shower. She took her time putting lotion on, brushing her teeth, and combing her hair. There were two thick white terrycloth robes hanging on the bathroom hook. She grabbed one and put it on to cover her naked body. It was soft and fluffy and felt divine. The she yelled, "All right, folks, I'm clean and smelling like a rose. Let's make these French Canadian cooks rustle us up some grub."

When she came out, Lee and Jared were in their beds alone. There was no sign of Melina or Roslyn. Emily said, "Hey, you two, what happened to our guests?"

Jared said, "Emily, get your ass in this bed."

In an hour the telephone rang. It was the guitar player, Jimmy.

"Jared—some shit has gone down," Jimmy said.

"What's going on?" Jared asked.

"I'm down in the lobby. Joe Carter got robbed and shot in his room. There were three chicks in there. You know the one with the red hair and that Asian-looking one with the hair down to her butt? Well, their buddy—the one with the real short blond hair—left the club with Joe. She was in his room. They robbed him, man—the three of them, about a half hour ago, and Tony King walked in on the shit. Joe's on his way to the hospital with a leg wound, and Tony beat the shit out of the redhead with the gun. The cops are down here now. You'd better get your ass up. You call the shots for the Knightcaps, so these people are going to want to talk to you. Lee brought them bitches from the club to your room. They'll want him, too. You guys better get moving," Jimmy said.

# Chapter Thirty-three

# *Paula*

Paula ended up with thirteen stitches as a result of her encounter with Killer. Horace kept me for two weeks straight and then returned me to her, along with Sydni. She didn't treat me much better, but she never hit me anymore and I never had to eat off the floor again. I was doing very well in school and was in the Honors program. Paula still had her boyfriends, and I kept my mouth shut about them. Whenever I went to Grandma's, Earl would come around and take Sydni and me to a movie or the museum. Sometimes he took us to his house to see the fish. We liked him a lot, and he and Horace were good friends.

Paula had gotten a job at a bar two nights a week and on weekends. She got really dressed up the nights she went to work. She also still worked at the department store.

Horace didn't bother with Paula at all. The only time she got to see Renee was when Horace arranged to leave Renee at Grandma's. She was seeing a lot of Floyd. Floyd was henpecked and did everything Paula told him to do. She told him she needed a bigger place and he saved up some money and rented her a house. It had three bedrooms, so we each had a room to ourselves. He stayed there often.

Floyd usually picked her up from the bar. She started to drink a lot. When she got drunk, she was pretty simple. Sometimes she would pee on herself because she couldn't get her clothes off fast enough to make it to the bathroom. If she came home alone drunk, she would sometimes stay in for a while and then call a cab to go out riding around. If she didn't have money to pay the driver, she'd bring him in or give him a lamp or something out of the house.

A few times she decided to fly on a plane somewhere and woke up Sydni and me to go to the airport with her. Since she had no credit cards, she'd try to write a check, but the people at the airline desk would see how intoxicated she was and refuse to take it. A few times she actually made it on the plane and we'd end up in some strange city. She would locate her friends, who'd invite us to go to their house for the day. Then she would attempt to get us back to Philadelphia. Usually she couldn't get us back home the next day because the banks were open and the airlines could check her balance. So Floyd or Grandma would have to wire money for us to get back home.

One year, I had a leading role as the "Ghost of Christmas Past" in *A Christmas Carol*. I was very excited. I had learned all my lines in one day and was the best at every rehearsal. On the night of the school play, everybody was coming to see me—Horace, Grandpa, Grandma, Renee, Emily, and Sydni. Even Earl.

The play started at seven p.m., and there was no sign of Paula. The play went on and things were going great. All of a sudden we heard a lot of noise in the auditorium. I peeped out from behind the curtain and saw Paula staggering down the school aisle, drunk as a skunk and barefoot. I wanted to crawl under the stage from embarrassment. I couldn't believe it! Everyone was looking at her. Horace and Earl jumped up to get her out, but they weren't quick enough, and Paula ran down the aisle onto the center of the stage.

She talked to the audience. Horace and Earl tried to get her off the stage, but she ran around in circles as they chased her. She fell, and when they got to her she started to scream, "Leave me alone. I want to say my piece. I'll fix that Amber Gray. You know what, people? I'm her goddamn mother and she is the worst child you ever want to know. She ain't no ghost, she's for real."

Horace grabbed her feet, Earl got her by the arms, and they dragged her out of the auditorium. Half the audience was laughing, the other half was in shock.

When they got her outside, Earl said, "Let's put her in your car, Horace, and take her home."

"I'm not putting this bitch in my car, and I'm not missing Amber's performance. Come on, I'll think of something."

Earl noticed two Dumpsters behind the school yard. He looked at Horace and pointed. Horace laughed. "Yeah, man."

Paula was on the ground, screaming and cursing as she tried to get away, but Earl had his foot on her neck. Horace got his jumper cables and an oily old towel from his car. The two of them removed all of her clothes, including her underwear. They tied her up with the cables, tied

Earl's bandana around her mouth, and wrapped the towel around her head. Then they put her in the Dumpster and closed the lid. Horace hid her clothing underneath the Dumpster.

They looked at each other. Earl pointed to the Dumpster. "That's trash, ain't it?" They gave each other a high five and returned to the school auditorium. They were confident that the naked Paula, even if she did eventually free herself, would not disrupt the performance.

One night Paula came home from the bar with Floyd. She put on a beautiful nightgown, redid her makeup, and combed her hair, adding a final touch of hair spray. She sat on the edge of the bed and waited for Floyd, who was in the shower. She decided to have a cigarette, took out a Newport, and lit a match. Then Paula screamed.

Sydni and I ran out of our rooms. Paula was running, jumping, and screaming. Her hair was on fire, burning like a tree. We tried to smother the fire with a sheet, but it kept burning. I ran to the phone to call the police. By now Paula was on the floor rolling her head around to put the fire out. The smell was absolutely awful. Floyd, who was still in the shower, hadn't heard a thing. Finally Sydni ran into the bathroom and screamed at him. He ran out, buck naked and dripping wet, and grabbed his pants when he saw us staring at him. He wrapped Paula's entire head in a blanket, led her into the bathroom, put her head in the tub, and turned on the water. When the fire was out, he drove her to the hospital in his car.

Sydni and I kept on screaming until the police finally came. We told them what had happened and they called Grandma. She told them to bring us to her house.

Well, compared to all the hair Paula used to have, she was as bald as she could be for over four months. It seemed like it took forever for her hair to grow back. Every time Horace saw her he started to laugh, and each week he sent her four cans of hair spray, a carton of cigarettes, and a giant box of matches. She had a fit every time the box came to the house.

I spent a lot of weekends and school nights at Horace's house. He would take me to school when he got in from work. I liked Emily a lot. She was fun. She took good care of all of us. Sometimes, Sydni stayed over too. Paula still hated me, but at least she didn't beat the daylights out of me.

One afternoon I was at home working on a school science project—a papier-mâché globe. Horace had bought all the materials for me. I had gotten the globe together and was painting it, when I accidentally knocked the paint can off the table and all over Paula's rug. I tried to clean it up, but couldn't. Sydni stood paralyzed with fear. I was scared Paula would kill me for sure, and I didn't want to be there when she got home.

Hysterical, I called Horace's house to ask him what to do and to pick us up. Emily said he wasn't home. I was screaming because I was scared. She said she didn't know where Horace and Renee were, but she offered to try to reach Earl. She called back in about five minutes and said Earl had left work and must be on his way home. She'd have him pick us up when he got in. I waited almost an hour, but Emily didn't call. So I called again and explained that I had to get over there because Paula was going to kill me for sure. She was due back from work any minute now. Emily told me to get my books together and pack a change of clothes for school. She would send a cab for me. I gave her our address and packed some things, praying to God I'd get out before Paula came home. I wrote a note saying I was sorry about the rug and that Emily had taken us to Horace's house. I put the note on her bed.

In ten minutes Emily and the cab were outside. I got my bag and wondered if I should take my globe with me, but I left it, grabbed Sydni instead, and ran to the cab. Emily was on the steps waiting for us when Paula walked up.

"What's going on?" Paula said

"I have to go to Horace's house," I answered.

"Wait a minute. What the hell is going on? Get your ass back into that house."

Emily scooped us up and threw us into the cab. We left Paula standing on the street. She went into the house, saw the paint spilled on the rug and all the mess from the project, and found the note. She was furious.

Horace got home with Renee about seven thirty. We told him what had happened and he said not to worry. He told Emily she had done the right thing by going to get me and reimbursed her for the cab fare.

He promised to buy me some more materials in the morning and to help me with the project so I could turn it in on time. I took a bath and got ready for bed. Paula hadn't called, thank God. Horace took a nap and got up around ten thirty p.m. to get ready for work. I was asleep in his bed when he left.

About twelve fifteen a.m., Horace got a call at work from Paula.

"Why did you send that bitch to my house to take my child? You've already given that bitch my baby, and now you have her come to my house to get in my business and take Amber and Sydni. You've got a lot of fucking nerve, Horace. I should call the cops on her."

Horace could tell she had been drinking. "Listen, Paula, Amber was scared to death. I wasn't home to pick her up, so Emily just did the next best thing to keep shit cool. Now, I'm at work and don't feel like going through a lot of shit with you. We'll deal with this tomorrow. By the way, I will pay to have your rug cleaned, get Amber's project done, and clean up the mess at your house if you like. Let's not get all bent out of shape about this thing."

"I'm sick of that bitch Emily. You're probably fucking her and planning on making a nice happy home and family and using my kids to do it."

Horace said, "Kiss my ass," and hung up.

At 1:10 a.m. Emily heard a knock on the door. She couldn't imagine who it could be at that hour. She knew Jared was out of town for the next couple of days. She went to the window and peered out. It was Paula! She moved away from the window.

Paula screamed and banged on the door, yelling Emily's name and demanding she open the door. Then she screamed for Renee, Sydni, and me. We woke up and scrambled around the house. Emily called Horace's job and left word that there was an emergency at his home. All of a sudden we heard a crash and breaking glass downstairs. Paula had broken a windowpane and was entering the house. Emily called the police and asked them to hurry. She was terrified, and Renee and I were both crying.

Emily ran down the stairs as Paula rushed in. She grabbed Emily by the throat and they began to fight. I tried to help Emily, but Paula knocked me away. The phone rang, distracting us all. Emily moved toward it and Paula reached for a statuette from Horace's mantle and struck Emily on the head. She was out cold with one blow. Paula stood over her body and called her a meddling bitch. I grabbed Renee and Sydni and headed for Horace's bedroom. The phone stopped ringing.

The police hadn't arrived yet. I slammed Horace's door and managed to connect the small latch. Paula was yelling, kicking and pushing the door to break it down. Renee was screaming. Sydni was quiet as usual. I ran into the closet and found Horace's money box. I planned to grab some money, climb out the window with Renee and Sydni, run for a cab or a bus, and ask the driver to help Emily. When I opened the box, I saw money and a gun.

The bedroom door suddenly crashed in. Paula was inside the room looking for me. I closed the closet door, but it didn't have a lock. Paula charged toward the closet, but she tripped over Renee. I grabbed the gun and kicked the closet door open. I fired three shots, hitting Paula twice. She fell to the floor.

I didn't make a sound. I kept the gun in one hand, grabbed my sister with the other, and headed downstairs. Sydni followed close behind. Emily was still on the floor and she wasn't moving. I thought she was dead. Finally the police arrived. I gave the officer the gun, put Renee on the couch, and gave her a toy to play with. I went over to Emily and tried to lift her head. The officer told me not to move her. He called for an ambulance and told me to sit down.

I said, "My mother is upstairs. I shot her."

One officer went to Emily and the other one went to see about Paula. The officer couldn't revive Emily. The other officer came down the stairs, Paula was in front of him. She was shouting that I had shot her. At that point I heard brakes screeching outside. Horace ran into the house. He screamed when he saw Emily on the living room floor and ran to her.

Paula was sitting at the bottom of the stairs. "That little bitch shot me, and I had to lie on the floor and play dead to keep her from killing me! She's crazy! She's going to reform school for sure now." Then she pointed to Horace. "He's a terrible person. I've been taking all kinds of shit off him. A few months ago he put me in a trash can. He left me there naked. He stole my clothes and tied me up and everything. I started to call you people to tell you about that, but I didn't want to get him in trouble. Now he stole my kids and made me get shot. You police officers have got to do something about him."

Her words ran together. She was as high as a kite or drunk for real. Horace just looked at her with a blank expression. He knelt over Emily, but the officers told him to move away. The ambulance arrived and the paramedics placed Emily and Paula on stretchers and carried them out. I sobbed as the ambulance took Emily away. The police stayed at the house to get a full report from Horace and me, then escorted all of us to the police station. Since I acted in self-defense, no charges were filed against me. No charges were filed against Horace either because the gun was legally registered to him. We left the station a little after three a.m. and went straight to the hospital to see Emily. She was still unconscious.

Horace called Grandma from the hospital and told her everything. She left home immediately. Horace wanted Sydni, Renee, and me to go back home with Grandma when she left, but I started to cry because I wanted to stay at the hospital with Emily. I wanted to be there when she woke up. Finally Horace agreed to let me stay.

At the hospital, a guard was inside the emergency room near Paula's bed. Paula had suffered two graze wounds, one on the side of her foot and the other on her wrist. She had been arrested and charged with everything from breaking and entering to attempted murder. She was handcuffed to her bed. Grandma went in to see her, but the police officer asked her to step back outside. He explained that Paula was under arrest and wasn't allowed to talk to anyone. He would be taking Paula to jail upon her release from the hospital. Grandma pleaded with him, and, finally, he allowed her to see Paula. He accompanied her inside and stayed with her while she spoke to Paula. After five minutes, he said she had to leave. Grandma walked out and came over to us with sadness in her eyes. She left and took Sydni and Renee with her. Horace peeped in to try to see Paula. She lay on the hospital bed staring at the ceiling. Horace had never seen her this quiet or calm.

Horace and I were allowed to stay with Emily in the intensive care unit. An IV was placed in her arm for medication, and she was on oxygen. Horace and I sat quietly by her bed and prayed together for her. Then Horace decided it was time to call Earl. He went to his car to get his address book out of the glove compartment and called Earl and gave him the bad news. Earl called his sister Regina and they arrived at the hospital in twenty minutes. They were in shock. Horace blamed himself. I blamed myself. The four of us sat by her bed and waited for a miracle.

The Knightcaps were performing in Houston. For some reason Jared was having a rough evening. He was depressed and didn't feel right. The guys had noticed he was not himself. When they returned to the hotel, Lee said, "Hey, what's up with you, brother? You coming down with something or are you just in a bad mood?"

"I don't know. I feel kind of weird. It's just a strange thing. I've got a bad feeling."

"Is it this spot or something? Is the hotel going to catch on fire? You know Mom always says you're psychic."

"I don't know, Lee. I just feel like something is wrong."

Jared put two pillows against the headboard of the bed and started to think. Then he tried to sleep, but he was too restless and fidgety. He tossed and turned for a couple of hours. He called his mom to check on her, and she was fine. He woke Stephanie up out of a deep sleep and told her he'd talk to her in a couple of days. Then he called Emily and let the phone ring seventeen times. No answer. Then he knew something was wrong. Emily should have been in that house with Renee while Horace was at work. When he called Emily in the middle of the night she was always there. He got up and paced the floor. He woke Lee up and told him about the calls he had made. He started to get dressed.

"Where are you going? Are you going back to Philly?"

"No, I'm going down to the lobby to make a bunch of phone calls."

"Make them here."

"No, man, I've got to be by myself. I have to find out what is going on with Emily. I have a bad feeling, man. Something is just not right."

"Listen, Jared, you're jumping the gun without a real reason. When was the last time you talked to Emily?"

"Sunday night."

"Well, it's only Tuesday. Think back. Maybe she said she had some plans or something."

Jared was irritated. "I *am* Emily's fucking plans! I know her. She would be home at this time of night. I've got a weird-ass fucking feeling that something is dead wrong, Lee. I know it, man."

Lee was getting worried now. "Jared, call home. Talk to Mom again. Wake her up. Ask her if Emily's there or if she heard from her tonight. You know how she gets crazy sometimes when we go to work. Maybe she's there. You never actually asked Mom when you called if Emily was there."

"She's not there."

"Goddamnit, call Mom or I will."

Jared called Connie again. "Hey, Mom, I'm sorry to wake you up again."

"Jared, what's wrong? Why do you keep calling here, waking me up?"

"Mom, is Emily there with you?"

"No, Jared, Emily is not here."

"Have you talked to her since I left?"

"She called me around two o'clock this afternoon."

"Was she sick or anything?"

"No, she seemed fine. Jared, what the heck is going on?"

"Maybe nothing, Mom. I've just had a rough night and a bad feeling. I can't locate Emily. I'm worried about her."

"Maybe she unplugged her phone, Jared. Maybe she was tired."

"Mom, Emily is not unplugging any telephone when I'm away. You know what I mean, Mom. The phone is not unplugged."

"Well, Jared, I don't know what to say. The only thing that bothers me about this thing is that you've always been able to sense stuff. Now I'll be up all night worried, too."

"Okay, Mom, I'm going to let you go. I'll give you a buzz tomorrow. If you hear anything from Emily, tell her to call me at the Houston Hyatt. I'm in room 936."

"Okay, Jared. Try to get some rest."

Jared hung up. Lee said, "Well, you know Emily showed up at four thirty in the morning in Toronto. Maybe she's on her way here."

Jared was praying that was the case.

# Chapter Thirty-four

# Reba

*I*t had been three days since Reba had arrived home. She decided to give Doug a call. She missed him terribly and wanted to find out how he was and if he still wanted her. His phone rang and he answered.

"Hey, Dexter," said Reba.

"How are you, baby? I have been dying to talk to you. How are things going?"

"Things are going okay. I had to turn into a drill sergeant, but I'm handling the new position rather well. How are you?"

"I'm doing pretty good. My foot is healing up. I have a few heart problems, but I guess I'll live."

"What's up with your heart?"

"Oh, I picked up some tramp about a week ago in Virginia and she broke my heart. It's on the mend."

Reba laughed. "Listen, Dexter, I've got something I need to ask you."

"Okay, shoot."

"Well, the question is: Do you still want me?"

Doug hesitated and then said, "Yes."

"Well, I've got a plan. I can't go into it fully, but I need to know if you want me to leave Johnny and come to be with you and if my kids are welcome. I mean all six of them. I can give you some time to think about it if you like." There was silence. Reba tapped her foot nervously.

Finally, Doug replied, "To be perfectly honest—and I don't want to upset you, baby—I've been going back and forth with this thing between you and me. I'm scared. This isn't a regular run-of-the-mill commitment—this is big-time because so many lives are going to be affected."

Reba listened and knew exactly what he was talking about. There was silence on the phone. Both were deep in thought. "Doug, I'm scared, too. But I'm more afraid of *not* uprooting myself and the kids to be with you. I'm petrified of us not being together. I'm on fast forward with you. I can't seem to get into reverse," Reba said.

"I'm so glad you admitted it too. I was almost afraid to let you know I was afraid," Doug said. There was silence again. "Listen—fuck it. Get yourself together and pack the kids up, too. Come on down. Shit. The worse thing that can happen is we'll all end up hating each other. If that happens, I'll move to my sister's house. You guys can have the damn house." They both laughed.

"So, Mr. Ransome, we're welcome?" Reba asked.

"So, it's a package deal and I get half a dozen kids and a woman who can't cook?"

"Yeah, baby, that's what you get."

"Guess what? You got a deal and a man who is in love and terrified of all of you—and myself. I must be crazy. Wait until my sister hears this shit. When are you coming?"

Reba whooped with joy. "I have a plan. It will take some time. Just be patient. I'll be there. You aren't going to hear from me a lot because I'm working on a few things. Just trust me, okay? Don't get pissed if you don't hear from me. I'll try to drop you a line or call when I can. Think about what you are going to do about space in the house or if you feel we need to move. I can save up some money toward a bigger house for us if that's what you want. I plan to help out as much as I can. By the way, I love you, I really do, and I miss you like crazy. I don't have time to tell you what happened when I got home. I'm hanging in here until we get together."

"Okay, Reba, you've got all my numbers. Keep in touch when you can."

Reba looked around at the house. It didn't look too bad. She wanted to get all her business straight before Johnny came home. He hadn't been keeping any late nights since her return. She picked up the telephone and made another call.

"Hello," said Peggy.

"Hi, Peggy, this is Reba. Can I come down to talk to you?"

"Yes, Reba, come on down. When did you get back?"

"Three days ago. I'm on my way."

Reba walked into Peggy's house and they both headed for the kitchen. Peggy poured two glasses of lemonade and sat down, impatient to hear the news.

"Peggy, I am leaving Johnny."

Peggy took a sip of lemonade and nodded at Reba to continue.

"I'm in love with Doug and he wants me and the kids," Reba explained. "I'm divorcing Johnny. He makes me sick. I'm ready to get well, and this man is the perfect medicine."

"When and how are you going to do this?"

"Well, there are some things I have to get in order before I go. First I have to get my kids together so they are responsible and know how to act. Also, I need to learn how to cook and how to dress. That's why I'm here. Do you think you could give me some lessons?"

Peggy stared at Reba for a long time. She knew Reba was serious, but she had to talk to her about what she was about to do. "Reba, you have been married to Johnny for a long time. The kids have always lived here. You have help here with them if you need it. We don't know much about Doug. Do you feel this is the best thing for yourself and the kids? You've only been back three days. Why don't you give yourself some more time to think? This could be a bad move. Does the man have enough room for all of you?"

"I've spoken to him. He wants us all."

Peggy nodded slowly. "All right, Reba, what's the plan?"

"The plan is that you will teach me how to cook and help me out with my clothes. I'll pay you."

"Reba, you don't have to pay me. I love you like you were my daughter."

Reba smiled shyly. "You don't know how much that means to me." She wiped away a tear. "So when can we start?"

"I'll tell you what. Let's plan on meeting every Thursday evening at eight. This way you'll be finished with the kids, dinner, and homework. I'll get some recipes together and we'll start next Thursday."

Reba got up from the table and hugged Peggy. Tears welled up in her eyes. She said to Peggy, "You have changed my life. Just giving me a job for the weekend has changed my entire existence. I don't know how to thank you."

When Reba returned home, Johnny was there. He looked at her, rolled his eyes, and walked to the kitchen. Reba followed him in.

"What's for dinner?" he said.

Reba replied sarcastically, "Oh, what's for dinner?" She pulled open a drawer and took out an apron and tied it around her waist. "Oh, what's for dinner? Let me see. Let's see what the old wifey-poo can get together for hubby-pie. Take your pick. Chicken marsala?" She threw a can of

Campbell's pork and beans from the cabinet to the counter. "Steak teriyaki or teriyaki steak, or whatever way it goes?" Out came the second can of beans. "Or how about veal parmigiana? Oh, no, strike that, no veal parmigiana—remember, we don't eat red stuff anymore. How about fettuccine alfredo—you like that?" The third can of beans went flying across the kitchen.

Johnny was ducking and staring at her. He wanted to smack her simple. Then she grabbed a loaf of bread and hurled it across the kitchen. It hit the refrigerator.

"There's your dinner, Mr. Penster." She switched out of the room.

Reba picked up the telephone and called the Nobles to see if they had heard from Lucy.

"Hi, Mr. Noble. This is Reba Penster, how are you?"

"I'm fine, Reba. How are you? Did you have a nice time in Virginia?"

"Yes, I did. I was wondering if Lucy was back or if you had heard from her."

"Lucy called last night and she is having a great time in the Bahamas. We expect her back over the weekend."

"That is fantastic! If she calls again, please ask her to call me. I miss her."

"Okay, Reba, I'll give her the message."

"The Bahamas!" Reba murmured to herself as she hung up. "Lucy hit the jackpot. Damn." She imagined Lucy and Kevin lying on the beach. She was so happy for Lucy.

Reba went to see the kids and to survey their rooms, which were looking pretty good. She checked the notes and charts where the kids kept track of their chores, and asked about their homework. Then she went back to her room.

In a few minutes Johnny walked in. He sat on the bed like a beaten man. "Reba, can we talk?"

"Talk about what?"

"Can we talk about you and me? Can we pull this thing together? I'm willing to do some serious changing to make you happy. Can we give it a shot?"

"Johnny, I do not want to mix you up or confuse you. I don't want to lead you on. I just want out."

"Reba, tell me something. Do you really have someone else, or is this bullshit?"

"What I have or do not have happens to be none of your business anymore. I've had a rough time with you for too long. I'm burned out and tired. I just want out. You can't do anything to change the way I feel. I wish I were angry with you for the way you've made my life all these years. If I were angry with you, you'd have a chance because it would mean I cared. But there is no anger. I do not have the energy or desire to keep at this thing. Do you understand?"

"Reba, listen. This is for real. I swear on the kids, I have never cheated on you. I just got caught up in the bars, the card games, and the clubs. You know, just messing with the guys and stuff. I never did anything wrong and I never had anyone else. Come on, Reba, let's get this thing back together."

Reba looked up at him and smiled. From the top of her closet, behind all the junk, she pulled out three composition books with rubber bands around them. She opened them up one by one and started reading. She had listed every date she had sex with him and every date he had stayed out all night. She had women's names and phone numbers and two addresses. She had notes of prescriptions she had filled for trichomonas on forty-seven occasions during their marriage. He had claimed that once you have trich it never goes away.

Then she read a letter out loud, one of six that she had found in Johnny's things and hidden in her books.

*Dear Johnny:*

*You are the wildest man I have ever known. A real outlaw in bed. Thank you so much for rescuing me from Jack and for these two beautiful boys we have together. Clyde looks exactly like you and Herman is indeed the apple of my eye. I am just sorry that we did not meet sooner, before you married that sad drab thing we laugh so many nights about. I know that you really love me and if it were not for your children with her, you would be here with us full time. I really appreciate the way you come to us on holidays, even though you have that "other family," and how you provide so well for us. We really had a great time camping last weekend. These boys of ours have the best dad in the world. I made tomato soup tonight and thought of you. I'll be glad to see you when the weekend rolls around. You have my life and my heart and I know that as soon as Reba's kids get out of the way, you'll be here full time.*

*Thanks for the perfume. You are truly the love of my life.*

*Tamara*

Reba put the letter away. She pulled out the five others and held them up for Johnny to see. She then put them back in the books and clutched them to her chest with her arms folded. Johnny walked out of the bedroom.

For the next three nights, Johnny came straight home from work and tried to talk to Reba. The first night he came in and asked about dinner again. Reba threw a can of Spam at him and it hit him on the nose. The next night he came in and asked her to go to dinner with him. She politely picked up a Super Soaker water gun that Andrew had left on the kitchen counter fully loaded, pulled the trigger, and emptied half of it all over Johnny. Then she put it down, told him to kiss her ass, and walked out of the kitchen, leaving him soaking wet. The third night he came home with flowers and a gourmet dinner from downtown. She dumped everything into the sink and ran water over it. The next night he didn't come straight home from work and didn't call.

While he was out, Reba thought about all the years she had invested in him. The longer he stayed out the madder she got. Even though she didn't want him anymore, she was still infuriated at the fact that he was probably out fucking as he had been for years.

Reba was a Cancer—the mothering sign. Sensitive, moody, and thrifty. Cancers are also very passive. They can take a lot of shit from a mate, and often do so in order to stay together. But Reba had Scorpio rising and a moon in Scorpio. That meant she could be vindictive. The worst thing to do in life is to cross a Scorp. They will freely give their heart and their soul, but the recipient had better know how to care for it. A Scorpio heart is fragile and should not be broken. Scorps thrive on revenge. They are the best at it. They are calculators and concentrators. They lay in the cut and wait for the right time to take revenge—when it's least expected. They plot their revenge and laugh the whole time. They are organized and will indeed have the last word. They are water signs, full of emotion, the most complex sign in the zodiac and the hardest people to share relationships with.

Every time a half hour passed and Johnny had not arrived, Reba got a new trash bag from the kitchen and put some of his things in it. By one a.m. she had nine trash bags filled with clothing, jewelry, shoes, and socks. Everything Johnny owned was in them. She took the bags downstairs and placed them by the front door. The next day was trash pickup. Just as she put the last bag at the front door, Johnny stuck his key in the lock.

Reba opened the door. He looked at her, surprised, and braced himself for a fight. Instead, she smiled. "Hi, Johnny. How are you? I was about to put the trash out because you were so late. Can you put the bags on the curb?"

Johnny, shocked, said, "Sure," and took the bags out to the street. Reba went upstairs and went to bed. Johnny didn't dare to get in bed with her after getting home so late, so he settled down in the basement.

Reba was up bright and early at five thirty a.m. It was a big day for her. She was having her first cooking lesson with Peggy in the evening. She prepared breakfast for the kids while Johnny was still snoozing away in the basement. Reba hoped he would oversleep so she and the kids could leave before he realized that his belongings were missing. She set the table, mixed pancake batter, and put sausage in the oven on low. Then she ran upstairs to shower.

After her shower, Johnny still had not awakened. She quickly dressed and got the kids up.

"Okay, guys, let's get going. You had your baths last night. Let's wash faces and brush teeth and get dressed. Then come downstairs for your breakfast. Be quiet. Your father is sleeping in the basement and I don't want you to wake him. Don't go into the basement for anything."

It was six forty-five a.m. now and she decided to give Doug a quick call. She reversed the charges so Johnny wouldn't find out his number. Doug answered and accepted the call.

"Hi, Dexter," she said.

"Hey, baby, this is a nice surprise. My day will probably go real well."

"I hope so. This is just a quick call to tell you I love you and I am on the case. Do ya miss me?"

"Yes, I miss you, but I got a couple of girls to spend the night with me last night, so I'm not terribly lonely. I'm just being honest with you."

Reba's tone changed. "You want to run that by me again?"

Doug said, "Hold on a minute." Reba could hear a rustling noise and then a young female voice said, "Hi."

Reba said, "May I speak with Doug?"

The girl passed the phone to Doug. "Yes, Reba?"

"What's going on—change of heart?"

"No, not really." Doug chuckled. "You just met my niece Sandi. She and her sister, Max, spent the night with me last night. I got you, didn't I, Reba?"

"You make me sick. I've got to go. The kids are on their way down to breakfast."

"You're cooking?" said Doug.

"Yes, I am."

"Well, I guess all the kids will end up in the nurse's office before three o'clock."

Reba snapped, "Go to hell, Doug. Talk to you later." She hung up, got the kids fed and off to school, and left for work.

Johnny woke up after eight a.m. He was tired and decided to take the day off. No Reba, no kids. It would be a wonderful day, and he intended to be gone by their return. He turned over and went back to sleep. He woke up again around noon and decided to shower, get the paper, and go down to the diner for breakfast. When he opened his dresser drawer for underwear, he found it empty. He figured Reba had washed clothes last night, so he went to the basement. Nothing there. Then he remembered that the kids had all these "duties," so he checked their rooms, thinking they hadn't distributed the clean laundry. He came up empty-handed. He searched the basement again and also looked in the washer and dryer. Bewildered, he went back into his bedroom and checked all the drawers one more time. He found all Reba's things in her drawers and nothing in any of his. He checked the closet where Reba's things were, but he couldn't locate any of his stuff. He sat on the bed and tried to figure it out. Johnny couldn't come up with anything. He thought the best thing to do was to call Reba at work.

"Reba, I am walking around naked because I cannot find any clean underwear or any of the rest of my clothes. Where are they? Did the kids put them somewhere?"

"You put your clothes outside last night. Did you forget that? You put them out with the trash. Why are you calling me about them? Don't you remember you took the trash out last night?" She never came up for air.

"What are you talking about, woman? You asked me to put the trash out last night. The only thing I put out last night was the trash."

"That's right, Johnny. Yes, you did. Your clothes were in the trash bags. You put your shit out in the trash. Why are you bothering me at work about your stuff that you put in the trash?"

Johnny was frantic. Still on the line with Reba, he was living a nightmare. Reba babbled on, but he didn't know what she was saying. He looked around the room frantically for some evidence that he lived there. There was nothing. He opened the closet and looked again. Nothing. He was flabbergasted. "Reba, woman, did you put *all* my stuff in those bags or have you hidden some things someplace?"

"I didn't hide a damn thing, and I have to get back to work. They're not paying me to help you find your belongings. You have to learn to keep up with your own shit." She hung up.

Johnny ran over to the window and looked outside to see if the trash men had taken the bags away. There were only empty trash cans on the street. He had missed them. All of his things were gone.

He sat down on the bed and put his face in his hands. He was getting sick of Reba. He didn't know what to do with her. He went upstairs to the kids' rooms and tried to find some clothes. He tried on the kids' underwear, but nothing fit him. He went back to his room and put on the dirty underwear and clothes from the day before. He checked his wallet. He had nineteen dollars and wouldn't get paid for another week. He was in deep shit.

"Hello, I'm Johnny Penster, Reba's husband, I'd like to speak to my wife. Please let her know that I am here."

The receptionist quickly went to retrieve Reba. Reba walked out to the library lobby. "Yes?" she said.

"I need to talk to you."

Reba motioned for him to step outside.

"Are you trying to make me hurt you, Reba? Why in the world did you throw all of my things in the trash?"

"Why did you throw my life in the trash? Let me tell you something, goddamnit, Johnny Penster. From here on in, don't you question me about a fucking thing that I do or say. You got that? You keep up with your own shit, you feed yourself, and don't you try to fuck me. Do not call me on my job or come down here again. You got that? Now, I do not give a damn what happened to your clothes. If you had your black ass home last night with your family, doing your homework, you would not have misplaced your belongings. Now, I do not give a damn if you continue to live in our house, or if you go. I just need you to leave me the hell alone. Quite frankly, I would prefer you packed your shit—well, now you have no shit to pack. I would rather you moved out of the house. I think that under the circumstances, us not having a marriage and all, you ought to leave the kids and me."

"That's my house and I refuse to leave. You got that, Reba?"

Reba walked away and then stopped for a moment to look back at Johnny who was leaning against his car. She growled, "You better get a watchdog."

# Chapter Thirty-five

# *Lucy*

*A*fter three glorious days of sunbathing, hikes, restaurants, gambling, and having every one of Lucy's fantasies fulfilled, Kevin and Lucy got on a plane headed for Norfolk. They spent the entire flight wrapped in each other's arms, discussing the last six days and making plans to keep everything intact. Lucy wanted to cry. She hated to see it all end. They retrieved their luggage and sped off to the Château Hotel, where it all began. Kevin checked them in. He planned to spend the night there with Lucy and put her on a train to Philadelphia in the morning. Settled in their room, Kevin lay across the bed deep in thought.

Lucy broke the silence. "Hey, San Jose, I've got some calls to make. Can I take my attention away from you for about an hour?"

"You need a whole hour? You want me to take a walk?" Kevin said.

"No, stay. I'm just letting you know I can't pay attention to you for an hour. Is that okay? I know you're addicted to me being all over you. Can you handle the withdrawal without going into convulsions?"

Kevin replied, "It's cool, baby. Do what you have to do. I think I'll make a run down to the lobby to call my stash to tell her that I'm back from babysitting my niece for the past few days and I can meet her later."

Kevin headed for the door, but Lucy grabbed him, and wrestled him to the floor. She managed to get on top of him and hold his hands down. She took one of his hands and put it between her legs.

"Navy man, huh? You just lost the battle, baby. Wait until I tell Uncle Sam about this. They may be a little worried about you protecting the country."

She lifted her head and planted a kiss on his lips. They relaxed for a moment. He gently caressed her buttocks, stuffed into the cutoff jeans he had bought for her in the Bahamas. He made love to her on the floor. When it was over, he yanked the telephone cord, making the phone fall to the floor, and dragged it over to them. He handed the receiver to Lucy and said, "Talk away, baby."

Lucy had two calls to make. The first was to her parents. She told them how much fun she had had in the Bahamas and introduced them to Kevin. Kevin chatted with them for a couple of minutes and told them how much he was looking forward to meeting them. Lucy let them know she was back safely in Norfolk, her train was scheduled to leave the next day at eleven thirty in the morning, and she would be home before eight p.m. Her father mentioned that Reba had been looking for her.

Lucy called Reba and Johnny answered the phone.

"Hi, Johnny. Is Reba there?"

"Who is this?"

"This is Lucy."

"Well, well, well," he said sarcastically, "the last of the all-time models is alive and kicking. Are you in Philly yet, or did you miss your bus, too?"

"Yes, Johnny, I missed the bus. Is Reba there?"

"No, she ain't here. I don't know where she is and if you can give me any information on how she turned into Attila the Hun, I would appreciate it."

Lucy giggled and said, "I'll call back later." She hung up and whispered to Kevin, who was falling asleep, "Johnny is pissed."

"What else is new?" Kevin muttered.

Lucy grabbed the bedspread off the bed and covered her and Kevin's naked bodies, and they fell asleep on the floor.

They woke up a little after ten thirty p.m. and went out for a bite to eat. Over the meal, they chatted about what a good time they'd had.

Kevin looked in Lucy's eyes and said, "I'll be in Philly next weekend on business."

"What business?"

"None of your business."

"Bullshit, none of my business."

"Who are you cursing at, young lady?"

"You."

"You wanna fight?"

"Maybe."

He grabbed her hand and, with his free hand, reached into his pocket. He stuffed something into her palm and closed her fingers around it. He bent down to kiss her hand and released it.

"I love you, Philly. Marry me."

Lucy looked into Kevin's eyes and knew this was the "moment." He looked so cute over there, a really sweet guy. She loved him, but she had the devil in her. She was getting ready to cut up. She wanted to get Kevin back for some of his sarcasm and playing jokes on her. She had something for the brother now.

Kevin was getting worried and becoming anxious for an answer. Lucy held the ring up to the small lamp at their dinner table and examined it without saying a word. She looked over at Kevin again.

In his seductive "I am the man" voice, Kevin said, "You like that ring, don't you, baby? I guess we're just going to have to marry each other and spend the rest of our lives figuring out the details of life." He smiled, gaining back his self-confidence.

Lucy said coldly, "Shut up, Kevin. Where did you get this ring? You're playing some stupid game again, aren't you? I'm not marrying you."

Kevin's face went blank. He was surprised and disappointed at her reaction, but also a bit amused.

"You little maggot, don't you make fun of me."

"I'm not making fun of you."

"You're crazy, Lucy! Let me ask you something."

"What, Kevin? What, what, what?"

"Do you love me?"

"I might."

He shook his head. "You know what, you are really crazy, girl. What is wrong with you?"

"There's nothing wrong with me other than the fact that I am sleepy and tired and I want to go back to the hotel."

Kevin shouted, "Do you want to marry me or not?"

Lucy smirked. "I might."

Kevin was sick of her antics and demanded, "Give me my damn ring back before I choke you."

By now they had an audience. Lucy stood up with the ring in her hand. "Get on your knees like a man and ask me, and maybe I'll respond in a more satisfactory manner."

Embarrassed, Kevin looked around at all the people staring at them. He whispered to Lucy, "If you do not stop this, if you do not come out of this restaurant right now, I swear you'll be sorry. You'd better stop playing with me, Lucy."

She smiled and pointed to the floor, shouting, "Ask me on your knees."

Kevin whispered again, "I'm going to count to three, Lucy, and you'll be sorry."

Lucy chuckled. "On your knees, mister, right now, like a man."

He counted to three. Lucy, still pointing to the floor, wouldn't budge. Kevin stood up and addressed his "audience." He recited all but one of Lucy's fantasies. "And guess what else? I'm going outside to bang her in the car. That's her all-time favorite thing. We've been down in the Bahamas doing it in strange cars for four days."

Lucy wanted to kill him! She was livid. She didn't believe he would go that low. She ran out of the restaurant with the ring. Kevin laughed and the audience applauded. He threw fifty dollars on the table, bowed to his audience, and left.

When he got outside, Lucy was sitting on top of his car. She was mad as hell.

"You asked for it, Lucy. I begged you."

"You went too far, Kevin."

"Oh, come on, how mad can you be? Get off the car."

"Nope."

"You're going to get hurt when I drive off."

"I'm already hurt."

"You are not. Stop playing. Come on, get your butt off the car."

"Nope."

"Okay, Miss Philly. I've got to run. Now you just hang on." Kevin got into the car and started it up.

Lucy screamed, "I know you are crazy now! You'd better not drive this car with me on top of it."

"Then you'd better get your booty off and get in."

"Nope."

Kevin turned the car off and got out. He tried to pull Lucy off the car, but she kept moving around. Finally, he climbed up on the car and dragged her off. She attempted to walk away from him, but he grabbed her hand and pulled her body close to his.

He whispered in her ear, "You are the sexiest, craziest thing I have ever met. I like your legs. They are my favorite things on you, baby. They are so soft and smooth. They turn me on."

Bending down in front of her, he kissed her knees and caressed the backs of her thighs. He lifted her feet, one by one, slipped her sandals off, and began to kiss her feet and toes. Finally she gave in and moaned with pleasure. She bent over to kiss his head. He pushed her face away, interrupting her kiss. "Will you marry me? I'm on my knees."

"Yes, Mr. Graham, I will marry you."

Lucy handed the diamond ring to Kevin and he placed it on her finger. He got up and kissed her on her forehead. "I'm sorry."

He walked her around to her side of the car and put her in, closing the door gently. They drove back to the hotel in silence. Lucy stared at her engagement ring, which sparkled in the dark, and gently kissed his face. She had found the man of her dreams. When they got to their room, they sat on the bed. Lucy had a serious look on her face.

"What are you thinking about, Philly?" Kevin said.

"Can I really tell you the truth? I mean, can I be honest without you making fun of me or laughing?"

"Lucy, just tell me."

"I don't know," said Lucy. "I just don't know about this."

Kevin felt a sinking feeling in his stomach.

"Kevin, I have not been in a situation like this before. I'm not this bourgeois highfalutin' person. I'm just Lucy. There's something I need to do right now about your proposal and I am reluctant to do it. I don't know if I can let you see the real me in this situation."

"Look, since I met you, you have been peeing in bushes, running off to Timbuktu with me, fucking my brains out in strange cars, and lying on the tops of cars pouting like a baby. I just can't figure out why you're so scared to be real now. Let's have it, baby. What's the next fantasy? Give it to me—I can take it. I won't ask for the ring back."

With that she immediately started to jump up and down and scream like a maniac. She was jogging a mile a minute in one spot. Her hands were in the air as if she had won the Boston Marathon. She had the biggest smile on her face he had ever seen. She was squealing. She shouted, tears streaming down her face. "I'm so damn happy I don't know what the hell to do. I have got to call Philadelphia! I want to tell everybody! I have to find Reba, and I have to call Peggy, because I am going to have the biggest, most beautiful wedding anybody has ever had. I want a banner attached to a helicopter that reads, 'Lucy Noble has a fine man and she loves him to death. He is the man of her dreams and they are getting married!' That's what I'm thinking about, San Jose."

He said, "Come here."

When the kiss was over and she was able to pull away from him, Lucy said, "Give me the telephone, please."

Reba wondered who was ringing her phone this time of night. "Hello," she answered.

"Reba! Reba! Thank God you're home. It's Lucy."

"Girl, I have been waiting to hear from you! I'm so glad you called. How are you? What the hell is going on? How is Kevin?"

"Kevin is fine! I am out of my mind. I just love him so much!"

"Way to go, Luce. You must have had a bang-up time in the Bahamas."

"Girl, I can't tell you how good a time we had. Here, I'll let Kevin tell you, but don't hang up. I got news." She handed Kevin the phone.

"Hey, Reba, I see you made it back. How are you?"

"I'm fine and I'm kicking ass in Philadelphia. I own this town. Tell me about your trip."

"Well, we did have a great time. I am in love with this crazy woman. She is wild and precisely what I need in my life. Your pal is something else."

Lucy grinned and motioned for him to give her the phone. She was afraid he would give Reba the news before she had a chance to.

"Reba, listen to this. Sit down," Lucy said with excitement.

"I'm sitting down. Now what the hell is going on?"

"Well, you used the right word. 'On.' I am on, Kevin is on, and a diamond ring is *on my finger*! Kevin and I are getting married!"

At first Reba was speechless. Then she started to scream, and Lucy joined in.

Kevin watched Lucy with amusement and decided to leave the girls to their conversation "I'm going to the bar. Meet me down there when you're done." Lucy gave him a quick kiss and shooed him out the door.

"Oh, Reba, he is just fantastic. He fell out of the sky from heaven, a present from the Almighty Himself. The Bahamas were unbelievable— so beautiful. Palm trees, girl. The hotel made the Château look like a rooming house." She told Reba all about the fantasies, the food, the beach, and how Kevin proposed to her.

Reba was in tears. "I'm so happy for you. When will you be home?"

"I'll be home tomorrow night. Call Peggy! Tell her she's about to make the most beautiful wedding dress in the world for her goddaughter. I'm going to be Mrs. Kevin Graham!"

"Okay, girl, I'll do it before I go to bed."

"Now, I don't want to be selfish and hog the entire conversation, so tell me what happened with you and Doug."

"Well, it's good stuff, too. We're getting together permanently."

They both started screaming again. Then Lucy said, "How are you managing that? What the hell are you doing? Where's Johnny? I talked to him earlier."

"Johnny has moved into the basement. I cannot stand him. I've been a bad girl since you've been away. I put all his shit in the trash. I mean every damn thing. I told him to get out. He refused. I've been cursing his ass out every day since I got back. He's been kissing my ass and it hasn't been working. Girl, he was bringing flowers in here, gourmet food, trying to get me to go out with him, trying to fuck me, trying to talk to me. Things he never did, not *once* in fourteen years. He went from Mr. Hyde to Dr. Jekyll. Oh, yeah, Lucy, he was working really hard on me until I put all his shit in the trash. After that he got so pissed that he moved to the basement."

"So what's he doing for clothes and stuff? Walking around naked?"

"No, he has the outfit he was wearing when I threw the rest of his stuff out. He's fuming because he put his own things on the street for the trash pickup."

Lucy was confused. "What do you mean *he* put it out?"

Reba explained how Johnny's clothes had been taken away. "I'll give you the rest of the details later. But let me tell you this, I had a private talk with Howard, the electrician at my job. I want a divorce and I want to make sure I get my due in the settlement. I mean, the house and money for the kids. You know Johnny would probably try to beat me in the end. Well, I told Howard I needed him to do some work in my house. I He's going to wire my phones, so I can tape all the conversations coming in and going out. I'm collecting evidence of all the low-down, nasty stuff Johnny does. I have some other evidence, written evidence, but I want to be sure I am completely covered. You see, the dirt I have is kind of old, so I want to have some current information to prove he is still messing around just in case he tries to say that it was a long time ago and he straightened up.

"So the day after I got home I spoke to Howard and he came over while no one was home. Girl, he put tape recorders in the pop-out ceilings of the basement. No one knows they are there except him, you, and me. He has them wired somehow to the phone system. Every time the phone rings or someone makes a call, the conversation is taped. I've been sneaking into the house checking the tapes."

"Don't they run out or something?"

"No, I pay Howard to come here with me on his lunch hour. He waits upstairs after he sets me up to listen to them in the basement. When I'm done, he puts a new one in. It's costing me, but it's worth it. Johnny's still messing around big-time, baby, and I got the shit on tape. Just like Watergate."

"What about *your* conversations? They'll be on tape, too. Don't you talk to Doug?"

"Oh, no, I'm smarter than that. Howard erases my stuff before I give the tapes to my attorney."

"You have an attorney already?'

"No, but I'm getting one very soon."

"Okay, let's get off of this now. Tell me about Doug, how did that go?"

"I had a wonderful time in Annapolis with Doug. Lucy, he loves me. He is taking the whole kit and caboodle. All six of these brats and me. Can you believe it? Sometimes I can't. Peggy is teaching me how to cook and dress, and I'm getting some money together to move down there. He is amazing! I love him so much. I am divorcing this asshole. Do you hear me? I am getting my walking papers and they will be expensive for Johnny Penster. I hate him so much I want to pee in the apple juice bottle."

"What?"

"I'll explain that later. I've got a few things to tidy up here in Philly and arrange for a job in Annapolis and then I am leaving. I can't wait."

"This is such fantastic news," said Lucy. "We'll get together Saturday night to talk about everything. I have to stay home with *Mommy and Daddy* tomorrow night because they have missed their little baby. I'll tell them the news about Kevin and me when I get home. If you see them, don't say a word."

"Okay."

"Look, I've got to run. My baby is at the bar and I don't want him to get drunk waiting for me. Somebody like you might sit down next to him and I'll never see him again."

"You're crazy, Lucy."

"Yeah, I know, and before I forget, you damn well better be sure this conversation gets erased because you've got all my business on it now. All my fantasies better not end up being played in divorce court."

"I've got you covered, Luce. See you soon."

# Chapter Thirty-six

# *Sheila*

*I*t was almost time for Pam to leave for Sheila's house. She was lying on her bed with her hand on her stomach. She could feel the baby moving. She was close to her sixth month. She had hidden it well, wearing big clothes and staying out of her parents' way. She was eating everything at home, at Sheila's house, and at restaurants with the money she had earned babysitting. She still didn't know what she was going to do about her pregnancy, but she knew time was running out. Vernon hadn't come up with a dime and he was scared to death of her parents. For now, she was keeping her size a secret and trying not to be noticed by Sheila when she showed up to babysit.

Most Sundays when Pam arrived, Sheila was dressed and ready to go out with Leonard. Pam would dash in and head for Auntie Len's room where she'd stay until Sheila left. When she got there this Sunday evening, Sheila was running late. She was in the basement folding the laundry and had put the kids to work with her.

Pam yelled "Hello" down the stairs to Sheila and the kids and went to Lenora's room. When she waddled into the beautiful room, she was shocked to see Auntie Len gathering her things together. She was always gone by Pam's arrival.

This was the first time they had officially met. Lenora took a look at Pam and immediately noticed her stomach. "Hello Pam, I didn't know you were expecting. When are you due?"

Pam put her finger to her mouth and said, "Shh. Please."

Lenora got up and closed the door.

Pam said, "Do me a favor. Grab my jacket off the banister and hand it to me in case Sheila and the kids come in here."

Lenora obliged her and came back into the room, closing the door.

"Pam, when is the baby due?"

"It's due in a few months, I think, and I'm due to die any day when my parents find out."

Lenora looked startled. "You mean your parents don't know?"

"Nope, I've been hiding it all this time. How I've been doing it, I don't know. I do know I will be dead before it is born. I'm just waiting to die."

"Where's the father?"

"He's home with his parents."

"How old is the young man?"

"Eighteen."

"What does he do? Does he have a job?"

Pam sighed. "No job, Miss Len, he goes to college. We've been seeing each other for about a year and a half. He'll finish college if my family doesn't kill him first."

"Oh, my," said Lenora. "What do you two plan to do about this other than dying?"

Pam started to cry. "I don't know. I cannot keep this baby and I don't know what to do with it. I can't seem to make it go away."

Lenora almost laughed. Instead, she held her. "Have you seen a doctor about this?"

"No, ma'am, no doctor, nobody. I've just been talking to Vernon for four months. We were trying to figure out what to do and time kept moving on, and now we have this." Pam pointed to her stomach.

"What about marriage?"

"I can't marry that boy. He's nice, but he's simple and irresponsible. He can't even take care of himself."

By now they could hear Sheila and the kids in the living room. Sheila yelled up the stairs that she was leaving.

Lenora shouted back, "I am chatting with Pam. Go on with Leonard and I'll see you Monday. We'll be down in a few minutes." Sheila kissed the kids good-bye and left.

Lenora asked Pam, "Is there any way I can help you keep the baby? Would you like me to talk to your parents since you think they're going to kill you? Or do you want me to speak to Vernon's parents for you?"

"No," said Pam. "I don't want to keep the baby. I want to go to college and I need to get rid of simple Vernon. I know what I need. I need an abortion. I was trying to save money to have one, but every time I get some money, I buy food. I can't stop eating."

"Pam, are you definitely sure you do not want to keep the child? Or maybe put it up for adoption and then perhaps go to college?"

"No, I do not want to have the baby and give it away. My parents wouldn't even let me do that. I just want to have an abortion and get on with my life. That's the deal. That's what I want to do."

"Pam, abortions cost money if you aren't in a hospital using insurance. Since you can't do that without your parents finding out, you have to get some money. Do you know anyone who can help with that?"

"The only person I know with money is my Aunt Libby, but I don't know if she would keep my secret or help me since I'm so far along. I would have gone to her long ago, but I was waiting for Vernon to figure something out. He said he would. He told me he would get a job and get some money together. He never came through."

Lenora gave this some serious thought. She wanted to help Pam and felt sorry for her. "I'm going to offer you some help. I want you to listen to me and keep what I say in confidence. Do you understand?"

Pam looked puzzled. She thought about Lenora's bankbook. Maybe she was going to give or lend her the money. She was feeling better already.

"Listen, Pam, I can help you to get an abortion. You have to follow my instructions. Do you think you can do that? Will you trust me and do what I tell you to do and keep your mouth shut?"

Pam nodded. "Yes."

"Now, you can't even tell Vernon what we are going to do."

Pam looked surprised. "I've got to tell Vernon. It's his baby. I tell Vernon everything."

"Pam, you cannot tell Vernon or anyone else."

"You mean he can't even come to the hospital to see me or help me through this?"

"No," said Lenora. "He cannot help you get through this. Now, do you want my help or not?"

"Yes, I want your help. I promise, if you help me, I will not tell a soul."

"Okay, I am going to fix this for you. Stay here in bed. I'm going down to feed the kids and make sure they are settled. I'm going to make a couple of calls. I may take you somewhere with me tonight to get this taken care of. I'll let you know as soon as I can. Try to relax."

Lenora closed her bedroom door and went downstairs. Once the kids were settled, she started to make calls. First, she checked to make sure there was an opening for Pam at the medical residence. Then she called her former patient, Tracey, and asked her to come to Sheila's house. She needed Tracy to babysit overnight until about six a.m. since she didn't have anyone else to stay with the kids. She offered her forty dollars for the favor.

Finally, Lenora called Leonard's house and asked to speak to Sheila. Sheila was making dinner for Leonard at his home that evening. Sheila got on the line, worried that something was wrong at home.

Lenora said, "Listen, baby, I'm going to stay home tonight. I'm kind of tired and Pam is coming down with a cold or something. So why don't you take advantage of this and spend the whole night with your man. We'll see you when you get in tomorrow night."

"Wow," said Sheila, "that's a good deal, but I'm sorry to hear about Pam. I didn't have time to see or talk to her at all when she got there. Are you sure you don't need me to come home?"

"No, baby, you just stay right there. I can take care of things here. Just relax. I'm taking the phone off the hook so we can all rest. We'll see you tomorrow. Say hi to Leonard for me."

Lenora went up to her bedroom and told Pam they would leave together as soon as the babysitter arrived. She ordered a cab to pick them up in an hour and fifteen minutes. Lenora explained to the kids that her very good friend, Tracey, was coming over to take care of them because she and Pam were going to the library to do some homework. "If you are very good and go to bed by eight thirty, I'll take you all to a movie after school on Thursday." They all happily agreed.

Tracey finally arrived. Lenora introduced her to the kids and took her upstairs to meet Pam. "Tracey, this is Pam. She is pregnant and in trouble. Can you have a talk with her? She is going to the medical residence tonight because of this problem. It's her first time." Lenora left the two of them together.

"How far along are you, Pam?" asked Tracey.

"About six months."

"Oh, boy, you waited a long time. I had to do the same thing two months ago. I was scared to death."

"What do they do?" asked Pam.

"Well, there's this procedure. They have to put a tube in you, which makes you get these bad cramps. They wait and then the baby works itself out of you."

"Who does it to you? The doctor?"

"No, Lenora does it. She did my abortion and she was very good. I spent the night and came home the next day."

Pam was stunned to hear that Lenora actually did abortions. She couldn't imagine her doing that. Then she thought about all the money and pretty things Lenora had and realized that was how she acquired them.

"Did you see your baby come out?"

"Yep."

"How many months were you?"

"I was a little over three months. It was scary, but better than getting my ass killed by my mom. It was safe and it seems everybody goes to the medical residence."

"Where is it?

"It's in a house about twenty-five minutes from here. People work there and all."

"Nurses?"

"Yeah, two of them and Lenora. They have food, too."

Lenora yelled up the stairs for Pam to come on down. The cab had arrived. She told Tracey to leave the phones off the hook. Nervously, Pam put her coat on. Tracey gave her a hug and she assured her. With her heart pounding with fear, Pam left in the cab with Lenora.

When they arrived at the "medical residence," Lenora's assistants, Lizzie and Joanie, were waiting. Lenora introduced them to Pam. She explained Pam's situation to them and told them how far along she was. Pam was not only nervous, she was downright terrified of what was going to happen. God, she wished Vernon could have come with her. Even if he was simple, she could have used him tonight.

Lenora had seen so many frightened girls come through there. She reassured Pam again. "Everything will be fine, Pam. Lizze will escort you upstairs into a room. I'll be up shortly."

When they got up the stairs, Pam heard a whimpering sound coming from one of the rooms. She tried to go in, but Lizzie pulled her into her own room. She told her to undress and get into bed. "Lenora will explain everything to you soon." Pam could still hear the woman whimpering. She realized it must be the pain from the cramps.

Lenora came up, checked on Sharon, the girl in the other room, and then came into Pam's room. She explained the procedure. She showed Pam the equipment she would use, where in her body she would place it, and what she would feel and could expect. "We will be responsible for disposing of the aborted tissue."

Pam had a million questions. "Is my coochie going to bleed? Do you have to cut anything? Do I have to drink anything? Are you sure Vernon shouldn't be here? When will the cramps start? Do I need stitches? How many hours will it be before the baby comes out? Will it come out dead? Can *I* die? How far do you stick that thing up me? Will I be sick when I leave here? Can you give me some pills to knock me out? Will I ever be able to have any children?"

Then she started to cry. She wanted her mother wanted her Aunt Libby, even wanted Vernon.

Lenora realized she had made a mistake. "Pam, maybe this is a bad idea. You can get dressed and we'll get you a cab to take you back to Sheila's house." Pam lay there for over an hour and a half trying to calm down. Finally, she decided to go through with it.

Lenora went downstairs. She still wasn't sure if she should do the abortion. In fifteen minutes, she returned with two blue pills and some water. "These are Xanax. Tranquilizers. They calm you. Take them. Shut up. Don't get out of this bed unless you have to go down the hall to the bathroom. I'll be back in an hour and we'll get this done."

Upon her return, she began the procedure, inserting the catheter through Pam's cervix and into her uterus. Pam was completely calm. When the procedure was finished, Lenora went downstairs to wait. She anticipated it would take about twelve hours to be over. She planned to leave the residence early by cab, go home to discharge Tracey, get the kids off to school, and finally return to Pam.

Lenora set her alarm for four o'clock and ordered a cab for five thirty. Joanie had left for the night and Lizzie was playing solitaire in the kitchen.

A little after two thirty, Sharon screamed for help. Lenora and Lizzie ran to her room. The fetus was coming out. The two women assisted Sharon and wrapped the dead female fetus in a towel and put it in a trash bag in the back yard.

They gave the frightened Sharon a bath, changed the linen on her bed and gave her a sedative. Unless she had any problems, they would order a cab to pick her up at ten o'clock. They checked on Pam, who was resting quietly. Lenora asked if she was having cramps.

"Yes, but they don't hurt very much."

"Okay, I'll be downstairs."

Pam could feel the baby moving inside her. It seemed to be doing somersaults. At five thirty, all was calm and Lenora left as planned. Lenora paid Tracey when she got home and got the kids ready for school. Once they were out of the house, she quickly showered and dressed. At eight thirty she reconnected the telephone and ordered a cab to come immediately.

When Lenora arrived, a police car was parked outside the residence. She could hear sirens and figured there must have been a fire, but she didn't see any smoke or fire trucks when she approached the residence. She jumped out of the cab and ran into the house. Lizzie was handcuffed on the living room couch. A police officer dashed over to Lenora and asked who she was and whether she lived there. Lenora felt her hands start to tremble. She gave her name and said she didn't live there. Another officer was on the phone in the kitchen explaining to someone that an ambulance was on the way. As he uttered the words, an ambulance careened into the driveway. The medics ran into the house and upstairs with stretchers. The police officer followed.

Frantically, Lenora asked what was going on. Lizzie was crying and shaking her head. "Something went wrong with the girl you brought, Pam. She started bleeding like crazy. The baby came out. He's alive upstairs. He was turning colors—blue. I was scared. I couldn't dispose of him. I couldn't leave Pam. She looks really messed up. I tried to call you at your house, but the line was busy. I didn't know what else to do, so I called the police. I thought Pam and the baby were going to die. The officers talked to Pam and then they told me I was under arrest."

The officer who had been on the phone came out of the kitchen. He read Lenora her rights and handcuffed her. As Lenora and Lizzie sat in the living room, Pam and her baby, followed by Sharon, were carried down the stairs on stretchers. A paddy wagon had been ordered to take Lenora and Lizzie to jail.

Around four o'clock Sheila received a telephone call at work from Beverly Resnick, telling her that Pam was in the hospital and had delivered a baby boy. She went on to explain that Lenora had performed an illegal abortion and that the baby was fighting for his life, but Pam was coming along fine after almost hemorrhaging to death.

Sheila was flabbergasted. She immediately left work and went to the hospital. Beverly and Buzzy were waiting for her. When Sheila arrived, Beverly asked her to take a walk with her.

"Sheila, you and I have been friends for ages," Beverly said. "You've got to be straight with me. Did you have any idea that Lenora was in this line of work?"

"Beverly, I swear to you I knew nothing. I didn't even know Pam was pregnant."

"Well, I believe that, because we had no idea either. This is the worst mess I have ever had in my family. Libby is ready to hire a hit man to kill everybody who worked at the medical residence."

"Medical residence? What the hell is a medical residence?"

"Well, from what Pam tells me, it's what they call the house where the abortion was performed. They've been running a business there for a long time. Pam says another girl named Sharon was also brought into the hospital."

"Is her baby here, too?" asked Sheila.

"No," said Beverly. "The police have the dead fetus. They got it out of the trash can in the backyard of the house."

Sheila was speechless. Finally she said, "Well, Beverly, let's not forget you introduced me to Lenora. You also thought—just like me—that she was a wonderful woman. If she was able to snow you, you know she was capable of deceiving me, too. In my wildest dreams, I would never have figured her for this. You wait until I get home to talk to her, and fire her. I can't wait."

"Sheila, she's not at your house. She's in jail. The police arrested her and another woman early this morning."

"What! Wait a minute. I've got to call my house. I thought she was there with my kids. Just stay where you are until I find a phone."

Sheila ran over to the pay phone and called home. Finally Derek answered. "Derek, it's me. Is everything okay there?"

"Yeah, Mom, I'm watching the kids. Auntie Len and Pam aren't here and Tracey isn't either. No one was here when I got home from school. I came in through the window."

Sheila was confused. "Derek, who is Tracey?"

"Tracey is Auntie Len's friend who babysat us last night when Pam and Auntie Len went out."

"Derek, I won't be home for a while. Do me a favor, get a pencil and paper and come back to the phone."

Derek went to the dining room and brought back a pad and pen. "Okay, Mom, I've got it."

"I'm going to give you three telephone numbers. Cousin Terri, Peggy Kinard, and Leonard. I'll spell their names for you and give you the phone numbers. Write the phone numbers under their names. Do you understand?"

"Yes."

Sheila dictated the numbers carefully and made Derek recite them back to her. He had them all correct.

"Now, I want you to call them in order. One at a time. I want you to say that I had an emergency and I'm at the hospital with a friend of mine. Tell them you guys are at home alone and someone needs to come over to make dinner and stay with you until I come home. Now, if you call Terri first and she tells you she can come, don't call the others. If Terri says she can't come, then you call Peggy. If Peggy can't come, then you call Leonard. Do you understand what to do, Derek?"

"Yes, Mom, I can do this."

"Okay, you are my man. I'll call back in twenty minutes to check on you. I'm at Potters Mercy Hospital. Don't worry about me."

"Hey, Mom, who's sick?"

"Pam."

"Tell her I hope she feels better, and don't you worry about us."

"Okay, baby, I'll talk to you soon. I love you."

Sheila didn't know how she got through that call with so much on her mind. She rushed back over to Beverly.

"I'm telling you, Beverly, this shit is blowing my mind with Lenora and Pam. I can't believe it. I had no inkling whatsoever that Lenora was involved in this. She told us she played bingo on Sunday nights and spent the night with some lady friend of hers. I never suspected anything different. Damn. I'm thinking this old woman is putting markers on I-19 and G-53, and here she is playing doctor and damn near killing everybody. This shit is a bitch. Everybody's got a racket. It's a good thing her ass is in jail because I'd certainly kick it for her."

Beverly said, "Let me give you the news about Pam's baby. He has a lot of problems. He was blue."

Sheila made a face. "He was blue in color?"

"Yes. He is so sick. They have him on machines. I don't think he is going to make it. You know, we had to give him a name today. It's such a shame about that baby. He's in there fighting for his life."

"How much did he weigh?"

"A little over three pounds."

"He could make it," said Sheila.

"I don't know," said Beverly, "He has a lot of lung problems and didn't get enough oxygen. I just don't know. What I can't understand is why Lenora did this to Pam knowing how far along she was."

"How far along was she?"

"Six months."

"Holy shit," gasped Sheila. "Lenora is out of her mind. She needs to be in jail."

"And guess what 'Sharon' they brought in with them?"

Sheila looked at her and said, "No!"

"Yep, Perry's niece."

Sheila shook her head. "You know, when I called home, Derek told me that somebody named Tracey, a friend of Lenora's, stayed at my house with him and the kids last night. I wonder who she is?"

"I can tell you that. She's a seventeen-year-old former patient of Lenora's."

"Well, I'll be damned," Sheila said. She went back to the phone to call Derek again. "Who's coming, son?"

"Terri can come and stay until nine thirty."

"Okay, Derek, you did a good job."

When Sheila returned, she said, "Let's go upstairs to see Pam. By the way, what did she name the baby?"

"Daniel Michael."

"I want to meet Daniel Michael if I'm allowed," Sheila said.

When they got to Pam's room, she was dozing off. Buzzy was holding her hand. Beverly hugged Buzzy and told him he could go home and she would stay the night. He insisted on staying. Their conversation awakened Pam. She looked up at Sheila in shame.

"I'm sorry, Miss Sheila."

Sheila went over and kissed her. "I am glad you are okay and I hope Daniel Michael pulls through. I'm also sorry you couldn't trust any of us. I guess that says a lot for us. You and Vernon have managed to make a real mess of things. I have to call this just like I see it, you know me."

Beverly said, "What the hell were you thinking about, Pam? Why would you wait until you were six months pregnant to pull a stunt like this? And by the way, why in the world would you let Lenora do it? Couldn't you find your way to the hospital? I really can't understand

Lenora. She must be crazy. I can't for the life of me figure out why she even did it."

"I begged her. I talked to her for a long time and I was crying and scared and I begged her. That's why she did it. She offered to talk to you and Daddy and even Vernon's parents. I said no. That's why she did it. I feel so bad that she is in jail. I'm the one who should be in jail."

A nurse in the room overheard their conversation. When it was over she called Beverly, Buzzy, and Sheila out of the room. She said, "May I give you some advice about Pam?" Beverly nodded. "Please don't lose sight of the fact that she is a child. Your child. She made a bad decision with this pregnancy because she was frightened to death of confiding in the people she loved. You have to understand that she almost died because she was in two bad relationships, one with her family and one with the father of her baby. You're coming down on her too hard. How many of us have had to face being afraid of the responsibilities of an unborn child? Pam is no different from the rest of us, including myself. She doesn't have it all yet. She's not a mature woman. She's a mere teenager. What's done is done. Work on a stronger relationship with her. If she doesn't trust you, teach her to. But whatever you do, be grateful she is alive and work from there. Do everything you can to save your child. We all make wrong choices. You have to take some responsibility in this, too. It would be good if you showed her more compassion. Her son, your grandson, is upstairs fighting for his life, and Pam has got enough on her mind knowing she put him in that situation. Believe me, I speak from experience."

Sheila related to what the nurse said. She leaned against the wall and thought about her life. Tears streamed down her face. Beverly and Buzzy cried in each other's arms. They got themselves together and went back into Pam's room. Beverly hugged Pam and kissed her on the forehead. Buzzy held his daughter's hand.

A doctor appeared and asked to speak with Pam and her parents. Sheila left the room and sat in the lobby. Buzzy came down in about twenty minutes. His eyes were red.

"Daniel died," he said.

Sheila went out to her car and cried. She was sorry for them all. She felt responsible, too. How was Pam going to get through this? She knew Lenora was in an enormous amount of trouble and couldn't help but feel sorry for her as well.

The next day Sheila bought the most beautiful newborn outfit she could find, and Daniel was buried in it four days later. Lenora was charged with two counts of manslaughter and a laundry list of other charges because of Sharon's and Pam's abortions. She had an option for bail but was so distraught and depressed that she didn't care. She wouldn't even hire a lawyer. She pleaded guilty and asked to stay in jail.

Sheila visited her and talked with her. Lenora wanted to give Sheila everything she had at her house, including her savings. She told her to take half the money and give it to Pam for college, and to keep the rest. Sheila refused, but Lenora pleaded with her to take what she was offering and use it to move to a nicer place. She told Sheila that she loved her and the kids as if they were her own.

Lenora got out of jail four years later. No charges were filed against Pam, who broke up with Vernon and went on to college.

A few months later, Sheila moved to a four-bedroom house with a huge backyard. She enrolled in nursing school and finished her program a year later. She and Leonard were married in a quiet ceremony on Valentine's Day at City Hall.

# Chapter Thirty-seven

# *Reba*

Johnny went home mad as hell with Reba. He didn't know what he was going to do. He didn't even have clothes to wear to his job the next day. Everything he had was on his back. He had nineteen dollars to his name. He felt he needed everything: a divorce, a home, money, clothes—the works. He sat on the couch trying to think of a way to solve his problems. He couldn't get a dime from the credit union at his job. He couldn't get a bank loan without Reba cosigning for it. His family couldn't loan him any money, and he didn't want to go to them anyway. Life was a bitch right about now.

He was so frustrated and confused that he decided to call the city dump. Maybe they could tell him exactly where the trash collected from his block was dumped, and he could go there and try to find his belongings. He called the City of Philadelphia Department of Sanitation and went from department to department until someone talked to him.

Finally, he was connected to Loretta Warren, who seemed to have a brain and was working in the right department. He felt like a fool when Ms. Warren explained that his trash bags were among hundreds of thousands of bags and that none were cataloged and labeled by their origin. She also let him know that she had never before received a call from anyone requesting to look through garbage bags at the dump.

He felt even worse when she asked him how everything he owned ended up in the trash in the first place. The wasted—and embarrassing—conversation made him even angrier with Reba.

He was running out of time. It was two o'clock in the afternoon. Pretty soon the kids would be back from school and Reba the Robber would be home around six. He wanted to have a plan for his own sanity before she got home. After much thought and pacing, he finally came up with something. He ran upstairs and went through their household documents and insurance policies. He came across what he was looking for—their homeowner's insurance policy. Bingo!

He called his insurance agent to report a theft. He explained that he had packed all of his belongings in suitcases because he was planning to move. He had placed all the luggage and bags on his front steps and was about to load them in his car when the telephone rang. He became engrossed in the phone conversation and when he returned, everything was missing. The agent gave him the information he needed to contact the claims department of his insurance company. Johnny called them and repeated his story. The clerk advised him that a claim file would be set up and that he would receive a call from the insurance adjuster assigned to handle the matter. He would have to provide a police report number and a list of stolen items when the representative called. He gave his home and work telephone numbers, but insisted they phone him at work on his direct line.

Johnny took the time to go over the coverages of his policy. He and Reba had taken out replacement coverage for all of their household items, so he would be compensated for everything at full current value, no matter how old it was. He listed the items and added a lot of expensive things he had never owned. He intended to make a killing! By the time he finished, he had "lost" snakeskin shoes, a portable color TV, expensive suits, two lizard belts, camera equipment, jewelry, leather pants, coats, boots, bottles of cologne, hats, sweaters, bathrobes, and fishing equipment. The total was $11,345.57.

Then he called the police, who arrived in about twenty minutes. They wrote down the details of his story and gave him the report number, the precinct telephone number, and their badge numbers. In five days he could pick up a copy of the report.

Johnny was feeling better already. He called Tamara at work and explained what Reba had done to him. He told her that he really needed some money, about a thousand dollars, to get him straight.

Tamara was reluctant to withdraw her vacation club money from the bank, but it was the only extra money she had to give him. She felt she had to help him because he had been with her the night before, and that was probably what had set Reba off and caused this whole mess.

To reassure her, Johnny said, "I have something in the works to get a lot of cash. I'll be able to pay you back within a month."

"Johnny, *what* do you have in the works to get my money back to me? You know I'm planning to take the kids to Florida in a few months and I will need that money. I don't want us to fall out over this. What are you doing?"

"Well, I'm not so dumb, you know. I came up with this scheme. I called the insurance company for my homeowner's policy and put in a claim. I told them my stuff was stolen. I have coverage on my policy for theft. They are going to open a claim and pay it." Then he bragged, "Look, I added in shit that I never even had, and I'm going to get a whole lot of cash for it. I filed a police report and everything. The police were here today."

She analyzed this as she was listened to him. "Don't you have to have receipts for all that stuff in order to get the money?"

"No, I doubt it, I've been living here and buying shit for a hundred years. They won't expect me to have receipts for everything. People don't hold on to everything."

"I don't know about this."

"Well, if I need receipts I can come up with some if I go through all our papers. The rest they'll have to do without. I'll see what I have and turn them in. Relax, Tamara, this will fly. I just have to be careful that Reba the Robber doesn't find out, so I'm praying the insurance company contacts me at work. They probably will because they work during the day. I can't imagine claims representatives calling people up and asking them questions after business hours. Hell, those people are tired when they get home from work just like the rest of us. You just get on the stick and try to get me something to hold me over until this thing is done."

"You told them the house was robbed?"

"No, I told them I had packed all my stuff because I was going to move and I had it on the steps. I said I was about to put it in the car when the phone rang. I went to answer it and when I got back outside, the stuff was gone. As long as they don't talk to Reba the Robber, and I'm making sure they don't, they won't know I actually put the shit out in the trash myself."

"Okay, I guess you know what you are doing."

Johnny continued to work out his plan. He felt the best thing would be to stay in the basement to avoid Reba until he had some money. It would be a cooling-off period for the two of them. When he got the money from Tamara, he intended to purchase things he needed to hold him over. He would not be a fool and keep his new stuff in the house so this could happen again. He would hide his things in the trunk of his car. He'd have to be up every morning before the crew got up so he could get his things out of the car. Whatever could not fit in the car, he'd leave at Tamara's house. He'd ask her to take his clothes to the cleaners each week and also do his laundry. He didn't want Reba to know he had much of anything right now. Having to do all these things would be a hassle, but he could do it. Once he collected the insurance money, he planned to split for good.

Now he had to figure out the insurance shit. Reba could not find out his plan. He would have to get home before she did every day to check the mail. He also had to check the answering machine several times a day in case a message was left for him by the insurance company. He was praying they wouldn't want to talk to Reba.

With the money Tamara had given him, Johnny went shopping. He bought everything he needed and had a few hundred dollars left, so he decided to put some money away in case he had any other problems. He gassed up his car, picked up a bargain bottle of wine, and headed for Tamara's place. He checked his messages at home and the insurance company had not called.

Reba got home at her usual time, checked the kids, made dinner, and decided to give Peggy a call. She asked Peggy if she could stop by for a chat. Peggy was glad to hear from her and told her to come right over. When Reba arrived, they headed up to Peggy's bedroom to get comfortable. Reba told Peggy about what had happened with Johnny and joked about him hunting all over the house for his belongings. Peggy thought it was funny as hell, and they laughed hysterically at Johnny.

"You'd better stop doing so many devilish things, Reba. I don't want the man to kill you before you get to be with Doug."

"You know what? I can't stand Johnny. He loves Red Cheek apple juice. You know the kind in the brown jar? He drinks the stuff nonstop. He comes back from the market with four or five half gallons of it every other day. He should be shitting his brains out. I hate him so much I feel like peeing in that big old jar, and putting it back in the refrigerator. I'd love to know he was drinking some piss—especially mine. I swear, if I didn't think the kids would get hold of the stuff, I'd do it."

Peggy laughed until she cried. They chatted a bit more about Lucy and Kevin, and were both glad she would be coming home soon. "I just miss her so much," Peggy said. "I'm dying to hear about what happened in the Bahamas. I think Lucy has hit the jackpot."

"You need to plan one of those weekend fashion shows every year—make it an annual affair. You did a good job. You should start a lonely-hearts club or something to rescue all the damsels in distress. You're pretty damn good at making things work out for them. Give me five, Mrs. Kinard!"

They slapped palms and Reba asked "Can I run down and grab Nina for a cooking lesson? Are you up for it?"

"Well, it's getting late—but I'm game. Let's check out what I have on hand. If I have enough stuff you're on."

They went down to the kitchen and Peggy looked in the cabinets and the refrigerator. "Well, I think we can do it. Go get her. Hurry. I don't want to be up all night with you guys. Scoot, Reba."

Reba arrived with Nina for their first cooking lesson and they were pretty excited. Peggy gave them aprons and cute little chef hats.

"What are we making, Peggy?" asked Reba.

"Okay, ladies, we're making three delicious dishes. Here are the recipes, which are step-by-step and very detailed. Even the boys will be able to make them. We're making candied yams, macaroni and cheese, and shrimp and rice. I've got all the ingredients laid out to start. I'll walk you through each recipe, and when we are finished you can take the food home for tomorrow's dinner. Let's get started."

"Miss Peggy, it's so nice of you to do this for us," Nina said while putting her hat on. "I've been looking forward to this since Mom told me about it. Once I get it all down, I'm having my friends over at our house."

"That's great, Nina. You know your mom is like a daughter to me. Now, I feel like I have a granddaughter," Peggy said, kissing Nina on the forehead. "I never had any kids of my own and lost my husband a long time ago. I love being a seamstress, but cooking is also a great hobby for me. As soon as you're a little older, you have to do some modeling for me. Lucy really likes it and is great at it—and she has never been to modeling school."

As they got organized, Nina asked, "Where's your family, Miss Peggy?"

"Well, I have a sister, Greer, and she lives in Boston. She doesn't have any kids, either. It's just us. Our parents died long ago. So I don't have any nieces and nephews. Lucy's a great godchild—I do have her."

"I'm a good girl, and I can use an auntie if you want me," Nina offered. A smile spread across Peggy's face. She was touched by Nina's words. "Does your sister come down often? I don't remember ever seeing her around," Nina continued.

"Well, she is a workaholic and a gym nut. She was here a little over a year ago to visit. Next time she comes down, I'll be sure you meet her."

"Okay, guys—the macaroni is boiling and so are the yams. Let's clean the shrimp and get going," said Reba.


## BAKED MACARONI AND CHEESE CASSEROLE

Preheat oven to 400 degrees.
1 lb. sharp New York cheddar cheese
1 lb. Vermont sharp cheese
1 lb. Longhorn style Colby cheese
2 lb. elbow macaroni
1 12 oz. can Carnation evaporated milk
1-½ sticks of butter
1 teaspoon salt
1 teaspoon black pepper
2 eggs
1 cup whole milk
paprika

1. Cut the cheese in cubes and mix together in a bowl.
2. Boil macaroni in salted water and add a splash of vegetable oil. When cooked rinse it thoroughly with warm water using a colander.
3. In a saucepan, add a can of Carnation with a stick of butter and a handful of the assorted cheese cubes. Add a pinch of salt and pepper. Let it simmer on a very low heat. Be careful not to burn it. Don't scorch it. You just want it to melt and become a sauce.

4. Put cooked macaroni in a large pan for seasoning and mixing. You can use a large aluminum disposable pan for this.
5. Add salt and pepper to taste.
6. Beat 2 eggs with a fork in a separate bowl.
7. Stir eggs into the cooked pasta. Add salt and pepper to taste. Mix thoroughly together.
8. Add one cup of milk to the pasta. Continue to mix together. Taste and add more salt and pepper if needed.
9. Add in the rest of the cheese cubes. Mix cheese in thoroughly.
10. Add in the cheese sauce and mix thoroughly.
11. Take ½ stick of butter and cut it into "pats" (little pieces). Hide all the "pats" inside the mixture.
12. Get out your casserole (or any large baking dish) and transfer macaroni to it. If it is nonstick, that's great. If not, spray your dish with Pam cooking spray so your casserole won't stick.
13. Sprinkle paprika and dust with salt and pepper for coloring. Cover dish.
14. Place casserole in the oven and cook for 1 hour or until bubbling. Uncover and let it brown for about 15 minutes.

Leftovers are great for lunch or dinner. When reheating, add a little milk so it's not dry. Serves eight.


CANDIED YAMS

Preheat oven to 400 degrees.
  6 large yams
  2-½ sticks of butter
  4 tablespoons ground cinnamon
  2 teaspoons ground nutmeg
  1 cup dark brown sugar
  1 cup light brown sugar
  1 cup white sugar
  3 tablespoons vanilla extract

1 fresh lemon
1 16 oz. can pineapple chunks

1. Boil yams until tender—about 1 hour—rinse, peel, and let cool. Slice thick diagonally.
2. In a saucepan put a splash of water, 1 stick of butter, 1 tablespoon of cinnamon, ¼ teaspoon of nutmeg, ¼ cup of each of the sugars, and 1 teaspoon of vanilla extract. Melt together on low heat.
2. Layer ⅓ of the amount of yams in a large ungreased aluminum baking pan.
3. Dust the first layer of yams with a coating of white sugar, dark brown sugar, light brown sugar, cinnamon, and nutmeg.
4. Carefully drizzle 1 tablespoon of vanilla extract over the layer.
5. Squeeze ⅓ fresh lemon over this.
6. Using ½ stick of butter, make "pats" and place on top.
7. Pour the entire amount of the heated mixture of the sugars, butter, cinnamon, nutmeg, and vanilla over layer of yams.
8. Repeat the process of layering.
9. On the last layer of yams, pour a can of pineapple chunks and juice on top of the casserole, dust the pineapple with the three sugars, cinnamon, and nutmeg and drizzle a little vanilla on the top.
10. Squeeze leftover lemon juice over the casserole.
11. Bake covered at 400 degrees for 1 hour and 15 minutes. It should be bubbling nicely. Uncover and let it remain in the oven for 15 minutes. Then remove. Serves ten.

## SHRIMP AND RICE WITH PEPPERS AND ONIONS

3 lb. medium size fresh shrimp (gray in color)
2 boxes Uncle Ben's Long Grain and Wild Rice
Salt and pepper
¼ teaspoon Old Bay seasoning
2 large green bell peppers

2 large onions
1 stick of butter
1 tablespoon Worcestershire sauce
1 tablespoon soy sauce

1. Remove shells and rinse shrimp in cold water. Devein shrimp. (Slit back with a knife to remove the black "guts.")
2. As soon as you have completed the shrimp, start your rice. Follow the instructions on the rice package.
3. Season shrimp with salt, pepper, and Old Bay seasoning. Set aside.
4. Split the green peppers in half and take out seeds. Then cut the peppers in wide strips.
5. Peel the onions and rinse them off. Cut the onions in thick and circular slices.
6. In a large skillet, place stick of butter in a pan. Melt it over a low heat. Do not scorch it. When melted, add in Worcestershire and soy sauce. (Remember that soy sauce is salty, so do not use too much. Also keep in mind your shrimp has already been seasoned with salt.)
7. Add in the green peppers and onions and let them cook a short time (less than 5 minutes) just until they become "limp." Do not overcook. You do not want them mushy. As they are cooking on medium/low heat, season with salt and pepper. (A little Accent flavor enhancer also makes them taste great.)
8. Add shrimp, mixing them in. Stir carefully.
9. Cover pan and cook about 12 minutes or until shrimp are opaque.
10. Serve the shrimp, peppers, and onions over a bed of rice. Serves six.

Johnny had eaten dinner with Tamara and the kids. He put away some of the things he had bought, got a quick piece, and headed for home. He went straight to the basement where the laundry crew was at work. He chatted with them and waited until they were finished and all was quiet to go back to his car for his new pajamas, robe, and some socks because the basement was chilly. He also brought along shaving items, toothpaste, deodorant, and lotion. When he returned to the basement, he made up the couch bed and retired for the night.

The next morning Johnny was up before everyone else. He took a shower, got an outfit from the car, and dressed quickly to go to Tamara's place. He gave her his clothes from the previous day and explained that she was in charge of keeping his things clean.

At work, he began checking his answering machine at home at nine o'clock. He stayed close to his phone in case the insurance company called him there. He decided against taking any lunch breaks outside the office until the matter was resolved. He waited all day but received no calls from them. He was worried. There were no messages on the tape at home either.

Reba and Howard, the electrician, arrived at her house at one forty-five that afternoon to check the tapes. She watched him carefully remove the machine from the basement ceiling and rewind the tape to play the messages of the previous day. He waited in the kitchen so Reba would have some privacy. She heard the conversation between herself and Johnny when he called her at work asking about his clothes. She found it amusing and and couldn't help laughing. The next conversation was between Johnny and the City Sanitation Department. Her eyes lit up as she listened. She was convinced now that her husband had to be the stupidest person in the world. He was actually trying to arrange to go through garbage bags at the city dump. She loved every moment of this. Reba wished that Simple Simon had gone down there to look through all that garbage and been bitten in the ass by one of those giant rats. Maybe he would have developed rabies and died. Then she would have gotten everything for sure.

The next call was between him and Lucy, and she learned her new name, Attila the Hun. Next was the call to the insurance agent. Reba could not believe it. "That slick motherfucker!" she exclaimed. Next came the call to the police department, and then, for the first time in fourteen years, she listened to Johnny talking with his woman, Tamara. This was quite interesting to Reba the Robber.

There were some hang-up calls after that, so Reba surmised that "Not So Dumb Johnny" was checking to see if the insurance company had called. Calls to Peggy and Lucy's call to her late last night from Norfolk came next. The last call on the tape was Reba calling Peggy to inform her that Lucy had gotten engaged. There were a couple of calls in the middle for the kids.

Reba sat in the basement in amazement and delight. She had Johnny's ass for sure now! She was so glad she had put all Johnny's shit in those trash bags that night. It was a stroke of genius. She sat there for a long time, forgetting that Howard was upstairs and that she had to get back to work. She dashed up to the kitchen and asked Howard to remove the tape and insert another one. She instructed him not to erase anything. He gave her the tape and she rushed out with it. Back at the library, she put the tape in an envelope, sealed and dated it, and hid it in the bottom of her desk drawer.

Thinking about everything, she decided that Howard should make duplicates of all the tapes from now on. Reba knew nothing about electronics, technology, or even the copying of a tape. She thought Nina might know how to do that stuff, but she didn't want to involve the kids. When she had a perfect tape, she would turn the volume completely down and have him copy it that way, so he wouldn't know her business. She didn't mind him knowing Johnny ran around, but insurance fraud was criminal. She couldn't trust anybody with this information, especially since she was still unaware of what Johnny was going to do.

Reba planned to open a safe deposit box at the bank where she would keep a set of tapes as well as a set hidden in her office at work. "That damn Johnny." Howard was going to run Reba's pocketbook crazy. All that running over to her house every day and duplicating tapes was going to cost her. But no matter what it took, she would keep that machine in the ceiling going night and day. She wasn't sure of what the hell she was going to do with the information. For the time being, she was going to wait and see how things played out. Any way it went, Johnny was going to be in deep shit. Either she would be the one to pile the shit on him, or the insurance company would. In any case, his ass was grass.

—

# Chapter Thirty-eight

# *Emily and Jared*

lose to two hours had passed and Emily had still not awakened. Grandma was in tears. Paula had been released from the hospital and was on her way to the police station. Horace tried to console her, but had absolutely no sympathy for Paula. After he and Grandma had talked, she wanted to speak to Emily's family to give them her apologies.

Earl and his sister Regina listened to Grandma's story about how she had tried so hard with Paula, but just couldn't control her. She let them know how very sorry she was that Paula was the cause of Emily's injuries. She hoped Emily would pull through and would pray for her. They accepted her apology and Grandma left the hospital.

Another hour and a half passed. Emily remained in a coma. At seven fifteen a.m., Horace called Benny and explained what had happened during the night. He asked him to go to his house because he had remembered the place was left wide open.

Benny was shocked to see the house torn up with glass everywhere. He decided to put it back in order and arranged for new glass to be installed in the door before Horace got home. While he was cleaning, Horace's telephone rang and Benny answered it.

"Horace, this is Jared, Emily's friend. How are you?"

Benny answered, "This is not Horace. I'm sorry, he is not in."

"May I speak with Emily?"

"I'm sorry, she's not here."

"To whom am I speaking?"

"I'm Benny, a friend of Horace's."

"Nice to meet you, Benny. I'm Jared, Emily's boyfriend. I've been trying to reach her all night and I'm pretty worried. Have you seen or heard from her?"

"Jared, maybe I shouldn't be giving you this news, but I'm going to do it anyway."

A cold feeling of dread washed over Jared. "What news?"

"There was some trouble here last night. Emily was seriously injured and is in the hospital. Horace is with her."

Jared tried to get himself together. He felt like he was going to choke. Finally he sputtered, "What happened? What hospital? How is she?"

"Well, she is at St. Carthage in the intensive care unit. She's in a coma and has been all night."

"Oh, my God," Jared whispered. "Oh, my God. Please tell me what happened."

"Amber's crazy mother came over here drunk. She broke into the place and attacked Emily. She hit her on the head with something and Emily hasn't come to yet."

Jared needed to get off the telephone. He thanked Benny and hung up. Lee was in the next bed asleep. Jared's body trembled as he tried to absorb the terrible news. He shook Lee out of his sleep and told him what had happened to Emily. Lee was in total disbelief.

Jared called St. Carthage. They connected him to the intensive care unit.

"Hello, I would like to speak with Horace Alston. He should be with one of your patients, Emily Frazier. How is Emily? Please, I need to know if she'll make it." Jared could barely breathe.

"Sir, calm down. Who are you?"

"A friend. I mean her boyfriend," he shouted. Jared was becoming impatient.

"I'm sorry, sir. I can not give you any information about that patient. But hold on, sir." Hearing the desperation in his voice, she did bring Horace to the phone.

"Hi, Jared."

"Horace, please tell me what's going on there. How is Emily? Has she come to? I spoke with Benny a little while ago and he told me what happened. Just tell me how Emily is doing."

"Jared, she is unconscious. I don't like to use the word 'coma.' That scares me. She has a gash on her head that has been stitched up. I'm here with her brother and sister and Amber. We have been praying and talking to her all night. She won't wake up."

"Do they think she is going to make it, Horace?"

"They don't know, man."

"Look, I'm in Houston and was scheduled to fly back tomorrow afternoon. I have a show tonight. I'm going to work something out to come home today instead. I have to get a flight. Let me give you the number where I am in case anything happens. Can you grab a paper and pencil?"

"Hold on." Horace grabbed a pen and a piece of paper off the nurses' station.

"Shoot."

"I'm at the Houston Hyatt, Downtown, room 936. The telephone number is 713-546-0900. If you call and I'm not in the room, you can speak to my brother, Lee, and leave me a message with him. If no one is in the room, leave a voice-mail message and also a message with the desk. Please. I've got to try to pull some strings to get out of here. Can you do one more thing for me?"

"What is that, Jared?"

"Does she have a phone in her room?"

"Yes."

"Listen, can you go in there and call me right back from her bedside. I want her to hear my voice. She's got to hear my voice, man."

"I'm on my way. You just stay put." Horace quickly returned to the room and called Jared.

"I'm putting the phone to her ear now," Horace said.

"Thanks, man."

Jared took a deep breath and started. "Now listen, baby, you're not going out this way, you hear me? You've got to wake up for me. You've got to wake up for everybody. Come on back, Emily. You hear me, baby? Come on back. Now, I am in Houston and when I hang up I am going to pull some serious strings to get back home to you right away. You've got to hang in there for me, baby. I need you. You've got my mom and Lee both worried to death, too. Who's going to take care of Renee if you don't wake up? Emily, baby, this ain't it and you can't leave. Stop being such a punk and wake up."

Horace removed the phone from her ear and spoke to Jared. "Okay, Jared, do what you can and I'll keep you posted."

"All right, Horace, I'm going to run. I've got to get things together. Thanks, and I'll see you as soon as I can."

Horace sat down and put his face in his hands. He said to Earl, "Please go out to the nurses' station. I don't have any pull here, but you're her brother. Please make arrangements with them to let her man in whenever he gets here. That may be what she needs to wake up. She's crazy about him. Maybe that's what it will take."

Earl looked at Regina. She nodded and said, "Go."

Earl returned in a few minutes. "What's Jared's last name?"

Horace looked bewildered. "I don't know. Shit, I never knew his last name. Maybe I should call him back."

I replied, "Wells. I read it on one of his records that Emily showed me. His name is Jared Wells."

Jared was in his hotel room talking with Kelly, Damon, Lee, and Rodney. He had insisted on them coming to him because he didn't want to miss any calls from Horace. They were pissed off because they had worked the night before and gone to bed at some ungodly hour in the morning, and now it wasn't even nine a.m. They were all in their pajamas and tired, and just not ready for drama. "Listen," Jared said, "you guys do what you have to do. Let Ralph get off congas and fill in for me, or you can skip the songs that I sing lead. You can even cancel the show, or whatever. But I'm telling you, I've got to split today. That's the way it is. I'm sorry."

They all looked at each other and then at Jared. "This is fourteen grand, Jared," Rodney said. "We can't blow that."

"This is Emily, Rodney, I can't blow that."

"Can't you just wait until tomorrow morning?" said Damon. "Just one more day? Maybe she'll come around."

"And what if she doesn't come around and lies up there and dies today while we're talking about money? You think I'll be able to handle that?"

Lee said, "Look, just pull Ralph off congas. Get him fitted and tailored for Jared's uniform and let Jared split. Shit, Ralph can sing the damn songs better than Jared."

Jared gave Lee a "you didn't have to go that far" look.

"Well," said Damon, "we can try it. Does everybody agree?"

Jared abruptly answered, "Yeah, everybody agrees. Everybody agrees, everybody agrees," and threw his hands up.

"Where's Ralph? What room is he in?"

"He's in 916 rooming with Joe Carter," Lee answered.

The guys sorted out the logistics of the new lineup. Jared said, "Somebody go down there and wake his ass up to get him going. Also, tell Slick Rick it's about time he started acting like a road manager and to get my uniform out. Let the hotel know that Ralph has to be fitted by six o'clock tonight. Get those guys moving! If they give you any static, fire them! I'm not taking any shit today."

The phone rang and Lee grabbed it. "Hello . . . hold on." Lee covered the mouthpiece and mouthed to Jared, "It's Stephanie."

Jared moaned and rubbed his temples. "Oh, shit." He took a deep breath and took the phone.

"Hi, baby, what's up?"

"What's going on? How are the shows going? Why did you wake me up in the middle of the night? You miss me or something?"

"Yeah, I think I did miss you. Everything is going well and I'm in a meeting right now. I can't talk."

"When are you coming home?"

"Uh, tomorrow night, or maybe the next day if we get sold out and they want another show."

"Damn, you've been gone nearly two weeks. How was Seattle last week?"

"It went just fine. Look, Steff, I've really got to run. I have to talk to you later."

"Okay, I guess I'll see you as soon as you get back?"

"Okay."

Jared decided to go down to the lobby to call his mother and his office, and try to get a flight. He didn't want to tie up the phone in the hotel room in case Horace called. As he was about to leave the room, Lee picked up the phone. Jared snapped, "What are you doing, you can't tie that line up."

"Look, Jared, Emily or no Emily—and you know I love her madly—I'm starving. I'm calling room service. You want something?"

Jared paused a minute. "No, I'll get something downstairs."

Jared changed his flight and called Connie. She was devastated and wanted to go to the hospital but he warned her that she probably wouldn't be able to see Emily. He planned to get a cab from the airport when his flight got in at 11:39 p.m. The two-hour time change pissed him off because he would arrive at the hospital after midnight, and he would have to raise hell to see her. He didn't care—no one would stop him from seeing Emily.

Jared returned to the room and started to pack. He was worn out. He still hadn't eaten a thing. It was nearly eleven a.m. He called room service and ordered breakfast. He devoured pancakes, steak, and eggs. By one o'clock, he was just about to call the hospital again when the phone rang. "Hello," he said, praying it was Horace.

"Hi, you've got a package at the hospital." It was Emily.

"Jesus Christ" were the first words Jared spoke. The next were "Thank you, Lord." Then he whispered to Emily, "Welcome back, baby, I've been waiting for you."

Emily started to talk very slowly. "I just heard what happened. I can't remember much."

"How are you feeling?"

"Well, I've got a bad headache and the top of my head hurts."

"Don't you sweat that, baby. They'll give you something to make you feel better and when I get there I'll help out with that, too."

"Where are you?"

"I'm in Houston and I'm packed to come there tonight. You miss me?"

"I don't know."

"What do you mean, you don't know?"

"I don't know much of anything right now."

"Where's Horace?"

"He's here, and so are Regina and Earl and Amber."

"Let me speak to Horace. I'll talk to you again before I hang up."

"Hey, Jared, we've got our girl back," said Horace.

"Thank God. Listen, a lot is going on. I made arrangements to leave here and I should be back in Philly around eleven thirty tonight. Can you fill me in real quick on how she is? What are the doctors saying?"

"Well, she just came around. The nurse has called the doctor, but he hasn't come by yet. She looks okay. She's just kind of slow."

"Yeah, I can imagine she is, taking a blow like she did."

"At least she's complaining about the pain. It's a good sign that she is talking. I'm just so glad to see her eyes open that I don't know what to do. We have all been scared to death."

"Does she need anything? I can send my mom shopping."

"Well, they don't want us bringing much to the ICU. I spoke to them about that already and we have to wait until she's in a regular room. She has to stay here a while for more tests. They have to do another CT scan of her brain, plus an MRI and some other tests. She's in a neck brace now. They don't want her to move her neck. I don't think they want to give her any serious pain medication yet. They don't want to mask the symptoms. She has a pretty bad concussion. She's also pretty bruised up."

"Where?"

"On her thighs and legs from the fight she had with the maniac."

"Where *is* the maniac?"

"Well, we've got reckless endangerment of a child, breaking and entering, assault, attempted murder, and God knows what else. I would say the maniac is in jail for a long time."

"Do you need my mom to pick up anything at all for her?"

"I'm going to run home to pack Emily a bag. Then I have to put my house back together. Nobody has to run around shopping for her, I can find her things at home okay."

Emily motioned for the phone. "Wait a minute, she wants to talk to you."

"Hi," said Emily.

"You already said that," Jared joked.

"Don't you be so smart."

"I had enough brains to bring you back to life."

"I heard your voice when I was sleeping," said Emily.

"Oh, yeah, what did I say?"

"You said you loved me."

"Now I know you've been dreaming." He laughed. "Everybody in Houston wants to kick your ass, baby. I've made them all crazy. I'm flying home without them and Ralph is standing in for me."

"No, Jared. I'll be okay until you all get finished. When will you be done?"

"The last show is tonight, but I'm leaving to come see about you."

"I want you to finish up. I'll be okay."

"Why don't you want me to come right away? I don't mind."

"I don't want you to switch planes. I just don't. Don't come, Jared. Come when everyone else does."

"Oh, come on, Emily, stop that. Everything's going to be fine."

"Jared, you know what I want you to do for me?"

"What, baby?"

"The song."

"What song?"

"The one you were working on. Sing the words for me. I can't remember them, but I remember the song. You know."

"You mean 'Miss You'?"

"Yeah, 'Miss You'."

"Emily, you need to get some rest. You've been through a lot. Let's get off the phone and I'll see you tonight."

"No, Jared. Stay there. That plane, there's going to be a problem. Don't switch planes. Sing to me right now. Sing 'Miss You'."

Jared started to sing into the telephone.

> When I wake up I look at the sky
> And I wonder why I miss you, love
> Seeing you and not seeing you makes me feel so blue
> I miss you, love

"Now Emily, that's enough. I'm not going to sing the whole song. I've got to go, and you better rest. I'll see you tonight. Here's a kiss and I guess since I have been going crazy all night and all day I must love you. Take care of yourself. See you soon, baby."

"Bye, Jared."

Horace, Regina, and Earl stared at the smile on Emily's face, so happy she was coming around.

The doctor came in and explained Emily's condition. She had to stay in the hospital another week for tests and the results. If the tests came out okay, she could go home.

Horace left after the doctor was finished and went home. He was surprised to find his door locked and the windows replaced. Benny sure was a good friend. He packed a bag for Emily, took a nap, and planned to return to the hospital that evening. He would take time off work until he got a sitter for Renee. He wanted Emily to get a whole lot of rest.

Grandma told Grandpa all the news about Paula, and he just shook his head. He didn't feel sorry for Paula. He was glad she was in jail. Grandma called the police station to find out how much it would cost to get Paula out of jail. She would need fifteen thousand dollars. Grandma didn't have that kind of money and didn't know where to get it. Even Libby couldn't get that kind of cash without selling or remortgaging her property. Anyway, she didn't think Libby would help with Paula.

She gave it some thought and called Libby anyway, crying. She told her everything. Then she asked Libby if she could get the money or lend her even part of it. Libby politely explained that it was about time Paula took some responsibility and paid for the things she did to people. She was not going into hock to help out the town tramp, whether it was Grandma's daughter or not.

Grandma got out the phone book and started to look for lawyers. She called two and explained the situation to each. When she hung up the phone, she was crying again. She told Grandpa, "She'll just have to stay in jail."

Grandpa said, "Maybe one of those no-good niggers she's been running around and laying up with all the time can foot the bill."

"Flight 477 is ready for boarding." Jared stopped reading the newspaper, got his ticket out, and proceeded to the gate. "Pretty full flight," he thought as he saw the crowd.

The itinerary included a stop in Atlanta and then it was on to Philly. He couldn't wait to get home. He took his seat and got comfortable. He planned to work on some new tunes for the group during the flight. He fastened his seatbelt and finished up an article in the newspaper. He checked his watch. The flight was twenty minutes past departure time. The pilot came on the loudspeaker and advised that they would be taking off a little late due to a malfunction in the galley, but they expected to have it corrected shortly.

Jared summoned the flight attendant. "What's wrong, exactly? Why are we late departing?"

"A part to the coffee system isn't operating correctly. We are servicing it and then we'll be taking off."

Jared looked at her strangely. He glanced around the plane at all of the passengers. He abruptly got his suitcase from the overhead compartment, picked up his newspaper and songwriting book, grabbed his jacket, and headed for the exit. He told the flight attendant, "I've changed my mind. If something isn't working properly now, *before* the plane takes off, it can go without me."

He hopped in a cab and returned to the hotel. He took his clothes off, took another shower, and went to bed. Lee came in and saw him sleeping. He couldn't figure out what happened. He shook him awake.

"What's up, man? I thought you were on your way back home."

"I was, until the plane started falling apart before it even started up. I'm leaving with you guys tomorrow."

"You know Ralph got your uniform fixed to fit him. Do you want us to switch back so you can do the show?"

"I want to go to sleep. He can do the show. Just leave me here. Hell, don't even tell anybody I came back. Don't say a word. That way there will be less confusion. I'll take the night off."

"Stephanie called again," said Lee.

"I've got to snatch Stephanie's hangout card for a couple of days until I see about Emily. Just cover me when she calls. I've got some things I have to figure out."

It was nearly seven o'clock. Jared wondered about his life as he tried to drift off to sleep. He was so tired. Tired from the road, tired of juggling Stephanie and Emily, tired of seeing so many strangers, tired of rehearsals, and of so much traveling. He loved singing, but lately life seemed exceptionally fast paced, chaotic, and hectic. What in the world was he going to do with Emily now? If she didn't get back to normal pretty quickly, he would have to help out with her. He felt a responsibility to do that. "Jesus," he thought, "Emily with head trouble." She was the last person who needed that. She was already as crazy as she could be. With her head injury, she might really be a nut for a while. But he couldn't get rid of her. He didn't want to.

Emily had a problem—a phobia. She could not stand the sight of Jared packing to go on the road. It was a strange thing. She'd start to cry like a baby, pulling stuff out of the suitcase as he was trying to pack. After a few bouts of this, they had decided she would not be around when he prepared for a trip. It was enough to deal with him being gone. So they arranged a code. He would say, "I've got an important meeting," and give her a time. Emily always left two hours prior to the meeting. No one understood it, but she never under any circumstances watched him pack unless she was going with him.

On these occasions, Emily was fine after he was on his way. She'd do her thing with the kids, see Sheila for lunch or dinner or a movie, drop by to see Connie, and keep up with her family. She never bothered him while he was at work with a lot of phone calls. She never asked a lot of questions or checked up on him. In fact, she rarely called him on the road—he did the calling. She was fine unless she smelled a rat, and then she made up her mind to kill it. She didn't do that often, but when she did it was for Jared's protection. The women on the road chasing entertainers were something else. They were capable of putting drugs in people's drinks, saving sperm in diaphragms, robbery, and Lord knew what else. They had their own agenda. Emily was convinced that Jared needed backup, and she was it.

That night, Jared tried to figure out how he was going to handle his life. He didn't want to give up Stephanie either. He loved her. He was used to her and he felt an obligation to her too. He enjoyed the times they spent together, but Stephanie was always talking to him about marriage. He held her off by explaining that he wasn't ready and needed to do all the things he wanted before settling down. He couldn't do the "marriage thing" right until he felt settled. She was unhappy about that and worried about losing him.

His main reason for not getting an apartment was knowing that he couldn't control these women if he had his own spot. He considered the times that he might want to just have some fun or go out on a date with someone else. He knew that his freedom would truly be at stake if he moved away from his mother's house. These women couldn't take over Connie's place. Finally, he drifted off to sleep.

The joint was jumping and the Knightcaps successfully rocked the packed house at Houston's Club Kismet. Ralph did a bang-up job standing in for Jared. While the band was having a drink at the bar after the show, one of the patrons mentioned to the bartender that he had heard about a plane crash. A plane that left Houston that afternoon and stopped in Atlanta had gone down. The bartender confirmed that he had heard the story and that the plane was headed for Philadelphia. The members of the band froze. Jimmy, who played lead guitar, asked, "Are you sure the flight stopped in Atlanta and was bound for Philly?"

The bartender replied, "I don't recall the actual flight number, but I do remember it was American Airlines going to Philadelphia from here, and the crash occurred some time after takeoff from Atlanta. That's all I know."

Jimmy turned to the other members of the band, "Jared's flight stopped in Atlanta."

They rushed to the dressing room. Rodney and Kelly were still there, almost ready to leave.

Jimmy went up to Rodney and said carefully, "A plane went down. It left from here headed for Philly. It stopped in Atlanta. Sounds like Jared's flight."

"What?" cried Rodney. "No, not my brother's plane!"

"Oh, no, man, oh, no," moaned Kelly.

"We've got to get to a TV or a phone." Rodney looked around frantically.

Jimmy said, "Where's Lee and Damon?"

"They met some people and went out to breakfast. They said they'd see us in the morning," Kelly replied.

Jimmy looked at everyone in the room. "Does anybody know what airline Jared was booked on? Did he stay with American or did he switch airlines to get out?"

Rodney said solemnly, "He stayed on American."

They all ran out of the dressing room looking for a pay phone. Rodney got through to American Airlines, and they confirmed that a flight from Houston to Philadelphia via Atlanta had crashed.

"Were there any survivors?"

"Yes, sir. But at this point, details are sketchy."

"Do you have a list of the survivors?"

"No, sir, that information has not become available yet."

Rodney hung up. They scrambled to get their belongings. On the street, Kelly hailed a cab and he, Rodney, Jimmy, and George, the saxophone player, jumped in. Rodney told the driver, "The Houston Hyatt, please, man, as quick as you can."

"Which one?"

"Downtown," said Rodney.

Jimmy asked the driver to turn the radio on in case the news report came on. "I can't believe it," Jimmy said. "I don't believe it. This has been some weird shit today. Emily and Jared. You know, I could be wrong, but I bet you Jared is alive. Something goes on with Emily and Jared. Something spacey. It's been that way all along from the very beginning. If Emily is alive, I'll bet you Jared is. They've got a funny thing going on. Think back." He looked directly at Rodney. "Remember when Connie got pissed off with you, Jared, and Lee a couple of months ago because all those chicks were coming to the house and calling nonstop and it was making her all crazy?"

Rodney, who was already upset and irritated and didn't want to hear this shit from Jimmy, said, "What does that have to do with this, Jimmy? You've always got some story. You're starting to act like that crazy bitch on the *Golden Girls,* you know, the blond from St. Olaf, Betty White. You better stop watching that show."

"Listen man," insisted Jimmy. "Remember, Connie was just so mad and sick of you guys and told you to get out? Remember when the three of you had to move in an hour and ended up in the Holiday Inn in Philly?"

"Yeah," said Rodney.

"Now the way I heard it from Jared was that he had not talked to Emily in about three days before Connie put you all out of the house. That Friday was the third day and the day you split from Connie's to the Holiday Inn."

"Yeah, yeah, yeah—so what."

"Well, the way I got it from Jared was that Emily had gone to bed that Friday and dreamed about Jared all night. She woke up upset Saturday morning. She figured we were away working because it was a weekend. But she stayed upset all morning crying and shit because she hadn't heard from Jared and didn't know exactly where he was. You know she's okay as long as she knows where he is. I heard she was pacing the floor and worried to death. So, she calls Connie's looking for Jared. Connie is still pissed off and tells Emily why she put your asses out and that you guys were also mad at her. She told Emily you all packed up and left and didn't tell her where you were going, and that she really didn't give a shit as long as her house was empty and quiet."

Now everybody was interested in this conversation, including the cab driver.

Rodney confirmed, "Yeah, that's what happened. We didn't tell her where we were going and when we left we really didn't know what hotel we were going to."

"Well, listen to this," said Jimmy. "I heard Emily really tried to get the info out of Connie and Connie said she didn't know. She even told Connie she had been dreaming about Jared all night and had been upset all morning and hadn't heard from him in three days. Well, Connie just told her that she couldn't help her and she didn't really care where you guys were. Then they hung up. Know what happened next?"

Everybody looked at him to continue.

"Less than five minutes after Connie and Emily hung up their phones,

Emily's phone rang and it was Jared. Jared said that as soon as Emily answered and realized it was him, the first thing she said to him was 'Tell me you just talked to your mom. Tell me you just hung up from Connie and called me.' "

"Jared answered, 'I haven't talked to her. We're not speaking and she kicked me, Rodney, and Lee out of the house.' He said Emily asked again, 'Are you sure? Are you lying? Did you talk to your mom? Did she ask you to call me?' Jared told her no and that he had no intentions of calling Connie. Emily went on to tell Jared the whole story. So, what I'm trying to say is those two have some sort of connection. I really believe that. After all this shit today and my knowing that story, I swear and I would bet cash money and everything I own that Jared is not dead. You may think I'm crazy, but I believe those two are chained up for the duration. When they go down or out, it will be together. I seriously believe that. Trust me, something goes on with those two.

"And here's another thing," Jimmy continued convincing his audience. "Remember that time Emily showed up unexpectedly in Toronto? Think about this. Jared and Emily had been hooked up for months before that. Emily had never shown up unexpectedly anywhere. Now think back. The couple of times she was on the road, Jared brought her from jumpstreet. Remember there were three chicks at the club in Toronto that night? It was that Chinese looking one with all the hair and the redhead and the one with the real short blond hair. Three of them together. Well, Lee left with the Chinese looking one and the redhead and took them back to his and Jared's room, right? Well, the other one ended up leaving with Joe Carter. Joe told me later that the chick's handbag fell over in the room and she was carrying a pistol. Now, she was friends with the other two chicks. They were at the club that night together. She tried to give him some story that she carried the gun for protection. Joe picked it up off the floor and got her ass out of there with it. Who's to say what those broads in Jared and Lee's room really had in store for them that night? Then up pops Emily in the middle of the night changing the plan. She may have saved his ass that night. Now you guys can think what you want, including that I'm crazy and off base, but I can tell you this—Jared and Emily are operating on something else. It's totally different and much stronger than what the rest of us have been given. They've got something extra. It's sure-fire protection and backup from somewhere, something, or somebody."

Everyone was silent. Rodney, thinking back, knew that part of what

Jimmy said was true. He knew Connie hadn't known where they were. That might have been a mere coincidence, but whatever it was or wasn't, he agreed it was weird

The cab pulled up to the hotel. They paid the driver and dashed into the hotel. They stopped at the desk for messages, but there were none.

"I'd better get upstairs and call my mother. I know she probably saw the news on television and is going out of her mind," Rodney said.

"Let's stop by to see if Lee is in his room," Jimmy said.

"He can't be back this soon. He left about fifteen minutes before you guys came to get us. Let's go to my room and turn on the TV and call my mom. She's probably left me a message anyway."

There were no messages in Rodney's room. He thought this was strange. Why hadn't Connie called? She always watched the late news. They turned on the TV and flipped channels, trying to find information about the crash. Finally, Rodney picked up the phone and called Connie. He woke her out of a sound sleep.

"Mom, it's me. I heard the news. Oh, Mom, I am worried and scared to death. Isn't it terrible? We just heard. I'll be home in the morning. I'm trying to get more information on the crash. We are praying Jared survived. I guess you've talked to the airlines. I know you must be devastated. Did they say anything about Jared? Exactly where did the plane go down—did they tell you? Do they have a passenger list?"

"Rodney, baby, pull yourself together and listen to me. I'm surprised to hear from you like this. Your brother is fine. He didn't take that flight. I figured you knew since you're right there with him. Why don't you know?"

"Know what, Mom?" Connie explained how Emily's premonition had convinced Jared to get off the plane.

Connie went on to say, "I talked to him tonight. He was in his hotel room asleep when I called him. You can calm down and thank God like I've been doing. You can also thank God for Emily. Boy, you better bless her tonight when you say your prayers. Go find your brother and hug him, baby. I know how you feel, being scared for Jared and all, because I saw it on the news and I went wild. I did call the airlines and then I tried to reach you. When I couldn't, I tried to reach Lee in Jared's room. Lee wasn't there and Jared answered the phone. I could have come through the phone and kissed that boy."

The others, impatient for news, huddled around him, hoping he would put their fears to rest. "Mom, I love you, but I've got to go. I'll see you tomorrow."

"I swear and promise to tell you the truth, Rodney."

"Remember when you put us out a couple of months ago?"

"Yes."

"Well, I know Emily called the house for Jared that Saturday morning. Had you found out from someone at the office or anywhere where we were and had them call Jared and tell him to call Emily right away or anything like that? Tell the truth, Mom."

"Rodney, first of all, if you remember, your office is closed on Saturdays and you know I don't have any other numbers. Also, I was absolutely furious with all of you and I wouldn't have called anybody to talk to them about you guys. So, the answer is no. If Emily and Jared found each other that morning, they did it on their own."

"Okay, Mom, I'll see you tomorrow."

Rodney hung up the phone and shouted, "Simple Simon never made the plane. He's down the hall as snug as a bug. He got off the plane before it left here. He got off because the fucking coffeemaker was broken! Do you believe it! Mom said Emily had told him earlier to stay here and not switch planes. She said the plane was going to have problems. She saved his life."

They ran down the hall to Jared's room and banged on the door. Jared jumped out of bed and opened the door.

"Well, look who survived a plane crash and got back to Houston so quickly," Rodney said sarcastically.

He hugged his brother and kissed him. The others joined in and they all picked him up and threw him on his bed.

Jimmy said, "Man, you scared the shit out of us tonight. We just heard about the crash after the show."

Kelly joined in. "Man, why didn't you call the club and let us know you hadn't gone to Philly?"

"I was tired, I didn't want to work or come to the club, so I passed out. So you thought I was dead, huh? All four of you have been crying all night, huh?"

"Yeah, everybody was crying except me. I knew you were still with us," Jimmy said.

The hotel room door opened and in walked Lee, Damon, and the rest of the band.

"What took you guys so long?" Jimmy asked.

"We went to IHOP looking for Lee and Damon. That's the only place open for breakfast this time of night. We figured they had to be there. Lee told us that Jared was alive and well, so we had breakfast. We tried to call you guys, but Rod's line was busy. So here we are."

Lee asked, "Jared, have you talked to Emily tonight?"

"Yeah, man, I left word for her at the hospital. They have taken her out of ICU. I'll see her tomorrow."

"Hi, baby. Wake up. I'm here. You saved my life." Jared kissed Emily's forehead. She stirred and opened her eyes.

"Hey, Jared. Hi, sweetie. I see you didn't get on the wrong plane. I'm so glad you're here. Give me a hug."

Jared placed his head on her chest and gently squeezed her shoulders and kissed her on the neck. "When are you getting out of here?" he asked.

"I've got about three more days."

"How are you feeling? What hurts?"

"I have some dizzy spells and my neck and head hurt a lot. They're giving me something for the pain."

"Look, my mom and I will help when you get out. Don't worry about anything, we'll work it all out. I'm not staying long because you need your rest. I'll be home if you want to call me and I'll be back here later. Guess what?"

"What?"

"I'm crazy about you."

Over the next few weeks, Emily was cared for by Horace, Connie, Amber, Jared, Earl, and Regina. She and Jared had certainly become closer. He took Emily to her doctor's appointments, they took long walks together in Fairmount Park, and spent a lot of time talking. Jared continued his relationship with Stephanie, but she got very little of his time.

Soon after the calm had returned to their lives, Emily began to worry about another matter—Jared's finances, which were run through his managers. For some reason, she believed the group was being cheated out of royalties. She was having dreams and visions of Jared being "stuck up" in his office. Finally, she placed a call to Astrid.

"Hey, Astrid, it's Emily. How are you, baby?"

"I'm good, girl. When are you coming by the office? We miss you."

"How about if I come by today? I'm feeling okay and I can get a cab. Do you want to have lunch with me?" Emily asked.

"Sounds great to me. Can you get here around one thirty?" Astrid asked.

"You look great!" Astrid screamed when she saw Emily. "Damn. You sure you are sick?"

"Yeah, I'm still a bit woozy, but I'm getting there. How have you been?" Emily answered.

"I'm doing fine. Let's run down to the luncheonette. It's rib day."

"Yeah, girl. That sounds good. Let's get moving."

Over lunch they chatted and Emily returned to the office with Astrid to "hang out." As soon as Astrid got settled at her desk, Emily began to browse around. She found her way to the accounting office, which was empty. She rooted through things, finding the folders with contracts and show dates. Then she searched through accounts payable and receivable and came across copies of checks and sums paid to management for the gigs. She had come with her briefcase—not something she normally brought to the office—but she told Astrid that her health insurance information and medical records were inside, because she had an appointment later at a doctor's office. Emily stuffed all the folders into her briefcase and returned to the lobby area where Astrid was working.

"I'm back. Getting tired. It sure is quiet around here today. Where is everybody?" Emily asked.

"Management is at a meeting with Butterball at WDAS and Serena is due back at three thirty from a school meeting for her son. Let's just thank God for the peace and quiet."

"Yeah—I guess," Emily said, looking around and yawning. "I'm getting tired. I'm going to grab a cab. If I go to the doctor's office early, maybe I'll get out quicker. Thanks for lunch, sweetie. I'll come by here next week when Jared gets off the road. I'll talk to you. Bye."

Emily went to the corner to the luncheonette and ordered a soda. She sat in a booth and examined the contracts and deposit checks. She took notes, then decided to go to Kinko's to have everything copied.

"Hi, baby, how are you feeling? Do you miss me," Jared asked.

"Of course I do not miss you. I'm busy."

"Yeah, right. How many things did you lose or forget today? You probably forgot you miss me. You know you're missing a few screws," Jared joked.

"Yeah—I am missing a few screws," Emily said seductively. "When are you coming home?"

"In four days. Sunday afternoon. I'll see you then."

"Listen, Jared. Remember when you worked New Orleans for that Jeff Fly person? Do you remember how much that contracted for? Wasn't it seven or eight thousand?" Emily asked.

"Let's see—no—you're wrong. We got that for thirteen five. You went to that meeting with me. I guess your head really is messed up."

"Oh, okay. I just wanted to know because I had lunch with Astrid today and was by the office. I ordered gumbo at lunch and it reminded me of New Orleans and when you did that show there. Okay, baby, I gotta run."

Emily stared at the check paid for the New Orleans concert. It was for eighteen thousand five hundred dollars. At least on that one, the Knight-caps had been ripped off. Emily planned to go through every document, every show date, and every check.

It took her three weeks to get all her ducks in a row, and then she presented all the evidence to Jared. The total take of the embezzlement—the robbery of the Knightcaps—amounted to more than seven hundred fifty three thousand dollars over two and a half years. Unbelievable!

Many things changed after Emily's recovery. Trouble erupted in the management of the Knightcaps. Fighting began among themselves. Members of the group blamed Jared for royalties stolen and squandered by management. Things got so heated that Jared, Rodney, and Lee left the group. The disintegration of his dream, the group that he had founded, so frustrated him that he relocated to California, leaving Emily. Depressed and lonely, he joined a religious group.

Men and women were housed separately, and husbands and wives could not sleep together. They studied the Bible in their quarters. During the day the men were required to go out on the streets or ride public transportation to ask for monetary donations which had to be turned over to the leader of the organization. Of the proceeds, they were given twenty-five dollars per day. The members were forbidden to have any contact with their families—no telephone calls or mail.

Emily was frantic and distraught because she couldn't contact Jared.

Rodney and Lee, still in Philadelphia, also had no way to reach him. Emily stayed in touch with Connie by telephone and would drop by to see her every once in a while, but found it too painful to be at the house. There were too many memories.

One evening Emily was on her way to work at the restaurant and decided to see Connie, who was home alone. At once Emily could see that Connie had been crying. She missed her son so much she couldn't stand it. She lit a candle in her bedroom window every night before she went to sleep and prayed to see or hear from him. It had been over a year. Emily decided to call out from work and stay with Connie to comfort her. They talked and watched TV for most of the evening. When Connie was going to bed, she lit the candle. Emily sat on the side of her bed and looked at the candle. She opened the Bible to the twenty-third Psalm and said, "He will be home. You may not believe me, but he will be home. I am here and this will bring him here. You're going to hear from him, Connie, don't worry."

Emily went into Jared's sister's bedroom and got into bed. As she lay there, she thought about everything that had happened between the two of them since they met. She concentrated on each event and emotion they shared. She went to sleep and dreamed about him.

The next morning she had breakfast with Connie, called Horace, and told him she couldn't work for a couple of days. She and Connie spent the day together at the supermarket, doing laundry, and making dinner. That night, Connie lit the candle again. The next morning Connie went into town to pay some bills while Emily stayed at the house. At around two o'clock that afternoon, Emily, starving, decided to make a pepper-steak sandwich. She was at the stove, flipping the steak when she heard the door open. She yelled, "Hey, Connie, you're back, huh? I got lunch going." Connie didn't answer.

Emily felt someone behind her. She turned around and was stunned to see Jared. They just stared at each other, neither speaking a word. He grabbed her hand to lead her out of the kitchen, but she pulled back.

"Wait a minute, I've got this food cooking."

"You better turn it off or it's going to burn up."

She pulled back again. He pulled her toward him.

"No. I've got something to tell you."

"I'll hear about it later. Come on."

She knew he wanted her right then and there. She was in a relationship with someone else, and although it was far from perfect, she was determined not to sleep with Jared. He was not just going to waltz into her life after all that time and think they would start up where they had left off. It wasn't going to be that way. She couldn't have her life turned upside down with no plan, even if she did still love him. Also, it had always been "one man at a time" for her, and she had one at the moment.

She yanked her body away from him. He yanked her back. He reached over and turned off the stove, and without saying a word, he pulled her out of the kitchen. She moved backward, fighting him off. He tried to restrain her and pull her up the stairs with him, but he didn't want to hurt her or cause her to fall. Emily continued to struggle and pleaded, "You've got to let me talk to you." If he actually got her down on a bed, that would be it.

"Whatever it is, I don't want to hear about it now, Emily. Let's go."

They passed by his sister's bedroom, which contained a twin bed, but he didn't stop there with her. This was going to be a rough one, he thought, and he would need a full size bed to overpower Emily. He wouldn't dare use his mother's bed out of respect. He finally made it to the third floor without actually dragging Emily up the stairs. She walked reluctantly, resisting along the way. He threw her on the bed and climbed on top of her. He kissed and caressed her, but she continued to fight him off. He moved down and snatched her panties down and lifted her housedress, which belonged to his mother.

Emily shouted, "That's not fair!"

He went down on her. Emily stopped screaming. She was completely silent. Then she started moaning. She placed her hands gently on his head and ran her fingers through his hair, which was done in neatly tracked cornrows. He made love to her for over an hour. She told him she loved him. That was the only "talk" that was spoken. He didn't ask her what she needed to explain and she never mentioned it.

When it was over, they got dressed and were sitting on the couch eating pepper-steak sandwiches when Connie walked in. She was astonished. Emily said, "Look what the wind blew in." He stayed there for a week and then returned to California.

Even though Emily and Jared were apart over the next three years, there would be other occasions when the vibes they got from each other would reunite them again.

Without knowing it, Emily had canceled out every other man who would ever come her way, for she truly was in love with Jared. By the same token, he had yet to realize that the two of them were bound together as soul mates forever. It was as if they were wearing invisible handcuffs, truly undetected by themselves, or anyone else. They would have no control over the situation. The power of their deep love and affection for each other would envelop the two of them and seal their love, thus prohibiting any human being from permanently coming between them. Their love would also serve as a strong antibiotic against other people who came into their lives. No one would ever be able to hold their own against their union.

Over the years, Emily and Jared would test or try to ignore this power. Any attempt to take a different road or deviate from the "master plan" would make them run into the stormy weather of misery—and so would their accomplices, who were truly impostors. Though it was far too early for them to know, they were extremely fortunate to have each other. It was impossible for two handcuffed people to fall at the same time. Stumble together they may, but never fall united. Emily and Jared would share such a special association, and their lives would be intertwined with self-confidence and respect, not mangled with jealousy. Jealousy fueled by insecurity, disabling one mate from allowing the other to remain free and honest at all times, and insecurity precipitated by fear would never be a part of their experience. Jared and Emily had no one to fear. The effects of their love would be so strong it would seem supernatural, but would be all the more intriguing because it was real. Their relationship and their love were protected by a higher being, the Man Upstairs. That was far better than million-dollar insurance policies on their lives.

So in the end, they would succumb and surrender to each other. Their relationship would survive and flourish through physical separation, without the nourishment of sex or the consistency of telephone calls. Signals, vibes, mental telepathy, and dreams would often be their source of communication when they were not physically together. One would even be able to sense when the other was in need due to sickness, danger, or trouble.

So Jared may have thought at the onset that she was a quick and cute piece of ass who would not pose much of a problem. Emily may have thought she had merely caught the man of her dreams who would make her happy indefinitely. But the two of them were in for the shock and surprise of their lives. Emily and Jared were about to learn the power of real friendship coupled with true love. In the interim, they would not un-derstand. They would abandon each other and start new relationships. But when the deal was done, they would indeed be one. Last night, they had embarked on an amazing journey, unbeknownst to either of them. This was magic.

# Chapter Thirty-nine

# *Reba*

*I*t took two more days before a sweating Johnny finally received a telephone call at his office.

"Mr. Penster, my name is Marlene Prescott and I am your claims representative from Ryers Property and Casualty Insurance Company. I am calling in reference to your homeowner's insurance claim for your loss of May 16, 1989. I will be handling the matter."

Johnny breathed a sigh of relief that they had reached him at work and quickly jotted her name down. "Good morning, Ms. Prescott, thank you for calling."

"First, I would like to give you the claim number and provide you with my direct telephone number. Can you take this information down?"

"Yes, I'm ready."

"Okay, your claim number is HOT845784-051689. You must always reference this number when telephoning or sending correspondence so that we can document the information to the proper file."

"I understand," said Johnny.

"Now let me give you my direct number and the address of the claims office, in case you are forwarding documents to me. Anything you mail should be marked to my attention." Johnny took down the information.

"Okay, thanks, Ms. Prescott."

"Now, we have to set up a date and time to do a recorded statement regarding this loss. It's a routine requirement when processing a claim. I need to know if you would be willing to give the company permission to record a statement from you detailing the events that occurred on the date of your loss."

Johnny took a moment to think. He was worried, but he said, "Of course, no problem. How is it done? Do I come out to your company or do you call me here?"

"The statement, which is part of our investigation, will take place at your home. I will meet with you there."

"Jesus," thought Johnny. "All right" he agreed. "When would you like to set it up?"

"Let me check my schedule. How about Tuesday, June 3, at ten thirty a.m.?" Marlene asked.

"Let me see. Can you hold on?" He wanted to vomit, but he took a deep breath and said, "That will be fine."

"Now, let's go over the property address again," Marlene continued. "I have you residing at 2214 Marshall Street, Philadelphia, Pennsylvania. Is that correct?"

"Yes, Ms. Prescott, that is my address."

"I wanted to check your address with you, as my file indicates that you were in the process of relocating when this loss occurred. I take it you had a change of plans?"

"Yes, I decided to continue residing at my home."

"Okay, Mr. Penster, I'll see you on the third at ten thirty."

"Okay," said Johnny, relieved that the conversation was over.

This shit was giving him a headache already. Well, at least the ball was rolling.


Reba had continued to sneak Howard into the house to check the tapes. She found out that Tamara was taking care of Johnny's clothes and that he was going by her house in the mornings. They didn't talk about the insurance claim. Reba decided not to call Doug from the house anymore. If she needed to talk to him, she would catch up with him at work.

Things were going good with the cooking lessons, and the kids kept up their end of the agreements about the chores. Reba decided they were pretty decent kids. She wondered how they would react when she told them they were all moving away. That would be trouble, she thought. She planned to take them down to meet Doug and would get a couple of hotel rooms. She'd talk to Doug about that when she caught up with him.

Lucy had finally returned home. She and Reba had filled each other in on everything and laughed and joked about all of their adventures. She began planning her wedding with the help of Peggy. The date was set for Friday, October 14, just five months away. Everyone decided it should be held at the Château, where the two met. Kevin's entire family was com-

ing from San Jose and other parts of the country. This was such an exciting time for Lucy. She planned to invite all her family, all the models,
and all of her friends in the neighborhood. A bus would take everyone
down to Norfolk. It would be a weekend event. Lucy wanted two recep-
tions, one at the Château and one the following day at an amusement
park in Virginia. Lucy was going all out. Her parents were taking a second mortgage on their house and using part of their savings. Nothing but
the best for their little girl. Her honeymoon would, of course, be a surprise. Kevin was planning that.

The gown Peggy designed for Lucy was unimaginable. Lucy didn't
want a "princess" dress. She wanted a bad, beautiful, bitch dress. So the
gown was tight-fitting, white silk satin, and hand beaded. The beads glittered like diamonds. The top was sheer from the neckline to the beginning of the breast line. In back, forty tiny buttons closed with small
loops from her neck to her rear end. The train was Italian pleated lace,
circular, and entirely beaded. The headpiece resembled a turban with an
attached sheer veil.

Lucy chose seven bridesmaids and groomsmen. Reba was maid of
honor. Angie was a bridesmaid because she had organized the night out
in Norfolk where Lucy and Kevin met. The rest of the bridal party included Kevin's two sisters, Glenda and Monica; Lucy's cousin, Cynthia,
who lived in West Philadelphia; Kevin's godsister, Portia, from Denver;
Sonja; and Lucy's friend Shelly from work. Renee was the perfect flower
girl and Reba's seven-year-old, Andrew, was the ring bearer.

Lucy collected bridal magazines for tips on accessories and invitations.
She buzzed around like a mad woman. Kevin and Lucy planned to fly
out to San Jose so that Lucy could meet his parents. Lucy's parents were
also going along, and they had plans for his parents to come to Philadelphia for an engagement "get to know you" party. Lucy also had a big surprise for Kevin.

Reba got home one evening and was looking through the mail. She came
across a letter addressed to John and Rebecca Penster from Ryers Property and Casualty Insurance Company. "Bingo!" she said.

She carefully steamed the envelope open over the teakettle. The letter
was from a Marlene Prescott, confirming a telephone conversation of
May 19, and stating that she would be present at their home on June 3 to

take a recorded statement from Johnny. Reba shook her head. He was something else! She wondered how the call got past the tapes and surmised that either the slickster must have called the company from somewhere else or they had called him at work.

She was glad she had the date and time, so she wouldn't run into Johnny, especially with Howard with her. She carefully placed the letter back inside the envelope, resealed it, and put it back in the stack of mail. She told the kids to order pizzas and got into bed, pretending to be asleep. She wanted Johnny to think that she'd had a hard day at work and was too tired to do anything, including read the mail. She stayed in her bedroom for the rest of the night and left for work the next morning after Johnny left for Tamara's.

The next week and a half flew by. Reba had arranged with Doug to bring the kids down for a visit after school closed. She spoke to the kids about the trip, but not about Doug, only about one of the models she had met on her trip. She said their destination was a big surprise and that they should get their money together so they could buy things. She didn't even tell Nina the truth.

So it was just a weekend trip to them. They would get to stay in a hotel and go swimming. That was good enough for them, and they started to plan and to pack as soon as she told them. The kids immediately told Johnny when he got home that day. He questioned Reba, and she politely told him to kiss her ass and switched out of sight. He wondered how he kept from killing her.

The doorbell rang on June 3 and Johnny met Marlene Prescott face to face.

"Good morning. Are you Mr. Penster?"

"Yes, and you must be Marlene." Johnny was trying to be friendly so she wouldn't be so tough on him.

"Yes. May I come in?"

"Certainly."

He led her into the living room. She looked around. She had been puzzled about this claim; it was interesting to her because he was leaving his wife. She noticed everything was neatly in place.

"I wish my house was this clean," she said.

He chuckled. "My wife has all the kids doing chores, and between her, me, and them, we keep it together."

"How many children do you have?"

"Six. Five crazy boys and a tough teenage girl."

"That's a lovely family, Mr. Penster. Why were you thinking of moving?"

"My mother had a stroke and has been in and out of the hospital. My dad is having a time taking care of her alone. He wanted me to help out for awhile."

"That's a shame. Well, let's get on with this. I'm going to need to set up the machine for recording. Why don't we get settled at your dining room table if you don't mind."

"No, that's fine. Come this way."

He led her into the dining room. She set up the machine and began. "Now I'm about to turn the machine on. As soon as I do, I will begin to ask you questions and you should answer them truthfully. I'll test the machine first to make sure it's working properly. Okay?" She turned on the machine. "Marlene Prescott, testing." She stopped, rewound, and played it back. "Okay, we're ready, Mr. Penster."

She pressed the record button. "This is Marlene Prescott of Ryers Property and Casualty Insurance Company. It is Tuesday, June 3, 1989, and I am at the home of John and Rebecca Penster, located at 2214 Marshall Street in Philadelphia, Pennsylvania. I am alone with Mr. Penster for the purpose of taking this recorded statement relevant to his homeowner's insurance claim regarding the theft of his property, which occurred on May 16, 1989. Mr. Penster, do I have your permission to record the information you are about to give me regarding this claim?"

"Yes, you have my permission."

Then she took out a Bible and asked him to place his right hand on it. Johnny was shocked and uneasy. He placed his hand on the Bible.

"Do you swear to tell the truth, the whole truth, and nothing but the truth, so help you God?"

"I do."

"Now, Mr. Penster, please tell me your name, spelling your first and last name."

"John, J-O-H-N, Penster, P-E-N-S-T-E-R."

"May I have your birth date and social security number?"

"Birth date is August 8, 1956, and my social security number is 154-56-8768."

"How long have you lived at this residence?" she continued.

"Since June of 1974."

"What is your marital status?"

"Married."

"Does your wife currently reside with you at this residence?"

"Yes."

"Who else resides here?"

"My six children."

"And their names are?"

"Andrew, Nina . . ." He stopped. He was nervous—the kids' names were all rolling around in his head. He was getting Reba's kids mixed up with Geraldine's and Tamara's. Marlene waited patiently. "Andrew, Nina, Aaron, Rudy, Alexander, and Craig."

"And their birthdates?"

"Miss, I can't remember all those kids' birthdays. I can't help you on that one. I might be able to come up with some months. Hell, I got six kids. My memory is shot."

She smiled. "Okay, Mr. Penster. Where are you employed?"

"I am the Assistant Administrator for the Human Resources Department of the Budman Oil Company."

"Where is that located, and how long have you been employed there?"

"It is located at 3360 Huntingdon Pike in Philadelphia and I have been there for eleven years."

"Who would be your immediate supervisor?"

"Jack Elman."

"Would you spell his last name for me?"

"E-L-M-A-N."

"May I have Mr. Elman's direct telephone number?"

"215-566-3409."

"Okay, Mr. Penster. Why don't you tell me everything that happened regarding the theft of your items on May 16, 1989?"

"Well, I had taken the day off to get packed up. I got all my clothing, jewelry, and personal items together. I packed them in suitcases and bags. I had all of my stuff in the living room and had moved it to the steps. The phone rang just as I was about to load the things into the car. I went back to the kitchen to answer the phone. I was afraid it might be my dad calling about my mom. So I ran back to get the phone. When I got off the phone, I came back to the steps and my things were gone."

"And what time did this occur, Mr. Penster?"

"This was about ten thirty in the morning."

"Was anyone at home with you when this occurred?"

"No, my wife was at work and the kids were in school."

"And exactly where does your wife work?"

"Well, she was not here."

"I understand that, but I need to know where she works for our records on this claim."

"She works at the Commonwealth Free Library of Philadelphia."

"And where is that located?"

"Barclay Square, Philadelphia, Pennsylvania."

"And what is her telephone number at her employment?"

"215-437-3400."

"Any extension?"

"506."

"Now, Mr. Penster, you indicated the ringing of the telephone distracted you from immediately loading your packed belongings into your vehicle?"

"Yes."

"May I have the name of the person who telephoned you at that time?"

Johnny paused. He was sick of this shit now. He didn't know what to say. Marlene was smart. She was taking it all in, waiting, recording, and taking notes. Her antennas were going up now for sure.

"Tamara Weston called me."

"Do you have a telephone number for Ms. Weston?"

"Uh, yes—her telephone number is 215-238-1514."

"Is that her home or work telephone number?"

"It is her work telephone number. I am reluctant to give out a home telephone number."

"Okay, this will be fine. Let's move on. Now, after you realized your things were gone from the steps, what did you do?"

"I panicked and looked up and down the street for the perpetrators. Then I looked to see if any of my neighbors were on the street, to ask if they had seen anyone take my things."

"Did you see anyone?"

"No."

"Okay, what happened next?"

"I called the police."

"You called the police immediately—that was your first call?"

"Yes."

"Then what?"

"I was waiting for them to come, and then I called my insurance agent. Then the police came and I talked to them. They gave me this paper with their names and told me to get the report and also to list what had been taken."

"Did you make a list?"

"Yes—here it is."

Marlene studied the list. "I'll need to take these papers with me and make copies of them for my file and return them to you by mail."

"Okay."

"Has anything like this ever happened to you before, even if you did not report it?"

"No."

"All right, do you swear that the information and facts you have provided in this conversation are true and correct?"

"Yes."

"I am now going to turn the machine off."

After she turned the tape off, she explained Johnny's coverage to him. She would complete her investigation and if everything was in order, the check would be processed and mailed to him. A release would have to be signed by both Johnny and his wife, as they were joint owners on the policy and the check would be made payable to both of them.

He said, "Okay." Then he added, "I have a few questions."

"Sure."

"I have replacement coverage, so your company will be paying me to replace my items without depreciating them down?"

"Correct."

"Do I need receipts for everything? I don't have each and every receipt for the things taken. I've lived here and accumulated things for a long time."

"We understand that and take that into consideration. However, we will need what you have and also any photographs you may have depicting your stolen items."

"Okay. Now, my other question is, how long does all of this take? I mean your investigation and all?"

"Probably about three weeks."

"Will anyone else come to talk to me?"

"Probably not to the house. However, I am sure I will be in touch with you if I have any additional questions or require any more information. By the way, where do your parents live?"

"They live in Trenton, New Jersey."

"Okay, Mr. Penster, it's time for me to leave. It was nice to meet you and I'll work as quickly as I can to get this resolved."

"Thank you," he said, and led her out of the house.

As soon as he closed the door and she drove off, he went crazy. "Oh shit! Oh shit! Oh shit!" he screamed. He was terrified this thing was going to blow up in his face.

He quickly called Tamara at work. As soon as she answered he said, "Look, baby, you've got to help me out with this insurance shit."

"I don't have another dime and I am sick and tired of keeping up with your clothes. Now what?"

"Well, that woman from the insurance company just left. She asked me a zillion questions about everything and everybody in the damn world. I wanted to put a muzzle on that bitch. Oh, man, I've got problems."

"What kind of problems?"

"Well, she wanted to know who I was talking to when the phone rang and I left the clothes to answer it."

"So?"

"So, I couldn't come up with anyone right away and I was on the spot. I told her it was you and I had to give her your work phone number. She may call you."

"What! I know you're lying."

"I had to, Tamara. What else was I supposed to do?"

"You were supposed to shut the fuck up first and then tell her that you have been so shaken up you can't remember who called. Shit, I don't need you getting me mixed up in this mess."

"Look, calm down. Maybe she won't even call you. Let's just see what happens. Also, I could have a snag in this mess because they are making the check out to Reba and me and Reba has to sign the release. I need you to do that."

"I'm not doing shit!"

"Well, if you don't I either have to forge Reba's name on the check or forget the whole thing and you don't get your money back."

"Johnny, hang this phone up so I can sit here and figure out how you got to be so stupid." She hung up.

Next he called his parents. "Hi, Daddy, it's me."

"Hey, Johnny, How are you?"

"I'm good, Daddy."

"How are Reba and the kids doing? When are you all coming to see us? I miss those big-headed boys and my baby Nina."

"Everybody is fine. I'm not sure when we're coming that way, Daddy. I have to talk to you about something."

"What's the matter, son? Is something wrong?"

"Well, I kind of got myself into a problem here. Some of my clothes were accidentally stolen."

"What do you mean 'accidentally' stolen? How does somebody 'accidentally' steal something?"

"Well, I mean I had them on the steps outside. All my stuff."

"Why in the world, Johnny, would you put all your stuff on your steps? Where were you going with it?"

"I packed my stuff up and I was going to your house to stay for a while because Reba and I are at each other's throats."

"Why?"

"I can't get into all of that, Daddy. I just need you to know that my stuff was stolen off the steps and I called the insurance company to file a claim to get money to replace my things. I only have the underwear and outfit I was wearing left. I needed some clothes, and all my personal items and fishing stuff were taken, too."

"I never knew you went fishing. When did you start fishing? I thought you were scared of water and boats."

"Well, I started fishing a while ago. Listen, Daddy, a lady from the insurance company was here to make a report. I told her that I was planning to move to your house that day and she might call you. I didn't want her in my business, so I told her I was coming there because mom had a stroke and I had to help you take care of her."

"What, Johnny? You used your mom? I don't like that—you could be jinxing her. I really don't like this."

"Well, Daddy, if she calls and you tell her anything different, she'll know I lied and I may not get the money. I need that money."

"Look, son, how much money are they thinking about giving you? What's the tab? Maybe I can help."

"Well, all my stuff came to about eleven thousand dollars."

"What, boy! Do you think everybody is crazy? There ain't eleven thousand dollars worth of stuff in that whole house! Fishing equipment! I'm ashamed of you and I know you're lying about something. I'm going to call Reba."

Johnny panicked again. "Daddy, don't call Reba. Please. Please do not call Reba. Daddy, can you just tell the lady if she calls that Mom has been sick and you had asked me to come home? Can you just do that?"

"Listen, Johnny, I don't know what the hell is going on there, but I do not want you involving me and your mom—who you impolitely haven't even asked about once during this conversation because you are so damn selfish—in any of your schemes. Now, maybe, to keep your black ass out of jail, if your mother happens to have a cold when this woman calls, I'll tell her she is sick. But don't think I'm going to leave my windows open or turn the heat down or snatch the covers off my wife while she's sleeping at night to assist her in catching a cold. You got that, boy? Now you better know I ain't telling any bold-faced lies to save your ass when I smell a rat as big as a cat. You're not fooling me. I've known you all your life. If your stuff was packed up or stolen or on the steps, I lay you ten to one Reba packed it. You've been driving that sweet child out of her mind since you married her. In addition, by the way, as soon as your mother comes home from work, I mean if she can walk in spite of her ailments, and doesn't have any comprehension problems due to her recent stroke, I'll try to explain to her what you asked us to do. And maybe I can help her understand that what we brought into the world and so carefully raised has turned out to be an idiot. I just hope she doesn't have a real stroke then. You better go to church and pray, boy." He hung up on Johnny.

Johnny called his job and told them he was sick and would not come in to work that day. He was scared to death. He went down to the basement to figure out how to get out of this mess. He was seriously considering telling Reba everything and dropping the claim. He felt he wasn't going to get away with it and she would find out through the insurance company or his parents. He was running scared, out of time and ideas. He decided to sleep on the whole idea and attack it the next day.

Reba got home from work, went to her cooking lesson, and went straight to bed upon her return. She never saw Johnny that night. The next day, she and Howard came back to the house to review the tapes from the last two days. Reba was delighted with what she had learned. Within the next week and a half, Howard had copies of every single tape and they were still going strong. Everything was arranged for her and the kids to visit Doug in Annapolis. Reba had planned their trip for the weekend after school closed in June or for the Fourth of July weekend, depending on how things went for her.

Johnny went to Tamara's place the next morning. He talked to her about everything, but she was still pissed off. He decided during his workday that he wouldn't tell Reba. He was going to take his chances with everything.

Two weeks passed, and he heard nothing from Marlene Prescott or anyone else. He had picked up a copy of the police report and some photos from their picture albums that showed some of the "stolen" items. He also sent all the receipts he had in his possession to the insurance company. He came up with eighteen receipts covering some of the things Reba had packed up. Everything went off by mail to Marlene Prescott a week after her visit. He called her to confirm she had received them and waited to see what happened next. He didn't receive a call from his mom and dad to say that they had heard from the insurance company. All was quiet.

On June 23, to his surprise, he found an envelope from Ryers Property and Casualty Insurance Company in the mail when he got home. It was addressed to Mr. and Mrs. John Penster. He ran down to the basement with it and tore it open. It was a release for settlement of their claim.

"Bingo!" he screamed.

He called Tamara. He told her that he had the release and that everything had gone through fine. She was relaxed now and was looking forward to the cash she would get. She also knew that he would give her a lot extra. She told him to bring it over right away, and if it looked okay, she would sign it. He hurried to her house.

She carefully examined it and believed that since neither she nor anyone else had gotten a call, it was probably going to fly. The release was for $10,845.57. She signed Rebecca Penster's name and dated it. He signed his name above hers and dated it. They shook hands, kissed, and made love. He went to the main post office, which was open all night, and mailed the release back to Ms. Prescott. He felt like a million dollars. As soon as the mailman came again bearing gifts, he was going to tell Reba to kiss his ass.

Reba decided on the Fourth of July for their trip. She wanted the kids to have holiday fun. If she took them to Maryland after school let out, then she would have to plan something else for the Fourth. Money was too tight for two big outings. She was doing fine with her cooking lessons and the kids were still having fun with the arrangements she had made with them. She felt better about herself and was starting to look pretty sharp. Peggy had kept her promise and was teaching her how to dress, and Lucy had taken her to have her hair cut.

Reba and Peggy had become tight. Peggy would miss her terribly when she moved to Annapolis. Since Reba had been spending so much time with Howard, she had gotten to know him better and decided to introduce him to Peggy. She wanted to introduce them soon, so they would be well acquainted and perhaps even dating by the time Lucy's wedding came up. Howard had to be close to Peggy's age or maybe a tad younger. He was a nice man and was kind of handsome. Reba thought they would make a fine couple. His wife had died two years ago. Perfect.

On July 2, lo and behold there was another envelope from Ryers Property and Casualty Insurance Company. Johnny hit the jackpot. It was a check for $10,845.57. They had paid for everything, less the five hundred dollar deductible. He was ecstatic! He jumped off the couch, did a little dance, and then ran to the telephone in the kitchen. Thank God Reba and the crew were not home, he thought. He was dancing and shuffling his feet while he dialed Tamara's number. He couldn't hold still as he talked to her.

"I did it, I did it, I did it. I've got the moolah moolah, baby. I got the checky wecky in my hand. They sent it! I told you so. I'm on my way over there right now. It's party time. I'm a rich guy now. You better be nice to me. I've got almost eleven grand!"

"You better bring me my cut, plus what you owe me for financing you and being your washwoman, or I'll turn you in."

"Oh, shut up. I'm coming," he said. He hung up the phone and jumped in his car.

Tamara saw the check and her eyes lit up like a Christmas tree. She was the one dancing now, with the check in her hand and no music. "Let's jam," she shouted. "Turn on the radio and find something jumping."

Johnny obeyed, and they started partying. The music was blasting, and the kids were looking at them as if they had gone nuts. Tamara and Johnny looked through her albums and sang the O'Jays' lyrics, "Money

Money Money" and continued to jam. Then they sat down and talked. They decided he would put the check through his credit union and wait for it to clear. Then he would draw it all out and put it in Tamara's account so Reba couldn't touch it in the divorce settlement. He was definitely going to divorce that bitch.

Reba and the kids got in late from shopping for their trip. The kids had lots of new clothes and had bought a few things on their own with the money they had saved up. The kids had been packing and unpacking ever since they found out they were going on a trip. They had crossed the days off the calendar and were really excited about the train ride down. Doug was all excited, too. He planned to bring his nieces over to meet the kids so Nina would be able to have some girl talk.

Reba called Peggy to tell her all about her co-worker, Howard. Peggy said she'd love to meet him. Now all Reba had to do was run it by Howard.

Johnny stayed with Tamara all night celebrating. The next day, he went straight to his credit union and deposited the check at the teller's window. "Miss, when will those funds be available to me?" he asked.

"Well, it is a four-day hold and we have a holiday, so you may draw on them on July 8."

Johnny said, "Fine," and walked out the door.

He got to work a little late, but he didn't care. He was just glad all the tension and strain were off. He wasn't worried about anything. It was time to kick back. For the Fourth of July, he'd get some fireworks and spend the day with Tamara and the kids. He'd eat some barbecue. Life was good. That bitch he married was taking his kids somewhere, so he didn't have to worry about showing up at home just to make things look good. He had money, which meant he had power. He was the man.

The 4:45 p.m. train departed from Philadelphia on schedule and was due in Annapolis at 8:20 P.M. Doug and the girls were picking them up and taking them to the hotel. Reba was excited to see her man, finally. She had big plans and was glad Nina was there to help out with the kids. Doug had also arranged to get a sitter in case Nina and his nieces wanted to go somewhere, or if they wanted the kids out of their hair for a while. He took care of everything and wanted to make sure everyone had an enjoyable time. He was dying to see Reba again and was looking forward to meeting the kids.

Reba tried to be cool, but she literally jumped into Doug's arms when she saw him at the station. Then she introduced everyone. She told them that Doug was a special friend she had met in Norfolk. He was not the "model" she had told them they were seeing—there had been a change of plans. They were polite and friendly to him. Nina immediately knew the deal and decided wisely to keep her mouth shut until the appropriate time. Doug introduced sixteen-year-old Sandi and fourteen-year-old Max, and they headed to the hotel.

The next three days were a blast. Swimming, amusement park rides, games, and lunches and dinners out produced an abundance of smiles. Doug also took them all to Baltimore Harbor. The kids had fun and loved the old tire swings at his house. Nina never even had time to interrogate Reba. She was having so much fun that she didn't care who Doug really was or what he had going with her mother. She and Doug's nieces got along splendidly. Reba and Doug had managed to sneak away a few times over the three days, and she realized just how much she really loved and cared for him. They talked a lot and decided they could not wait to get together permanently. On July 7, she left her man at the train station and headed back to Philadelphia with her children.

On July 8, Johnny Penster presented himself at the credit union to withdraw his fortune. He was going to be late for work again, but he wasn't going anywhere without his money. While he was waiting at the window, he went over in his mind all the things he was going to do with the money. He wanted to move, give Tamara a nice chunk, and move them into a new house with him. He decided they would move across town somewhere so he would not have to see Reba. He wanted to get his own spot rather than move into Tamara's place, in case it didn't work out. This way, she would have to leave if there was a problem. He had it all figured out.

The teller checked his account balance and informed Johnny that his check had not cleared. She said there was some sort of problem and that he should call the company that issued it. He was frantic and immediately asked to use the telephone across the room. He looked through his papers, found Marlene Prescott's telephone number, and called her.

"Good morning. Marlene Prescott speaking."

"Good morning, Ms. Prescott. This is John Penster and I am at my bank. I received my claim check about a week ago. I deposited it into my account a few days ago and for some reason the funds are not available. I was told to call you."

"Mr. Penster, can you hold on while I get your file? It is not at my desk. I'll just be a few minutes."

He could feel himself getting nervous and aggravated not knowing what the problem was. After what seemed like an eternity she returned to the phone. "Okay, now I have the file. Yes, Mr. Penster, there is a problem and our company was forced to stop payment on that check."

Johnny panicked. He tried to gain his composure so she wouldn't notice he was upset. "What type of problem? I signed the release and I sent in all the papers. What type of problem could there be?"

"Well, there was a problem with the police report. We could not reach you over the holiday to discuss it. Would you like to come out to my office and we can try to clear it up?"

"When should I come?"

She told him to hold on. He held on nearly three minutes. "I happen to be free this morning at eleven thirty. Is that good for you?"

"Yes, that's fine. I'll be there."

"Okay, I'll see you then."

Johnny was going out of his mind with worry. He went to the police station and tried to speak with the officers who had come to his house. He thought maybe they had made some kind of mistake on the report or omitted something. He wanted to see the report again. The officers were out on the street. The only way he could get a report was to go to City Hall, so he drove there, paid ten dollars to obtain one, and anxiously snatched it out of the clerk's hand. He examined it thoroughly. All the information was correct—he could find nothing wrong. He headed to the insurance company, thinking, "Damn, this place is in the suburbs of East Hell." He thought he'd never find it. He had to stop three times to get directions, but finally he arrived. He told the receptionist he had a meeting with Marlene Prescott. She rang Ms. Prescott, asked him to have a seat, and said Marlene would be with him shortly. The five-minute wait seemed like an eternity.

When Ms. Prescott finally appeared, she smiled, spoke pleasantly, and invited him back to the conference room. They walked down the long hallway and entered the room. As soon as he stepped inside, she extended her hand, offering him a seat. He was nervous and a little angry that things had not worked out well at the bank. He sat down. He looked around the room. It was a beautiful large room with cream-colored walls, walnut baseboards, and soft mauve carpeting. A large oval walnut conference table with twelve chairs around it dominated the room. Johnny observed everything and thought to himself, "These people must have plenty of money."

Johnny pulled the police report out of his jacket pocket. "Ms. Prescott, I picked up my police report on the way here. I have examined it thoroughly and I cannot figure out what the problem is with it." He handed it to her, and she looked at it and flipped the page over to the attached list of stolen articles. As she studied the list, he grew more nervous and uneasy, but tried not to show it. She handed the report back to him.

"Mr. Penster, before we get started, I need to ask your permission again to record these statements."

He was pissed. He lost it. "All that stuff again! We have to go through all that again? What happened to the last statement? Did you lose it or something?"

"Mr. Penster, this is a different meeting with different circumstances. I will need to tape this conversation in order to complete the processing of your claim. I cannot complete it without the statement. Now, if you would rather not give the recorded statement today, that will be fine and we can adjourn this meeting."

"If we adjourn the meeting can you still issue me another check today that I can cash?"

"No, Mr. Penster, I have to go over your file first and I have questions. I have to record your statements."

He wanted to choke the living shit out of this robot. "Okay, let's get it over with. I just can't believe we have to do this thing all over again."

"So, I have your permission to record our conversation this morning?"

"Yeah, yeah, yeah. You have my permission. Now get out the Bible and all so I can swear and get this over with and get to work."

She retrieved a tape player from the closet. She tested it and it was working. Throughout this, he was rolling his eyes.

"Okay, Mr. John Penster, do I have your permission to record our conversation this morning, Thursday, July 8, 1989, which is taking place at Ryers Property and Casualty Insurance Company?"

"I told you five minutes ago that it was okay to tape this stuff."

She took the Bible out of the closet and gave it to him. He slammed his hand down on it before she could say a word and blurted out, with his head going side to side, "I swear to tell the whole truth and nothing but the truth so help me God about all of my things stolen on my steps on May 16, 1989."

"Mr. Penster, let's start with the police report. Are you certain that this list attached to it is correct and that you packed all of these items listed?"

"Yes, I'm certain the list is correct."

"Would you look the list over for me?"

Johnny took the list from her and examined it. "It is correct."

"And these items were all stolen from your steps on May 16, 1989?"

"Yes."

She walked over to another small table, which had a telephone on it. She picked up the phone and dialed a number. "This is Marlene. You can bring them in now."

Johnny's stomach did a somersault. Beads of sweat were popping up on his forehead and armpits. In a few seconds, two men entered the room carrying trash bags. Marlene pointed to the corner of the room and they put the bags on the floor against the wall. One man left the room and the other began taking items from the bags. The other man made two more trips with more bags. After unloading nine bags, they left the room. Johnny was completely bewildered and angry. He was pissed to see those damn fucking trash bags.

Ms. Prescott said, "As you can see, Mr. Penster, fortunately we have recovered your belongings. You must be very glad to see your things. Let's walk over and go through the items."

He was frozen.

"Oh, boy," he managed to say, "I am so surprised to get the good news. How did you find my stuff?"

Marlene said, "Well, first of all, let's make sure it is your stuff."

He got up from his chair and walked unsteadily to the corner of the room. By then he needed to take a shit. Clothing, underwear, cologne, and personal items were all over the place. He looked through the things and said, "This is my stuff."

"Please go through and check for everything." She was watching him carefully. When he finished, she said, "Is everything there?"

"No, everything is not there."

"What is missing?"

He was trying to remember all the things he had added to the list.

"My fishing equipment and some of my belts and some other stuff. I can't remember everything, but that's okay, I can do without the other stuff. I'm just happy to have this stuff back. May I go and load it in my car now? I need to get to work."

"No, not yet. Aren't your suitcases missing? Remember, you said you packed your things in suitcases and bags?"

"Oh, yes. I'm so surprised and have had such a long morning that I didn't realize the suitcases aren't over there."

"I think you are also missing your TV."

Johnny hit himself lightly on the head and laughed. "I'm just overwhelmed today and it's been such a long process. Please forgive me for being so slow to notice what's missing and not missing."

Then she said, "As I explained to you earlier, there was a problem with the police report."

He was truly frustrated and confused now. "What is the problem?"

"There is something else that we encountered during our investigation." She went to the closet and got his file. She removed a box of cassette tapes from the file and put them on the large conference room table. He was completely bewildered. Then she brought out another tape player, set it up, and inserted a larger tape from the box. That tape was labeled May 16, 1989. She went back to the telephone, dialed a number, and said, "Okay, we're ready."

Johnny wanted to shit, but he was too nervous and scared to leave the room. He was thinking, "Ready for what?" He didn't know what was going on. In a few seconds, Reba walked in the door and took a seat.

"Hi, Johnny."

He was shocked and speechless for the second time in that room. He looked at her as if she were a ghost.

Marlene said to Johnny, "The problem with the police report is that it is fraudulent."

She pushed the play button on the machine. The first call they listened to was from Johnny to Reba at her job asking about his clothing and other belongings. The second was to the city dump and the third was to his insurance agent. Then they listened to his conversations with the insurance company, the police department, and Tamara. He put his face in his hands while listening to all the lies he had told. He was absolutely petrified. A million things were running through his mind. He didn't know what they were going to do with him.

Reba sat quietly, tapping her foot, and never took her eyes off of him the entire time. She was shaking her head and tears were rolling down her face as she listened to all the conversations between him and Tamara.

Marlene Prescott felt sorry for Reba, and Reba was going to make sure she did. They were there for three hours, listening to tape after tape of Johnny and Tamara and also the tape of Johnny and his dad. Ryers Property and Casualty Insurance Company had everything on the two of them and they had their $10,845.57 check back, which they had issued to Johnny as bait. They had been on to him for quite a while. They had Tamara's forged signature of Rebecca Penster. They had worked through the Philadelphia Police Department, the Philadelphia Sheriff's Office, and the Montgomery County Sheriff's Office to set up the arrests of John Penster and Tamara Weston for conspiracy, insurance fraud, forgery, filing a fraudulent police report, and theft by deception. Johnny could not say a word. Reba's eyes pierced him. He sank in his chair with his face in his hands.

It was telephone time again and Marlene Prescott marched over to the little table and dialed another number. In less than five seconds, two uniformed police officers came in with a warrant for the arrest of John Penster. They read Johnny his rights and escorted him to the Police Administration Building where Tamara had already been taken. They had picked her up at her job a couple of hours earlier. She was hysterical in her cell when he got there.

After they left, Marlene had a cup of coffee with Reba. "Mrs. Penster, tell me something. Where have your husband's things been all this time?"

Reba answered, "In the trunk of my car. Nine trash bags taking up my entire trunk all this time. I removed the things from the sidewalk early that morning because I knew I would never get him out of the house if he had no clothes. So I was planning to return them to him. I just wanted to make him sweat for a while. Then after I started listening to the tapes, I decided not to return them to him."

Marlene smiled. "You're pretty smart. Thank you for cooperating with us and saving Ryers a lot of money."

Johnny and Tamara managed to get out of jail on bail and they both got probation. Reba filed for divorce, used the tapes to prove adultery, and ended up with the house and a large chunk of Johnny's paycheck. Johnny was forced to move in with Tamara. The arrangement was tense because Tamara found out about Geraldine and her children. Johnny had to pay child support for them, too, so there wasn't much cash. Tamara and her kids never did get their thousand dollars back and did not make it to Florida.

Reba sold her house and moved to Annapolis at the end of August, prior to her divorce being granted. She went down early to register the kids for school. She got Johnny to sign papers and agree not to try to get any money from her. She told him that if he attempted to take one penny of the proceeds from the sale of the house, she would have a chat with his boss, Mr. Elman, and explain that Johnny had committed insurance fraud right from his workplace. She would not hesitate to take the tapes to his boss.

Doug sold his house, and with the money from the sale of both houses, they purchased a six-bedroom home with a pool in Annapolis.

Reba's children adjusted very well in their new environment, and Reba landed a job with the assistance of Marlene Prescott.

# Chapter Forty

# *Lucy*

"Hold still, Lucy!" Peggy snapped. "How am I supposed to get you in this dress if you keep moving around?"

"Okay, okay. I'm just so nervous and excited. Jesus Christ, I can't believe this day has finally arrived."

Angie chimed in, "You've got the baddest wedding dress I have ever seen. Can I have it when you're done?"

Lucy smiled. "No, you're liable to go down to the strip joint in it." They laughed.

The busload of neighborhood guests had arrived, the cake was a masterpiece, and the hotel was packed with people from all over the country coming to see Kevin and Lucy do their thing.

Reba, Doug, and the kids had stayed up almost all night with Peggy and Howard, telling Howard about how Lucy had met Kevin at the fashion show. The rehearsal went wonderfully and Lucy and the Grahams were already an attached family. After the rehearsal dinner, all the models and the guys from the original Norfolk trip hit Hannibal's again.

The ceremony was due to start in an hour and a half. Peggy had finally gotten Lucy into her dress, her makeup and hair were done, but it was too early for everything. Lucy just couldn't wait. After Peggy got her dressed, she left Lucy's room and headed for her own. Howard heard her put her key into the lock and quickly rushed to open the door for her. He was such a gentlemen and so attentive. When she walked in, she had a full house. Kevin and his parents and Reba were there. Peggy asked, "Reba, what the heck are you still doing in our room? Aren't you sick of us?"

"Nope. I miss you desperately."

"You want to come back to Philly and move down the street?"

"Nope."

They laughed.

Mrs. Graham chimed in, "How's the bride?"

"Listen, Camille, that girl is so nervous. I hope she doesn't go crazy before two o'clock. She's dressed and ready. I guess she'll go downstairs in a minute and just stand by the altar and wait for Kevin."

They all laughed.

Kevin said, "Well, I'd better get out of here and get ready myself."

After he left, they chatted a bit and the room emptied. Peggy started to arrange her outfit and makeup.

"I'm going to get a shower now, so I can be out of your way, honey," said Howard.

When he was ready, he kissed Peggy and headed for the lobby bar. Peggy smiled as she watched him leave the room. She loved being with Howard and he certainly filled the void in her life. They were spending a lot of time together and were leaning toward moving in together. She liked the way he opened car doors for her and helped her with her chair at restaurants. She liked the softness of his voice and the breakfasts in bed he made for her whenever he stayed over on the weekends. They had long friendly chats on the phone when they were not together. She liked his son, Donald, and the fact that he stopped by sometimes with his kids. This helped Peggy to feel welcome in their lives. She felt like family. She was thankful that Reba had placed them together.

Howard made it to the bar where he spotted Bernie and Roger. Howard ordered a glass of Pinot Grigio. He preferred a cold beer, but he was afraid it would make his breath smell.

"Well, we've got some event going down in the next hour. My man Kevin is ditching us this time for good. No more singles nights out for him," said Roger.

"Yeah, Lucy is going to have him washing the dishes and cleaning out the sink."

They laughed. "Did you guys give him a bachelor party?" asked Howard.

Bernie answered, "Did we? It was unbelievable. He had a blast. It was too much fun. We had strippers all over this hotel last weekend while Lucy was in Philly. Then at the end of the night, when everything was quiet, we had something waiting in Kevin's bed for him."

Howard's eyes lit up. "Oh, really?"

"Yes, really, man. We paid her and even paid for her lingerie."

Howard was surprised and really did not approve.

"Guess what?" said Roger.

"What?" said Howard.

"You should have seen Kevin's face and heard him scream when he got into his bed and found a seventy-seven-year-old white woman in there in all that makeup and sexy underwear. She looked just like that woman in the Wendy's commercial who said 'Where's the beef?' And that's what we paid her to say. We were listening outside the door. When we heard him scream and start running around inside, we ran down to the bar and sat there as if we knew nothing. He threw his clothes on and made a bee-line to the bar. As soon as we saw him, it was over. We lost it and couldn't stop laughing at him. It was great."

Howard laughed heartily, just imagining it. They traded a few more stories and then noticed the time.

"Hey, we'd better get going. It's one forty-five. Let's split."

Everyone was assembled in the room for the ceremony. The decorators employed by the Château had outdone themselves. The place was magnificent. After the bridesmaids, groomsmen, flower girl, and ring bearer made it to the podium, Lucy stood at the entranceway of the room. She was drop-dead gorgeous. Her father and mother escorted her to the podium. Kevin was in awe of her beauty and gave her a wink. They took their seats. Reverend Maysley officiated and when they were pronounced husband and wife, Lucy squealed and stomped her foot. She put both of her hands on Kevin's face and passionately kissed him. The crowd cheered with delight. Everyone waited for the two of them to leave the podium so they could form a receiving line. Lucy took her husband's hand and led him behind the podium where Reverend Maysley stood. "Excuse us. The bride has an announcement to make."

Kevin looked bewildered. Lucy spoke into the microphone. "Could everyone please go immediately to the main terrace and wait there for us? We will join you there."

The guests obliged and scrambled out of the room. Lucy and Kevin made their way outside to the terrace hand in hand. They stood in front of the crowd.

Lucy said, "Look up in the sky. Just watch."

Everyone lifted their heads. In a few seconds, a helicopter slowly flew by. Attached was a long banner. It read: LUCY NOBLE AND KEVIN GRAHAM MARRIED UP TODAY. CINDERELLA'S NOT THE ONLY ONE WHO SNAGGED A PRINCE.

# Epilogue

y life was truly in an uproar for a while. I was in the middle of a custody battle. Horace was going to sue Grandma for full custody of me. Paula was still in jail and had at least four more years to serve. My daddy, Lance, was also currently serving his prison term for shooting Perry Shoreman all those years ago. Horace and Grandma took me to the prison to see Paula several times and she treated me badly each time. She blamed me for what she had done to Emily and hated me for shooting her.

I have not been to the prison in over a year. I will not go again. Grandma refused to give me to Horace because Paula had told her I did not belong to him or with him. Grandma felt sorry for Paula because she was in jail. Paula told Grandma she would commit suicide in prison if I went to live with Horace. I know that Paula was just trying to continue to punish me from her jail cell. Grandma told the county workers assigned to monitor our care that she felt it was best that Sydni and I be raised together by her and Grandpa. Horace not being a blood relative hurt our case.

It doesn't help much that two years ago, while Paula was in the city jail awaiting trial, I was only fourteen and pretty depressed with my situation. I had met a Muslim guy at the bakery and we became friends. His name was Hasson Azizz. He gave me gifts and I started to visit the mosque with him. These weren't really "dates," but I was meeting him there and attending the meetings. I met a few Muslim sisters who were around my age.

Attending my public school was awful. The kids stole, fought, and used foul language. I hated it. I also missed the calmness and normal family routine of being at Horace's house. Grandma still went to the card games and the Rockaway bar. It seemed like Paula all over again because Grandma also had boyfriends. She was even carrying on with the man renting our second floor. I didn't like what she was doing to

Grandpa or how she treated him. I told Horace I wanted to stay with him. He thought it was a fine idea, but Grandma sided with Paula. She accepted her opinion and the check that was available to her from the county for Sydni and me. I had to stay put.

One day I wanted to go to the store and Grandma told me to take the key so I could get back in without her having to come to the door. I hated to take that key because it never worked for me. I would always end up ringing the bell and she would start to shout at me for disturbing her. She never hit me like Paula used to, but she was mean. After I came from the store, I tried the key. As usual, it didn't work. No matter how much I kept turning and twisting it, I was forced to ring the bell. She was so mad she started screaming at me. It hurt my feelings and I cried.

I went over to the bakery the next day and told Hasson about it. I called Horace and he came to pick me up there. I introduced him to Hasson. While Horace and I were driving to his house, I explained what a good friend Hasson was to me. I told Horace he had given me the fancy Gucci handbag I was carrying and some other nice presents. I also told him that Hasson had taken me to the mosque and I had learned all about his religion. Horace never said a word. He just listened. I thought he might be against my friendship with Hasson, but he wasn't.

It was explained to me at the mosque that women's hair had to be covered at all times when they left the house. They wore a *kimorah,* which is a scarf and headpiece. When in full *hijab,* their bodies were completely covered. Only their eyes could be exposed. Muslim women did this for protection. It kept outsiders from becoming aroused by their beauty, thus ensuring that they were not sexually assaulted. Learning about it intrigued me.

Grandma knew about Hasson and that he was twenty-seven years old. He brought her goods from the bakery sometimes and had dinner with us on Sundays. He repaired things in the house for Grandma and gave her money if she was short. I told Horace how nice Hasson was to her.

Hasson had a Muslim wife. I also learned that Muslim men are allowed to have more than one wife. That surprised me. I had never met his wife when I went to the mosque or the bakery. I hadn't been to his home and didn't know where he lived.

Usually I went to the bakery on Tuesdays and Thursdays. One Thursday when I arrived, Hasson gave me a *kimorah* and a full *hijab* as a present for Ramadan. In the Muslim religion, this holiday is a fasting period. When that thirty-day period is over, the Eid Al-Fitr holiday occurs. It is a time of gift giving.

The garb Hasson gave me was colorful and very beautiful. He told me I could put it on in the restroom. Then he asked me to attend the mosque with him that evening. I enjoyed dressing up and pretending to be a Muslim. This would be so much fun for me—just like Halloween.

What Hasson didn't know was that there was a cat on the prowl named Horace Alston. Horace smelled a rat named Hasson trying to squash a mouse named Amber Gray. Little did I know that Horace had Emily watching a few hours every day outside the bakery while he was home with Renee. On this particular day, Emily was in Earl's car with her best buddy, Sheila, behind the wheel.

As soon as Hasson and I stepped out of the bakery and began walking down the steps toward his car, I spotted Emily leaning against the car smoking a cigarette. They didn't recognize me in my new outfit and they didn't know Hasson. "Hey," I shouted, and waved to them. I wanted to show off my new clothes.

Emily froze for a second, then she ran over to me. Staring at me in a confused manner, she said in a low voice, "Amber?"

"Yes, it's me. Look at the new stuff Hasson got me. I'm going to the mosque with him to see the other girls."

Flabbergasted, Emily lunged for me. Hasson swiftly pulled me away. I was in the middle.

Hasson ordered, "Amber, stay beside me." Sheila was on her way over to us by then.

Emily shouted, "Give me this child!"

Hasson tried to yank me away, but he wasn't quick enough for Sheila. She jumped on his back and they both fell to the ground. Sheila's old boxing skills came back to her and she pounded away at Hasson. I was frozen still and felt sorry for him at the same time. Sheila grabbed me and threw me into the car. Emily jumped in and we sped off. Hasson was still on the ground.

When we arrived at Horace's house, he didn't recognize me. As soon as we walked in, Emily said, "Here is your child." She snatched the drape off my head.

Horace was stunned. He took me into his arms. "What the hell is all this shit you have on? Have you been in Iran or somewhere?"

Emily said, "She's been right at that damn Muslim bakery. That's where we found her butt. She and that cradle robber were probably going on a date. Sheila beat the shit out of him and left him on the street for dead like she did her late husband. He must be damn near thirty years old!"

Horace was absolutely livid. He thanked Sheila and Emily, then sank to the couch with his face in his hands.

Sheila knew we had a lot to talk about and decided to leave. "Look, I'm going to run. I'll give you guys a buzz tomorrow. Amber, you'd better stay put or your ass will be the next one I come after. You got that? Don't make me hurt you and don't you forget that I know where that nigga, your 'friend,' works. I guess you know I'm crazy and I'll kill him."

Horace had a long talk with me right away. I sat on that couch and listened to him preach to me for over two hours. In the end, he hugged me and told me he loved me. Then Emily chimed in, reassuring me that I'd made a bad decision, but that given all I had been through, I was forgiven and loved. We talked about setting goals and moving on.

Horace paced the floor, shaking his head. Finally, he sat down with me to make plans. He planned to file a petition with the court to get permanent custody of me and try to adopt me. I would trust him. In the meantime, he would get me into another school. It would be a nice, private school. Horace arranged for me to start piano lessons on Saturdays at the Martin Music School and also got me enrolled in the writing workshop held two evenings a week at the downtown YMCA. He wanted me to get focused so I could choose a goal and a profession. I would work hard to do well and apply to college. Then he said, "That's enough talking for this night."

The next thing he did was take me over to Grandma's house. She wasn't home, but Grandpa let him in and was glad to see him. I walked in behind Horace and Grandpa scooped me up just like he used to when I was four years old. Sydni came running out to see Horace.

Horace sat down in the kitchen and had a beer with Grandpa. Horace told him the whole story about Hasson. Grandpa was blown away and even more pissed off that Grandma had approved of my friendship with him. We waited about an hour and still Grandma hadn't come home. Horace asked Grandpa to tell Grandma he would speak to her the following day. When I got ready to go, Sydni started to cry. Horace said, "You can come back to my house for the night if you want to."

Sydni flew to her bedroom, grabbed some clothes and her school-books. Horace suggested that I pack a few things too.

When we got back to Horace's house, Emily talked to me again, asked me about sex, my period, and condoms. I told her I had not had sex or even kissed Hasson. She was relieved. Horace went for pizza for us all. We got in Horace's bed, all five of us, and ate pizza and watched TV.

We fell asleep one by one. Horace left for work. After he got back home the next morning, he drove Sydni and me to school. Then he started to put his plan into action. He went to Libby's house to get all the information on the whereabouts of my daddy Lance. He immediately wrote him a letter explaining everything and asked Lance to put his name on the visiting list so he could come to talk to him.

He got Peggy Kinard's telephone number and called to ask for her help in finding some information on the private schools in Philadelphia. With her class, she would know where I should attend school. He also asked Peggy if she wouldn't mind taking me to church with her on Sundays. She thought that was a marvelous idea.

He called the Philadelphia Bar Association for the names and telephone numbers of three attorneys who practiced family law. He made appointments with each of them early the next week. Then he called the hospital and made friends with the clerk in the medical records department. He charmed her into copying my medical records from the time when Paula had bitten me. He could pick them up late that afternoon or the next day.

He called County Care at Broad and Reed Streets to let them know he needed the records of Renee's stay there when Grandma was arrested. Then he contacted the police department to see how soon he could get a copy of the police incident reports from Grandma's arrests on New Year's Eve that year and for the illegal numbers. I was surprised Grandpa had told Horace all about Grandma being locked up for gambling at Libby's.

Horace sat down and gazed at Paula for a few seconds. Paula then said, "Why are you here?" He answered, "I'd like to form a truce. I'm here to make peace. How's jail life? I put some money on your books so you could buy cigarettes. I thought I'd be nice and not include any hair spray or matches. Wanna either bury the hatchet or at least call a truce?" Horace asked.

"I'm faring pretty well. Thanks. What made you come here?" Paula asked.

"A few things. You and I were hanging for a long time. It's a damn shame things didn't work out, because I really dug you. I tried too hard too long—but you had an agenda quite different from mine. No hard feelings, though. We're cool."

"Horace, I'm who I am and you're who you are. We don't mix. That's the problem. Label me a tramp again or maybe I'm just adventurous. Whatever. Personally, I stopped caring about or putting any energy into who or what you wanted me to be a long time ago." Paula looked worn out and haggered. Her hair was brushed back from her face—those cute bangs that made her look younger were gone. There was no spark in her eyes.

"Okay. No further explanation needed regarding our absent flame for each other. I'm here to ask a favor," Horace said.

"What?" Paula held up a Newport to be lit by the guard.

"I want to give all the kids a life. A good stable life. I'd like to adopt Amber and Sydni. That's what I want. Are you game? You certainly can't do anything for them in here."

"I want my mother to keep Amber and Sydni," Paula said.

"Yeah, I imagine you do because she collects a hefty check for them. I know she's probably splitting it with you. I'm willing to see that you get the money from me. I'll set up an account for you at my bank. Will that work? Can we agree on that?" Horace asked.

"You know what? It seems all you've ever been concerned about were those kids. That's one of the things that always pissed me off about you. You're forever yapping about those kids, what they need and should have. Sometimes I think you never gave a damn about me. That's one of the reasons I ran around on your ass. I wanted someone who was interested in me. Nobody's ever cared about me just for myself."

"Look, Paula, I started off digging you. Just you. I was your man, so of course I wanted to be involved with you and help out with your children. You should have appreciated that—not been pissed off or jealous. But that's neither here nor there now. We have a problem. You're going to be in jail for quite a while. I can help with the kids. I love them. They deserve a better life and some stability. Why don't you give them a shot for a change?" Horace asked.

"I'll consider it. I really will, but my preference is that they stay with my mother."

"Well, you give it some thought and let me give you some additional food for thought. If you don't sign them over to me, I'm going to fuck with Fannie. Maybe the Department of Human Services might be interested to learn about her two arrests and the fact that Renee ended up in County Care as a result of one. Also, you need to know that people talk," Horace said.

"So what, they talk. I don't give a shit about what people say about my family," Paula answered, rolling her eyes at Horace.

"Well, that depends on what they're talking *about.* I got word that you had an abortion about a year ago at a medical residence. Miss Lenora Bush happens to be very friendly with Sheila. Sheila and Emily, being as tight as thieves, the news got back to me. Don't make me play that card, Paula. If I don't get the kids from you now, I may surely get them if you and your mother are doing time side by side. If I were you, I'd take the money and run. The next phone call you need to make is to your mother, because I'm going to pay her a visit soon."

Paula thought he was a real pain in the ass. "What abortion? I never had any abortion," she lied.

Horace contemplated every date he'd had with her, all the money he had spent, and how many times he had caught her wrong. He thought about how she had damn near killed Emily and how she always managed to manipulate every good and unsuspecting person who entered her life. He considered what a rotten, abusive mother she had been. He hated her for depriving her children of the love and stability they so deserved. He finally answered, "Okay, Miss Paula. You keep right on suffering from amnesia. I'd better get going, baby."

Paula was shocked he had found out about that abortion shit and Fannie's arrest on New Year's Eve. She didn't want any more trouble and she didn't know how far Horace could get with the custody battle, but Fannie did have two prior arrests. She knew the Department of Human Services could rule in Horace's favor because they might want to keep the kids together. Worst case scenario was Sydni and Amber could end up in foster care if Horace was successful in proving Fannie unfit. Horace wasn't a blood relative. The county didn't have to award him custody even if they found Fannie unfit. Paula had a lot to think about. She also knew she could use any money he was willing to give her to sign them over. She looked over at Horace and said, "I'll get back to you."

Horace knew where the Muslim bakery was, so he headed there about one p.m. He should have passed out long ago after working all night, but his adrenaline was flowing. He was on a roll. He went into the bakery and looked around. He saw Hasson behind the counter with some bruises on his face and a girl at the register. He walked up to the counter. The man came over to wait on him.

Horace was pleasant. He ordered a few bean pies, some carrot cake, and a pound cake. The guy wrapped up the goods and gave him the total. Horace paid him, but didn't remove the bags from the counter. The guy was confused. "Will there be something else?"

"I don't know yet. What's your name, brother? I remember seeing you here before. I just can't remember your name," Horace said.

"Hasson."

"Nice to see you again, Hasson." Horace extended his hand.

When Hasson extended his hand to meet his, Horace grabbed him by the wrist with one hand and by the collar with the other. He pulled Hasson over the counter and yanked him to the floor. The pastries in the bags came with him, along with other items displayed on top of the glass case. The cashier and the patrons in the bakery looked on, surprised and frightened.

Horace dragged Hasson out of the store and into his car. He threw him into the backseat, which he had to share with a friend of Horace's— Killer. He locked the door. Hasson was petrified. Killer didn't take his eyes off him. Horace ran around the other side of the car, jumped into the driver's seat, and sped off. Benny was in the front passenger's seat and turned around to face Hasson. He was holding a gun. While he was driving, Horace asked Hasson questions about what he had done with me while we were together.

He drove toward downtown Philadelphia and into the park. He located an area where the city had a display of historical things used in colonial times. Horace stopped the car, snatched Hasson out of the backseat, and laid him down on the grass. He motioned for Benny to give him his gun and he put it to Hasson's head. Hasson's eyes were blinking wildly and he was moaning. Horace told Benny to bring Killer out of the car. Hasson cried and pleaded with them not to let the dog eat him up and not to shoot him. As Killer approached, Hasson froze.

Horace smelled shit. Hasson had suddenly developed a case of diarrhea. They had literally scared the shit out of him. Horace grabbed him around the neck and began to choke him. Then he let him go. He told Hasson what a disgusting person he thought he was, and that if he ever came near me again, he would kill him. He went on to inform him that he had have a talk with Grandma on Sunday. Horace wanted Hasson to explain to Grandma that if she fought Horace for custody of me, he would cooperate with Horace. He would force Hasson to lie, telling the authorities, police, support unit, and the court system that she had sold me to him and he had been paying her money in order to date me.

Hasson promised and swore on his life that he would do it. Horace threatened that if he tried to get him into trouble for the events of that day by telling the police, he would definitely kill him, and before he would actually kill him, Hasson would meet up with Killer again. Then he sat him up, letting him take a long look at Killer's enormous head and colossal teeth. He pointed to the dog and said, "That's Killer. Do you understand me, Hasson? Are we going to have a problem? Will you be at Fannie's house on Sunday?"

Hasson answered, "I swear to God and Allah that I will take care of everything."

Horace yanked him up from the ground. "Don't think I don't know what you were planning. You are despicable and you have to be punished. Do you know what a pillory is, Hasson?"

"No."

"A pillory is a wooden frame used for public punishment. It has a hole for your head and two holes for your arms. It exposes you to public scorn." Horace turned Hasson's head in another direction and pointed his finger.

"You see that thing back over there—that's a pillory."

Horace motioned for Benny to help him. They dragged Hasson to the pillory and placed his head and arms inside the holes. He was crying and screaming. They got a rope and tied his feet to the base.

Then Horace said to Hasson, "Don't forget I've got a trump card, man. Don't make me play it. She's fourteen years old. Don't forget you ain't fifteen and a suitable date."

Horace and Benny got into the car. They didn't care how long he stayed out there, but Horace told Benny, "That asshole better get himself rescued and present himself at Fannie's house before Sunday." They could hear him screaming as they drove off.

Horace drove to Grandma's house. He rang the bell and she answered. He spoke politely, and she invited him to the kitchen to sit down.

"Fannie, you and I have to talk. I'll go first, and please don't interrupt me. Now, I am not going to take you through all the lies and bullshit and waste time like that. I'm going to let you know my plans. You can make the decision that you feel is best for you. You don't have to make the decision best for Amber, because you aren't capable of doing that correctly. Remember: Don't speak. I am not going to bring Amber back here. I am planning to keep her. I am going through the court. If I have to dig up Perry Fucking Mason, if I have to spend a million dollars, if I have to drag your arrest records into court, or if I have to cause you to depart this life sooner than you expect, I will have that child. Now you can decide to fight or you can surrender. Just keep in mind that you and that bitch daughter of yours will not get past me. You got that? Are there any questions, or do you have something to say before I walk out the door and go home to my kids?"

Grandma said, "What about Sydni?"

"Oh, what about Sydni?" he said sarcastically. "Wasn't it you who said they should be raised *together?* You figure out what about Sydni. You'll come up with something. And, by the way, you'll be getting a call from your deadbeat daughter. She should have some instructions for you." He walked out of the house. We never ended up in court fighting.

My new school is awesome. I am a junior in high school. I feel good being in a beautiful private school with a giant yard. There are guinea pigs named Willie and Elvis in the science classrooms for the younger kids who attend the elementary school. There is also a huge colorful parrot named Delilah in the lobby of the main building. A rabbit named Joshua hangs out in his cage in the girls' locker room, enticing us to show up for gym. It costs a lot of money to go to this wonderful school and Horace is paying for it all. It is nice there because the kids don't fight or steal. The classrooms are much smaller than the ones in public school and the kids get more special attention.

My classmates treat me nice, which helps to keep me from feeling like an outsider. I love all the teachers and they like me. I listen and learn a lot. I am an honor student with expectations of becoming a doctor. My favorite subjects are science and history. All periods of history intrigue me.

We have a special class at my school called "It Amazes Me." In this class we are required to write a brief report on any subject that amazes us. Then we explain it orally to the class. I have participated many times. The last time, I explained how people's accents amaze me. I cannot understand why people in the United States speak differently in different parts of the same country. The whole thing amazes me. It even occurs in Philadelphia. People who live in South Philadelphia talk differently from those in other parts of Philadelphia. The South Philly people sound rougher. The white people in the Kensington section sound tougher and more streetwise than other whites in Philadelphia.

Those who live in the South, like South Carolina and Georgia, have that southern drawl. Why? The people in Massachusetts and Rhode Island sound like they just got off that pilgrim boat from England. New Yorkers—you can tell where they come from as soon as they open their mouth. Well, the one thing I just don't understand is why we can't all just talk the same. Where did all these accents come from?

It sure feels good to be Amber Alston. I left Philadelphia and now reside in a house on a hill located at 729 Prairie Lane, Rydal, Pennsylvania, with my adopted daddy, Mr. Horace Alston, and my two sisters, Sydni Alston and Renee Alston. We also still have the wildest nanny in the world, Miss Emily Frazier.

# Departures

Adrienne Bellamy

# A CONVERSATION WITH ADRIENNE BELLAMY

�֍

*Q. What inspired you to write* Departures *and what questions did you ask yourself when you were working on it?*

A. Frankly, my longtime love of writing was my initial inspiration. I've always liked being able to make people laugh. I've been a bit of an entertainer all of my life to my family, friends, and colleagues at past jobs. When I decided to write *Departures*, the only question I asked myself was "Can I do it?" I was unsure, so I had to rely on test readers every step of the way for reassurance and criticism. I wanted to make sure my product was perfect and my words and situations would penetrate my readers.

*Q. Paula is totally ruthless. What about her character and her situation inspired your portrayal of her?*

A. I love children and have two of my own. I am a protective worrywart parent. I have observed, read, and heard about unfit mothers. I am particularly interested in how people are able to mistreat and abuse their children. This is how Paula was born to *Departures*. Because I am strong, I wanted Amber to be strong enough to sustain the abuse Paula was inflicting upon her. Because I detest abuse and I am a bit of a vindictive person (Scorpio Rising) I was able to get back at Paula through the wonderful Horace.

*Q. There are many characters in this novel. Who is your favorite character and why?*

A. Emily is my very favorite. I love her self-confidence. She is strong. I love how she and Jared operated each other. She is a woman who is totally secure and not infested with jealousy. I love their support and connection with each other.

*Q. What was your vision when you began writing* Departures? *What got you started when you actually began the first paragraph?*

A. In my mind I saw a little girl walking down the street pulling a red wagon. The wagon was filled with empty soda bottles that she was taking to the grocery store for a refund. As she passed the houses on the way, I created the characters from the people living inside.

*Q. What was the hardest scene you had to write in* Departures?

A. The spaghetti scene and the abortions. There was a rage in me when Amber had to deal with the spaghetti. I remember backing away from my computer and ending up on the floor of my bedroom crying my eyes out for that child. I truly wanted to kill Paula, the character I created. I am a writer who many times knows not what she will write. I never know where a chapter will take me. Most of the time I am a writer whose material comes into her head and goes through to her fingers and upon the screen of her computer monitor. So, I was indeed shocked at what appeared with Amber and the spaghetti. I knew beforehand I would write about abortion. When I did the research on it, I was upset to have to deal with such a sensitive issue. I felt I needed to be graphic in the explanation of the procedure and I cringed when writing it.

*Q. What were your favorite chapters and scenes in* Departures?

A. I have many. This is a tough one. I love the rules that Reba gave to her children when preparing them to leave their father. The church scene with the minister had me in stitches. When *Departures* made its debut, I read that chapter to over two hundred people on a Sunday afternoon book signing. They were hysterical laughing. Lastly, I must say that the hotel scene with Emily and the Toronto girls had me roaring with laughter.

*Q. Were any of your characters actually derived from real people?*

A. *Departures* is a book of fiction. However, there are things about people in my life that jumpstarted me in the development of some characters. Those characters are Paula, Amber, Jared, Emily, Peggy, Lance, and Oscar.

*Q. Are there certain times during the day that you write? Do you ever get writer's block?*

A. When I began *Departures*, I was juggling four jobs. I was a full-time paralegal at a law firm during the day. At night, I worked two hours as a companion to a wheelchair-bound muscular dystrophy patient. A few months later, I switched full-time jobs and went to work for an invest-ment firm. On weekends during the day, I was a paralegal for a local at-torney. Weekday mornings, I was up at five thirty and off to be the nanny for a seven-year old whose single mom was attending medical school. I would arrive at her home as she was leaving and take a snooze until it was time to wake seven-year-old Andrew up for school. I'd get him ready, drop him off at school, and go to my full-time job. Also while writing *Departures* I was employed part-time interviewing parents and children who had been injured in motor vehicle accidents. This was a study program at Children's Hospital of Philadelphia. It seems that left little time for writing, but I wrote in between coming and going and often in the middle of the night. I came down with writer's block on many occasions; however, it never lasted long. I believe six weeks was the longest period I experienced. I am a writer who will not write if I don't feel I have good material. Many times material would come to me while I was driving. I'd try to retain it by jotting a few words down at a stoplight or often just turning around and going back home to my computer if I was on a personal errand.

Q. *How much of* Departures *is based on your own experiences?*

A. About one-fourth of the situations in the book. A few scenes were written almost exactly as they happened to me. Others I prepared from a little that occurred and then I'd simply blow it out of proportion, adding fictional events.

Q. *Are you working on another project?*

A. I have completed two additional novels, *Connecting* and *Arrivals,* sequels to *Departures.* Some of the characters from *Departures* are featured in these novels. I have begun a fourth novel titled *Illusions* that takes us totally out of the *Departures* neighborhood. I am scheduled to begin my fifth novel in August of 2004. That will be an astrology book. I was inspired to write about astrology as many of my readers simply love the stuff and are pleased with the little "taste" they had in *Departures.* I plan to get back to the *Departures* neighborhood characters by writing an additional sequel to *Departures* in 2005.

Q. *At any point in your writing of* Departures *did you know how the book would end?*

A. Yes. Midway through I knew exactly how Amber would get away from Paula. In fact, I wrote the ending chapter a month prior to the book being completed. Often I jump to another character when I have the "juice" and know what's going to happen with someone else in the book. I also often leave a chapter unfinished if I run out of steam for that situation or get writer's block. Later, I'll get something and go back for the finish.

Q. *Can you tell me some of the ways you get material?*

A. I have gotten material through my dreams—while sleeping. I often try to figure out how to keep people alive thorough medication and health care—so I come up with a lot of material that way. I was in my kitchen one morning and reached for a bag of coffee beans. I slit the bag and accidentally dropped it on my kitchen floor. As I looked down at the beans, I came up with a storyline that resulted in five chapters of an upcoming novel. My test readers absolutely loved it and the character in that novel connected with those beans has "walked away with my book." In my writing I also like to teach my readers so I touch upon subjects and go into detail on a subject so they walk away learning something.

*Q. Can you share with me some of the compliments you have received from your readers?*

A. People love my work because it is easy reading—no giant words that a not-so-articulate person would have to have a dictionary next to them while reading. This makes my work appeal to all types of people. I purposely watch the words I use so all will understand. I've also been praised for my descriptions of people, places, and things. Many readers have said, "I've never been there but I felt I was there after you described it." My readers also like my characters because they can relate to them. Many say, "I'm Reba" or "I know these people!" "I have a cousin who acts just like that!"

*Q. What chapter or scene in* Departures *caused the most controversy, discussion, or sparked the readers?*

A. There are two. The funeral/graveyard scene and the Pisces chapter are always the topic of discussion. Hands down, readers loved it. Even the injured Pisces wanted more!

*Q. Who are your favorite writers?*

A. Wally Lamb, John Grisham, Vincent Bugliosi, Terry McMillan, and Danielle Steel.

*Q. Did you learn something about yourself when writing this book?*

A. I learned I am really funny, crazy, mean, and vindictive. I also realized how much I love children and good parents. I also learned how important it is that we all know that there are some very decent and strong African American men in this world.

*Q. You write a lot about astrology. How do you know so much about it? Have you studied it?*

A. I have read up on astrology for years. I am not an expert. I find it intriguing and I totally believe in it. In all my relationships (co-workers, bosses, lovers, friends, and relatives) I have used the assistance of astrology to guide me in the way I handled those relationships. I have raised and handled my children using astrology. My daughters are Leo and Aquarius—exact opposites. The Leo I have to handle with kid gloves. I have to request, ask, and be gentle if I want something done. She requires praise. Whenever I would make commands—nothing got done. I had to realize and understand that lions are king of the jungle and we are their loyal subjects. We are beneath them. Knowing my astrology and their personalities, I knew how to approach her. Praise and flattery will always put you ahead with them. The Aquarian with the bad temper always did me in. However, I also knew I had the smartest person in the zodiac in my house. I had to learn to deal with her belligerence, which is part of her characteristic. You'll always walk on eggshells with an Aquarian female, even though they are true humanitarians. They will always belong to a group of something. Maybe it will be a church, cult, sorority, or singing ensemble.

# QUESTIONS FOR DISCUSSION

�֍

1. Motherhood is one of the most important topics in *Departures*. What characteristics make a good parent? How do you feel about the parenting of Reba, Sheila, and Horace? What do you think makes Paula such a bad parent? Why do you think Sydni is so quiet and nothing like the feisty Amber?

2. Paula seems to just love money and sex. What do you think she really wants?

3. Relationships are a major part of *Departures* and all are very different. Compare the relationships of Kevin and Lucy, Reba, Johnny, and Doug, and Emily and Jared. Which is your favorite and why?

4. How do you feel about Lenora's part-time job and the deceit? Do you feel she was right to help Pam Resnick? Do you feel she should have gone to prison?

5. In *Departures*, Sheila, Amber, Emily, and Reba all seem to have a coping mechanism and a lot of strength. Paula seems to be without one—not unless she's using men and money. I'm not sure what she's searching for or trying to achieve. She seems to have a lot of underlying problems.

What's your take on her? Do you feel Grandma Fannie's upbringing is the root of all Paula's evil?

6. Discuss the different ways in which the lives of these characters might progress.